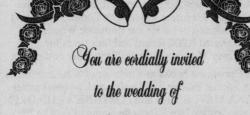

You are cordially invited

to the wedding of

Joanna Vail and Casey Clinton

&

Molly Clelland and Sam Frazier

These strong, caring women have agreed to marry

their sexy, charismatic grooms not for love or passion,

but because of a child.

Little do they know

that something more is in store for them....

CHRISTINE RIMMER

Since the publication of her first romance in 1987, *New York Times* Extended bestselling author Christine Rimmer has written over thirty-five novels for Silhouette Books. A reader favorite, Christine has seen her stories appear not only on the prestigious *Times* list, but on the Waldenbooks and *USA Today* bestseller lists, as well. She has won the *Romantic Times Magazine* Reviewer's Choice Award, and has been nominated twice for the Romance Writers of America's coveted RITA Award and four times for *Romantic Times Magazine*'s Series Storyteller of the Year.

Look for Christine's books in a number of Silhouette series, including Special Edition and Desire, and the continuities MONTANA MAVERICKS and FORTUNE'S CHILDREN. She has also written two Silhouette single titles, *The Taming of Billy Jones,* released in 1998, and *The Bravo Billionaire,* coming to your local bookstore in September. Also watch for *The Marriage Agreement* in August and *The Marriage Conspiracy* in October, both from Silhouette Special Edition.

LAURIE PAIGE

says, "One of the nicest things about writing romances is researching locales, careers and ideas. In the interest of authenticity, most writers will try anything…once." Along with her writing adventures, Laurie has been a NASA engineer, a past president of the Romance Writers of America (twice!), a mother and a grandmother (twice, also!). She was twice a Romance Writers of America RITA Award finalist for Best Traditional Romance and has won awards from *Romantic Times Magazine* for best Silhouette Special Edition and Best Silhouette Romance. She has also been presented with *Affaire de Coeur*'s Readers' Choice Silver Pen Award for Favorite Contemporary Author. Recently resettled in Northern California, Laurie is looking to whatever experiences her next novel will send her on.

Her newest series from Silhouette Special Edition, THE WINDRAVEN LEGACY, begins in May 2001 with *Something To Talk About.* It continues in July with *When I See Your Face,* and concludes in September with *When I Dream of You.*

Convenient Vows

Christine Rimmer
Laurie Paige

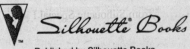

Silhouette Books

Published by Silhouette Books

America's Publisher of Contemporary Romance

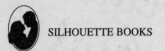 SILHOUETTE BOOKS

ISBN 0-373-21718-8

by Request

CONVENIENT VOWS

Copyright © 2001 by Harlequin Books S.A.

The publisher acknowledges the copyright holders of the individual works as follows:

DOUBLE DARE
Copyright © 1991 by Christine Rimmer

MOLLY DARLING
Copyright © 1996 by Olivia M. Hall

This edition published by arrangement with Harlequin Books S.A.

Visit Silhouette at www.eHarlequin.com

Printed in U.S.A.

CONTENTS

Dear Reader,

If you've read even a few of my books, you know how much I adore the marriage-of-convenience story. I've written a number of them over the years. I've even created my own marriage-of-convenience series, CONVENIENTLY YOURS, stories in which the hero and heroine always start out "in name only" and end up falling in love.

In *Double Dare*, best friends Casey Clinton and Joanna Vail decide to tie the knot for the sake of a child—and before you know it, there's a lot more than friendship going on between the two of them....

The very best to you and yours,

Christine Rimmer

Double Dare
Christine Rimmer

For my parents, Auralee and Tom Smith,
who had love enough to give me my start in life—twice

Chapter One

"Joey?" the little boy asked.

Joanna paused in the act of turning off the light by the bed. "It's time to go to sleep, Mike," she said.

"I know, but Joey—"

She switched off the light. "No buts. Snuggle down." She tugged the sheet up around him. He smelled of toothpaste. When she kissed his cheek she thought that his skin was like some incredibly fine yet resilient flower. "'Night."

"Joey, just so you know. I won't go live with Uncle Burnett."

Joanna was glad the room was dark. Because of it, Mike couldn't see her expression. He was a bright boy. She probably should have guessed he might realize what was going on.

"Don't worry. It'll all work out for the best." The

'words were inane, but she heard herself saying them anyway as she stroked the fine hair back from his forehead.

"Uncle Burnett's always working. And Aunt Amanda's always smiling and asking me to be careful around her things." His tone turned plaintive. "I try to be careful, Joey. But jeez, I'm only almost six." He surged up from under the blanket and grabbed her in a ferocious hug.

"I want to be with you and Uncle Case," he whispered fiercely in her ear. "You could stay with us forever, if you wanted. You could paint your pictures here, Joey, just as good as down there by Disneyland. Say you will. Please, say yes."

Joanna hugged him back, saying nothing. Tears of love burned her eyes, and she willed them not to spill over and upset Mike even more. She wanted to say yes, to promise him all he desired. But making him a wild, unconsidered promise would be worse for him than for most five-year-olds. When he was still a baby he'd lost his father and his mother had died just five weeks ago. He deserved, as much as possible, only the kind of promises that could be kept.

Gently, she took his arms from around her neck and guided him back beneath the sheet. His narrow face was softly defined against the pillow. He watched her trustingly, full of conviction that a single word from her could guarantee his happiness.

Though she couldn't just say yes, neither could she deny him. "I'll do everything I can to see that you stay with your Uncle Case," she said.

His mouth, as small and neat as his mother's had been, curved upward. He uttered his favorite word:

"Excellent." Then he said, "Now I can go to sleep." He rolled over on his side and tucked his fist beneath his chin.

Joanna watched his lashes come to rest on his cheeks. Then tiptoed out the door.

Before joining the family conference in the living room, Joanna paused in the hall bathroom. As she dabbed at her smudged mascara and ran a comb through her hair, she sent a little prayer to heaven that tonight would see an end to the conflict over who would have custody of Mike.

Actually, Joanna was feeling responsible. After Emily's funeral, Joanna hadn't returned to Southern California, where she'd lived for fourteen years. Instead, she'd stayed on in Sacramento to help out with Mike—and found herself getting increasingly involved in the dispute over Mike's future.

Tonight had been her idea. She'd talked Casey into fixing his famous Chicken Teriyaki, and she'd made the dessert crepes herself. She'd casually mentioned a "friendly talk" when she'd extended the invitation to Casey's older brother, Burnett, and his wife, Amanda. Joanna's plan had been to approach the disagreement in a civilized fashion, to create a relaxed, noncombative atmosphere in which to discuss the problem.

"Relaxed. Noncombative," she muttered to herself as she walked down the hall to the living room. She saw Burnett first. He stood beside the bar, clutching his wineglass a little too tightly. His stern face was slightly flushed.

Judging by Burnett's expression, things weren't going well. Joanna swallowed the knot in her throat and shifted her glance to Casey. He sat slouched in his favorite soft leather chair, one leg tossed over a chair arm and the other planted on the floor.

The differences between the brothers had always fascinated Joanna, making her wonder how two men could come from the same set of parents and yet be so diametrically opposite. There *were* family similarities: both had brown hair—though Burnett's was much darker—and the strong Clinton nose. But Casey had light, arresting eyes, while Burnett's were shadowy dark. Burnett stood a commanding six foot three and possessed an imposing physique. Casey was shorter, and cut from much finer stuff. He was Michelangelo's *David*, while Burnett could have been a latter-day Goliath.

In Joanna's memory, there had never been a subject on which Casey and Burnett had agreed. The clash over Mike was just another case in point—with one important difference. This time, a young child's future was at stake.

Forcing a composed smile, Joanna left the shadow of the hallway and moved to Casey's side. No one spoke. The short distance across the floor seemed like a hundred miles.

At the light touch of her hand on his shoulder, Casey glanced up. To a casual observer, he would have appeared utterly relaxed. But Joanna was not a casual observer. Casey Clinton had been her best friend for twenty-two years, ever since the day his mother, Lillian, had moved her family in next door to Joanna and her parents. Now, as Joanna looked down at him, the watchful silence lurking in his eyes struck her immediately, as did the barely perceptible tightness around his mouth.

"Did Mike give you any trouble?" he asked. Joanna knew the question was rhetorical. His mind was on the contest of wills between himself and his brother.

Joanna grinned at her friend, willing away the tension that filled the room. "He's like any five-year-old. He takes half an hour to brush his teeth. And then, of course, comes the story. And that final trip to the bathroom. But he did settle down finally."

The hostile silence descended again. Joanna glanced at Amanda, Burnett's wife. The porcelain-skinned blonde hovered near the French doors that led to the backyard. She stared out into the summer night as if there were something fascinating happening out by the pool.

Burnett drained his wineglass with an air of grim finality.

"More?" Joanna asked him politely, when he set his empty glass on the washed oak bar.

Burnett shook his head.

"I think I'd like another glass," Amanda chirped, her voice made shrill by her effort at nonchalance. "You just stay put. I spotted that bottle in the fridge." She laughed nervously. "I'll get it." Her heels clicked sharply on the pine-strip floor as she escaped to the kitchen. Joanna decided not to remind her that there was also a bottle in the bar icebox, right next to the feet of the glowering Burnett.

She couldn't blame Amanda for trying to find any excuse to leave the room. The Clinton brothers were going head-to-head, and that meant a possible explosion if Burnett lost his cool.

The silence after the sound of Amanda's clicking

heels faded away reminded Joanna of a huge rubber band, stretching, stretching. To the snapping point.

Then Burnett broke the silence. "I only want what's best for my nephew." His deep voice vibrated with barely restrained animosity. "And I'm not going to let you prevent me from doing the right thing, no matter what foolish decisions Emily might have made."

"She was Mike's mother—" Casey began.

"She was confused," Burnett cut in with a haughty wave of his hand. "She never got over Michael's death. And she was always unrealistically indulgent toward you. I'll be frank. She looked up to you with stars in her eyes—her dashing brother, Casey, who dreamed of *flight*—" Burnett uttered the word as if it were an obscenity "—who deserted the family at eighteen to join the navy, and then came back to spend half his inheritance on a run-down airfield."

Burnett paused significantly. Joanna understood his ploy. He was hoping to put Casey on the defensive by getting him to defend Clinton Airfield. But Casey didn't bite. There was no reason to. The facts spoke for themselves. He had left the navy because his eyesight had deteriorated just enough for him to be grounded from flying the fighter jets he loved. He'd come home and bought the airfield. True, it would never make Casey much money—but Casey ran Clinton Airfield because flying was what he knew and loved. He had done what he wanted with his life, and done well at it.

"You were Emily's favorite," Burnett went on, when Casey didn't defend his choice of career. "That's all I'm saying. And she found me, well, mundane, to say the least. So, in choosing to make you

Mike's legal guardian, she made an irresponsible decision. Besides, once she made up her mind, she was always as obstinate as you are.'' Burnett paused, then added with a sneer, ''Whether she was right or not.''

''I have no trouble supporting Mike,'' Casey said, remaining coolly reasonable. ''I'm willing to spend time with him. And I love him. I wouldn't say that Emily made such a bad choice.''

''Casey, you're a bachelor,'' Burnett replied. He flicked a dismissive glance around the spacious, comfortable, but very masculine room. ''Your life lacks the necessary feminine touch.'' He shot Joanna a disparaging glance. ''Except for Joanna's *generous* help, which we all know is only temporary at best.''

''I'll be here to help out as long as Casey needs me,'' Joanna insisted in a level voice.

''Oh, come now, Joanna.'' Burnett eyed her with aloof disdain. ''You're hardly cut out for domesticity. You'll be running back to L.A. to bury yourself in your canvasses and paintbrushes the first chance you get. You're simply not the type of woman who can be counted upon to take care of a child.''

Beneath her hand, Joanna felt the slow tightening of Casey's muscles. She squeezed his shoulder gently, communicating in the subtle touch that she could handle his brother's calculated insults. She kept her face carefully composed, though the thread of bitterness in Burnett's tone had distressed her.

I should have realized, she thought. He's never completely forgiven me.

Fourteen years ago, Joanna had come dangerously close to marrying Burnett. Casey had changed her mind for her. And he'd done it in a very unconventional way. Burnett himself had actually broken things off, and over the years Joanna had allowed herself to believe that bygones were bygones. But as she faced Burnett now over another issue altogether, she saw she was mistaken. Burnett still thought that she'd made a fool of him, and deep down he still nurtured resentment toward her.

Joanna realized it had been foolish for her to have arranged this family dinner. She should have stayed out of it, and let Burnett and Casey fight it out in their own way. But now it was too late.

"I'll say it again, Burnett." Joanna's voice remained steady and firm. "I'll be here to help out as long as Casey needs me."

Burnett's lips curled contemptuously. "How convenient for him."

Out of the corner of her eye, she spied Casey's dangling foot. It was clad in a high-top sneaker and it had begun beating rhythmically in the air. Joanna swallowed. If she didn't put Burnett firmly in his place on this issue, Casey would do it for her. And the Lord only knew how he would manage that.

That was the thing about Casey. He could be pushed so far and never even raise his voice. He'd be smiling. And reasonable, and even rather good-natured. And then *it* would happen. He'd toss a curve that the most experienced verbal batter could never hit. As his friend, Joanna would be the one wearing the catcher's glove.

Straightening her shoulders, Joanna said, "It's not a matter of Casey's convenience. It goes far beyond that. I'm Casey's friend, and I'll always be there for him if he needs me. Furthermore, Emily herself asked me to help out.''

''When exactly did she do that?'' Burnett demanded.

Casey cut in. ''Burnett,'' he said, ''she doesn't owe you any explanations.''

''It's okay.'' Joanna smiled down into Casey's eyes, willing him not to say or do anything he'd regret later. Then she looked back at Burnett. ''It was a couple of years ago. Emily brought Mike down to visit Disneyland. They stayed in West Hollywood with me. We talked.'' Joanna paused, remembering Emily's pixieish face as she sat across from her at her own kitchen table, seeing again the melancholy in Emily's eyes…

''It took me a year to believe that Michael was really dead,'' Emily had confided, her sad eyes focused on some faraway place. Mike, Sr. had been killed in a freak motorcycle accident a few years before that. Those who knew how much Emily loved her husband had feared for a while that Emily would never recover from the loss.

''In some ways, I still don't believe he's gone,'' Emily had said. ''I still look up from something I'm doing and expect to see him there, sitting across from me, or standing in the doorway. And when I'm finally aware that he's not really there, there's this horrible moment, this emptiness, when I realize he's never going to be there again…'' Emily's voice had trailed off then; she'd forced a smile. ''Sorry. You asked,'' she'd said a moment later, with an embarrassed little clearing of her throat. ''Sometimes I wish I had what you have with your painting, Joey. Something to lose myself in, you know?''

Joanna had nodded. For a time they'd fallen into a companionable silence, and Joanna, with her artist's habit of observation, had recorded the moment in her mind. Two women, one dark-haired and one light, sitting at a kitchen table bathed in a hard wedge of blinding morning sun.

"I've always thought of you as a sister, did you know that?" Emily had said at last.

And then she'd begun to talk about the will she'd made…

"You talked about what?" Burnett prompted, yanking Joanna's thoughts back to the present.

Joanna sighed, letting her precious memories of Emily fade into the past. Then slowly and carefully she began to explain what Emily had told her.

"Emily said she wanted her wishes clearly understood, in case anything happened to her. She said she wanted Casey to raise Mike. She said she'd asked Casey and he had agreed. She also said that she'd explained her feelings to your mother and that Lillian understood completely."

"You don't have to tell me why she didn't choose Mother," Burnett cut in gruffly. "Mother deserves a few years of freedom. What I want to know is, why did she decide against me?" Burnett could not entirely mask the thread of anguish beneath his stiffly spoken words. For a man who exerted such rigid control over every aspect of his life, accepting the death of a loved one was no mean feat. Joanna felt compassion for him rise up within her. Burnett could be a hard man, but he still had feelings. She really didn't want to tell him why Emily had chosen Casey over him. The reason would hurt him.

"Joanna," Burnett said, prodding her. "I asked you a direct question."

Once again Joanna looked rather hopelessly at Casey. His eyes said, There's no getting around it now. You'll have to tell him.

Joanna dragged in a breath and faced Burnett squarely. "She felt you had a problem with showing love. She said she could never leave Mike to be raised without love."

An awful silence ensued. Then Burnett said, too quietly. "Of course I don't believe that. I—" he paused over the word, as if it were in bad taste to say it in mixed company "—*love* Mike. And I know what he needs." He paused to look for his wife. "Amanda?" She appeared on cue, as if, after having left the kitchen, she'd been lurking behind the big areca palm in the foyer. She glided to Burnett's side, and he put his arm around her.

"Amanda and I," Burnett continued, "have talked this over." They smiled at each other, automatically and without any discernable warmth. Joanna thought they looked like a commercial for the perfect couple. He, handsome and dark. She, lovely and blond. "And we know we're in the right."

Casey said, "It doesn't matter what you know, Burnett. Mike's staying with me." His foot kept tapping. Relentlessly.

Burnett turned his cold smile on his brother. "No, Casey. He is not staying with you."

Joanna had a horrible, sinking feeling in her stomach. Burnett had moved right past blustery rage, which was awful but could be handled, to cold-blooded calculation. And Casey's foot kept tapping faster and faster.

Burnett threw out his challenge.

"We've taken it to a lawyer, Casey," Burnett said.

Casey moved his shoulder just enough to shake off Joanna's restraining hand. "You're planning to *sue* me for custody? You'll drag Mike through the courts just to prove Emily wrong for choosing me over you?" In spite of the anger implicit in his words, he asked the question very calmly.

"I want to raise the boy because it's the right thing for him," Burnett said crisply. "And I'll win, too. You know I will. My lawyers agree with me. A two-parent home will be best for Mike."

"I see," said Casey. "That's your case, then? That I'm single, and you're not."

"You can't win in this, Casey."

For a moment, Casey stared at his brother.

And then, very slowly, he smiled. "Don't bet on it, Big Brother."

Joanna's stomach tightened with dread. Something completely impossible would be coming out of Casey's mouth next, Joanna knew it with every fiber of her being.

Casey went on. "You'd better see your lawyers again, then. And this time be sure to give them our news."

"What news?" Burnett asked suspiciously.

Casey snared Joanna's hand. His touch was warm against Joanna's skin which now felt cold with dread.

Casey squeezed her hand. He shot her a look that managed to be both fond and crackling with challenge. How well she knew that look. A dare. They had dared each other often over the years. And what did the dares usually get them? Trouble.

Joanna gave Casey's hand a returning squeeze. A desperate squeeze. A squeeze that said *this is no time for dares....*

But Casey Clinton ignored her unspoken plea.

He said, "Joey and I have decided to get married."

Chapter Two

Amanda gave a strangled little squeak that sounded like the cry of a trapped mouse. After that, you could have heard a pin drop in Fresno, two hundred miles away.

Joanna could have killed Casey right then. She *would* have killed him if it wasn't absolutely imperative that they present a united front.

"You're lying," said Burnett at last.

Casey said nothing. Maintaining a murderous grip on her best friend's hand, Joanna spoke the words she'd never in a million years expected to utter. "It's true, Burnett. Casey and I are getting married right away."

Burnett glared at Joanna for suspended seconds, as if the force of his will could make her retract her words. When she didn't recant, he pounded a fist on the bar and bellowed, "This is outrageous!"

Looking stunned, Amanda clutched her husband's arm. "Can they do that, darling?" she asked in a bewildered little-girl voice.

Burnett ignored her. His eyes were on Joanna. "You're lying, aren't you? Both of you. Just admit the truth now."

Joanna almost did just that. But then she thought of how that would make Casey look, how Burnett would hold it up as more evidence that Casey was too irresponsible to raise a child.

"We're getting married," Joanna repeated, and waited for Casey to say the same.

But he was silent. Joanna eased her death grip on his hand and wondered if he was already trying to formulate a way out of the mess he'd gotten them into. It was, strangely, as if they were kids again and Casey had set off the fire alarm down on the corner just to see what it would sound like. He'd been caught, of course, and punished. But not before Joanna had tried to protect him by claiming she was the culprit.

Burnett turned on Casey again. "You're just stirring up trouble. Because you can't win in this, you want to create as much static as you can before you finally give in."

"Mike's staying with me," Casey said quietly. "And now—it's been a hell of an evening, and I'm tired." He swung his dangling foot to the ground and stood up, letting go of Joanna's hand in the process.

Though she was furious with him, his touch had been reassuring. For a moment, standing there alone, Joanna felt cast adrift. But then she reminded herself that they were still in this dilemma together. And together they could find a way out.

They needed to talk, that was all. But first, they must get rid of Burnett and Amanda.

Joanna trotted briskly to the dining alcove where Amanda had left her handbag. Then she hustled back to the living room. She handed Amanda the purse.

"Thanks for coming." She smiled at Amanda, and then turned a level stare on the scowling Burnett. "I'm sorry it couldn't have been a more…mutually satisfying evening."

Casey came and stood behind Burnett. Between the two of them, he and Joanna managed to herd the other couple toward the door.

"This isn't the end of it," Burnett warned. "This incredible announcement of yours only makes me more determined to see that that child gets a proper home."

"Good night, Big Brother," said Casey, hanging back a little and feigning a jaunty wave.

Burnett was still growling when Joanna closed the door.

Feeling suddenly deflated, Joanna leaned against the door. She reached down to slip off her high-heeled sandals, which she let drop by the areca palm in the corner nearby.

Suddenly the brightly lit, roomy house seemed very quiet. Joanna stared down at her toes for a minute, curling and uncurling them against the cool stone vestibule floor. Then she looked up at Casey.

He stood near the entrance to the living room, his hands in the pockets of his loose tan slacks. He wore an inscrutable expression. He seemed to be studying her.

She had no idea why she felt so defensive.

"What?" she asked, in that cryptic verbal shorthand that they often used with each other.

"What do you mean, what?"

"What are you staring at?" Her question came out sounding as defensive as she was feeling.

"You." His mouth wore a hint of a smile.

"Well, I know that. But why?"

"Why what?"

She knew that he knew what she'd meant, but she slowly explained anyway. "Why are you staring at me?"

"It's okay," he said, as if he were talking to himself.

"What's okay?"

"Staring at you," he said. "I like it, always have. That's important, don't you think? That you like staring at the person you're going to spend the rest of your life with."

Joanna groaned aloud. He *couldn't* be thinking of actually going through with it—could he? "Now, just a minute—" she began.

But he didn't let her finish. "Come on," he said, and covered the distance between them.

"Where?" Wary of him after what he'd done, she shrank against the door, her hands behind her back. He reached out and felt for her wrist, pulling it out from behind her.

"Outside," he said. And then he towed her along behind him as he made for the French doors on the other side of the living room. "I'm sick of being cooped up in here."

He paused long enough to scoop up two glasses and get the bottle of wine from under the bar.

Beyond the French doors, it was a beautiful evening, mild for July in the Sacramento Valley, which was known for its hot summer days and oppressively warm nights.

"Much better," he said, when they stood by the night-lighted pool.

Since Casey's house was in a development outside of Sacramento, the lights of the central valley sprawl could be seen as a glow on the horizon. A half-moon beamed down on them. And the stars, though paled by the city lights, still looked close enough to touch.

"Too bad about the moon," Casey mused, much too lightheartedly for Joanna's peace of mind. "I swear, Joey. If I'd known what was going to happen tonight, I would have put in an order for a big, fat full moon."

Joanna gave a low growl of frustration, freed her wrist, hiked up her skirt and sat down at the edge of the pool, dangling her feet in the water and not looking at him. Casey sat beside her, but back from the edge. She heard him pull the cork from the bottle and pour out the chilled wine.

Then she felt the cold kiss of a glass on her arm as he touched her with it by way of offering it to her. Instinctively, she jerked away.

Casey chuckled. "Whew. You *are* steamed, aren't you?"

She turned her head enough so she could glare at him. "What do you expect?" Grudgingly, she took her wine from him.

He raised his glass to her. "Tears of joy that I'm willing to make an honest woman of you after all these years?"

"An honest woman? You make an honest woman out of a mistress or a lover. Not out of your very best friend whom you've never done more than kiss."

"I was thinking more on the lines of emotionally honest," he told her, still in that infuriatingly nonchalant tone.

"What are you saying? We're friends. That's emotionally honest."

"Joey, you certainly are defensive about this."

Joanna gaped at him. This conversation was not going at all the way she'd meant it to. Not that she'd had time to decide exactly how it should go. She hadn't even had time to so much as draw in a calming breath since he'd announced to Burnett that they were headed for the altar.

"Defensive is not the issue," she snapped.

"Oh, no. Then what is?"

"How we're going to get out of it."

He leaned back on an elbow. He was still grinning. "Maybe I don't want to get out of it. Maybe it's time I settled down and learned to live with emotional commitment."

"Fine. You do that. Just leave me out of it."

"I'm sorry, Joey." He didn't look at all contrite. "But I can't leave you out of it. You're too perfect."

"You're nuts." She glared at him, and then looked away into the lights at the bottom of the pool. "I'm not cut out for domesticity. Burnett was right about that much, at least."

"That doesn't matter." Joanna turned once again to stare disbelievingly at him. "Cooking and cleaning always get done one way or another," he said. "What

I'm talking about is how perfect you and I really are for each other.''

He set his glass aside, drew up his knees and wrapped his arms around them. ''I don't know why I didn't see it before. The obvious solution to the problem is for us to get married. I mean, we're both committed to Mike. And to each other in all the ways that count. You're always there for me, and vice versa. We have a history together, things in common that go back years and years. We practically read each other's minds—''

She cut him off. ''But we're not in love with each other.'' She looked away toward the lava rock fountain that bubbled into the pool on the other side.

For a moment, he was silent. She thought she'd finally given him pause. But then he said, ''It's a stupid idea anyway, that people should marry because they're in love. Why base a lifetime commitment on two sets of crazed hormones?''

''I'd prefer to be in love, thank you.''

He seemed to have no reply for that. She continued to stare at the fountain. Then she heard his teasing voice again.

''Joey...'' He reached out and smoothed her hair from underneath, the pad of his index finger whispering along her neck. It was the kind of thing he did all the time, a fond gesture of caring, of closeness. But, suddenly, for the first time in years, it seemed charged with new meaning.

''Don't—'' She ducked away.

He withdrew his hand. ''Come on. It's not such a bad idea.''

"It's impossible," she said, still refusing to look at him.

There was a long silence. Over by the fountain, a cricket chirped.

Joanna felt trapped. When Casey had made the announcement, she hadn't even considered that he would actually want to go through with it. Now, she not only had to think of a way to ease out of the bind with Burnett, but she also had to convince her friend that a marriage between the two of them was totally out of the question.

Casey chuckled.

"What?" she said, automatically turning around to look at him again, wanting, as always, to share in the joke.

"Just thinking."

"Thinking what?"

"If you painted us now, what you'd call it."

Joanna knew she shouldn't ask what. "What?"

"The Marriage Proposal?"

She tried gentle reason. "It's really not a good idea, Casey. You have to accept that, then we can start thinking about how we're going to handle Burnett."

His gray-blue eyes still held a hint of teasing humor. "Why is it such a bad idea? Have you been holding out on me? Is there a new man in your life?" He gave her his gorgeous fly-boy smile.

She refused to smile back, though maintaining a serious expression took some effort. Casey had always had a devastating smile. Too often, he could get her to do anything he wanted just by smiling like that. "No," she said. "There's no one."

"Not for me, either. See? We're just getting to be

a couple of confirmed bachelors. Marriage. To each other. It's the only answer."

Joanna groaned. "Why are you being so stubborn about this?"

He stopped smiling and said nothing for a moment. The cricket kept up its cheerful song. "I have Mike to think about," he finally said.

Their eyes locked. He *would* have to bring the focus around to Mike.

She thought of Burnett, willing to throw them all into a lengthy court battle to get his way. And she thought of Mike, who could end up the *almost*-six-year-old victim of a lifelong war for dominance between two brothers. If Casey were married, Burnett would have no case at all—as long as the marriage provided a stable environment in which to raise a child.

If they decided to go through with it they would have to convince everyone that they were marrying because they wanted to bind their lives together in the truest sense of the word. Mike would only be benefiting from a decision that Casey and Joanna would have made anyway.

It wouldn't be so difficult to make the world believe they were in love, Joanna mused. No one else really understood the nature of their friendship anyway. Burnett, she was sure, actually believed that she and Casey had been lovers for years. Why not just let everyone think that they'd finally decided to make it legal?

The upstairs room she was staying in would be fine for a permanent studio. She could make Sacramento her base, rather than her West Hollywood apartment. And getting back and forth to Los Angeles to maintain her professional contacts there would present no problem. After all, Casey did own an airfield.

"You know it would work," Casey said softly, as if he could tell from her expression exactly what was going on in her mind.

"No, I don't," she lied, angry at her own mind for wandering off into dangerous conjecture about something she had no intention of doing.

"Yes, you do."

"I don't."

"Do."

"Don't."

"Do…"

They both sounded the way they had when they were children. Against her will, Joanna felt a smile coming on. "Will you stop it?" she begged.

"Then marry me." He grabbed her hand and started towing her to her feet.

"Casey…" she pleaded, trying to object.

But he was already taking her wine, setting it aside and pulling her toward the umbrella-shaded glass-topped picnic table on the edge of the lawn.

"Sit here," he said, and pushed her down into a padded lawn chair.

"Casey, no—"

He knelt before her. "Joanna, my darling—"

"Get up, you rat."

"Marry me and I'll give you two sunsets in one day, one on the ground and—"

"One in the air. I've heard it before." And she had, too. Years ago, in high school, he'd asked her what romantic words to say to a girl. She'd told him. In detail. And now she heard the flowery adolescent phrases she'd invented for him coming right back at her.

"I'll give you the sky—" he went on.

"Right. And the top of the clouds—"

"We'll touch the stars—"

"I know, I know. And swing from the moon."

"Joanna, I adore you. Let me take you to heaven on the wings of the night."

"I don't believe you're doing this."

He put his hand over the little alligator embroidered on his shirt. "I can't live without you."

"Fine. You won't have to. Lately, I'm here all the time anyway."

"Marry me."

"Not on your life."

The look of feigned ardor left his eyes; instead, they sparked with challenge. "I dare you to marry me."

Joanna decided the wiser course would be to pretend he hadn't said that. She said, "I'm not cut out to be a wife. The subject is closed." She held out her hand to him. "Come on. Stand up. You make me nervous when you're on your knees."

He took her hand and stood. "The dare's been made, Joey. Accept it."

She straightened the full peasant skirt of her dress over her crossed knees. "One of these days, you're going to have to grow up," she said, not looking at him.

"I *am* grown-up, Joey. The question is, are you?"

Joanna glanced up sharply at him. His gaze was probing, intense. She felt, for a moment, that inside him was a man who was a stranger to her.

But then he smiled, and he was just Casey again.

He shrugged and left to retrieve their glasses and the bottle of wine over by the rim of the pool. Joanna watched him, her artist's mind intrigued by the lean economy of his movements, by the way the pool lights shot brightness upward over his face as he bent to get the glasses, bathing his features in an eerie, rippling glow.

He returned and set her glass beside her on the picnic table. "I'm turning in," he said.

"You can't," she protested. "We have to talk about how we're going to handle Burnett."

"We'll get married right away," he told her. "That'll handle the problem just fine." His tone was the same as the one he would have used to tell her he was headed for the corner store to get a loaf of bread and a carton of milk.

"Absolutely not," she said.

"Joey," he reached down and chucked her under the chin, "a dare's a dare. Say yes."

"I'm not going to marry you."

"Remember Graeagle, Joey," he said cryptically. "Once you swore you'd marry Burnett and I swore you wouldn't. Who was right then?"

"You were," she readily agreed. "You said marriage would keep me from doing what I was meant to do."

"I said marriage to *the wrong guy* would be a disaster."

"And all of a sudden, after all these years, you've decided *you're* the right guy?"

"Look. I know we can be happy together. And we can give Mike what he needs. Think about that."

"Casey—"

But he would hear no more. He bent and kissed her on the forehead.

And then he went back inside.

Joanna sat alone for a while. Then she checked on Mike in his ground floor bedroom, reclaimed her sandals from the vestibule and climbed the stairs.

At the top of the landing she hesitated, considering going on to Casey's room. But she decided she had no idea what she wanted to say to him right then. She shook her head and opened the first door at the top of the stairs.

Once alone in the room that she'd started to think of as "hers" over the past five weeks, Joanna stepped out of her dress and tossed it across the back of a chair. Leaving on her slip she dropped her sandals by her drawing board.

Right after Emily died and Joanna had decided to remain for an open-ended visit, Casey had insisted that she set up the room as a studio. Besides the drawing board and easel, there were materials for stretching canvasses as well as a long folding table covered with art supplies.

The big bay windows on two of the walls drew the sun into the room, so that in the daytime it was washed with light. Though the view was of landscaped yards and gracious homes rather than the tarred rooftops of West Hollywood, the space itself was not that much different from the living room in her apartment, which Joanna used as her studio space at home.

For a moment, in the darkness, Joanna spared a guilty thought for all the work she hadn't been doing lately. She considered throwing on a robe and then sketching for a while before she went to bed. But she gave up on the idea; her mind was simply too preoccupied with her best friend and his outrageous announcement.

We can be happy together, Casey's words replayed in her head. And we can give Mike what he needs... Remember Graeagle...

The crazy events in Graeagle, the tiny Sierra foothill town where the Clintons owned a vacation cabin, had happened fourteen years ago. It was the summer that they had graduated from high school, the summer after Joanna's father died. Looking back, Joanna realized that she'd started seeing Burnett because her mother had approved of him. Joanna had wanted, impossibly, to make it up to her mother for losing her father. She'd longed to ease her mother's pain by becoming the kind of daughter that her mother had always wanted her to be.

But Casey Clinton had had other plans. And his actions then had been every bit as outrageous as those of tonight.

In hindsight, Joanna knew that her friend's outrageousness had saved her from a life she had never been meant to live. She would always be grateful to him for that.

But, she told herself firmly, being grateful doesn't mean I should marry him now.

In the small, functional bathroom that shared a wall with Casey's large, sybaritic one, she brushed her teeth. Then she returned to her room and climbed beneath the covers of a daybed.

Sleep, however, didn't come. She kept thinking about Graeagle.

Late on a Saturday afternoon in July, Casey had come to the door of her mother's house with some absurd story about needing her help getting his Bronco started. Totally unsuspecting, Joanna had followed him next door to his mother's garage where he'd grabbed her from behind, trussed her up like a prize turkey and driven off with her wedged behind the seats so no one would see he was abducting her.

Joanna smiled into the darkness. It had been an uncomfortable ride, bouncing around back there, whining and pleading while Casey occasionally tossed a sympathetic remark over his shoulder at her.

I hate to do this, Joey, but you didn't leave me any damn choice... Someday, you'll thank me for this... You're my best friend, I can't let you ruin your life....

When the bouncing and rolling of the truck had finally stopped, Casey had dragged her out by the feet, slung her over his shoulder and carried her, bucking and squirming, into the cabin. There, he'd locked her in for an entire night and for half of the next day while he badgered her relentlessly to break it off with his brother. He urged her to go to UCLA as she'd planned.

But he hadn't been able to keep her locked up forever. In the early afternoon, she'd grabbed his keys and bolted out the door.

He'd caught up with her at the tin-roofed garage, but she'd eluded him. So he'd chased her out behind the house, bringing her down on a scratchy bed of pine needles beneath the tall trees. They'd struggled.

He'd gained the top position, his bluejeaned knees planted on either side of her hips. She'd kept trying to punch him. But then he'd captured her wrists, pinning them to the prickly bed of pine needles beneath them.

He'd begged her to listen to reason, but she had only fought harder, insisting she loved Burnett. He'd called her a liar, and then announced bluntly that he knew she'd never made love with his brother.

"Your body knows the truth," he'd told her. "It shies away from him. Your body knows my brother will never let you be your real self. You can say you're waiting for marriage and all that, and a lot of people might even believe you. But this is Casey you're talking to, Joey. I'd never buy a story like that from you. You're not the type to hold out for a ring on your finger. If the trust and love were there, you'd be all over a guy like paint."

Not wanting to hear the truth in his words, Joanna had begun struggling again, demanding he let her up.

"Not yet." A cunning gleam had lit in his eyes. "I'm going to prove I'm right first..."

And then he'd kissed her. The only *real* kiss they'd ever shared.

With that kiss, Casey had proved she was lying to herself. Had she truly been in love with Burnett, then Casey's kiss never could have stirred her the way it did.

Joanna punched her pillow and rearranged it under her head. The kiss, really, had meant nothing, she told herself. There was no need to give it too much thought. He'd kissed her and she'd liked it; Casey had only done it because he wanted her to reconsider her plan to marry Burnett.

It was what followed the kiss that was important. He'd asked her, for the sake of their friendship, to stay until dark. She'd agreed. And through the rest of that afternoon and evening she had come back in touch

with who she really was and what she wanted to do
with her life. Casey had provided her with a sketch
pad and soft pencils, and insisted that she spend the
time drawing.

By the time they returned to Sacramento, Joanna
knew Casey was right, though she didn't know how
she was going to break it off with Burnett.

She needn't have worried. As soon as Burnett heard
that she'd stayed with Casey longer than she'd had to,
he'd asked for his ring back.

Joanna had felt ten pounds lighter after she'd
handed it to him.

She'd left to look for an apartment near UCLA two
weeks later. She saw Casey just once before she left.
He came over with the sketch pad she'd left in his
Bronco. He was wearing dark glasses that didn't completely cover either the big shiner or the bruise on his
left cheek.

"You should see Burnett," he'd offered wryly as
he'd handed her the pad.

"No, thanks. Do you want to come in?"

"Uh-uh. Gotta go. See you…" And he'd left. He
was headed for the navy, on his way toward fulfilling
his dream of testing fighter jets. He hadn't promised
to write, or to look her up between basic training and
whatever came next for him. She'd understood. They
were each starting a new life, and holding on to the
old was too dangerous then.

She'd put the sketch pad away in her closet, because
at that moment it would have made her sad to look at
the drawings inside. When she moved to Los Angeles
she forgot about the drawings. And when her mother
took the insurance windfall from her father's death and

moved into the big brick house in South Land Park, the sketch pad somehow was lost. But it was okay. There was so much to paint in the world, so many scenes and moments to capture. An afternoon and evening spent in Graeagle with her best friend wasn't something that clamored for her attention as time went by.

Now, though, as she lay awake in her studio in her best friend's house, she wondered what had happened to the sketch pad. She wondered if the sketches were as good as she had thought they were.

Probably not, she decided, so it was just as well that she'd never know. Let them remain perfect in her memory.

Joanna rolled over and faced the wall. She closed her eyes. In no time at all, she was dreaming.

"Joey?" The soft whisper came to her out of the darkness.

The dream she'd been having melted around her, and Joanna found herself sitting up in the daybed in Casey's house, clutching the blanket to her breasts. With her free hand, she rubbed the grogginess from her eyes and raked her hair back from her face.

"Casey?" She could see the outline of his torso, the beautiful, spare musculature of his shoulders, and the shadow of his head against the window. He was half sitting, with one leg resting on the window seat in the bay window opposite her bed. The only item of clothing he had on were the slacks he'd worn that night.

She squinted at him, trying to focus on him. It was dark, but he was outlined in moonlight. "What is it?"

She knew he was watching her, though she couldn't see his eyes. "I couldn't sleep," he said.

She clutched the covers a little closer against herself, feeling at a disadvantage, half-asleep and bathed in moonlight before the eyes she knew so well but in the darkness couldn't see.

He was behaving so uncharacteristically, entering her room without warning. If there was one thing they had both always respected, it was each other's privacy. But then, she reminded herself, everything between them had suddenly changed. He had dared her to marry him.

And never had she been able to refuse one of his dares.

"Thinking about us?" she asked.

"Yeah."

When he didn't go on, she tried to bridge the awkward silence by saying, "I was dreaming."

"About what?"

Joanna secured the sheet around herself and leaned back against the bolsters. She closed her eyes briefly, calling up the dream he'd interrupted.

"It was at the first Chilly Lilly's," she said, referring to the chain of ice cream stores that Casey's mother had started and Burnett now operated. "I was twelve again, and I was calling for you. When you came, you were an adult. I was all upset that you'd gone and grown up without me."

He turned his head, and she saw his profile, the strong Clinton nose making it resemble a profile on a Roman coin. "Sounds pretty scary to me," he said. He remained turned away from her, looking out the window at the shingled roof of the house next door.

"It wasn't scary. Not really,' she said.

"It was only a dream, anyway," he said when she didn't go on.

"Yes. Just a dream."

He stood up then. "I can't stop thinking about this," he said, and she knew he was referring to their possible marriage. "I want us to settle the matter." His voice, low and serious, lacked any trace of his usual humor.

Her throat felt thick. It was so eerie. Limned in moonlight, he could have been anyone. He could have been the dark prince of her most primal romantic fantasy. Her own private Heathcliff, her other half come to claim her.

"Tonight?" she asked, the question husky and hesitant.

"Yeah. I want you to say yes. I know it can work. We can make it work."

She thought about how much she owed him, and the promises she'd made to both his sister and to Mike.

"Say yes," he prompted.

He moved toward her, a shadow with substance crossing the smooth wood floor.

Her answer surprised her with its steadiness. "All right," she said. "I'll marry you, Casey."

He came no closer. He nodded. "Good night, then, Joey," he said, and was gone.

Chapter Three

"The garden looks lovely," Casey's mother, Lillian, said. Lillian was standing at the window, gazing down on the guests in the garden below.

Joanna stared at her own reflection in the vanity table mirror, finding it hard to believe that the bride who gazed back at her was really herself.

"How your mother managed to orchestrate all this in less than two weeks is beyond my comprehension," Lillian remarked.

Joanna brushed at the skirt of her magnolia-white crepe georgette dress, her thoughts turning to her own mother. Joanna had been surprised at how readily Marie Vail had sanctioned this marriage.

All through Joanna's childhood Marie's fondest wish had been that "that wild Casey Clinton" would drop off the face of the earth—and take Joanna's art supplies along with him.

But, over the years, when she'd seen how happy Joanna was with the life she'd chosen, Marie had changed her opinion. All she'd asked for, when Joanna told her that she and Casey were going to get married, was the privilege of giving her daughter a garden wedding in her own backyard.

Lillian turned from the window and smiled at Joanna, her hazel eyes lighting in appreciation. "You look beautiful."

Joanna made a face at herself in the mirror and then smoothed the low sweetheart neckline of her dress. "I feel kind of frazzled."

"Well, no one will guess. You look stunningly composed." Lillian left the window to come and stand behind her. Setting her clutch purse on a corner of the vanity table, Lillian bent over and brushed her cheek against Joanna's. The touch was feather-light, in consideration of Joanna's hair, which had been swept up in a soft Gibson girl style and threaded with tiny white silk flowers.

"My son's a lucky man," Lillian breathed in her ear.

Joanna immediately felt her frayed nerves relaxing. For Joanna, Lillian Clinton had always had the ability to put things in perspective. All it took was a reassuring touch from Casey's mother and the roughest challenge seemed easily surmountable.

She smiled at Lillian in the mirror.

"Is Casey even here?" she asked wryly. "I've spent so much time getting ready for today that we've hardly seen each other lately. If he's changed his mind about marrying me, I wouldn't even know."

Though Joanna didn't mention it, her work had also

suffered. She hadn't picked up a brush or her sketch pad since the night Casey had told his brother about the marriage. And Lord knew she hadn't been doing all that much before that. Since Emily's funeral, her creative life seemed to have come to a standstill.

Joanna couldn't afford the hiatus, either. The small gallery in Los Angeles that exhibited her work had agreed to give her her own show in September. She'd promised Althea Gatin, the gallery owner, some new pieces. But she hadn't come up with even a ghost of an idea for anything new. In the past two months, her life had changed so drastically that she was beginning to wonder if things would ever seem normal again.

Lillian's hand rested comfortingly on her shoulder. Joanna gave it a companionable squeeze.

"I'm sure things will settle down after today," Joanna said, pushing her anxieties about her work to the back of her mind.

"And you don't need to worry," Lillian teased. "I saw Casey not five minutes ago. He looked fine. Not the least likely to leave you waiting at the altar." Lillian scooped up her clutch purse from the table and stepped back. "Now stand up and let's admire you."

Joanna obligingly pushed back the vanity stool and went to twirl before the mirrored wall of the closet. The calf-length dress floated around her deliciously, the crepe so light it was like a spun breeze. The long raglan sleeves draped softly in tiny gathers that were repeated at either side of the silk-buttoned bodice.

"Something old?" Lillian asked.

Joanna shot her a puzzled look before catching on. "I completely forgot."

Lillian pretended to look disapproving. "Well, the dress is new. How about borrowed?"

Joanna grinned smugly, and touched the pearl clip that nestled with the little flowers in her hair. "This is Mother's."

"And blue?"

Joanna lifted a froth of white crepe to reveal her powder-blue garter.

"Good, but you need something old," Lillian insisted. "It's a tradition."

"It doesn't matter. I've never been a very traditional woman anyway."

"Don't say that," Lillian chided, "or you'll ruin my surprise." Wearing a Mona Lisa smile, she slipped the catch on her clutch purse and extracted a midnight-blue satin bag.

"Maybe this will help." The satin bag was old, creased in places, but very fine. Lillian loosened the drawstring. "Hold out your hand."

Joanna obeyed and a five-strand pearl choker, bound with an enhancer of ice-bright diamonds, dropped into her palm. Joanna had seen the necklace once before, on the day that Emily had married Michael Nevis.

"It belonged to my grandmother," Lillian said. "She gave it to my mother on the day of her wedding, and my mother handed it down to me when I married. I was fortunate to see my own daughter wear it on her wedding day." Lillian's voice had become, suddenly, very low and controlled. "And then it came back to me...when Emily died."

Joanna looked up from the pearls as Lillian glanced away.

"Lillian?"

"Oh, this is awful. I wasn't going to cry."

Diffidently, Joanna touched Lillian's shoulder. The older woman stiffened, and then swayed toward Joanna, allowing Joanna to wrap comforting arms around her.

"I'll muss your beautiful hair,' Lillian sighed.

"So what?" Joanna held on.

"Oh, Joey. I miss her so."

"I know. We all do."

"And how she'd have loved to have been here today. You and Casey were two of her favorite people, you know."

Down in the yard, the pianist Marie had hired was playing a slow ballad that had been popular a decade before.

For a moment, Joanna wished fervently that she hadn't chosen the song. It was too sad for a wedding. But then, in her mind, she saw Emily...

As a skinny little girl in pink shorts with scabs on her knees, hanging upside down from a jungle gym bar: "Casey, Joey, watch me now!"

At thirteen, her strawberry-blond hair sticking out in scouring-pad curls, confiding feminine secrets: "His name is Bobby Jordan, he's a freshman and I think he likes me. It's the perm, I think. It makes me look older."

At fifteen, registering true horror: "Joey, you're an artist! If you marry Burnett, you'll never forgive yourself. *I'll* never forgive you. It's too grotesque to believe!"

At eighteen, hazel eyes aglow: "His name is Michael Nevis, and I love him, Joey, oh so much..."

At twenty-four, two years ago, sitting in a bright

swath of morning sun, her face drawn and vulnerable: "Joey, if Casey had any trouble managing alone, would you help out? And don't give me that nothing's-going-to-happen-to-you look. Sometimes in life, things do happen. Michael's death proved that to me. I want to know that my son will have every chance for love and happiness, whether I'm there or not..."

And in the hospital, just a few months ago, weakened so badly by the virus that had attacked her heart: "This is pointless, I know. But I keep thinking you'll all forget me." The freckles across her nose were barely noticeable, as if her illness had bleached them. "Isn't that silly?"

"No, it's not," Joanna remembered replying, "And we won't forget you. Not ever."

Emily's brave smile had an otherwordly luminosity, "Promise?"

"Promise."

To herself, now, as she held on to Lillian, Joanna silently promised again: We won't forget you, Emily. And we'll make sure that Mike has his chance for all the love and happiness we can give him.

Down in the yard, the song ended. Lillian gave Joanna an extra squeeze, and then pulled away to dash at her damp cheeks with the back of her hand. "Now, give me those pearls. I want to see how they look on you."

Lillian took the necklace, fastening the shining line of diamonds beneath the cluster of dark curls that the hairdresser had let down in back and brushed over one of Joanna's shoulders. "Perfect," she said, when she was done.

Joanna touched the glowing strands. They shone

with a rich luster against her skin. "I promise I'll take good care of them."

"Do that," Lillian said. "For the rest of your life."

It took a moment for Lillian's meaning to register. Then Joanna quickly demurred. "Oh, no, Lillian. I couldn't."

"You can and you will. For loving my son, and making him the happiest man in the world at last."

Joanna wanted to cry. The pearls were so beautiful, and yet she felt that taking them would be dishonest. She did love Casey, but not in the way Lillian assumed.

We're doing the right thing, I know we are, she reminded herself silently. Casey and I will have a good life together. It'll work out. It *has* to work out, for Mike's sake.

In the garden below, the pianist had switched to Chopin. Soon, he'd be playing the wedding march. Joanna realized her knees were shaking.

It was really going to happen. She was getting married. To Casey.

Suddenly, it all seemed overwhelming. She, Joanna Vail, artist, a contented and confirmed bachelor by her own definition, was getting married within a matter of minutes.

"Joey? Are you all right?" Lillian's voice came to her.

"Yes," Joanna said, forcing herself to smile. "I'm fine. It's just, you know, wedding day jitters." She glanced at the mirror again, and remembered what she'd been trying to tell Lillian. "And I can't keep the pearls. It wouldn't be right."

"I don't want to hear any more about it." Lillian

made her voice stern. "Since it's highly unlikely I'll have another daughter, Casey's wife is the perfect choice for my grandmother's pearls. Now tell me you love them, and you'll treasure them always."

Joanna saw that any further debate would only hurt Lillian, and ruin her joy in presenting such a gift. Resolutely, Joanna pushed away her guilt at letting Lillian think she and Casey were in love. "I adore them," she said. "And I'll treasure them always."

"That's better." Lillian looked content.

Joanna went to the window and gazed out on a cloudless azure sky. The day was perfect for a wedding, sunny, but not too hot. She shifted her gaze downward, to the small gathering of people in the garden.

Beneath a trellis arbor twined with white roses and lilies of the valley, her mother was talking with the minister. Marie glanced up toward the window. Joanna leaned closer to the glass so that her mother could see her. Marie lifted her hand, and Joanna waved back in a signal the two of them had prearranged.

Marie's eager smile was bright as a new day. Joanna smiled back, feeling the tightness of emotion in her chest. Planning a wedding in ten days might be a nerve-racking experience for all concerned, but some good had come of it, too. Joanna felt closer to her mother now than she ever would have thought possible in the years she was growing up.

Joanna turned to Lillian. "Time to go down."

Lillian held out the bouquet of tuberoses and magnolias. Joanna accepted it with a hand that hardly shook at all.

* * *

Joanna stood by the side door, thinking vaguely that after this day the scent of tuberoses would always remind her of her wedding day.

The caterer's staff worked quietly by the sink and stove, clinking pans and spoons in a hushed, almost reverent manner. Beyond the kitchen windows, Joanna could see the backs of her friends and family, sitting patiently, waiting for her, the bride, to appear.

The wedding march began, and Joanna left the kitchen to walk up the garden steps to the slate stepping stones that made a natural aisle between the rows of chairs. She heard the muffled rustling as people shifted in their seats to watch her progress. She was aware of their upturned faces, glowing like moons as she passed.

She wondered, is this how every bride feels? Disoriented, floating, numbly abashed that all these people are staring at her?

The minister, a round and smiling man who presided over the church Marie attended, waited beneath the arbor, his face beaming. To the left stood Mike, the only attendant, holding a little tasseled pillow with the rings on it. He was wearing a boy's size cutaway morning coat, with a silk ascot tie and gray striped slacks. He looked very intense, clearly taking the responsibility of his job as ring bearer seriously.

Casey waited in front of the minister. As she moved slowly toward the empty space beside him, Joanna found herself unable to look directly at him. His clothing was identical to Mike's. He was dressed in a gray morning coat and striped slacks, with a white rose in his lapel. The late afternoon sun caught the gold highlights in his hair. Joanna glanced rather desperately over his shoulder, at the beaming minister, at the roses that twined on the arbor, at the clear summer sky, at anything but this man she'd grown up with who would become her husband within a matter of minutes.

The wedding march ended. Joanna was standing at Casey's side. She shot him a nervous, oblique glance and he turned to face the minister with her.

"Dearly beloved, we are gathered here…" the minister began.

Joanna watched the minister's smiling mouth move, and soon she heard the man beside her murmur, "I will."

Then it was her turn. Her voice was surprisingly firm and clear, even clearer than Casey's, she realized with a little flare of pride.

Mike stepped up with the tasseled pillow, and the minister explained the meaning of the rings.

"Like a circle, enclosing your love, infinite and everlasting…"

She looked down at the sprinkling of bronze hairs on the back of Casey's hand as she put the gold band on his finger, and she thought how warm his touch was—and gentle, too—as he slipped her ring in place.

Then the minister said Casey could kiss the bride. Casey put a finger under her chin and tipped her face up, and there was no choice for her but to really look at him.

"Hello, there," he mouthed silently. There were crinkles at the corners of his eyes. He was smiling that smile he always gave her when she was taking herself too seriously—it seemed to say "lighten up." He lifted an eyebrow and she was sure he was thinking the same thing she was; this was going to be their second real kiss.

In recent years, of course, they had often kissed each other. Those little offhand, pecking kisses that you gave someone you cared about when you greeted them, or when you were leaving them. Kisses that missed the person and hit the air around the person's head instead. Hello or see-you-later or how's-it-going kisses.

Their only real kiss had been fourteen years ago beneath the pines at Graeagle.

And now, here they were, on the verge of their second real kiss, and there were at least forty pairs of eyes watching them. Joanna thought of the innumerable lists her mother had made, and wished she had jotted on one of them, "practice kissing Casey." Because right now, she felt woefully unprepared.

Luckily, Casey seemed willing to meet the challenge. One arm slid to her waist and encircled it, bringing her against him. Since they were almost the same height, they made a surprisingly nice fit, Joanna decided with the objective part of her mind.

She heard a muffled chuckle from somewhere among the guests as Casey's index finger left off propping up her chin to trail down the side of her neck. Lightly, he slipped the finger up under his great-grandmother's antique pearl choker and brought her face close enough to his to get the job done.

Their lips met. His were coaxingly sweet as she somehow knew they would be, or maybe as she remembered them to be so long ago. Joanna's mouth gave under the tender pressure, opening just enough that he subtly traced the inner surface of her lips with

a playful tongue. She smiled into the kiss, feeling soft
and shy and exceedingly feminine. His arm was firm
and supportive at her waist, and his other hand twined
seductively in the mass of dark curls at her nape.

She sighed, because it was so lovely. And she totally forgot they had an audience at all until the minister coughed politely.

Casey stopped doing those magical things to her
mouth, and stepped away, looping her arm through
his. Bemused, she smiled at him. He winked in return,
but as subtly as his tongue had teased her lips, so no
one else could see. They walked back up the aisle side
by side.

Since the wedding was so small and informal, Marie
had been persuaded to dispense with a receiving line.
Still, once they'd cleared the last row of chairs, Joanna
and Casey found themselves surrounded by well-
wishers.

She was hugged and kissed. Her back was pounded
heartily by one of Casey's flight instructors. The Clinton Airfield office manager, Rhonda Popper, who used
a blue rinse on her gray hair and traditionally went to
work wearing jogging clothes, had actually worn a
dress for the occasion. She grabbed Joanna and commanded with husky fierceness, "You be good to him,
you hear?"

"I will," Joanna promised. Over Rhonda's shoulder, Joanna caught a glimpse of raven-black hair and
slanted blue eyes. Rhonda stepped away and Althea
Gatin took her place.

"You made it. I can hardly believe it." Joanna
forced a laugh, dreading the moment when the gallery

owner would ask how she was doing on the paintings for the show in September.

Althea bestowed an airy kiss on each of Joanna's cheeks. "I have to keep a watchful eye on my investments, you know." Althea grinned, then murmured in her ear, "I know this isn't the best timing, but I have to get back to L.A. tonight. After the crowd thins out a little, may I have a few moments to go over some business?"

"Sure," Joanna answered promptly, feeling guilty all over again that she'd had no time in the past weeks to think of her work.

"Good," Althea said. "Now, where's the champagne? Weddings always make me thirsty."

Joanna sighed as she watched Althea edge off toward the bar that had been set up down in the lower yard. Before she'd left Los Angeles for Emily's funeral, she'd promised Althea that on her return they'd sit down and make some solid decisions about the theme and scope of her show. But then, she hadn't returned. The few telephone conversations she'd had with Althea since then had been brief, and evasive on her part.

Joanna pushed her neglected work from her mind as the next group of well-wishers stepped up, and Joanna and Casey were again hugged and kissed and congratulated. Finally, the press of people eased—and Marie closed in. "Time for the pictures," she announced.

Joanna found herself standing again beneath the arbor, being snapped in a variety of groupings for the sake of posterity.

More than one shot included Amanda and Burnett,

as immediate family to the groom. The photographer posed Amanda just behind Joanna. As he busied himself placing the subjects and then framing the shot, Amanda whispered tightly into Joanna's ear.

"Joey, aren't those Emily's pearls?"

Joanna was spared a reply by the photographer's command that everybody smile and then his subsequent request for a few more shots of the newlyweds only.

She was soon in Casey's arms again, kissing him for the camera.

"Perfect," said the photographer. "You can stop now."

Joanna, enjoying once again the tender feel of Casey's lips against her own, pulled away with an embarrassed little laugh. Casey lifted his head and she caught a slumberous glint in his eyes, a look that reminded her of the night to come, when they'd be alone together as man and wife for the first time.

That feeling of unreality assailed her again—so much was happening all at once. She was experiencing a kind of emotional vertigo, as if she'd climbed too high too fast and now found herself teetering on the edge of a cliff.

She was *married* to Casey. And tonight, they would do the intimate things that married people did.

It occurred to her that, in all the hustle and bustle to get married, they had never once discussed how they would handle physical intimacy. How in the world could they have forgotten to deal with sex?

Rather frantically, Joanna glanced around the yard, looking for something to focus on, to distract her from further unnerving speculation about her first night as

Casey's wife. Her gaze settled on Mike, who was lurking over by the buffet tables, near the wedding cake. He stuck his finger in the frosting and was promptly shooed away by the caterer's assistant.

"Think," Casey said softly, noticing that her eyes were on Mike. "In four years, he'll be the age we were when we first met." He draped an arm across her shoulder. At first she relaxed against him in a comradely way, just as she'd done so many times before. It came to her again that he was her husband now. They were still the same people, yet everything had changed. She didn't move, though her body stiffened slightly. Casey's arm dropped away from her shoulder.

Seeing her opportunity, Althea Gatin approached with one of the flying instructors from the airfield. She patted her escort's arm. "Why don't you and Casey go talk about flight patterns or something. I've got business with the bride."

"Business?" Casey asked. "On our wedding day?"

"Sorry," Althea said. "But your new wife's been a little hard to pin down lately."

Casey laughed. "I understand."

Even through the haze of unreality that had settled over her, Joanna thought he sounded like he really did understand. She reminded herself to be grateful for that. Casey had always taken her work seriously.

She stared after him for a moment, as he walked away with Althea's escort. As he turned his head to speak to his companion, she could see his face in profile. She was impressed by how handsome he was, her new husband... Absurdly, Joanna felt her face flushing.

Althea wasted no time in leading Joanna to a redwood bench in the corner of the yard. "So, how are you doing with my pieces for September?"

Joanna forced her mind to concentrate on business, and cast desperately about for the words to reassure Althea that everything was fine. "I'm working on something…totally different. In fact, I need a little more time before I'll be ready to talk about it."

Althea gave her a glance from those mysteriously slanted eyes, and Joanna knew that the gallery owner hadn't been fooled in the least. "Nothing at all, huh?"

"Things should be settling down here now," Joanna said, wondering how many times she'd used that justification lately. "Then I'll be able to really get some work done."

Althea's sculpted mouth curved upward. "When? During your honeymoon?"

"We aren't taking a honeymoon," Joanna said levelly. Once or twice in the past few days, Casey had dropped some hints about a secluded mountain lodge he knew of in Idaho, but nothing had been agreed upon. Now, as Joanna thought about her career, she decided firmly that they were staying home and she was getting down to work.

"No honeymoon," Althea echoed. "That's a definite?"

"Definite."

"Then you're ready to take on another major commission?"

"What kind of commission?" Joanna stifled an urge to groan aloud, and reminded herself reprovingly that one didn't build a career by turning down work, no matter how behind one was.

"Wall art," Althea answered briskly. "Desert

Empire Savings. They've got six branches in Southern California and Arizona. Good money and relatively easy, though the total number of pieces would be considerable.''

"Did they ask for me, specifically?"

Althea nodded. ''Their representative came into the gallery last week and looked around. Her name is Niki Tori. She felt that those desertscapes you did out at Joshua Tree were stunning—her word—and she liked the Los Padres Forest series. But her greatest interest was in those three light-and-texture studies. If you ask me, that's the kind of thing she'll be after rather than anything too representational.

"She wants to meet with you, of course." Althea's voice had become far too offhand.

Joanna gave a fatalistic sigh. "You've already set an appointment, haven't you?"

"Nothing ventured—"

"When?"

"August first, a week from this coming Tuesday. Lunch." Althea chuckled wryly. "Lucky you're skipping the honeymoon, isn't it?"

"Very."

"Well?"

"All right. I'll meet with her. But we both know I'm backed up with the show. If she can't give me a reasonable time frame, I'll have to—"

"Don't say it," Althea cut in, only half jokingly. "Wait until you hear the figures. You won't be able to turn it down. And if we have to, we can put off the show."

Joanna rushed to veto that idea. "No, I don't want

to do that. It's a big step for me, and I don't want to lose it.''

''I didn't say cancel.''

''I know what you said. We'd put it off until you have another slot, which could mean a wait of as much as a year. Admit it.''

''Joanna, we'll work it out. And stop frowning. You'll get wrinkles before your time.''

Joanna said nothing for a moment, only looked down at her satin shoes. When she glanced back up, she'd concluded that the gallery owner was right—and not only about the wrinkles. She'd always known that it wouldn't be easy combining her career with a family. The last week or so she'd told herself that she'd manage it somehow. Some person she'd turn out to be if she went under at the first challenge.

''That's better,'' Althea said, approving the change in Joanna's expression. ''And since you'll be in L.A. for your meeting about the bank commission, we can get down to details on your show once you're through with your negotiations.''

''In other words, have something ready by then or else?''

''Well, it would be nice to know what I'm building a whole show out of. Now, I suppose I should let you get back to your wedding day.''

''Thanks,'' Joanna murmured dryly.

''That's quite all right. Where is my flyer?'' Althea scanned the yard. ''Oh, there he is...'' The gallery owner stood up and headed for the buffet tables.

Joanna was left alone on the bench—but not for long. Her Aunt Edna, her mother's sister, soon joined her. Then Nancy, one of Edna's six daughters, strolled over, bringing her own two daughters, and then another aunt, from her father's side of the family. They talked about what a perfect day it was and how wonderful it was that their Joey was at last beginning a family of her own.

She could see Althea and her flyer standing near the bar by the kitchen door. Althea was talking animatedly while her escort was listening.

Joanna couldn't see Casey anywhere.

"Don't you think so, Joanna?" her Aunt Edna was asking.

Joanna brought her attention back to the group of women around her. "I'm sorry. I was thinking of something else. What did you say?"

Aunt Edna smiled knowingly. "Never mind, dear. It's not important."

"If you're looking for Casey, I think I saw him go into the house a few minutes ago," Nancy said.

"Oh, really?" Joanna stood up. "I think I'll go find him."

As she walked away, she could hear her aunts and cousins agreeing on what a beautiful bride she made.

In the house, the kitchen was a beehive of activity, but Casey wasn't there. He wasn't in the big living room, either.

But Amanda was. She hovered near the entrance to the foyer, as if awaiting the signal for a quick getaway.

"Joanna, we were just thinking of leaving," Amanda hastened to explain in a breathless rush, as if she'd been caught doing something reprehensible. "But then Casey and Burnett got into a little discussion."

Dread tightened in Joanna's stomach. For the past

ten days, Burnett and his wife had kept a low profile. Joanna had hoped that they might continue to do so— at least until after the wedding. "Where are they?" she asked Amanda.

"Actually, I think they wanted a bit of privacy," Amanda said. "You know how men are."

"What exactly are they discussing, Amanda?"

Amanda glanced nervously around, as if hoping someone would appear to save her from this disagreeable conversation. "Now settle down, Joey. Let's not be hostile."

Joanna remained calm and reasonable. "I'm not hostile, Amanda. I just want to know what's going on."

"Oh, all right." Amanda's attitude of strained propitiation turned to one of resigned acceptance. She tugged Joanna into the shadow of the foyer and spoke in an intimate whisper. "It all started with the pearls," she chided, as if Joanna were a badly behaved child. "You really were naughty to take them, Joey. Those pearls belong in the Clinton family."

Joanna decided against making the obvious arguments: she *was* in the family now. And she hadn't *taken* them; Lillian had given them to her. "What did you do? Corner Lillian and demand to know if she'd given me her grandmother's pearls?"

Amanda's gaze slid guiltily away, then she stuck her chin in the air and said with wounded dignity, "I didn't *demand* anything. I simply asked politely is all."

"And then you went straight to Burnett with the news."

Amanda's eyes glittered like chips of blue ice. "I

certainly did. It's bad enough that you and Casey have engineered this fake marriage just so Casey can get his way against Burnett. But when it's all over and Burnett and I have been left to pick up the pieces, I can't bear the thought of you slipping off to Los Angeles with the family jewels.''

Joanna didn't know whether to laugh aloud at the twisted workings of Amanda's mind, or to grab the blonde by her delicate shoulders and shake her until her French twist came loose.

Until Emily's death, Joanna had had little opportunity to get to know Burnett's wife. The past weeks had done much to convince her that the less she knew about Amanda Clinton, the better. The woman was like some kind of nightmare Mrs. America, a Princess Grace with fangs.

''Where are they now?'' Joanna asked in as civil a tone as she could muster.

''Now, Joey, they want to talk in private.''

''I really don't care what they want.'' Joanna clasped Amanda's shoulders firmly, impaling her on a stare. ''Where are they?''

''Joey, please. You're wrinkling my dress.''

''Where?''

''Oh, all right.'' Amanda gave a weak little shake, and Joanna released her. ''Upstairs,'' Amanda confessed sulkily. ''But never tell me I didn't warn you to mind your own business.''

''But this *is* my business, Amanda.''

''You make everything your business,'' Amanda accused, her voice low and sibilant. ''That's the pushy, unfeminine kind of woman you are.''

''I'm sorry you feel that way, Amanda.''

"Oh no you're not. You don't care how anybody feels, just as long as you get your way."

Joanna left Burnett's wife wearing a disdainful pout and smoothing the silk of her sleeve.

She was already on the stairs when Marie called to her from the door to the kitchen. "Joanna, there you are." Joanna watched her mother approach, followed by Lillian. "Everyone's asking where the bride and groom have gone off to." Marie bustled up, Lillian close behind. Both women stood at the foot of the stairs and looked up at her expectantly.

Joanna hesitated in midstep. "I think Casey's upstairs with Burnett," she explained, eager to be gone. "I was just going to find him." She started to rush up the stairs again.

Her mother's voice stopped her. "Joanna? Is something wrong?" A worried frown had creased Marie's forehead. She'd begun to suspect that something disturbing was going on. "Joanna? What is it?"

"Nothing. Really." Joanna tried to keep her expression composed as she decided her next move. The last thing she wanted was to lead the two women in the middle of a fight. But, on the other hand, it was too late to insist that they stay behind without further worrying Marie.

Well, she finally reasoned rather desperately, when in doubt, do something. Joanna gulped and beamed a thousand watt smile at her mother. "Why don't you two come help me drag them back down to the party?"

"Certainly." The deep worry lines in Marie's forehead eased. "Come on, Lillian." Marie was already bustling up the stairs.

Chapter Four

When she reached the top step, Joanna could hear muffled masculine voices in the bedroom off the stairwell.

Without a pause, she swept into the room. "There you two are!" Her voice was absurdly breathy. "I've been looking all over for you."

Burnett, who was facing the far wall, turned and glowered. Casey, slouched in an armchair, lifted an eyebrow at her and then gave a low chuckle when he saw Marie and Lillian behind her.

Lillian stayed near the door wearing a pleasant, neutral smile. Marie, on the other hand, seemed to have assessed the situation at a glance. She bustled into the room. "Come along, now, Casey," Marie clucked. "Your guests are feeling neglected." She gave Burnett one of her best hostess smiles. "You two don't mind continuing your little talk later. Do you?"

Burnett said nothing for a moment, and Joanna found herself waiting fatalistically for the ax to fall. But when he spoke, it was in a perfectly civil tone.

"No, of course not. Amanda and I have to be going anyway." Confronted by his hostess, the bride and his own mother, he'd obviously decided it would be in bad taste to continue fighting with the groom.

"Oh. So soon?" Marie said. Joanna glanced sharply at her mother, whose expression was too guileless to believe.

"Yes, I'm afraid so," Burnett answered in a tone of feigned regret. He nodded at his brother. "Casey."

Wryly, Casey saluted him.

"Goodbye, Joanna," Burnett said with the strained nobility of a king being polite to one of the palace serving girls.

Joanna nodded, though she needn't have bothered. The tall, imposing figure was already passing Lillian at the door.

"We'll see them out," Marie announced, taking Lillian's arm and starting for the stairs. She turned briefly to her daughter and new son-in-law. "Come along, you two. You'll have a lifetime to be alone together. But now, your guests are waiting."

Casey uncurled from his chair and approached Joanna.

"What happened?" she asked.

He shook his head. "More of the same. We can talk about it tonight, after all this is over."

Joanna decided he was right, now was not the time.

"I think I'm ready for champagne," she said. "About a barrelful."

Casey took her arm and they descended the stairs to rejoin the party.

In the yard, the shadows grew longer as evening approached. The rituals of the wedding day continued, one after the other.

Joanna and Casey ate together at one of the small round tables that had been set up near the buffet. They cut the cake and fed each other sugary slices for the photographer's benefit. They drank champagne from each other's glasses, elbows linked, as her Aunt Edna's husband, Uncle Nathan, proposed toast after toast:

"To Life.

"To Health.

"To Love.

"To Happiness…"

And after darkness fell and the aisles of folding chairs had been cleared away, they danced on the lawn in the upper yard as a sliver of moon smiled down on them.

Joanna had always liked dancing with Casey. He knew how to lead, but he never made his partner aware that he was doing so. Joanna gave herself over to the music, a blissful lassitude invading her limbs.

"Nice," she sighed.

He made a low answering sound and pulled her closer.

The champagne was really doing the trick, she decided. "I think everything's going to be fine," she murmured in his ear. "As Uncle Nathan pointed out, we're alive and we're healthy. We love each other, um, in our own way. So I think this must be happiness I'm feeling right now.''

''*I* think you're feeling about four glasses of champagne.''

''You're right,'' she said. ''It's a bubbly kind of happiness. And I like it very much. I hope it never ends.''

''Is that what you'll say in the morning?''

''No, in the morning, I'll probably say, 'where's the aspirin?' ''

His low chuckle stirred her hair as he pulled her close again.

An hour later, Joanna stood on the staircase and tossed her bouquet. Althea, who'd been married more than once already, snatched it from the air. ''Oh, no!'' The gallery owner's trilling laugh rang out. ''Not again...''

A cousin of Casey's caught the garter and promptly displayed it on his sleeve.

Mike had fallen asleep on the living-room floor and Rhonda Popper had carried him up to one of the bedrooms. Casey and Joanna went to get him. They found him sleeping on his stomach in his T-shirt and slacks. Rhonda had thoughtfully seen to the removal of his coat, shirt and shoes. His head was turned to the side, his mouth open.

''Down for the count,'' Casey said softly. ''I wish I didn't have to disturb him.''

Casey scooped up his nephew and settled the boy's head on his shoulder. Mike's stockinged feet dangled below Casey's waist. His red-blond hair stood straight up from his head where he'd lain on it.

''He doesn't look too bothered,'' Joanna remarked,

as Mike gave a sleepy little snort and snuggled more comfortably into the curve of Casey's neck.

Casey captured her gaze over Mike's tousled head. As always, his crooked grin charmed her.

Joanna grinned back, thinking that the happiness of the rumpled child in Casey's arms was well worth the chaos of all the changes occurring in their lives.

"Let's go home," Casey said.

Joanna turned and led the way.

Mike slept through the congratulatory goodbyes, through being strapped into the back seat of the car, and even through the ride home, a noisy experience because of the clanging rattle of the cans that one of Casey's friends had tied to the muffler.

They put him to bed in his room without even undressing him, and he crawled beneath the covers, not really waking except to mutter, "Can we have waffles tomorrow, to celebrate?"

"You bet, now back to sleep." Joanna tugged the blankets up around him and settled him in. Then she and Casey left him to his dreams.

They went upstairs, talking softly about the day's events. It seemed perfectly natural for them to go to Casey's room.

Casey flicked on the two lamps by the bed, and the sparsely furnished space glowed with subtle light. When Casey had first shown her the room, four years ago, Joanna had been intrigued. Its spareness had surprised her. Before, Casey's taste had always run to the "tacky-sexy," as she used to tease him. He'd liked intense colors and water beds. But this room was different. Perhaps it reflected a more mature Casey.

The walls and ceiling were painted off-white. The big bed had a black iron frame, its four slender black posts capped with lethal looking spiked finials. The bed linen was creamy white, but the throw covers across the foot resembled a Moorish tapestry, in blood red, mustard and black. The short, close-woven carpet was the color of tanned leather, and the bedstands and chests were of dark, rich mahogany.

A pair of Tuscan mahogany columns defined a sitting area, which contained a small cinnamon-brown leather couch, two armchairs and a mother-of-pearl inlaid mahogany trunk that doubled as a low table. Like Joanna's room across the landing, this room had two large bay windows, one behind the couch and the other on the adjacent wall. There was also a whimsical round window, high above the bed, which Joanna had loved on sight. In the daytime, it let in a leaf-shadowed disc of sunlight that moved around the room as the hours advanced.

Joanna slipped out of her shoes and settled into one of the armchairs, immediately drawing her legs up under the diaphanous fabric of her dress. She felt utterly at ease. Her nervousness about the time when they'd finally be alone together as man and wife had faded away. Now that the moment was actually here, she recognized the absurdity of her fears. After all, they were still the same two people, best friends since childhood. On the deepest level, nothing had really changed.

Casey, however, seemed a little on edge. He prowled the room, shrugging out of his jacket, getting rid of his ascot and unbuttoning the wing collar of his stiff, starched shirt.

When he sat on the edge of the bed and shucked off his shoes, he appeared to relax. A smile played on his lips as they spoke of Marie's take-charge behavior with Burnett.

"I never thought I'd say this," he remarked after she'd told him how Marie and Lillian had caught her on the stairs. "But I think I could get to like your mother."

"Know what? I think I could, too."

"You've…explained the situation to her?" Casey asked. Joanna didn't miss the hesitation in the question. It meant he didn't like what he assumed she'd done, but was willing to be understanding about it.

The happy haze of contentment she'd found with the help of the champagne thinned a little. When she'd agreed to marry Casey, they'd decided it was important that everyone think they were marrying for love. That way, Burnett could never tell a judge that their union wasn't a real one. Now Casey was accusing her of telling her mother that they'd only married for Mike's sake. Joanna didn't like the implication that she couldn't keep her part of their bargain. "What situation do you mean, exactly?"

He stood up, his shoes in his hand. His quick glance at her was very tolerant, irritatingly so. "Don't be defensive."

"I'm not."

"Joey." He stood up, circled the bed and put the shoes away in the closet. Then he slid the door closed. "I can understand if you felt you had to tell your mother that we were doing all this to keep Burnett from getting Mike."

"She doesn't know."

He came to her side of the room and dropped into the chair opposite her. "Joey, we *have* to stay honest with each other, or this isn't going to work."

His self-righteous tone rankled. "I *am* being honest."

He kept looking at her, unbelieving. "I know your mother. She's too self-absorbed to be that perceptive on her own."

Never in her life would Joanna have imagined that she'd be defensive of Marie. But she was now. "Thank you very much. And what about *your* mother? She's still standing around with a vacant smile on her face while her sons tear at each other's throats—"

Casey stepped back as if she'd slapped him.

"I'm sorry," Joanna said quietly, ashamed of herself. "That was fighting dirty. I love Lillian, you know that."

"I know." Casey sprawled backward with a sigh, laying his hands on each arm of the chair. He looked up at the ceiling. "She's always tried not to take sides."

"I can understand that," Joanna conceded. "But, in this case, Mike's future is at stake."

"Tell me about it. But my mother is my mother. She's dealt with Burnett and me in the same way ever since I can remember. She's not likely to change now."

"I think it's sad," Joanna said. "To be such a great lady and then to have this one huge blind spot."

"Welcome to the human race."

Joanna realized he was waiting for her to explain exactly what she'd told her mother.

"All right," she said. "As far as what I told my mother—"

He chuckled. "Going to make a clean breast of it, huh?" His tone was blessedly light.

She entered into the banter with a feeling of relief. "If you make one more snide remark, I will tell you nothing. Nothing. Do you understand?"

"God, you're tough."

"It's true. I can be ruthless. So shut up and listen."

"Yes, ma'am."

"I *did* tell my mother that Burnett is angry because Emily left Mike with you. She'd be likely to find that out eventually anyway, and she'd only be hurt if she thought I hadn't trusted her enough to tell her myself. But as for the rest, we agreed to let everyone think we're in love." Joanna's tone lost its bantering lightness. She looked away from him, toward the mean looking finials on the white bed. "I'm doing my best."

"Hey." His single coaxing word hung on the air for a moment, and then she looked at him again. "I apologize for doubting you."

"It's all right." She let her gaze drift upward, to the round window above the bed. The branches of a live oak touched the glass outside, as if scratching to come in from the dark. She looked down again and idly began undoing the long row of tiny buttons on her sleeve.

"Tired?" Casey asked.

One by one, the buttons slipped from their holes. "A little, I guess. And sort of deflated."

"Come here," Casey said.

He held out his hand and she reached across to put

hers in it. He gave a tug. She left her own chair and dropped onto the arm of his.

His gaze roved her face. "Even if she's not in love, the bride is beautiful," he said. "And the groom's a fortunate man."

"Thanks, pal." She lifted her arms and began to remove the silk flowers woven into her hair. "Now tell me what happened with Burnett."

He watched the movement of her hands. She thought his gaze strayed down once or twice to where her dress clung closely to her breasts, responding to the movement of her lifted arms. As she slowly removed the adornments in her hair she realized he didn't make her uncomfortable at all. It seemed the most natural thing, as if it had always been that way. The two of them, talking over the events of the day, getting ready for bed.

"There's nothing much to tell," he said. "It was just more of the same."

She stretched out her arm to set the sprays of cloth flowers and the pearl clip on the mahogany chest and then settled back close to him, tugging on one of the points of his collar. "Come on. What did he say?"

Casually, Casey stroked the ropes of pearls at her neck, causing them to roll against her skin. She smiled, enjoying the feeling of being caressed by pearls. "He was angry about these," Casey said.

She reached behind her and unfastened the gleaming strands. "I know that. I talked to Amanda. She wasn't happy when she learned that your mother had given them to me."

"Amanda is a menace," Casey said.

She handed him the pearls, and her mother's pearl

hair clip. "Do you have a place you could put these?" He nodded and went to lay them in a small jewel case inside a bureau drawer.

He came back to the chair they'd been sharing, sat down and began winding a corkscrew of her hair around his finger. "I think, though, that the necklace was only an excuse." As he played with her hair, his expression became almost dreamy. "Burnett just wanted another opportunity to tell me he's going to be waiting for this marriage of ours to start falling apart." He pulled his finger from a shining curl and his voice grew somewhat brisk. "Which, in reality, means that he's talked to his lawyer and been told that he doesn't have much of a chance as long as I'm a married man. Now he has nothing to offer Mike that I can't offer. Less, actually, when you add Emily's own wishes, as stipulated in her will."

"Plus love and happiness, don't forget those," Joanna hastened to add.

Casey's face grew serious. "I haven't forgotten. Not for a minute."

Joanna stared into his light-filled eyes, and then she looked at his mouth. Down in the womanly center of her, something warm happened, a tiny fluttering, like a promise of desire. She wanted to explore it, coax it to grow stronger. But she was scared, too, because it reminded her that the axis of their friendship was changing—like a planet being tilted in the heavens by some new gravitational force. She feared what might happen, feared spinning wildly out of her known orbit, into empty space.

"Casey?" Her hand was on his chest, which was warm and solid beneath the stiff dress shirt.

"Yes?" he said.

It seemed the most natural thing to run her hand lightly over the round pectoral muscles that she could feel beneath his shirt. "You don't regret this, do you?"

"No." He sounded very sure. He traced the tip of her chin with the pad of his thumb. "Do you?"

"No, but—"

"But what?"

She couldn't help it. She moved her head closer, so that she could feel his gentle breath against her mouth. "It's all changing. And it scares me. And then again…"

"Yes?"

"Sometimes I like it. Sometimes I wonder…"

"Go on."

When she turned her head slightly, he captured her chin and made her keep looking at him.

"Sometimes you wonder what?" he asked.

She looked into his eyes and wondered again. The question had been in the back of her mind for a while now. It occurred to her especially at night when she slept alone, when her mind went its own way and started thinking of their past.

"What would have happened if," she whispered.

His mouth was so close, his eyes lit with that same languid intent that had burned in them when he'd kissed her for the photographs, beneath the arbor in the bright sunlight.

"What would have happened if what?"

"If you'd done more than kiss me fourteen years ago…"

His lips, breath-close, curled slightly upward.

"We'll never know." The fingers that had captured her chin stroked downward, skimming the line of her neck.

So marvelously strange. He'd touched no part of her that he hadn't touched a hundred times as her friend, and yet every touch was a discovery, brimful with shimmering and intimate intent.

He took a curling tendril of her hair that fell over her shoulder and lightly tugged it.

That brought her mouth down to his. "How about if we concentrate on what's happening right now?"

She kissed him on the word "now," tasting him teasingly, lightly, on a side to side movement as his breath whispered across her mouth. "All right."

The kiss deepened. He put a coaxing hand at her waist and she slid easily off the arm of the chair and into his lap.

The kiss went on and on, delicious and exploratory, as she felt his hands caressing her through the frothy material of her dress. His touch molded the round line of her hip, defined the long curve of thigh to her knee and then back up again. It was a questing touch, one that refused to be hurried.

Joanna shifted against his chest, wishing she could just melt right into him. She swept her arms up to encircle his neck so she could press herself more closely into his body.

And then he touched her breast.

It was a caressing, exploring touch, no different than the feel of his hands on the rest of her body.

But still, immeasurably different. It was the place they'd stopped so long ago, beneath the pines behind the cabin that weekend he'd kidnapped her to keep her from marrying his brother.

A turning point. Her heart seemed to lift and hover high up in her chest—because the invisible line was being bridged. They were approaching ground on which they'd never before trod together.

His touch burned through the sheer dress and through the wisps of silk below, unbearably intimate. In its cradle of lace, her nipple grew hard, blooming out toward his palm. Could he feel her body's readying response, through all the layers of bridal adornment that separated his flesh from hers?

Joanna froze, a tiny confused sound escaping her. Without even thinking about it, she jerked back and met his eyes. They burned into hers, knowing her.

It was scary how well he knew her. Naked before him, she would be so much more naked than before any other man.

"I— I'm not sure I'm ready for this," she got out on a shaky breath.

"I know." His voice held that huskiness that came from arousal, but his gaze was level. His cradling hand had already left her breast.

He swung her up against his chest as he stood up.

She laughed, the sound high and unsure. "Casey, what are you doing?"

"Putting you to bed."

Joanna looped her arms around his neck and buried her face in his collar, thinking that it would work out all right, steeling herself for the scariness of the coming intimacy in his big white bed.

Since her eyes were closed, she didn't realize that he wasn't carrying her to *his* bed until he nudged open

the door to the landing with his foot. He took her to
her own room and put her down on her feet in the
middle of the floor.

"Stay there," he said, and went around the big
room, rolling up the blinds until the space was softly
lit with the glow from the street lamps beyond the
windows. Then he approached the neat little daybed,
took the bolsters off and drew back the spread and
covers.

Joanna watched him, saying nothing, but thinking
that the bed was awfully small for two when they had
his big one in the room they'd just left. But then,
maybe he thought she'd feel more comfortable here,
in her own territory.

She decided not to mention her doubts about the
bed. He was being thoughtful, she wouldn't ruin it for
him. Besides, her silly heart was pounding harder by
the minute. If she dared to speak, she felt her heart
might leap out of her mouth and dance around the
dimly lit room.

He returned to her. "Hold out your hand."

She did. With great care, he unbuttoned her sleeve.
"The other one."

It was the one she'd already started, so he made
short work of it.

Then he smoothly and efficiently undid the front
buttons, opening the airy fabric and slipping it over
her shoulders, catching it before it touched the floor.
He carried the dress to the closet and hung it inside.

Joanna stood in her ivory silk braslip, waiting, until
he returned.

"What do you want to wear?" he asked, still standing by the open closet.

She blinked, confused. "Pardon me?" She felt her whole body flushing, and was glad for the dimness of the light.

"To bed."

"Oh, nothing," she answered. In summer, she rarely wore much to bed. But then she felt absurdly forward, and yet inept at the same time, so she added, "Just this slip, I guess."

She stared down at the lace-trimmed hem of that slip for a minute, realizing that it had never even occurred to her in the past weeks to buy a sexy nightgown for this landmark occasion. But then she decided it didn't matter. The way things were progressing Casey would be dressing her in it only to take it right off again.

He slid the closet door shut and started to walk toward her again. Quickly, she slithered out of her pantyhose, not sure she could bear having him help her out of them.

He held out his hand. Not sure exactly what he wanted, she dropped the panty hose in it. The wisp of nylon fell across his palm. He looked down at it, then glanced back at her with his crooked grin. He turned, and draped them across the chair by the closet.

She waited. He held out his hand again. Hesitantly, she laid hers in it.

"Come on," he said. "Get into bed." He pulled her toward the turned-down daybed. She followed his lead, climbing between the covers and lying there quietly while he pulled them up under her arms.

Then he sat on the side of the bed. "Sleep well, Joey."

She realized then that he wasn't going to stay. And

she experienced disappointment, mingled with relief. "This *is* our wedding night," she told him softly.

"We need to give it time."

"Chicken."

"No dares, Joey, okay? Not about this. You were the one who said everything's happening so fast. This is something we have control over. We don't have to be pushed into this too fast, just because it's our wedding night. This is the one thing in all of this that can be just between you and me. We can set a pace that's right for both of us."

"I suppose you're right," she allowed, though she felt out of sorts. The way he was leaving her now seemed another example of how strange things had become. He always seemed to be leaving the room at crucial moments, with nothing ever settled, with things always somehow up in the air.

"I know I'm right," he was saying. He stood up. "Good night, Joey."

"Good night," she heard herself answer. He left her, softly pulling her door shut behind him.

Joanna lay alone in her single bed on her wedding night and wondered what in the world was happening.

Remembering what had just transpired, she felt again the lovely, cradling touch of his hand on her breast, felt her nipple rising, blooming in its nest of lace.

It would have been all right, she was sure. It would have been fine if they'd gone on to fulfillment. But Casey had stopped it, using her slight hesitation as an excuse.

She wondered if he was having trouble getting aroused. They were, after all, best friends, with twenty-two years of strictly platonic closeness between them. Maybe when it came down to sex, Casey was realizing he wanted things to stay platonic.

Joanna didn't like to think that Casey could be finding it difficult to desire her, especially because she was finding it so effortless to desire him. Her body thrummed with unsatisfied anticipation.

They should talk about it, she decided.

She was out of the daybed and halfway to the door before her courage deserted her.

Things had changed between them in the past week and a half. So much of the old easy camaraderie was gone. She realized that to barge into his room in the middle of the night wearing only a slip to ask him if he found the idea of sex with her repugnant called for more nerve than Joanna possessed.

Besides that, the calming effects of the champagne she'd drunk at the wedding had worn off. She was left with a dull headache and a raging thirst.

Joanna detoured to the bathroom, where she washed down two aspirin with several glasses of tap water. Behind the door, her paint-spattered work shirt hung on a hook.

The idea of working suddenly had great appeal—especially when considering the alternatives of trying to sleep or seeking Casey out.

Joanna put on the shirt. Then she returned to the other room and took a sketch pad and a few sticks of charcoal from the long folding table that held her supplies. She carried them to the window seat that overlooked the front lawn and made herself comfortable.

She reached over to the black gooseneck lamp that

craned over her drawing table and adjusted it to shine down on the sketch pad in her lap.

She flipped open the cover and stared at a blank page.

She had no idea what would take shape there, no idea at all. And for a while, nothing did. For a while, she just sat, very still, her eyes focused out the window on the street where Casey lived, the street that was now where she lived, too.

And then her hand, clutching the stick of charcoal, began to move across the pad.

A soft smile on her lips, Joanna glanced out the window. The street lights suddenly went off, and an enterprising young girl on a bicycle passed along the sidewalk, pitching fat Sunday papers onto front driveways from a huge wire bin attached to her handlebars.

Dawn, Joanna thought, and shook her head. She'd spent her entire wedding night sitting alone alternately staring out the window and sketching out hasty renderings of whatever popped into her head. She looked down at the sketch pad. It was flipped to the last sheet.

Slowly, with growing excitement, she thumbed through the pages. Each one was filled with sketches.

By the growing light of dawn, Joanna knew what the sketches meant. They were a message from her creative self, that part of her so scarily silent for the past few weeks.

She had her theme for September's show. It was going to be families—hers and Casey's. And she would call the whole thing Family Album.

She would have several studies of Emily, from childhood to adulthood. She would show Mike, half-dressed in his formal attire as a ring bearer, asleep in her mother's upstairs bedroom. She'd have her own mother, talking to the minister beneath the arbor yesterday. And Burnett, at about fifteen, at Chilly Lilly's in that paper hat he used to wear when he worked behind the counter.

There were a thousand scenes for her to choose from, Joanna realized, and in her Los Angeles apartment were some already completed studies of Emily and a few posed portraits of Mike. She could show those to Althea next week, if she didn't get anything new ready before then.

Joanna set aside the sketch pad and headed for the door, her stomach fluttering with excitement. She wanted to tell Casey. He'd be so excited.

Chapter Five

He was sleeping half-under, half-out of the covers, wearing only a pair of white cotton briefs. Joanna closed the door very softly and crept to the side of the bed.

He really was a beautiful man, she decided, the artist in her still thrumming with purpose and exhilaration. Really physically beautiful, and almost as beautiful on the outside as in his spirit and heart.

She wished she'd brought her sketch pad.

She stood in pure sensual appreciation of him, not wanting to disturb the picture of male beauty in repose.

One tanned, lean foot lay in a relaxed pose on top of the sheet. She gazed at it, at the good bones, the high arch, the gleam of health and strength in the brown skin, the sprinkling of hairs across the toes and instep.

Her appreciative gaze glided upward, over a lean ankle, a hard bulge of calf, and the good, clear bones in the knee, all dusted with gleaming, wiry brown hair.

The three long, wrapping muscles of his thigh were pure poetry, braiding in smooth bulges beneath his golden skin up to the whiteness of his briefs and a clot of wrinkled sheet.

He held the sheet against his belly. His flanks showed hard muscle, the stomach slightly rippled in that lovely "washboard" effect. Crisp hair grew thickest in a trail up the solar plexus line and separated out into little whorls at the pectorals.

Her gaze tracked out and down again, over a golden bulge of deltoid muscle at the shoulder, to well-defined triceps and biceps, and good radials beneath the elbow.

"Have I got my shorts on backward or something?" Casey's drowsy voice made Joanna jump like a naughty child who'd been caught snatching forbidden cookies. Her glance shot up to his face. His eyes were half-open, watching her, and a lazy smile was on his lips.

She took an unconscious step back, felt a bedside chair against her knees, and dropped into it. "I had this idea…" she managed lamely, and then felt disgusted with herself. It was much more than just an *idea*. "Scratch that," she amended, "It was an inspiration, a *revelation!*"

He sat up and stretched. "And all before even one cup of coffee?"

"I was up all night. Thinking and sketching."

"And?"

"I've got it," she said, taking pleasure in drawing out her excitement. It was nice, she thought, to have someone to share a breakthrough with. "It's families. Our families."

"Great," he said. "Now translate."

"You know Althea's promised me my own show in September?"

"I remember you mentioning something to that effect."

"Well, she caught me yesterday and wanted to pin me down on what I'm planning to do for it. And I still couldn't tell her a thing, because I didn't have a thing. Furthermore, she told me I've got to meet a big potential client next week to discuss wall art for a bank chain."

"You didn't tell me that last night."

"I forgot. I mean, we had all those other things to talk about and well, maybe I didn't want to think about it because I was scared to death I was in way over my head."

He arched an eyebrow at her. "And are you?"

She grinned smugly. "Not anymore. Like I said, I've got it."

"Families, right?" he said, still not understanding.

"My big show. It's going to be the Clintons and the Vails. I've been thinking and sketching all night and I know just what I'm going for and how to go about getting it." In her enthusiasm, she shot off the chair and jumped onto the bed beside him. "Only I can't tell you that part, not in detail. You know that. That would take the punch out of it, to talk it to death." She stretched out, face down across the foot of the bed, all her tired muscles seeming to sigh and groan at once. "Oh, I'm exhausted. Just wrung out from being brilliant all night long."

He chuckled. "And so unassuming, too."

She rolled over and wrinkled her nose. "False modesty has never been my long suit." Idly, she combed her tangled hair out over the edge of the bed with her fingers, and then she noticed that the tips of her fingers were black with charcoal. "I'm a mess, huh?"

"Brilliance always has its price."

"Slick, Clinton," she shot back. "Very slick." She grinned at him, full of euphoric enthusiasm. She was so excited about her breakthrough that she'd almost managed to forget about the changes that were happening between the two of them.

"Why do I get the feeling this is going to put a crimp in my big surprise?" he asked.

Joanna looked up at him. "You have a surprise?"

He nodded. "I already made arrangements for Mother to take Mike. And you and I were leaving today, as a matter of fact."

"For where?"

"Would you believe Puerto Vallarta?"

"Mexico?"

"Last I checked, that's where they put Puerto Vallarta. I've been picturing us deep-sea fishing, and windsurfing."

"But it's tropical!" The words escaped her lips before she considered how critical they sounded. "I mean, right now I can't be anywhere tropical. It's completely wrong."

He looked hurt. "Thanks."

She wriggled upright and sat on her heels. "Oh, Casey. I'm sorry. I didn't mean it like that. I just meant that the stuff I'll be working on now won't have a tropical feel at all. It would set the wrong mood altogether.''

''I see.'' He didn't look as if he saw at all.

''And besides, there's my meeting next week.''

''Right. About the banks.''

Joanna looked down at her hands, all smudged with charcoal, which she'd folded on her thighs. ''I'm sorry. I should have told you last night that we'd have to postpone a honeymoon.''

''It's okay,'' he said. ''I knew when we decided to get married that your work would always be a consideration in any decision. It's no problem. I'll call Mother and tell her she's off the hook for baby-sitting. And tell you what? Maybe Mike and I will fly to L.A. with you.''

''I'll bet you cleared your schedule at the airfield and everything.'' Casey taught flying and oversaw the entire operation. Though his schedule was flexible, he still needed to spend a lot of time at work. To have arranged for more than a week off would not have been an easy matter.

''Will you stop feeling guilty about being who you are?'' Casey sounded as if he might be losing patience.

Joanna decided he had a point. ''You're right. I'm not a conventional person—and this isn't a conventional marriage.''

''That's better.'' He swung his legs over the side of the bed and stood up. Joanna's hands itched for a stick of charcoal and her sketch pad. A few of her new pieces would have Casey as the subject. Right now, as he walked away from her, the broad line of his back, tapering into his waist and down to hard hips was something to see. Also, his gluteals were nothing to sneeze at—from a purely aesthetic point of view, of course.

Unaware of her scrutiny, Casey went to the mahogany dresser and pulled out some gray sweats. He shoved his legs into them and tied them at the waist. Then he caught her watching him. He froze, and stared right back at her.

Joanna gulped, remembering how she'd almost paid him a visit in the middle of the night to talk about sex. Maybe now, in the bright light of day, in nonthreatening circumstances would be a good time to broach the subject.

"What?" he asked, as if cuing her.

"Hey, Joey! Uncle Case..." Mike stood in the doorway, dangling a balsa wood glider from one hand and still wearing his striped dress slacks from the day before. He looked from his uncle to Joanna and back again, sensing, as children often do, that he'd interrupted at an awkward moment.

"Ever heard of knocking?" Casey asked wryly.

"The door was half-open."

Joanna glanced at Casey and nodded. "I left it that way when I came in." She looked at Mike again. "It's all right. Come on in."

Mike looked doubtful for a moment, and then he crossed the threshold. "I'm starved."

"For waffles?" Joanna asked.

"Yep." He looked at Joanna's smeared hands. "But you better wash your hands first, Joey."

"She better wash her whole self," Casey winked at Joanna. "Go on. Take a shower. We'll get things moving on the waffle front." He scooped up a giggling Mike and set him on his shoulders. "Come on, kid.

Let's split this scene.'' They were at the door already. ''Duck,'' Casey ordered, and Mike did.

Joanna stood still for a moment, listening with pleasure to the childish voice and the deeper one, laughing and talking as they went down the stairs.

She felt a twinge of regret—for what hadn't quite been said before Mike burst in. But then she turned her mind back to her work and decided that time would take care of the problems between Casey and herself.

Casey called Lillian right after breakfast and told her they were staying home after all. Then he went about canceling their reservations.

By noon, Joanna's lack of sleep had caught up with her. They were out by the pool, and Casey ordered her upstairs when he caught her snoozing on her air mattress. She slept until dinner, which was barbecued ribs and corn on the cob eaten outside on the picnic table.

Once Mike was in bed, they sat outside for a while as the night grew darker. Joanna felt the urge to work again, like a strong thread pulling her upstairs where her drawing board, pastels, charcoal and paints waited.

Casey rolled his head over to her from the chaise longue next to hers and said. ''Go on. Go to it.''

''Would you mind?'' Her voice was sheepish.

''I said get lost.'' He turned his head back toward the stars and closed his eyes.

''Georgia O'Keefe and her husband lived separately.'' She mentioned a contemporary artist famous for her vivid paintings of desert flowers and animal skulls. ''He stayed in New York and she lived in Arizona.''

"Are you trying to make a point?"

"Just that it could be worse." Her voice held a sheepish note.

He still had his eyes closed, his face turned to the sky. "I didn't hear myself complaining. Was I complaining?"

"No, I was feeling guilty."

"Again?"

"I'm sorry."

"Are you still here?"

She rose quietly from the lawn chair and went to her studio.

And the night, again, slipped by in a magic haze of creative work.

At dawn, she showered and was on her way to Casey's room to wake him up, when another idea came to her, one she had to get down. She worked for another couple of hours, and then she smelled coffee.

Joanna followed her nose downstairs and straight to the coffeemaker that sat on the counter by the front window. She tossed a vague smile at Casey and Mike as she passed them. The boy and the man were sitting at a breakfast bar formed by a section of counter that projected into the room. They were surrounded by boxes of cold cereal.

Casey read the paper as he spooned shredded wheat into his mouth. Mike, Joanna's cursory glance revealed, was pouring something called Boffo Balls into his bowl, a cereal blinding in its brightness. Round balls in pink, yellow, green and blue tumbled out of the box.

Joanna poured her coffee.

"Joey, I think you should start sleeping at night

again. You don't look so good,'' Mike said from behind her. She could hear milk sloshing into his bowl.

"Um," Joanna murmured. Out the window, she
was watching a white station wagon pull up to the
curb. Amanda Clinton emerged from it and came up
the front walk. Joanna suddenly wished she could turn
around, mount the stairs again, climb into her daybed
and pull the covers over her head.

Chapter Six

Amanda stood at the door clutching a bag with a famous designer's initials all over it. "Hello, Joey." Her delft-blue eyes scanned Joanna's torn jeans, her rumpled work shirt and her wild, uncoiffed hair.

Amanda's bowed lips formed a slight moue of distaste, which she quickly banished. "Lillian said you weren't going on a trip after all, so I thought I would drop by this morning before my Women's Auxilliary meeting at the hospital." Amanda mentioned one of her numerous volunteer affiliations at normal volume, then she lowered her voice to a subdued murmur. "I think we need to get a few things cleared up, don't you—for little Mike's sake, if for no other reason."

Joanna longed to remind Amanda of that handy little device known as the telephone, and to add that she personally liked to be warned before hostile in-laws came calling at 8:30 a.m. But she didn't. Amanda was right, they did need to learn to get along with each other.

"Come in," Joanna said. "Want some coffee?"

"Yes, thank you."

Joanna led her to the kitchen, where she poured coffee for her new sister-in-law while Mike greeted her around a mouthful of Boffo Balls.

"'Morning, Amanda." Casey glanced at Joanna. Joanna nodded imperceptibly, signaling that nothing was happening that she couldn't handle. Casey returned to his paper.

"What kind of breakfast is this for a growing boy?" Amanda picked up the cereal box and began reading the ingredients on the side. "Joanna, the second ingredient is sugar."

"That's why he likes it so much," Casey remarked from behind the sports section.

Amanda clucked her tongue. "I suppose it's none of my business, but…"

Casey reached out and took the box away from her. "You're right, Amanda. It's none of your business." He set the box back on the counter with a smart thump.

"Well, pardon me." Amanda clutched her designer bag more tightly.

From behind his paper, Casey only grunted. Mike, wise beyond his years, said nothing, but went on contentedly crunching his sugar-packed breakfast.

Joanna slid around the end of the breakfast bar, carrying a small tray with two full cups and cream and sugar on it. "Why don't we go out back. It's such a beautiful morning, after all." She kept her voice purposely light and cheerful.

"Certainly," Amanda sniffed, and followed her out to sit beside the pool.

They sat across from each other beneath the umbrella at the round table, Joanna facing the pool and Amanda facing the house. Amanda blew lightly on her coffee before she sipped from it. Then she sat back in the padded chair, holding her cup in both hands.

"As you know," she began after a moment, "Burnett and I are quite distressed at what is happening in this family."

Amanda paused, as if waiting for Joanna to make some affirmative comment. To spur her on, Joanna said, "Oh?"

"And of course we all know what is going to happen in the end." She paused again. Joanna assumed she was expected to ask "What?" But she didn't.

Amanda frowned at the lack of response and continued. "But I suppose there's nothing to be gained by belaboring the obvious, so I'll get to the reason I came this morning." She paused again, but Joanna was just exasperated enough to be through making polite noises.

"We're going to have to *try* to get along, Joey. For Mike's sake. And of course, for dear Lillian who loves us all and wants only for us to be kind to each other."

Joanna smiled. "I agree with you completely."

Amanda blinked, reminding Joanna of a beautiful china doll she'd seen as a child in a toy store window, a china doll with eyes that could open and shut. "You do?"

"Sure. It'll be the best thing for everybody if we

can just let bygones be bygones." The words weren't hard for Joanna to say because she meant them, though she knew both Burnett and Amanda well enough to doubt that it would all be smooth sailing.

Joanna was an optimist at heart. She chose to believe that someday the Clinton brothers would work out their differences and she and Amanda would become, if not friends, at least cordial acquaintances.

"Well, I'm just wonderfully relieved," Amanda was saying. "And now, I think we need to put our heads together about the party."

Joanna took another bracing sip of coffee. "The what?"

"Joey," Amanda clucked her tongue in a patronizing way that was supremely irritating. "I realize you get terribly absorbed in those little paintings of yours, but you do have other responsibilities now. Mike's birthday. It's August second, a little over a week away. I thought we could resurrect the old family tradition and give him a party at the original Chilly Lilly's."

Joanna smiled to herself. Way back when, they'd had some great times at Lillian's first ice-cream shop. In her mind's eye, she could see them all as children, wearing party hats and scooping syrupy sundaes into their eager mouths. Once Casey had used his spoon as a slingshot, and started an ice-cream fight. By the time Burnett stopped it, there was mocha fudge dripping from the old-fashioned milk glass light fixture overhead and nuts and maraschino cherries in everyone's hair.

In the free-association way that her artist's mind worked, Joanna recalled the dream she'd had on the night she and Casey had decided to marry, the dream of the adult Casey at the ice-cream shop. That might be interesting, she thought. Two paintings: one of the ice-cream fight long ago, and one of the adult Casey standing in the archway of the storeroom in a sort of dreamlike Chilly Lilly's, with hazy green walls moving up into nothingness....

"Joey, have you heard a word I've said?" Amanda's exasperated complaint brought her back to the here and now.

"Sorry, just thinking. I think a party would be a great idea. Now when did you say you wanted to have it?"

"Mike's birthday. Wednesday, the second. It's rather short notice, but I'm sure if we start calling today, we can get a few of his little friends to agree to come."

Joanna remembered her meeting with the bank representative. "Fine. But can we make it the following Saturday? We're going out of town for a few days. I have some appointments in Los Angeles."

"You're dragging Mike down there on his *birthday?*" Amanda made it sound as if Joanna had just invented a new form of child abuse.

"Come on, Amanda. Mike loves to go places. And he'll still get his party, if we have it when we return."

"Joey, you are going to need to get your priorities in order, if you hope to make this absurd marriage of yours work."

Joanna took a slow, deep breath and replied quietly. "My priorities are in order, Amanda. Now, shall we set the date of the party for the fifth?"

"I suppose I'll have to do it all myself, since you're going to be so busy."

That was the final straw. "Tell you what, Amanda. Forget the party, all right? Casey and I will take Mike to Magic Mountain while we're in Southern California."

Realizing she'd pushed it too far, Amanda turned contrite. "Oh, no please. I was being silly. Of course I'd love to do it." For all her poise and prettiness, Amanda suddenly looked very lost. Joanna found herself feeling sorry for her, and wondering about the deep-rooted dissatisfaction Amanda must feel in her life to be so relentlessly looking for opportunities to aggravate an already difficult situation.

Families, Joanna thought wryly, remembering the words of one of her more eccentric artist-friends in Los Angeles.

Families give you the chance to get to know a lot of people with whom you would otherwise have nothing to do, her friend had said. In the case of Amanda Clinton, how right he was.

"Please, Joey," Amanda added. "I *want* to do it. I want to be involved."

Though her wiser self warned against it, Joanna couldn't say no to such a heartfelt plea. "All right."

Amanda smiled, looking relieved and almost grateful. "Oh, good. Now, I thought we could make it a surprise. I have a list that Lillian gave me of several of his friends. I'll call them right away. And I thought we could just let Chilly Lilly's give the party, since they do it so often for customers. They'll provide the favors and game suggestions and all that. Really, all we need to do is be there a little early to check things over. And I can do that, so you can bring Mike after everybody else is there."

Joanna had been mentally rearranging her schedule, trying to squeeze in some time for hunting down party hats and noisemakers. But the arrangements were obviously going to be quite simple, contrary to what Amanda had tried to make Joanna think at first. "That'll be fine," Joanna said.

Amanda pulled a leather appointment book from her bag and hastily jotted in it. "Wonderful. So that's Saturday the fifth at...two?"

"Fine."

"Well, then." Amanda put the appointment book back into her bag, and stood up. "I should be going, my meeting's at 9:30." Joanna started to get to her feet. "No, don't get up. I'll just go through the gate." Amanda smiled angelically. "Oh, Joey. I'm so glad we had this talk."

Joanna smiled back at her and murmured a low assent, not quite able to bring herself to say me too, since the "talk" hadn't really solved anything.

"I'm sorry I had to barge in on you without warning, but when I see that something needs to be confronted, I just do it, you understand?"

"Completely."

"And I want you to know I regret that little scene we had at your wedding, though I still feel you had no right to—"

"Amanda, I thought we were going to let bygones be bygones?"

"Oh, yes. Of course, you're right. Saturday the fifth, then. At two o'clock?"

"Sounds good."

Her slim back charm-school straight, Amanda glided toward the gate to the front yard.

Joanna remained in her seat, staring at the mosaic tile that rimmed the pool. She was trying to tell herself that things would be better between herself and Amanda from now on, and yet she could not really bring herself to believe it.

Lost in thought, she didn't sense Casey standing behind her until he put his hands on her shoulders. She jumped a little, and then grinned up at him.

"Is the dragon lady still breathing fire at her innocent in-laws?" he asked, half-teasingly. He began to knead the tired muscles in her upper back.

Joanna closed her eyes and let her head fall forward. "I can handle her." She sighed. "A little to the left. That's good. If you ever get tired of running Clinton Airfield, you could become a masseur."

"What's she up to now?"

"She wants us all to get along."

"That's refreshing, even if it's not very believable."

"And we're giving Mike a surprise party at Chilly Lilly's on the fifth, after we get back from Los Angeles."

"After *we* get back?" His fingers felt wonderful, working their soothing magic. His voice sounded pleased. "Does that mean you want us to go with you?"

She opened her eyes to slits and lifted her head a bit, so she could see his face above hers. "Sure, I do. Didn't we agree on that yesterday?" An uncertain look crossed his face, and then disappeared. It happened so fast, Joanna wasn't even sure she'd seen it. It surprised her because Casey so rarely looked uncertain. "I want you to come," she said levelly.

"I thought maybe you'd be ready for a break from us by now. Especially after a prebreakfast visit from the original wicked sister-in-law."

She took one of the hands that massaged her shoulder and interlaced her fingers with his. "A break from Amanda, definitely. But from you and Mike. Never." She pulled him around so they faced each other. "Is there something you're not telling me?"

"About what?"

"I don't know, lately..."

"Yes?"

She looked at him. Here they were again, two people who'd always had plenty to say to each other in the midst of another dangling conversation.

"Something's happened between us," she said bravely.

"Joey, it'll all work out," he said.

Joanna could tell by the tone of his voice that he didn't want to pursue the subject, and she didn't know quite how to approach it herself. There was the sex issue. It suddenly occurred to her she might bring it up in an oblique fashion by mentioning birth control.

Dragging in a breath, she managed to say, "I thought I'd get a doctor's appointment this week. Maybe go back on the Pill." The second of two serious relationships she'd shared had ended over a year before, and Joanna hadn't needed to worry about protecting herself from pregnancy since. A nervous laugh escaped her. "Everything's been so crazy. We hardly had time to think about preventing surprises." Not that we've needed to so far, she added grimly to herself.

"Right," he said. He was looking at her in that

unfathomable way he'd developed recently. "Good idea."

"I should, then," she heard herself continuing inanely, "go back on the Pill?"

"It always worked fine for you, didn't it?" he asked back.

"Yes, fine."

"Then, fine. Do it."

Casey, of course, knew all about her past close relationships with men. By the same token, he'd come to her to help him understand when a long-term relationship of his own had ended badly; his lover, Annie Devon, had accused him of being incapable of making a real commitment.

He'd ended up admitting to Joanna then that Annie had probably been right.

"Sometimes I think I'll never really fall in love in any lasting sense," Casey had confessed. "That it's just not in me. The idea of a lifetime commitment scares me to death. It makes me feel trapped, as if my big brother might finally win out and there I'll be, nose to the grindstone, grounded with a backbreaking load of responsibilities for the rest of my life."

He'd gone on to say that he knew in his mind that a deep relationship with a woman didn't have to be that way, but convincing his feelings of that was another matter altogether.

Joanna had teased him to lighten his mood. "Some smart girl will set her sights on you and not give up. She'll run you to ground. Eventually."

Never in the world would she have imagined then that he'd end up committed to Joanna herself.

Was that the root of the painful awkwardness between them now? Now that he was in the marriage, did he feel horribly trapped?

She'd asked him on their wedding night if he regretted what they'd done. He'd said no. If she kept harping at him about it, then he'd decide for sure that he'd made a giant mistake.

He was still standing in front of her, still wearing that inscrutable expression. She said, her voice hesitant, "Casey, I just feel like something's bothering you."

"Everything's fine," he said.

"You're sure?"

"Positive."

Joanna gave up. She said, sounding lame, "Well, great. Then as far as Los Angeles goes, we'll fly down together, the three of us, on Monday the thirty-first. We'll come back up on Friday in time for the party on Saturday."

"Fine," Casey said. "We can take the Citation." He mentioned his Cessna six-seater of which he was justifiably proud. "It'll be fun."

"Yes, fun," she said, and forced a smile.

Chapter Seven

Mike was cranky on the afternoon flight down to Los Angeles a week later, but Joanna hardly noticed. She was too keyed up over the coming interview with the Desert Empire Savings representative, and her meeting with Althea at the gallery after that.

They flew into Burbank Airport, then took an unpleasant cab ride to West Hollywood. The summer day was hot—in the high nineties. The air conditioning in the cab didn't work, and neither did the rear windows, so the three of them sat and sweltered.

When Joanna pushed open the door and confronted the long hall that ran the length of her upstairs apartment, a wave of air even hotter than that outside hit her in the face. Then she was aware of the smell of dust and paint solvents. For a moment, she stood there, perspiring in her light summer dress, peering over the threshold at what once had been her home. She wasn't giving up the flat; it was rent-controlled and ideal for her use whenever she needed to come to Los Angeles. But still it struck her, suddenly, that she really didn't live here anymore.

Behind her, Mike whined. "Do we have to stand here all day, Uncle Case? I'm hot."

Joanna turned to see Casey scooping the boy up in his arms. "Keep your shirt on, kid," Casey said. "We're getting there."

Mike leaned his head on Casey's shoulder. "My throat hurts," he mumbled. Then he sneezed.

Casey and Joanna exchanged a look over the boy's red-blond head. Then Joanna reached out and felt his forehead.

"He's warmer than he should be, even given that it's a hot day," she said. "I've got a thermometer in the medicine cabinet."

She led the way into the apartment, down the long hall to the extra bedroom, where Casey gently lowered Mike onto the bed and then returned to the door to bring in their suitcases. Joanna found the thermometer, stuck it in Mike's mouth and admonished him to keep it firmly under his tongue for four full minutes. She instructed him to watch the second hand on the clock by the bed. Then, while the boy stared intently at the clock and Casey went to the kitchen to get some cold drinks, Joanna started up the window air conditioners in both the bedrooms and in the studio-living room.

Mike's temperature was just over a hundred, so they tucked him into the bed and Casey made a quick trip to the corner store to buy throat lozenges and children's aspirin.

By dark, Mike was suffering from a full-blown case of the flu. He was feverish and coughing and tyrannical to both his uncle and Joanna. He finally dropped off to sleep at about ten o'clock.

Joanna and Casey ordered a large pizza and ate it at the kitchen table to the hum of the air conditioner and the occasional screams of sirens out in the Los Angeles night.

"He'll be on the mend by morning," Casey assured her.

Joanna smiled at him in vague agreement. She knew Mike would be fine. Right then, she was thinking of how she needed to put two finished paintings of Emily and another of Mike in her van the next morning, so she could show them to Althea after the meeting with the bank representative. The idea for the show at the gallery must be presented just so, to capture Althea's interest. The style of this show would lean toward photo-realism, and Althea's tastes ran to the more abstract.

"Anybody home in there?" she heard Casey teasing.

"Oh," Joanna laughed, embarrassed. "Sorry. Just thinking."

"Nervous about tomorrow?" he asked.

"A little."

"You'll be terrific," he told her. "And you should get to bed early, to be fresh."

She looked at him over the remains of their pizza. He had his chin on his fist, his elbow braced on the table. His strong neck looked very tanned where it disappeared into the collar of his blue sport shirt. "Yes," she said. "Early."

At that moment, Joanna discovered she was no longer thinking about her meetings the next day. Instead, her mind had conjured up an image of the way the man beside her had looked, asleep beneath the sheet the morning after their wedding. And then she found herself remembering the feel of his hand caressing her breast when he'd kissed her the night before that.

They'd been married a week and a half, and still they kept to their separate beds at either end of the landing in the house in Sacramento. Here in Los Angeles, she couldn't help thinking, Mike had the spare room. There was a Japanese futon bed in the studio/ living room, but wouldn't it be much more natural for her and Casey to just share the bed in her room?

She silently admitted to herself that every day since their hasty wedding she'd become more and more aware of her best friend as a man. The truth was that she had come to desire him, and she longed for him to share the sweet yearning that grew stronger day by day.

I want him, Joanna thought, marveling, really want him—and I'm scared to death he's never going to want me back....

Bewilderingly, she recalled a conversation she'd shared with Michelle Bennet, Casey's first steady girlfriend back in high school. They had been in the girl's rest room, where Michelle spent a lot of time touching up her makeup during breaks between classes. Joanna had purposely sought Michelle out, because she wanted to be on good terms with anyone who was important to her best friend.

"Casey says you two are just friends." Michelle,

who was pretty in a tough sort of way, had been piling more mascara onto her already impressive black eyelashes. Her inky eyes slid to Joanna's in the big mirror over the sinks.

"That's right," Joanna had replied.

Michelle lowered her voice to a whisper. "Come on. You mean you never even fooled around a little?"

"Nope," Joanna had said. "We've been friends forever." Precisely six years, at that time, but to the teenage Joanna, it had seemed like eternity. "We just don't think of each other that way."

"Weird," Michelle had decided after a moment.

Joanna had felt defensive. "What we have is special. Why ruin it with sex?"

"Hey," Michelle had retorted. "Do you see me arguing? You just keep what you got with him—and I'll take the rest." She'd leaned toward Joanna, so their images in the mirror were almost touching. And she'd whispered, her black eyes full of a feminine knowledge which Joanna had not possessed at the time. "I ain't complaining, Joey. Even though you're not interested, he's really great that way."

He's really great that way... Black-eyed Michelle's words echoed in her mind.

Joanna couldn't help but wonder: was he? And would she ever find out?

Joanna's face suddenly felt very warm. Beside her, Casey sat unmoving. He was watching her, his light eyes focused on the hollow of her throat, where she could feel the throb of her heightened pulse. And then his gaze traveled up, slowly, to her haphazardly pinned up hair that always became thicker and more unmanageable in the heat. Now, she had it anchored on her head with a huge plastic clip.

In a gesture that stunned her with its simple intimacy, Casey reached out and pinched the clip, removing it from her cloud of hair, which promptly fell full and wild around her face.

"Pretty," he said. "Thick and loose like that." He set the clip aside and lightly, in subtle strokes, combed her hair with his fingers, from her temples out to the wild-curling ends.

Joanna swallowed. It was almost as if he had read her mind. As if he knew what she wanted of him, and had simply decided to give it to her.

"What—" she had to swallow again "—what are you doing, Casey?"

"Touching," he said. "Is that all right?"

Joanna didn't trust herself to speak, so she nodded.

"I'm glad." He went on combing her hair with his fingers.

Lately, she didn't understand him at all. She knew him better than any other human being on earth. He was her best friend. Yet he'd left her alone on their wedding night and had barely touched her since. And now he was looking at her like…he was touching her like…

Joanna's thought faded off into a chaos of pure sensation as, holding her gaze captive, he laid two fingers against the throbbing pulse in the hollow of her throat. The absolute familiarity of the gesture took her breath away. Somehow, he *knew* she'd been aware of that pulse, of its quickening. And he touched it as if to share her excitement with her. Her breathing deepened, and she was suddenly conscious of her breasts rising and falling beneath the light cotton of her dress, of her nipples, hardening though he had not even touched them.

His fingers lay quiescent against her throat for seconds without end, as if he were absorbing her sensations, taking them inside himself, and then, through the fingertips that had received those sensations, passing them back to her, redoubled.

"What is happening, Casey?" she heard herself ask.

"Shall I stop?" he asked by way of reply. His fingers left the secret pulse in her throat to travel downward.

Joanna couldn't speak period.

With the flat of his palm, he very lightly rubbed her left breast where it strained erect beneath her loose cotton dress.

"Tell me to stop, Joey," he said. "If that's what you want, I'll understand." His voice had grown serious in its huskiness. He went on teasing her breast with his palm.

"Don't stop," she heard herself sigh, letting her head drop back as she strained her breasts toward him. He obliged her body's request by stroking the other breast.

Then he pulled his hand away. Joanna gave a tiny cry of loss and lifted her head.

He smiled at her, slowly, and nodded toward the window.

It took her a moment to understand. Making love in front of the window wasn't as private as he wanted it to be.

"In the bedroom?" she asked.

He stood up and took her hand. They stopped briefly

at the room where Mike slept and Joanna went in to feel his forehead and straighten the covers. Mike's breathing rattled a little from the congestion in his chest.

"His forehead is still warm," Joanna said. "But I think he's okay."

They went on to her room with its buff-colored walls and accents of the cool, soothing green found in the deepest part of a forest.

Casey sat on the edge of her bed and pulled his sport shirt over his head, tossing it on the fat green velvet chair in the corner.

Joanna hovered by the door, watching him, feeling suddenly as if she were moving in a dream. Casey was hunching over to remove his shoes when he stopped, without warning, and looked at her. He sat upright, one shoe off and one shoe on.

He said, "Have you changed your mind?"

She said, "No. I was just wondering, I guess—why now?"

He said, "I thought, the way you looked at me in the kitchen, that you were ready."

The dreamlike quality of the moment made her bold. She said, "I was ready on our wedding night."

He shrugged. "If you say so." He bent just long enough to slide off the other shoe and get rid of his socks. Then he stood up and approached her. He came within inches of her, and she could feel the radiant heat of his body reaching out to hers.

"But forget then. We can't change then. The question is, do you want me now, Joey?" he said.

"Yes." Her voice was firm and steady.

He stroked her bare arm, in an up-and-down movement. It caused little shivers to run over her skin. Then he slid both of his hands to her hips and, very slowly, he began to gather up the skirt of her dress.

The slow bunching and raising of her skirt was one of the most erotic sensations she'd ever experienced. It shocked her as much as aroused her that it should turn out to be Casey who would make her body vibrate with such overwhelming sensuality. In her previous intimate relationships, she'd enjoyed sex, but not like this, never so totally—and so far, Casey had done no more than touch her breast and slowly—oh, so slowly—raise her skirt.

The cool air from the window air conditioner caressed her legs as he uncovered them. Soon, the skirt was bunched in his fists at her waist.

He pulled her against his chest. And then he kissed her, lingeringly, his mouth teasing at first, and then closing possessively over hers. Joanna gave herself over to his mouth, as his hands rode her hips, rubbing her bunched skirt against the tender skin of her pelvis.

Then he pulled back. Joanna swayed unsteadily toward him, as if, during the lingering kiss, her body had become magnetized to his.

"Open your eyes, Joey," he said.

She did, slowly, and found herself looking into his.

He continued, his eyes holding hers. "I want to see your eyes while I look at you. All of you."

He pulled the loose dress up and over her head. She stood before him, her gaze locked with his. She was wearing only her sandals, her bikini panties and her bra.

He put his hands back on her hips, the warm touch sending a bolt of sensory lightning straight to the secret place between her thighs. Then he turned her around and guided her backward, until she was sitting on the end of the bed.

He knelt, and slipped her sandals off, one at a time. Feeling weak-limbed, she leaned back on her hands and looked at the strong muscles in his shoulders and arms, at his bent head, as he held her foot in his hands.

There was something so trusting in the way he revealed the back of his neck to her, something so honest and vulnerable. Within the heat and hunger he'd aroused in her body, her heart melted, too.

It seemed as though she had always known him. They had shared the need to find different lives than the ones their families had laid out for them. Casey had longed to fly; Joanna had wanted only to paint pictures that would capture the beauty and mystery of all creation. Always, they'd encouraged and nurtured each other's dreams.

But now, to see this other side of him. To see him as a man, offering her his bent head, the vulnerable back of his neck. To see the totality of him, her friend since childhood, was beautiful and terrifying and almost more than she could bear.

"Casey…" She breathed his name.

He raised his head. His eyes were full of heat and knowing. He said nothing. He didn't have to. He placed his hands, open, on either side of her ankles, clasping them. And then he slid his hands, slowly, up the sides of her calves, over her knees to her thighs, leaving a trail of sensual heat behind, so that the skin of her legs burned with his knowing of them. His eyes, meanwhile, held hers captive, daring her, as they'd so often done, but in a new way.

Daring her to see him, all of him, and to utterly surrender to what was happening between them now.

He slipped his middle fingers up over her hips, eliciting a gasp from her which made him smile.

He hooked her panties with his fingers and gave a gentle tug. Joanna lifted her hips so he could slide them off.

He took her bra next, in a leisurely fashion, enticing her first by massaging the curve of her waist, and by insinuating his fingers beneath her bra strap and lightly stroking the skin there with the back of his hand.

At last, as her eyes pleaded with his, he unhooked the front clasp and slid it over her arms and away. Her breasts, the dusky nipples already achingly hard, were revealed to him.

Did he call her beautiful? If not, he made her feel that way, as he moved up between her legs to make slow tender love to her breasts, both with his hands and his hungry, seeking mouth.

By then, Joanna had thrown her head back, too transported to maintain the heady contact with his eyes. But he allowed that, taking satisfaction, she perceived, in the way her body gave over completely to the magic in his touch and the tender urgings that came from his lips.

Gently, he pulled back again. And his hand strayed to the liquid center of her. He loved her there, with his touch, as she opened herself utterly to him. In that way, he brought her to shuddering satisfaction, until she fell back against the comforter, spent.

For endless moments, she lost the touch of his skin against hers. She bore the loss well at first, still pulsing with sweet afterglow. But then she missed him.

"Casey?" She lifted her heavy head from the pillow to see him just stepping out of his briefs at the foot of the bed.

"I'm here, Joey."

She looked at him. And she thought he was the handsomest, most perfectly formed man she had ever seen. He was fully aroused, and seeing that, she felt desire build in her again.

She held out her arms. Casey moved into them. The magical sensual dance of pleasure began again.

Joanna said his name over and over, as she revelled in the feel of his body against her, the teasing scrape of wiry chest hair against her tender breasts, in the hardness of his thighs against hers, and the sparring play of their tongues as their lips met and joined.

She touched him. And he astonished her again by giving himself up to her pleasuring hands just as moments before she had given herself to his. He let her bring him to completion like that, without even entering her. Joanna thought that marvelous, that he was willing, in lovemaking, to surrender as totally as he wanted her to. After that, they rested, his head against the soft curve of her neck.

They talked for a time about nothing of consequence, like new lovers sometimes do, more for the sound and play of voice to voice in the aftermath of passion than for any of the things that might have needed to be said.

Joanna left him, briefly, to turn off the air conditioners and open the windows, letting in the warm night air. Casey watched her, as she returned to him where he waited on the bed.

She saw that desire was moving again, a slow heat

in his eyes. Casey reached for her, brought her down to him and found her instantly ready for the total joining he sought.

He reared up over her, and came into her. Joanna opened for him like a flower for the sun, astounded by the wonder of it, marveling at herself and Casey, woman and man, after all these years.

They found fulfillment together that time, and as the waves of pleasure vibrated between their loved bodies, Joanna cried aloud with the beauty and the wonder and the joy of what he made her feel.

Afterward, unspeaking, he held her close for a time. Then they peeled back the covers of the bed and tucked themselves beneath the sheet.

As she drifted toward slumber wrapped in Casey's arms, Joanna felt certain, for the first time since their impetuous marriage, that everything would work out. Even if Casey feared being trapped in marriage, he was capable of desiring her. Beyond the emotional and mental affinities they shared, beyond their commitment to Mike's well-being, they could now count on the bond of physical pleasure as well.

The next morning, Mike was still feverish and fussy. Joanna coaxed him to drink some juice and read to him for a while, before Casey shooed her out of the bedroom to get ready for her lunch date.

After carting the canvasses down to her van, Joanna took a leisurely bath and dressed with care in a trim ice-pink gabardine dress.

Joanna met with Niki Tori, the interior designer from Desert Empire Savings, at an upscale California-cuisine restaurant in Century City at 12:30. Two hours later, she shook hands with Niki—they were on a first-name basis by then—and floated out into Century Plaza on cloud nine.

The specific figures would be worked out between Niki and Althea, who often acted as Joanna's agent, but the commission was definitely *on*. The time frame, which had been Joanna's main concern, was wonderfully broad. Niki didn't need the six massive acrylic texture studies or the series of smaller signed prints until the first of next year. Except for signing the contracts, Joanna could put the commission from her mind until she'd finished the collection of paintings for her show at the gallery.

The meeting with Althea at three o'clock was also a success, though there were one or two rocky moments. It took some convincing to make Althea warm to Joanna's idea.

"If I wanted Norman Rockwell, I'd go looking for back copies of the *Saturday Evening Post*," the gallery owner had remarked snidely.

But Joanna had brought out her charcoal sketches as well as the finished portraits of Emily and Mike.

Althea found the two studies of Emily, sitting in a bentwood chair in front of a black drop curtain, haunting. And she noted that, in the painting of Mike, Joanna had managed to capture that engaging combination of enthusiasm and solemnity that made the boy unique.

Soon enough, Joanna and Althea were poring over the charcoal sketches together and Althea was outlining her own ideas for how the show would be hung, explaining with conspicuous excitement how she'd move the tall display screens around to show each canvas to best advantage.

Joanna left the gallery at five, flushed with excitement and exhilaration. She couldn't wait to tell Casey all about it.

Though traffic was the usual Los Angeles rush hour nightmare, the San Vicente address of the gallery was less than two miles away from her apartment. Within fifteen minutes of waving goodbye to Althea, Joanna pulled into her parking space behind her apartment building.

Since she'd left the paintings with Althea, she only needed to tuck her sketch pad under her arm and race for the stairs, her joy at her success bubbling over into a happy laugh.

She took the steps to her door two at a time, in spite of the heat and the difficulty of such acrobatics in her elegant high-heeled shoes. She burst into the air-conditioned coolness of the apartment calling Casey's name.

"In here!" His voice came from the bathroom.

Joanna hurried down the long hall past Mike's open door and the room she and Casey had shared for the first time the night before. The bathroom door, at the end of the hall, was open.

She entered to find Casey kneeling by the tub and a naked, drooping Mike inside.

"What's the matter? How is he?" she asked.

Casey looked up at her. His eyes were bleak and full of fear. "His temperature just shot up. I don't understand it. It's a hundred and six."

Chapter Eight

Joanna dropped her purse and sketchbook on the counter behind her and knelt beside Casey at the tub. Using a big plastic cup from the kitchen, he was ladling the bathwater over the little boy's bowed shoulders.

"I called his pediatrician in Sacramento. He said I had to get his fever down, to give him the children's pain reliever and to put him in a lukewarm bath."

"Too cold, don't like cold," Mike said in an odd little sing-song, shaking his head. He remained upright, but barely. He was staring blankly at the tub fixtures.

"How long's he been like this?" Joanna asked.

"I don't know for sure. I guess he was getting worse all day, though I didn't want to acknowledge it. He got cranky after you left, and then he seemed tired, so I let him sleep. I checked on him at two and three and he was feverish, but not too bad. Then I left him alone for a while. About half an hour ago, I went to check on him and he was burning up.''

"When did you give him the pain reliever?''

"At least twenty minutes ago,'' Casey said. "Do you think we should get him to an emergency room?''

Joanna tested the water. "This is too warm,'' she said. "It's not going to lower his temperature any.''

Casey kept tenderly pouring the water over Mike. "I had it a little colder before. He cried. It made him uncomfortable.''

Joanna stuck her hand in the water and pulled the plug. Then she turned on the cold tap full blast. Mike jumped, and slid back away from the cold jet. "No, no, cold, cold...''

"What are you doing?'' Casey roughly shoved her aside and shut off the tap. "I told you, he doesn't like that.''

"It has to be colder, Casey.''

"No.'' He put the plug back in and turned on the taps again, to the same warm temperature.

Joanna stared at him, just beginning to put together what was happening inside him. Right then, she realized, he was thinking only a little more clearly than Mike himself. Casey Clinton had tested fighter jets for the navy after finishing second in his class. To this day, there was nothing he enjoyed more than hanging by the prop of his Stearman Biplane for endless seconds before dropping gracefully into a tailslide.

He was the kind of pilot who, even to the last moment, would keep thinking calmly of what strategy to take next to pull himself out of a low-level stall.

But at that moment, he was so terrified for his nephew that he couldn't accept that he would have to let the boy cry from the cold if they wanted to get his temperature down.

"We need to get him to the hospital," Casey was saying. "Joey, get something to put on him..." He reached for a bath towel.

"No." Joanna grabbed his arm. "You go call the doctor again."

He shook her off, anger sparking in his eyes. "What do you mean, call the doctor?" He swore. "The doctor's in Sacramento. We need help here!"

"You go call the doctor now," she demanded in a no-nonsense voice. "You ask him what lukewarm means. You ask him if Mike's going to have to cry a little from the cold if his fever is going to be lowered."

"What the hell do you know?" Then, he stood up and glared down at her. "You never had a kid! I never had a kid! What the hell do people like us know about something like this?"

She looked at him, and she didn't allow her gaze to waver. "Call. Now."

Miraculously, he did. Like someone in a trance, he turned and left the room.

He returned in a few minutes wearing a sheepish expression.

"Okay, do it," he said.

Joanna pulled the plug and began the process of cooling the water. Mike scooted backward to the end of the tub, shaking his head.

Casey said, "He'll be screaming in a few minutes."

"But his fever will go down," Joanna reminded him. "From what I understand about kids and high fevers, they get them—and they can be serious. But the important thing is not to let them go on for too long. We'll get his fever down and then we'll call the doctor back to find out what we should do next.''

Casey attempted a grin. ''Since when did you learn all this about kids?''

''It's secondhand,'' she told him, and then elaborated in an effort to distract him from his distress over Mike. ''Mostly from Aunt Edna. She did raise six kids, after all. And she always says she never could have done it if the little devils weren't so darn resilient. 'You give them love,' Aunt Edna always says, 'and they'll bounce back from anything.' ''

''Cold, cold,'' Mike mumbled. He'd started to shiver.

Casey's attempt at a smile faded. He was still hovering near the door. ''Maybe I should let you deal with this,'' he said.

Joanna considered this suggestion, while Mike's whimpering became more insistent.

True, the easiest course would be to tend to the nursing herself, since it upset Casey so much. But letting Casey off the hook in this painful duty would be the wrong approach. He was in for the duration when it came to raising Mike. And he needed to know that he could do whatever had to be done himself if the need arose.

Joanna said, ''Are we in this together or not?''

Mike was shaking all over now, and he'd started to cry. ''It's too cold!'' he insisted, between sobs. ''It's cold, cold, it's too cold!''

''God,'' Casey said. But he left the haven of the doorway and came to kneel beside her.

For the first time since Joanna had entered the bathroom, Mike's eyes cleared. He looked right at his uncle through a fat rain of tears. "Uncle Case, it's too cold! Turn it off, now!" He levered his small shaking body upright to grab the rim of the tub, and tried to climb out.

"You'll have to hold him down," Joanna said. "And I'll pour the water over his shoulders." Mike was halfway out of the tub. "Casey," Joanna said. "Please..." She reached toward Mike, to keep him in the tub, since Casey seemed to be frozen beside her.

But then Casey said quietly. "It's all right. I'll do it."

And he did. First, he took the boy's thin shoulders and gently but firmly pushed him back down in the cool water. Then he held him there, not relenting though at first Mike screamed and flailed his arms about.

As he held him, Casey spoke to Mike soothingly, until at last the child stopped fighting the pain of the cold water against his burning skin. In the end, Mike sat shivering and sobbing while Casey comforted him with soft words and Joanna ladled the cold water over his chest and shoulders.

Casey looked over at her, his mouth a grim line. "How long does this have to go on?"

Joanna had no idea, but she knew now was not the time to show Casey her ignorance. "I'd say we should give it a good fifteen minutes, at least. Give the water—and the pain reliever—a chance to really work."

"Terrific," Casey murmured, and then turned his attention back to Mike. "It's okay," he said. "Only a little while, kid, and you'll be feeling a lot better."

Joanna glanced at her watch to start timing, and then went back to pouring the water over the quivering child.

Somehow, the fifteen minutes passed, though Casey said later that it didn't seem like they ever would.

At last, Joanna said, "Okay. Take him out."

Casey scooped the shaking boy against his chest, while Joanna got a big towel to wrap around him.

Back in the spare room, they took his temperature. It was down four degrees to one hundred and two.

"Thank God," Casey breathed.

Joanna got him to drink some juice while Casey called the doctor again.

"He says to give him the pain reliever every four hours, and keep him drinking liquids," Casey reported. "If the fever goes back up, we call him right away. Otherwise, he gave me the name of a pediatrician in Van Nuys where we can take him tomorrow."

Mike's eyes were already drooping against his flushed cheeks. Tenderly, Joanna tucked the sheet around him and then she and Casey tiptoed from the room.

Casey went out for Chinese food as Joanna changed from her soaked dress to a pair of shorts and a tank top.

As the big orange sun disappeared behind the roof-tops, they took turns checking on Mike, and coaxing liquids down his throat. By midnight both Joanna and Casey felt that the worst was behind them.

They sat on the futon in the living room/studio, and Casey asked her how her meetings had gone. She proudly reported her success and he congratulated her.

"It's been quite a day for you," he said, then, and pulled her head down to rest on his shoulder.

She snuggled against him, feeling bone-weary, but content. "It's been pretty challenging for you, too," she said.

He made a sound in his throat. "Clearly I have a lot to learn about giving Mike what he needs."

"You love him. You hated to see him suffer." In a reassuring manner, Joanna put her hand on his chest. Beneath his light knit skirt, she could feel the steady beating of his heart.

"I was an idiot." He kissed the crown of her head, his breath teasing her hair. "Seeing Mike so sick reminded me of Emily," he confessed. "Of being powerless, of having to sit by and watch someone you love suffering, and not knowing what the hell to do about it. I started thinking that maybe Burnett was right."

She reached up, by feel, and put two fingers on his lips. "Don't say it. Don't even *think* it, Casey Clinton."

He spoke against her fingers. "Thank God you came in when you did or heaven knows what would have—"

Joanna interrupted again. "What *did* happen was that we got his fever down. I'll bet you he'll be well enough for his party Saturday. Really. Like Aunt Edna says—"

He chuckled. "I know, I know. 'Give 'em love, and they bounce back from anything.'"

"You got it."

"The question is," Casey murmured with another rueful chuckle, "will *we* survive?"

"I think we're doing okay," Joanna said.

"That's easy to say now. We're four hundred miles away from Burnett and Amanda. Getting through a one-hundred-and-six-degree fever is nothing compared to dealing with my family on a day-to-day basis."

"Burnett and Amanda are not your whole family," Joanna told him. "Your sister was like a sister to *me*. And your mother is a dear friend."

"Right," he said, not sounding too convinced. She fidgeted a little, trying to get comfortable on the small couch/bed. "Come on," he told her. "Swing your legs up here."

Obediently, Joanna swung her bare legs across his thighs. He laid a warm hand on her knee. Joanna squirmed a little. Not from discomfort, but from the memory of the pleasure they'd shared the night before.

Their bodies, at least, were totally at ease with each other again—and in a more intimate, and infinitely more pleasurable way than they had been when they were just friends.

In fact, after what they'd faced together this evening, she felt closer to him, more relaxed emotionally, than she had since the night they'd decided to get married. Maybe now would be a good time to talk about the distance she'd been feeling from him lately.

"Casey?"

"Um?"

"Remember when you and Annie broke up three years ago?"

"Yeah."

"She accused you of being afraid of commitment."

"I remember," he said.

"You told me then that you thought she was right.

That the idea of a lifetime commitment scared you to death.''

"That was then," he said. His voice, she thought, was much too expressionless.

"Casey, we need to talk about it. There's nothing wrong with your feeling that way, really. I can understand completely, I really can. I mean, every day I wonder—"

"What?"

"Well, I wonder if we did the right thing. I feel it's a big step for both of us, and I pray we'll make it work."

"Do you want out?" he demanded. "Is that what you're saying?"

Somehow, in the space of a few short exchanges, the conversation had gotten completely away from her. All the easy, relaxed feeling had evaporated. The air crackled with tension.

Joanna was sitting up straight by then, and she tried to pull her legs off of his thighs. But he held onto them.

"Just tell me," he said. "Do you want out?"

"Casey, I'm just trying to get us to talk about what's going on here."

"Do you want out?"

"No, no," she found herself hastening to reassure him. "Casey, really. It's working out fine for me. Honestly."

"Good."

"But Casey..." Hesitantly, she touched his forehead, smoothing his hair back.

"What?"

"You seem guarded. You were never guarded with me before."

He shrugged in a casual way. But the look in his eyes wasn't casual at all. "I put you in a difficult position, that's all," he said. "I feel badly about that. But you know what?"

"What?"

"I don't feel badly enough about it to let you off the hook."

"I didn't ask to be let off the hook."

He grinned, and his gaze slid down to her bare legs stretched out across his own. "Then what are we arguing about?"

"Well, we're not. Or at least, that wasn't my intention."

"Good. Come here." He pulled her closer, until she was actually sitting on his lap.

His body felt so good against hers, that Joanna gave up her attempt to get him to tell her what was going on inside him. Ultimately, she told herself, their marriage was necessary if he wanted to keep Mike. They were getting along well together, all things considered. And if he wanted to keep his doubts and fears to himself, that was his business. She certainly wasn't going to nag him into confiding in her.

Casey nuzzled her neck. Joanna sighed and snuggled closer to him.

She decided to give it one more try. "Casey?" Her voice was husky with the beginnings of desire.

"Yeah?" He began kissing her ear.

"I would do my best to understand anything you wanted to tell me."

"I know, Joey," he murmured into the ear he was

kissing. "You always have. And I do have something to tell you..."

"Yes?"

"I want to make love to you..."

"Casey Clinton," Joanna said. "That's not what I meant and you know it."

"Yeah, but do you *understand?*" His sexy whisper had a hint of laughter in it.

"Oh, I do understand," she told him, giving in to the sensual game he played so wonderfully. "Absolutely."

"Good."

Casey slowly ran his hand along her leg, lingering over the shape of her knee. Taking all the time in the world about it, his hand slid up her thigh to the hem of her shorts, where he teased her by slipping a finger under the hem and running it back and forth against her skin.

"Casey," she sighed.

"Want me to stop?"

"We should check on Mike."

"Right. I'll go." He set her neatly off his lap and stood up, oblivious of her small forlorn moan. He looked back at her, though, just before he reached the arch to the long hallway. "I could meet you in the bedroom in five minutes," he suggested. "It would save me another trip down this tunnel you call a hallway."

She gave him a naughty grin. "You don't want to try out my futon? It converts into a double bed." But then she thought of Mike. It was unlikely the boy would disturb them, but a locked door was the only way to be sure of that. "Oops. I forgot," she laughed. "We have a child."

He pretended to look regretful. "One of these days we'll have to come down here alone." He cast a speculative glance at her drawing board. "The erotic possibilities are endless."

"Casey, I'm shocked," she lied.

"You?" he scoffed. "Joey Vail, who dared me to take off all my clothes when we were twelve and dance naked in the vacant field four blocks from our houses?"

She hastened to correct him. "That wasn't about sex and you know it. That was a dare. No different than all the other times you dared me or I dared you."

He shook his head. "It *was* about sex," he said.

"What do you mean?"

"I mean I was damn thrilled you dared me to take off all my clothes with you. You played right into my most secret fantasies. I wanted to see you naked," he said. "I'd never seen a girl naked before, except Emily in the bathtub, and that didn't count. When I remember that dare, that's what I think of. Seeing you naked."

Joanna found she was blushing. "You never told me that before."

"You never asked." He grinned. "You were awful skinny," he added, "back when we were twelve."

"Why, you…" She picked up a small throw pillow and aimed it at his head.

"I was relieved last night," he went on blithely, "to see how much you've filled out." He ducked into the hallway just before the throw pillow connected with his head.

"Five minutes. The bedroom," he called back to her, though she couldn't see him.

"You were no Adonis yourself back then!" she called to him. She heard a distant chuckle in response.

Then she pulled herself to her feet, went to the kitchen to put the Chinese food cartons in the refrigerator and followed Casey down the long hallway.

When he joined her, he told her Mike was sleeping peacefully, and then he took her in his arms. They made love slowly at first, touching and teasing and getting to know each other's bodies all over again.

But as their desire escalated, their loving took on a frantic, hungry edge. Joanna reveled in it, in all the moods and tempos their lovemaking took. In the end, she clung to him, crying out his name, as he gave her her satisfaction and took his at the same time.

They lay together afterward, their moist bodies clinging together, and Joanna remembered the two of them, as they had been all those years ago, a pair of skinny children dancing naked underneath a spring sky.

Very gently, Casey pulled away. Joanna gave him a small moan in protest.

"Go to sleep," he told her. "I'll take the big chair in Mike's room, just to keep an eye on him."

Casey kissed her and pulled the sheet over her.

"You're a wonderful uncle," she murmured.

She felt his smile against her cheek as he kissed her once more. "'Night, Joey." And he was gone.

Before she surrendered to sleep, she experienced that sense of unease again. The night before she had told herself that their physical union was a good thing.

And it was. But tonight, she couldn't help suspecting that Casey had used the new excitement between them to avoid opening up about his fears and doubts.

Chapter Nine

The next day, Wednesday, was Mike's birthday. Casey and Joanna sang a chorus of "Happy Birthday to You," while they took his morning temperature. Then they clapped wildly when the thermometer came out reading 98.6.

The pediatrician pronounced Mike successfully on the mend and declared that he should be ready to fly home by Friday as planned. Joanna bought a cake at the supermarket and produced a few gifts that she'd wrapped and put in her suitcase before the trip down. She also brought along presents from his paternal grandparents that had arrived from the Midwest the week before. Packages to open made the day special, and also served to keep Saturday's party the surprise it was intended to be.

Still weak from his bout with fever, Mike went to

sleep before eight. And Casey and Joanna made slow, leisurely love in her forest-green bedroom.

Thursday, they remained in Los Angeles and Mike recuperated further. Early Friday they flew home.

In Sacramento, they took Mike to his own doctor, who advised an over-the-counter expectorant to get rid of the boy's lingering nighttime cough. During a moment when Mike was out of earshot, Joanna asked the doctor about the party the next day; the doctor said it should be fine as long as Mike went easy on the sweets and didn't overdo.

Saturday dawned a scorcher. It was well over eighty-five degrees by the pool when Joanna took a morning swim at nine o'clock to clear out the cobwebs from working late into the night. Casey returned at nine-thirty from the airfield where he'd gone to find out how Rhonda had managed in his absence. He and Mike both joined her in the pool. They played a rousing family game of Keep Away, with Joanna and Mike against Casey, who continually managed to leap from the water and snare the ball no matter what the other two did.

At noon, while they ate tuna sandwiches, Casey casually suggested that the three of them could drive over to Chilly Lilly's in an hour or two for ice cream.

"Is that where I'm having my party?" Mike asked.

Casey and Joanna looked at each other; somehow, Mike had figured it out. Casey cleared his throat, and Joanna knew he was about to ask, How did you know? Joanna shot him a pleading look. The agreement with Amanda was that the party would be a surprise; Joanna wanted to keep to the agreement, for the sake of improved family relations. She wanted to give Amanda no excuse, however thin, to stir up hostilities again.

"What makes you think you're having a party?" Joanna asked, her voice studiously noncommittal.

The six-year-old looked smug. "Uncle Burnett and Grandma Lilly didn't give me my presents yet, even though we've been home for a whole day." Mike swiped his nose with the back of his hand. Joanna frowned and handed him a tissue. "Oops, sorry," he said, taking the tissue and wiping his nose properly.

Mike passed back the used tissue. "So I'm right, huh?"

"Do you want to get ice cream or not?" Joanna asked.

"I get it," Mike said. "I'm supposed to pretend I'm surprised. Right?"

"Drink your milk," Joanna said, as Casey tried to keep from laughing.

Mike did his six-year-old best to act surprised when his friends jumped out at him from behind the ice-cream freezers. But he was too much a stranger to deception to make the behavior convincing.

"Wow, dinosaurs!" he said, commenting on the decorations after the squealing and greetings had died down. "I didn't expect dinosaur decorations. This is very excellent."

Over the boy's head, Amanda shot Joanna a chilly look for presumably having ruined her surprise. "I knew you'd like them Mike, so I picked them out especially," she said. "Now, how about a little game of pin the tail on Tyrannosaurus Rex."

"Wow, excellent," the boy said, and the game commenced.

Amanda had a number of entertainments lined up, and she conducted each of them with the skill of a social director. The children all received dinosaur activity books, and then connected the dots to make a Pterodactyl, the child who accomplished the task first winning the prize. They played Drop the Dinosaur in the Bottle, for which Amanda had provided an astonishing number of small, plastic Stegosauri.

In fact, as the party progressed, Joanna realized that Amanda had put a great deal of time and energy into this event. The number and variety of decorations and favors was way beyond anything Chilly Lilly's could ordinarily provide; when they had spoken of the party the previous week, Amanda had clearly stated she'd let the ice-cream shop furnish everything.

After feeling somewhat deceived at first, Joanna looked at Amanda's actions from a different perspective. She decided to be grateful that Mike's aunt was willing to do so much to give him the best party imaginable.

It was a little more difficult, however, to rationalize Amanda's cunningly treacherous behavior as the party progressed.

Subtly, in a hundred little ways, Amanda slighted Joanna. At one point she asked Lillian to help her jot down the children's names to put in a hat. She asked Casey and Burnett to move chairs and tables around to clear the floor for another game. She never invited Joanna to be involved in any way; but twice she asked Joanna to please get out of the way.

Joanna decided to be philosophical. She had known

that it was unlikely that she and Amanda would ever be close. Furthermore, Joanna saw no reason at all to compete with her sister-in-law for Mike's affection; that would be extremely destructive. She reminded herself that Amanda *was* the hostess and told herself to be grateful that Mike was having such a terrific time.

More than once, she intercepted chagrined glances from Lillian, who saw all too well what was going on. Joanna smiled reassuringly at her mother-in-law, trying to telegraph the message with her eyes that she was bearing up. Once or twice, Joanna thought she caught a self-satisfied gleam in Burnett's dark eyes; it occurred to her that he was very pleased with the efficient way his wife had pushed Joanna to the sidelines. Joanna determinedly told herself that she simply couldn't afford to react to Burnett's smug, exasperating behavior.

One thing Joanna had learned from years of battling her parents when she was an intense, dissatisfied teenager was that it took at least two family members at odds with each other to make a family fight. If she didn't let Burnett or his wife get to her, then no family battle would ensue.

Joanna was quite pleased with her mature approach—until she happened to glance at Casey.

He was sitting backward in a straight chair at the long table where everyone had gathered to sing the birthday song. He was staring, calmly, at Amanda at the other end as Amanda helped Mike cut the Brontosaurus-shaped ice-cream cake. He looked utterly and completely relaxed. He seemed to feel Joanna's eyes

on him and left off staring at his sister-in-law to acknowledge Joanna's glance.

He smiled at Joanna. The smile was ice-cold.

Joanna realized he was furious.

"Mike, honey, please," Amanda was saying in a
coyingly affectionate voice. "Use a tissue when you
wipe your nose." She whipped one out of her sleeve
and handed it to Mike who obediently made use of it.
"There," Amanda said, and then felt his forehead.
"Well, at least it doesn't feel as if you're feverish."
The day before, Joanna had spoken briefly over the
phone with Amanda and had told her about Mike's
illness in Los Angeles. It had seemed wiser to mention
it herself than to have Amanda find out secondhand;
no doubt Amanda would then accuse her of manufac-
turing a plot to keep family information from her.

Mike pushed Amanda's coddling hands away. "I'm
fine, Aunt Amanda. Really. Now let me cut my cake."

"I'm glad," Amanda said. "It wouldn't do if
Joanna had brought you out when you were still sick."

Casey stood up. "Amanda," he said. "I wonder if
I could have a word with you, in private."

"Casey…" Joanna began, falling silent when he
shot her a sharp look.

Burnett growled. "Now, just a minute here—"

Lillian, as usual, only smiled sheepishly.

Casey winked broadly at Burnett. "We'll be back
in a flash, Big Brother." He was already at Amanda's
side, taking her arm, and guiding her toward the store-
rooms in the back. "This is just something that can't
wait another minute. Joey, help Mike cut the cake,
would you?"

"Casey, I—" Joanna began.

"Do it," Casey cut her off, his tone pleasantly neutral for all the command in the words.

Amanda was too nonplussed by her brother-in-law's audacity to do anything but stare in astonishment. Then, she was dragged out of sight into the other room. For a moment, Joanna thought Burnett would follow, but then Lillian completely surprised her by placing a hand on his arm.

"Let it be, dear," she said pleasantly.

Burnett stayed where he was.

The children had already tuned out whatever boring adult things were going on among the grown-ups. One of the little boys had stolen one of the girl's Triceratops erasers and the girl began wailing. Mike was busy sawing the head off his ice-cream Brontosaurus.

"Yum, gumdrop eyeballs," he murmured, popping the eyeball in question into his mouth. Joanna reminded herself that the doctor had told her Mike was no longer contagious, so none of the other children were in danger of picking up his flu. Still, after reclaiming the wailing girl's eraser, she promptly took over the cake-cutting duties.

In a few minutes, Amanda and Casey rejoined the group. Joanna looked at Casey reproachfully; he had come so close to causing a fight on Mike's special day. Casey simply looked away, pretending not to catch the significance of her glance.

For the rest of the party, Amanda was scrupulously polite to Joanna, actively including her and, once or twice, even asking her opinion about what to do next. When at last the party came to a close, Joanna couldn't decide which had been worse: Amanda slighting her, or Amanda being so overwhelmingly solicitous.

* * *

That night, alone with Casey as they prepared for bed, Joanna asked him what he'd said to Burnett's wife.

Casey shrugged. "Nothing much. I reminded her that *I* have custody of Mike. And therefore, I determine with whom Mike associates and with whom he doesn't. She nobly decided that, for Mike's sake, she would have to be nice to you. She sees herself as the only constructive influence in Mike's life, and she considers it her duty, at any cost, to do what she can for him. She can't do that if she isn't allowed to see him."

Joanna shook her head. "Casey..." she cleared her throat, hesitating, because what she wanted to tell him was a criticism of what he'd done.

"What?" The question was pure challenge. His chest was bare, since he'd removed his shirt. He was sitting on the bed, getting out of his shoes and socks.

Joanna, already dressed in a short-sleeved nightshirt, was perched on the couch in the sitting area. "Well," she drew in a breath and forged on. "I don't know if threatening her really solves anything, that's all."

His mouth tightened as he stood up and tossed his shoes in the closet. "I did what I had to do. She left you alone after that, didn't she?"

"But it was descending to her level, in a sense, don't you think?"

"I told you what I think. It was necessary." He disappeared into the bathroom.

"But we want to learn to get along with her and Burnett," she said when he came back. "We don't want to go on forever digging at the same old wounds."

"She's not using you as a doormat, and that's final," Casey said. He yanked the zipper of his slacks down, stepped out of them and hung them in the closet. He turned and faced her, wearing only his snug white briefs.

"Now, can we drop it?" A trace of his usual humor sparked in his eyes. "It's bad enough that we have to deal with them from birthdays to Christmas to Easter and then back again. Let's leave them out of our bedroom, okay?"

Joanna, her bare legs gathered up under her on the couch, felt her face flushing—both with anticipation of what she knew would come soon, and with pleasure at the way he'd said *our bedroom.*

He held out his hand. She gladly jumped from the couch to take it. They went into his big bathroom together. He removed the contact lenses he wore and they brushed their teeth side by side in front of the huge mirror. They hadn't even rinsed the minty toothpaste from their mouths before they were kissing. Soon Casey was hoisting her up on the marble counter and showing her what erotic possibilities there were to be explored right there in front of the bathroom mirror between the double sinks.

All through the next week, Casey spent long hours at the airfield making up for lost time. Lillian came by often to take Mike for a few hours, or to drop him off at one of his friend's, so that Joanna could have the precious time she needed to work on the paintings for the gallery opening.

Late Wednesday afternoon, when Joanna was working on one of the studies of Casey at Chilly Lilly's and concentrating on capturing the play of artificial light on green tiles, Lillian returned with Mike. She asked Joanna to take an iced tea break with her out by the pool.

Joanna was so absorbed in her work that she almost requested a rain check. But then she glanced up and saw the anxious expression on Lillian's face.

"I sent Mike to his room to play," Lillian said. "I really do think we should talk."

Joanna blinked, coming out of her concentration on work and turning her attention to the real world. She smiled at Casey's mother. "Sure. Iced tea sounds great. Why don't you go on outside. I'll just clean up a little and be down in a jiffy."

Lillian was waiting for her at the glass table on the edge of the lawn, glasses of iced tea in front of her. Joanna sat down beneath the big umbrella and enjoyed a long, cool sip before urging with mock grimness, "Okay, what is it?"

"I'm not sure I should be here at all," Lillian began, clearly unsure. "I've thought about it and thought about it. And I'm still not sure I should be doing this."

"Okay," Joanna didn't know what else to say.

"It's about Amanda…"

"Yes. What about her?" Joanna said in a neutral tone.

"Well, I don't mean to speak ill of her, but she *has* been behaving terribly toward you."

Joanna focused on the shimmering reflection of the sun on the water in the pool. "We're two very different people," she said after a moment, trying her best to be fair. "Our personalities just don't mesh, I guess." Joanna looked back at Lillian. "Maybe in time—"

Lillian cut Joanna off with a slight wave of her hand. "She's extremely jealous of you, Joey, and you're sensitive enough to realize that."

"Well, yes. I've felt that."

"In part, she's jealous of the closeness you and I share. She longs to be the perfect daughter-in-law. It hurts her that I have such an easy, intimate relationship with you while I'm a little more reserved with her."

"I see," Joanna said. She hadn't really considered that Amanda might feel like an outsider when confronted with the closeness that Joanna and Lillian had shared for so many years.

"Furthermore," Lillian continued, "you were once engaged to her husband."

Joanna left off pondering Lillian's first point to deal with the old issue of her foolish engagement to Burnett. "But that was so long ago," Joanna protested. "And Burnett and I were so totally mismatched. It's absurd for Amanda to be jealous of that."

"Nonetheless, you and Burnett did once plan to marry. And Amanda's a little insecure about her relationship with Burnett right now."

Joanna sensed that Lillian was quickly approaching the crux of the matter. "You want to tell me why, is that it?" Joanna prompted. "But you're also worried that you'll be breaking Amanda's confidence if you talk to me about her relationship with Burnett."

"That's it exactly," Lillian replied. "But I've come here to ask you to keep on putting up with her, for the sake of the family. The way she's been behaving, that's a lot to ask. I feel that I should at least give you a reason to be tolerant of her.''

Joanna reached across the table and squeezed Lillian's hand briefly. ''Not if it's breaking a confidence. I'll keep trying to get along with her for you, and for Mike and Casey. I don't need any more reason than that.''

Lillian's next words were grim. ''Maybe you don't, but Casey does.''

''I'll talk to him. I'll get him to get along with her for my sake and yours and Mike's.'' Joanna forced a laugh. ''Whew. All this family intrigue is a lot of work. I didn't realize how easy I had it down in L.A., with only minor details to stew about, like how to pay the rent.''

Lillian laughed with Joanna, but the laugh was short. ''Seriously though, Joey, on Saturday I saw how fed up Casey is getting with Amanda and Burnett. If something isn't done, there's going to be a big, ugly split in this family. I can feel it.''

Joanna was silent. She was thinking that any incipient split was partly Lillian's fault, for never confronting the fundamental hostilities between her two sons. She said, hesitantly, ''Did you know that Burnett threatened Casey with a lawsuit to get custody of Mike?''

''Yes,'' Lillian admitted. She sounded infinitely sad. ''Burnett told me his plans. I tried to reason with him, but he is so pigheaded. And then, of course, you and Casey announced your marriage and that ended that.''

Joanna was silent. She was trying to keep from asking Lillian exactly how hard she'd tried to reason with Burnett on the issue of Mike's custody. But before she could diplomatically frame such a delicate question, Lillian went on.

"What I'm going to tell you is no secret in any formal sense. I mean, Amanda never specified that I not tell anyone."

"But she wouldn't like it if you did?"

"Probably not."

"Then I don't think you—"

Lillian didn't let her finish. "Joey, you need to know. You're part of the family. And you need to understand why Amanda is the way she is." Quickly, before Joanna could protest again, Lillian said, "Amanda wants desperately to have children. They've been trying for seven of the eight years they've been married. She's had difficulty conceiving. As a matter of fact, they've seen more than one doctor about the problem.

"A little over a year ago, she finally became pregnant. They were both ecstatic, though they told no one but me. They were waiting to get through the first trimester, to be sure everything was all right, before making any formal announcements. At eleven weeks she lost the baby."

Joanna looked out at the sparkling pool again. "Oh, Lord," she said, and she did feel real compassion for the perfect Amanda, whose deepest desire had so far eluded her.

Joanna turned back to Lillian again. "So Amanda and Burnett want Mike for more reasons than I at first understood," she said.

"Yes." Lillian agreed. "They both long for children, and they're afraid they'll never be able to have them." Lillian paused to sip from her tea, before she

added fervently. "Joey, I just know that in time
Amanda and Burnett will accept the situation and decide to adopt a child. As soon as they do that, they'll
let go of the idea of taking Mike away from you and
Casey. Everything will work out fine. If only we can
avert an all-out war in the meantime."

Joanna sighed, "I suppose you're hoping that I'll
pass this information on to Casey."

Lillian smiled sheepishly. "Unless you want me to
tell him."

Joanna considered her suggestion, and then realized
she'd have to talk with Casey about it anyway,
whether Lillian passed on the information first or not.
"It's all right," she said after a moment. "I'll discuss
it with him."

"Oh, thank you," Lillian said gratefully. "Maybe,
if you two are incredibly tolerant, we'll avoid any awful confrontations next month," she said.

Joanna shot her a questioning look. "Next month?"

"Labor Day weekend, at Graeagle," Lillian told
her.

Then Joanna remembered. The Graeagle weekend
was an annual event with the Clintons. The whole
family went. For three days. Joanna groaned inwardly
at the thought: herself and Casey, Burnett and
Amanda, Lillian and Mike, all sleeping under the same
roof and sharing each other's company for seventy-
two hours. It would be an exercise in tolerance, to put
it mildly.

"I don't know, Lillian," Joanna began carefully.
"Maybe this year we shouldn't push our luck."

Lillian's face fell. Joanna realized how much observing the family tradition meant to her mother-in-law.

"All right, count us in," Joanna said. "Somehow, we'll all manage to get along."

Chapter Ten

Casey didn't arrive home until late that evening. Running a small, private airfield was demanding. Rhonda Popper was willing to work in the office full-time for a pittance and plenty of flight hours, but the burden of most of the paperwork still fell on Casey's shoulders—a burden he accepted in order to keep costs down. The two weeks he'd taken off after the wedding had to be made up.

He found Joanna in her studio, where she was just finishing the second painting of him in the ice-cream shop. He came up behind her and kissed the back of her neck.

''Why is it that lately I find the smell of paint thinner erotic?'' he teased.

She leaned back into his chest, holding her palette and brush out in front of her and studying the painting she'd just finished. "Because you're a man of taste and discernment," she told him. "Did you look in on Mike?" she asked.

"Uh-huh. He's asleep for the night."

"Did you eat?"

"You bet." He nuzzled her neck. "As a matter of fact, I'm ready for dessert."

She giggled, and thought how nice it was to have Casey's arms to look forward to every night. It was surprising, really, how easy she'd found it to integrate him and Mike into her life. If it wasn't for their family difficulties and the fear she had that something was troubling Casey, she would have called her life perfect.

She rolled her head against his chest until she could kiss his chin. "Tell you what. Why don't you let me clean up a little in here and I'll meet you in the bedroom in fifteen minutes."

He kissed her mouth, quickly. "Deal," he said, and left her alone.

Joanna cleaned her brushes and took a quick shower. She joined Casey with two minutes to spare. For a while, they lay side by side on the big bed, talking about the events in their respective days.

Finally, she told him about what Lillian had revealed about Amanda's longing for a child. There was a silence after she was done. Casey was lying on his side, facing her, his head resting on his bent arm.

He levered himself up on an elbow and asked, "So what's the point?"

Joanna blinked, surprised at his sudden curtness. Until then, she had been feeling so contented, savoring the clean scent of his skin and hair after his evening shower, enjoying the sound of his voice as he talked to her and anticipating the moment when one of them would reach out and touch the other with intimate intent.

She sat up, crossing her bare legs Indian-fashion and smoothing the hem of her nightshirt over them. "Well, Casey," she said, "the point is that Amanda's had a difficult time."

"So that makes it all right for her to treat you like dirt?"

"Well, no, but—"

"That's what my mother's saying, isn't it? She wants you to let Amanda walk all over you because poor Amanda can't have a child. And she wants me to sit by and let it happen."

"Casey, please. Don't be like this."

Suddenly, he was off the bed and pacing the floor. "Damn it. She should have come to me, not dragged you into it."

"Casey, she offered to talk to you herself."

"Sure she did." He stopped pacing long enough to glare at Joanna. "As soon as she'd finished laying it all on you. Because she knew I wouldn't be as sympathetic as you, she took advantage of her relationship with you, figuring maybe you could do a better job of getting me in line."

"Come on," Joanna slid off the bed and approached him. "You know how Lillian is. We've talked about it a hundred times. On our own wedding night, when I was the one complaining about her, you said it yourself: Lillian is who she is. She hates conflict. You can't suddenly expect her to act like someone else."

"It's not your problem," he said.

She looked at him, eye to eye. "It is very much my problem," she told him. "It has been ever since you talked me into marrying you." He stared back at her, and she saw a bleakness in his light eyes. "Casey, what is it?" she heard herself pleading. "What's bothering you?"

"Nothing." He turned away and went to the sitting area. He stood near the couch looking out the bay window at the sloping lawn and the quiet nighttime street.

Joanna drew in a long, deep breath. "You feel guilty, is that it?" she asked him, "For getting me involved in all this?"

"You're damned right," he said, still staring out the window.

"Casey," Joanna paused, wanting to frame her thoughts carefully. "It was wrong of me to say you talked me into marrying you. I chose to get involved. You may have pressured me, but I wouldn't have given in to that pressure unless I knew it was the right decision."

"It's a bad deal for you, all around," he said. "You can be a good sport about it, but we both know what's what in the end."

Joanna stared at his back, not knowing what to say to bring him out of this strange dark mood. She didn't know how to reach him when he was like this.

In their years as friends, Joanna had been the one whose moods had been erratic; she was the one who had had a tendency to brood. Casey was the one who never overreacted, never took things too seriously. He could be outrageous, but he was usually patient with the failings of others—unlike now when he had so abruptly become furious with his mother's actions. Never before had she seen Casey angry with Lillian for trying to avoid a fight. Dealing with this new volatility in him made her feel like she was dealing with a total stranger.

And ten minutes ago, she'd been thinking how comfortable and cozy they were together...

Casey turned away from the window and looked across the room at her. As he so often did before bedtime, he wore only his loose khaki slacks. He crossed his arms over his beautiful chest. "Are there any more dead babies I should know about so I can work on being more understanding when my brother and his wife treat my wife like a dart board?"

"Casey, that's a lousy thing to say," Joanna said. "It's not worthy of you at all."

"Isn't it?" He dropped his arms to his sides and approached her, his bare feet soundless on the thick close-woven carpet.

"Are you trying to pick a fight with me?" she challenged.

He stopped opposite her and very slowly reached out to smooth a swatch of hair back over her shoulder. The small gesture, in spite of her ambivalence toward him then, was like a signal. His hand whispered along her neck, and she was trapped in the awareness of the pleasure his touch could bring her.

"Joey," he said. "What makes you think I want to fight?" His eyes dared her, and the dare was all about the delight they could be sharing right this minute.

"You do this to me all the time lately," she accused halfheartedly.

Lazily, he undid the top button of her nightshirt, and

then took the collar points and pulled them apart, so the tops of her breasts were revealed to him.

"Do what?" he asked.

"Make love instead of telling me what's going on inside you."

He undid another button, then looked from her breasts into her eyes. "What's going on inside me is I want to make love with you."

What could she say? He knew she would listen, if he chose to open up. But he didn't open up, and in the final analysis, that was his right.

His fingers moved nimbly, until her shirt was completely open. She tipped her head back, to watch his face, her eyelids heavy with building desire.

He cupped her bared breasts with his hands as his eyes held hers. Joanna sighed.

"I love it when you look like that," he said. "Your eyes all heavy, wanting me." He bent his head to her breast. She swayed on her feet, moaning aloud as he sucked a nipple into his mouth. She combed her fingers through his thick hair and held his head there, while he nipped and licked and blew cool air across the tender flesh, pleasuring her.

He stood up again and gathered her against his chest. His lips were breath-close. She strained toward them. He loosened his slacks and felt for her hand, guiding it to where she could feel the proud evidence of his hunger for her.

"This, at least," he said against her mouth, "is fine between us. Isn't it, Joey?"

"Oh, Casey..." Her hand closed around him, cupping him.

"Say yes," he whispered. "Say you like it."

"I do," she heard herself murmur. "I love it, I do..."

Then he gave her his mouth, kissing her deeply and with growing abandon until she felt she would melt there against him, melt into a molten pool of desire right there on the tan carpet six feet from his big, white bed.

Insistently, he pushed the nightshirt from her shoulders. She was nude for him except for her panties, which he soon removed as well.

Then he swung her up against his chest, carried her to the bed and laid her down on it. His eyes burned into hers as he took off the rest of his own clothes.

At last, gloriously naked, he joined her on the bed, loving her first with his mouth. Then, after she had touched heaven once, he entered her and together they found that magical place where mutual fulfillment overwhelmed them.

Later, as she held his head against her breast and lay sated, gazing up at the ceiling, she remembered about the Graeagle weekend.

"Casey?"

Languidly, he was tracing a figure eight on the smooth skin of her waist. "Um?"

"There was one other thing that Lillian mentioned..."

His lazily tracing finger grew still. "What?"

"The Graeagle weekend."

"What about it?"

"She expects us to go, that's all."

He raised his head and looked at her. "And you said we would."

"Well, except for the time you were overseas with the navy, you'd always gone before."

He rolled away from her to lie faceup, throwing an arm across his eyes. "This isn't before," he said.

"It's a month away," she tried optimistically, as if she was hoping the situation might change dramatically in that space of time.

"It's a bad idea," he said.

"Casey, I promised." Joanna didn't like herself very much at that moment. She knew she should have waited to consult him.

"It'll be a disaster," he said. "And Burnett and Amanda won't miss a trick when it comes to running you down."

"I'm an adult. I can take whatever they dish out."

He looked at her, moving his arm away from his eyes to his forehead. "You're just not in the pattern about this at all," he said, using a pilot's expression.

"What do you mean? I understand what's going on completely."

"They're chipping away at you, Joey. Little by little, they're trying to wear you down. They figure that you're the weak link in my claim on Mike."

"Oh, Casey. That's a little farfetched, don't you think?"

"No." The word was flat, unequivocal. "After what I saw at Mike's party Saturday, I don't think it's farfetched at all."

He went on, sounding weary and a little bitter, "Some things never change, and we're fools if we think that they can. When my father deserted us, Burnett was eleven. He took on the burdens of the man of the house then and he hasn't stopped trying to run all our lives since. My mother feels guilty; she always hesitates to criticize him because she knows she really leaned on him. She knows that without his business brains and willingness to work like a dog when he should have been out being a kid, none of us would be rich now.''

He was staring at Joanna, that scary bleakness in his eyes again. "The hostilities between Burnett and me go so deep, the bottom would be impossible to reach, Joey. There *is* love there, but it's all wound up with resentment and anger. I've always had all the freedom he could never allow himself, and I've never used it the way he thought I should."

Casey's words rang too true for Joanna's peace of mind. She shivered a little. Then she sat up and dragged the throw cover from the foot of the bed, wrapping it around her bare shoulders. "You really think Burnett and Amanda are so diabolical that they would consciously try to break up our marriage?" she asked.

Casey had turned on his side, facing her. With hooded eyes he had watched her wrap herself in the blanket. He himself remained splendidly nude, cloaked only in his considerable male grace. "Conscious or unconscious," he said, "what's the difference if the outcome is the same?"

"The difference is that I can take it." Joanna leaned over and kissed him on the nose in an attempt to lighten the mood, which had grown much too somber for her liking.

In the past, it had always been Casey who lightened the mood, she thought. But somehow, their marriage had switched things around. More and more, Joanna played the role of the optimist.

"It's not fair to you," Casey said.

"I can handle it," she told him for what seemed like the hundredth time. "For Mike's sake, I can handle a heck of a lot."

"Right," he said. "For Mike's sake." Then, abruptly, he sat up and began swinging his legs off the side of the bed.

Joanna watched, puzzled at first, as he gathered his clothes from the rumpled pile on the floor and proceeded to put them on again. "You're going out?" she asked, when she realized what was happening.

"Not out." He zipped up his slacks and went to the chest of drawers opposite the foot of the bed. He found a T-shirt and pulled it over his head, then spoke again as he tucked the shirt into his pants. "I brought home a stack of log sheets this high. I should get to them."

"But Casey—"

"What?" He paused by the closet to cast her a rather impatient look over his shoulder.

"Well, we were talking about something that's important—and all of a sudden you've got work that can't wait."

"The subject seems pretty much played out."

"But we didn't even decide about the weekend at Graeagle."

"Sure we did," he said. "You decided about that way before you even thought of consulting me."

Joanna drew a deep breath. "Okay. I was wrong. I'll tell Lillian that we won't be going this year."

"Hell, no," he said, his tone a mockery of lightness.

"The Graeagle weekend is a family tradition. And we can't go breaking with tradition, now can we?"

"Casey—"

"Look," he said. "We've run the subject of my family right into the ground and all the way to China. I'm sick and tired of it. And I do have work I need to do."

"It feels to me like you're running away," she said.

"Okay," he sighed. "I'm running away. And I have work to do."

"But Casey, I don't—"

He cut her off, fed up. "Just give it a rest, will you please, Joey?"

He came where she sat on the bed. He bent over to kiss her before leaving her for work she knew he'd invented. When she didn't immediately raise her face to his, he tipped her chin up with his hand. "Come on," he said. His touch was tender on the soft skin of her throat. "Let it be. Some things in life never get worked out."

Like what's bothering you? she thought, but didn't say. It would do no good to ask, anyway. He wouldn't tell her. And ironically, her desire to understand seemed to only drive a wider wedge between them.

"Smile?" he asked.

Obediently, she forced the corners of her mouth up. His lips met hers once, sweet and brief, and then he went downstairs.

Chapter Eleven

For Joanna, August passed in a sweltering haze of creative activity. The paintings for the gallery show seemed to almost paint themselves.

The paintings, at first studiously realistic, became more impressionistic, renderings of light and shadow, striking in their vividness, as Joanna let herself go.

Casey was busy, too, both with the airfield and with Mike. Still, he and Joanna found time to make love almost every night, and how good they were together in that most intimate of ways continued to take her breath away.

After the night they'd argued about the Greagle weekend, Joanna was careful to avoid the dangerous subjects that made her new husband turn away from her. She stopped asking him what was bothering him; she remained scrupulously neutral whenever anyone mentioned either his brother or his sister-in-law.

More than once, Amanda dropped by on what she said was a whim. Because Joanna knew Burnett's wife always wanted to see Mike, she was able to avoid any trouble by just leaving Amanda alone with the boy.

Sometimes, during a rare quiet moment when her latest canvas wasn't consuming all her attention, Joanna would find herself wondering sadly what had happened to the old ease she and Casey had always shared. When she wasn't looking her best friend had faded away and left in his place a cordial stranger who treated her with thoughtful consideration and kindness during the day—and set her nights on fire.

But then she would rouse herself from the negative speculations and go back to work, or play with Mike, or look up to see Casey watching her. They'd exchange smiles, and she'd want to ask, What is it, what's happened to us? But she wouldn't, because she knew it would do no good at all.

On Thursday, August thirty-first, Joanna put down her brush for the last time before the opening of her show in Los Angeles on September eighth. Most of the paintings had already been flown down to the gallery the week before; all that remained to be transported were the last ones she'd completed. She and Casey could take those with them on Tuesday, when he flew her down so she could work with Althea on the finishing touches for the show.

Joanna stood back from the big canvas she'd just completed. The late afternoon sun came through the bay window behind her and picked up the red heat of the dying sun in the painting.

It was a rendering of a certain magical moment during that long-ago weekend at Graeagle when both she and Casey had been eighteen. She'd painted the Mill Pond with a single small rowboat out in the middle, turning slowly in a circle as the sun dropped behind the western hills. In the boat there were two figures, one at either end. The figures were Casey and Joanna; they weren't detailed enough for anyone looking at them to ascertain their genders, let alone the fact that they were a boy and a girl of eighteen at a moment of crossroads in each of their short lives.

Casey had been headed for the navy shortly after that. Joanna had been planning to marry Burnett in the fall, but would end up going to UCLA and becoming an artist.

Graeagle, now mostly a vacation and retirement community, had once been a logging town. The big pond where the logs once floated, waiting to be milled, was virtually deserted when Casey had led her out there with the intention of going for a sunset swim.

By plowing through a few willow stands and stomping doggedly in marshy grass, they finally came to a place that Casey had declared acceptable.

Casey had coaxed Joanna into the abandoned boat that he had found in the rushes. As she started to slide the oars through the rowlocks, he had signaled to her not to bother; he swam the boat out toward the middle of the pond, strong legs beating beneath the water, one hand on the stern to guide the boat.

Slow, lazy ripples had moved out from the bow before her, shot with the colors of the dying sun. Out in the center, it was still, a peaceful kind of quiet made more so by the slight bobbing of the boat and the soft slap of water against the sides.

Sleek and agile as an eel, Casey had glided up over

the side and into the boat and had moved toward the back. Joanna naturally made the adjustment to his weight, moving forward a little and turning to face him, perching on the sailing thwart, while he took the seat in the stern.

The hot ball of the sun sunk halfway behind the mountains and hung there, bleeding its final colors into the darkening sky. Pale to the northeast, the moon seemed to be waiting for darkness and her chance to dominate.

Casey took an oar and gently dipped it in the water. The boat turned, slowly, in a circle, and the panorama of the pond, the sloping grassy land, the sentinel pines, the shadowy distant hills and the twilight sky were Joanna's to experience and know.

Then the swallows came, soaring effortlessly above, snatching unwary insects as they dipped and rose in strong and buoyant flight. Their occasional calls were unmusical, but the music in their flight alone was enough for Joanna.

The sun dropped from sight, leaving only an iridescent rim of pink and orange on the western horizon, and the swallows became like living shadows, wings spread in double chevrons against the dusky sky.

Joanna had felt transported in ecstasy by the sheer beauty of the world around her. She sat, the sketchbook that Casey had insisted she carry with her laid across her lap, her hands hooked beneath her pressed together knees. She drank it all in, as the night fell and the air cooled perceptibly against her sun-warmed skin.

"I'll miss you," Casey had said. He was on his way to the navy two weeks from that day.

Joanna, lowering her gaze from the sky, had looked at his face, shadowed across from her as he stopped his gentle circular rowing. The boat had stilled with Joanna facing the hills where the sun had gone.

''I'll miss you, too,'' she had said. She had felt, at that moment, an absolute confidence in the security of his friendship. She had felt that the boy across from her knew her exactly as she truly was, and accepted her without reservation. At that moment she had known she would not marry Burnett, and that she would go to Los Angeles after all....

Now, fourteen years later, the more mature Joanna turned abruptly from the painting embodying a moment of absolute affinity between herself and her best friend. She busied herself cleaning up, then she took a long, refreshing shower.

Out the small bathroom window, she could hear Casey and Mike splashing in the pool. She joined them after she'd finished her shower. She swam a few laps and then floated on a rubber raft in the scorching sun until Casey reminded her to either find some shade or slather herself in sunscreen.

That night Casey made love to her with an intensity and beauty even more stunning than all the incredible nights before. It seemed to Joanna that she became pure sensation. He explored and mastered every inch of her yearning body, bringing her once and then again to a shuddering satisfaction, cradling her close against him, and then starting all over again.

Finally, exhausted from delight, her head nestled in the crook of his arm and her legs entwined with his, she drifted toward a bottomless well of sleep.

"Joey..." his voice came to her, his breath playing across the crown of her head.

"Um?" She shifted a little, snuggling closer into his warmth against the air-conditioned coolness of the room.

"Joey, I..."

"Yes?"

Then there was a long silence, and the part of her mind that held on to a thread of consciousness knew she should prompt him, ask him to go on.

She forced sleep away, canted up on an elbow and pushed the mass of tangled hair away from her face. "What? Tell me."

For a moment, their eyes held, and she was sure that he was going to open up to her at last. She felt the beginnings of relief—and she felt dread.

Over the past weeks, she'd begun to fear more and more that the reason for the change in Casey was that, deep down, he didn't like being married. For Mike's sake, he was staying with it. But she was afraid that he'd call it off in a minute if the custody issue were resolved. He'd dared her to marry him; she'd accepted the challenge and now they were stuck with each other, for better or worse. For as free a spirit as Casey Clinton, Joanna feared, the bonds of matrimony felt too much like prison walls.

Casey was looking at her silently.

"Do you want out of this marriage, Casey?" she heard herself asking, her voice stark and low. "Is that it?"

"No," he said. "I don't. Do you?"

"No," she said.

They looked at each other across what seemed like

a huge chasm of silence. Joanna wondered then what else she could do. When she asked what was wrong, he always said nothing. She hated the rote exchanges: Do you regret?…No, do you?…

"What did you want to say?" she asked then.

"Never mind." He pulled her down against his chest, and tugged the sheet over them. "It's late. We should get some sleep to be fresh for tomorrow."

Tomorrow, Joanna thought grimly, when they would be leaving for Graeagle and the annual family Labor Day weekend.

Joanna lay close to her husband and dreaded the next three days with all her heart. The feeling of foreboding had increased over the past weeks, every time the subject of the weekend had come up: when she'd marked the dates on the calendar in the kitchen, when she'd learned that Burnett and Amanda would definitely be going, when Amanda had called a few days ago to instruct Joanna on what groceries to bring. Joanna couldn't shake the growing certainty that seething hostilities would flare into out-and-out conflict given three days of proximity between the Clinton brothers and their wives.

She should cancel, she thought, no matter what a family stir her backing out would cause. Going when she felt like this was comparable to blithely boarding an airplane after having noticed an Uzi sticking out of the flight bag of the passenger in front of you.

Fitfully, Joanna turned over, pulling away from Casey and seeking the cool sheets on her own side of the bed. At her back, she felt Casey shifting too, turning away, to his side.

For a while, she lay staring at the dim reflection of her sheet-covered body in the mirrored closet door.

Joanna wanted to scream. Or to cry. Or to beg Casey to be honest with her.

But then she realized that what she needed to do was to stop driving herself crazy over things she could do nothing about. In the past, Casey would have been the first to point that out to her.

But, she told herself firmly, this isn't the past. This is the present. Casey and I are married. We both want it to stay that way, for Mike's sake, no matter what doubts Casey feels he can't share with me. We said we'd go to Graeagle, and that's exactly what we're going to do. It's going to be fine. It's going to be fun.

Resolutely, Joanna rolled over and invaded her husband's side of the bed. She wrapped herself around his back, spoon-fashion, and was extremely gratified when he reached for her hand, pulling her arm around him at the crook of his waist and entwining his fingers with hers.

The next morning they were packed and on the road by nine. At Casey's suggestion, they took the scenic route to Graeagle, through Grass Valley and up Highway 49. They turned off at Bassetts Station and took the Gold Lake Forest Highway, driving past spectacular views of the Sierra Buttes. Then they traveled down into the Lakes Basin, past all the dirt road turnoffs that led to campgrounds at the myriad small lakes tucked in among the tall trees and rugged hills.

Mike, seated in the back of Casey's Chevy Blazer along with the suitcases and the bags of groceries, kept up a steady, excited stream of chatter throughout most of the three-hour drive.

Someday, he explained, he'd stop in Downieville and pan for gold... When could they climb the Buttes?... Did Casey and Joey think probably there were deer at Deer Lake and horses at Horse Lake?... And what about Gold Lake, huh? Was there probably lots of gold, a treasure in gold there, didn't they think?

Then there was Sand Pond. They'd gone swimming there last year. Could they please go again this year, too?

Casey and Joanna took turns good-naturedly dealing with the boy's endless queries. Joanna rolled down the window after they'd left Grass Valley and relished the feel of the clean mountain air flowing over her face and tangling her hair.

The sky overhead was the summer-blue of Casey's eyes, pale, but vibrant with light. The few fat clouds were cotton-white, more reminiscent of an artist's idealized rendering than of anything that might actually produce rain.

As they turned onto Highway 89, the road that cut right through Graeagle where it lay nestled in the Mohawk Valley, Joanna happened to glance at Casey. He felt her eyes on him and gave her a quick smile and a wink.

Joanna sat back in her seat, temporarily content with the world and her place in it. The night before she'd made the resolution not to let her negative thoughts get the best of her. So far, it seemed to be working out just fine. She was on her way to a holiday weekend with two people she loved. Everything else, she'd cope with.

They arrived at the cabin at noon, before any of the others. Joanna climbed from the Blazer and stretched, loosening up the kinks from the drive. She gave herself a moment to appreciate the cabin, which lay at the crest of a sloping natural lawn of wild clover and Bermuda grass.

Joanna had always liked the cabin, which was really more like a country cottage. It was painted rust-red, as were most of the dwellings that had originally been owned by a company that had once run a profitable lumber mill in the town. The tin roof peaked high, so winter snow would slide off, and the rustic stone chimney dominated the outside wall toward the garage.

Lillian had inherited the property from a wealthy bachelor uncle, along with the money that she'd used to start up the family chain of ice cream-shops.

Behind her, Joanna heard Mike hit the ground at a run.

"Hold on," Casey ordered from the other side of the Blazer. "Where do you think you're going, kid?"

"Just across the street, Uncle Case. I gotta check out the Mill Pond, and find out if Megan came." Megan, Joanna had learned, was a girl Mike's age whose family had vacationed here the year before.

"That street is the highway," Casey said, "and you're not to cross it without adult supervision. And before you do anything, we need to unload the truck."

"Aw, Uncle Case…"

"Then you have to have a sandwich."

Mike groaned, a long, theatrical sound. "*Uncle Case…*"

Casey chuckled. "Do it and get it over with."

Dramatically slumping his shoulders, his tennis

shoes dragging on the pebbled driveway, the boy went around to the rear of the truck where Casey handed him a bag of groceries.

Joanna smiled to herself as she got in line behind Mike to do her share of toting food and suitcases to the cabin. Casey had always been good with Mike, but invariably in the role of the indulgent uncle. When Emily died, Casey would no more have known how to keep the boy in line than Joanna would have known how to bring a navy fighter plane in on the postage stamp runway of an aircraft carrier.

But now, especially since the boy's scary bout with the flu in Los Angeles the month before, Casey seemed to have learned that being a parent wasn't all affection and indulgence. Sometimes doing what was right for a child was the hardest thing a parent could do, and often the child didn't like it one bit.

At this point, Joanna mused, Casey was completely capable of raising Mike on his own. His schedule was flexible, and he'd become accustomed to including the boy in his day-to-day existence.

If she and Casey hadn't ended up married, it would have been time for her to return to her own life in Los Angeles. Oddly, Joanna could hardly imagine herself going back to her apartment to pick up her old life. Somehow, imperceptibly, Casey's house had become her home and Casey and Mike a necessary part of her life.

Luckily for her, she thought with equal parts irony and guilt, Burnett and Amanda had made it imperative that Casey find a wife. Joanna chuckled to herself. The next time she longed to throw Amanda off the nearest available cliff, she'd simply remind herself that if it wasn't for Casey's brother and his wife, Joanna wouldn't be married to Casey now.

"What's that big grin about?" Casey asked, as he handed her a box piled with hot dog buns, paper plates and plastic flatware.

"Just thinking what a gorgeous day it is and what a lucky lady I am to be sharing it with my two favorite guys," she told him.

He grinned back at her. "That's what we love to hear." He passed her the keys to the cabin and she laughed as she juggled the bulky box in an effort to catch them.

Mike was waiting beneath the tin porch roof that ran along the front of the cabin like a high skirt. He was holding a bag of groceries, shifting impatiently from one foot to the other.

"C'mon, Joey. I got things to do!"

Obligingly, Joanna mounted the two steps and stuck the key into the lock beneath the old, yellowed porcelain knob.

The door swung open, and Mike edged past her, hurrying to the kitchen to set down his load and rush back out to the Blazer for more. Joanna took a minute to appreciate the interior, which to her was like somebody's fantasy of homeyness. The planked walls were painted in pale greens and gray-whites, and rag rugs were scattered over the fir floors. All the furniture seemed to have been handed down for generations—fat, faded and inviting. The sofa was upholstered in a rose-patterned fabric, with antimacassars on the arms and across the back.

Joanna followed Mike into the bright kitchen, where someone had added a handy pine-topped island and stenciled bunches of grapes in a row near the ceiling. The stencils were a new addition since the last time Joanna had visited the cabin. Joanna remembered that Lillian and Emily used to spend weekends here often, and remembered them talking about different changes they'd made. Joanna found the thought pleasing, of Emily and Lillian here together, supervising the installation of the island, or stenciling the walls. With a contented little grunt, Joanna set her box on the island next to the bag Mike had brought in before he'd trooped back outside for more.

Within an hour, they were completely unpacked and Mike, who'd made alarmingly short work of his sandwich, was off looking for Megan.

The boy had listened with growing impatience as Casey had reiterated that under no circumstances was he to cross the street alone to get to the Mill Pond. Visiting Megan's was allowed, since the girl's family rented a cottage on the same side of the highway as the Clinton cabin.

"Jeez, Uncle Case," Mike had finally interrupted. "I promise, I promise. I won't cross the street alone. Now, it would be totally excellent if I could please get going now."

At last, the boy had been released. Casey and Joanna had finished their own lunch at a more leisurely pace. Then Joanna had volunteered to clean up while Casey went out and replenished the woodpile.

Thunk. Joanna looked out the kitchen window to see Casey sink his ax into a big chunk of cedar. Joanna decided she felt cooped up. She'd lingered in the kitchen when she could be outside among the pines. She hung the dish towel back on its peg by the win-

dow and climbed the steep back stairwell to one of
the trio of second-floor bedrooms.

In the room that she and Casey would share, she
found her blank sketchbook along with a few soft pencils. Then she hurried back down the stairs and out
into the early-afternoon sun. She joined Casey in the
backyard and perched on a log beneath a cedar tree at
the edge of the clear, grassy space that defined the
cabin's backyard.

Flipping to a clean page, she spent more time trying
to capture the impression of the sky seen through a
web of pine needles, trying to depict the lambency of
random rays of sun peeking through the branches. It
wasn't easy to do without using color, but she found
her interest and absorption growing.

Joanna drew the trail that wound off into the woods,
trying to capture the way the shadows thickened, as
the branches of the trees meshed overhead. She drew
the woodpile, with the garage in the background. And
then, on the next page, quickly, just the ax head as
Casey brought it down with a thunk on a hunk of
wood.

Then she started on sketches of Casey, of his arms,
lifting up and then bringing down the ax. Of his feet,
in a pair of old laced up boots, planted in a pile of
wood chips. Of his back, beautifully muscled and
dewed with sweat as he rhythmically lifted and
brought down the ax.

And then Casey stopped, turning toward her and
wiping his forehead with the back of his gloved hand.
"Whew. Good for what ails you."

She caught that, too—the satisfied tiredness in his

hard body, and the moment when his hand blotted his forehead.

"Let me see," he teased, knowing she wouldn't show him. After all the years they'd been friends he was well aware of her personal creative eccentricities.

"Uh-uh. Sketching's private. Always," she muttered, and went on drawing. When she glanced up, he was stacking the wood in the lean-to box against the garage. She flipped the page and drew him throwing the wood in, her strokes quick and sure, not needing to look up at him again after one glance.

As her fingers flew over the white paper, a shadow fell across the sketchbook. Joanna looked up and found Casey standing over her, his work gloves in his hands. "I thought you were through working for a few days." She could hear the smile in his voice, though the midafternoon sun behind him made his grin hard to see.

She shaded her eyes against the glare and grinned right back, thinking that maybe this weekend would turn out to be just what they needed after all. "Bad habits die hard."

He bent quickly and set his gloves on the log. As he stood up again, he feinted for the sketchbook. "Let me see…"

She giggled, yanking it away and putting it behind her back. "No way, Casey Clinton."

"If you're going to draw pictures of me with my shirt off, I've got a right to take a look."

"Uh-uh." She stood up, stepping backward over the log. He advanced on her, drawing his eyebrows together to show her he meant business.

"Come on, Joey."

She backed away. "No."

"Yes." He advanced.

"No." She curved around and began backing toward the house.

"Yes." He followed.

"No!" She broke and ran for the back step, clutching her sketchbook and pencils, laughing out loud.

He brought her down to the sweet grass, in the middle of the yard. They wrestled together for possession of the sketchbook, more in fun than in earnest.

"Let me go!" Joanna cried.

"Give me that," Casey demanded.

"No."

"Yes…"

"No…"

"Yes."

Finally, with a huffing pretense of great effort, Joanna sent her sketchbook and pencils sailing over her head. She and Casey ceased their mock struggles as they heard the sketchbook land on the porch and saw the pencils bounce on their erasers and roll down the steps.

"Now you've done it," Casey said.

Joanna squinted up at him. "Done what?" He had captured both her hands and held them over her head. His sweaty, bare chest heaved against her breasts.

"Forced me to choose," he said.

She squinted even more, her expression bemused.

"To choose," he explained, "which I want more. To look at pictures of myself with my shirt off—"

"Or?"

"To keep rolling around in the grass with you."

"It's a tough choice," she conceded.

"But I think I'm ready to make it."

Joanna fell in with his game, squirming a little, just to make the choice more interesting. "Take your time," she advised, her voice grown somewhat husky. "Give it lots of thought."

With his thumbs, he rubbed the sensitive inner skin of her arms, where he held them captive against the grass. "Right." Then he repeated after her, as if trying to remind himself, "Give it lots of thought..."

"You always did have a tendency to rush into things," she teased.

He moved his head just enough to shade her face from the glaring brightness of the sun. She could see his expression then; he was pretending to look incredulous. "Me? Rush into things?"

"Yes, you."

"Never."

"Always."

"Uh-uh."

"Uh-huh."

He shook his head.

She nodded hers.

Then both of them burst into a silly fit of giggling.

And then the giggling passed as, enticingly, Casey touched her lower lip with the very tip of his tongue. And then very lightly he bit the place he'd licked. And then he started nibbling all around her mouth, little soft quick kisses.

Joanna was captivated, as she always was when Casey's lips met hers. Until Casey had started regularly kissing her, she'd never realized that it could be so much fun.

Half the fun, of course, was kissing Casey back—

which Joanna immediately began doing, stretched out on the grass under his damp, strong body beneath a hot late-summer sky.

She was just thinking how lovely it would be if they could just lie here forever, kissing lazily and pleasurably and letting the rest of the world take a hike, when the kitchen's screen door banged shut and footsteps could be heard on the porch.

The footsteps came to an abrupt halt. Joanna heard the sound of a soft feminine gasp. Then she heard a man clear his throat.

Casey swore feelingly against Joanna's mouth, and slowly raised his head. Joanna craned her neck and saw Burnett and Amanda standing side by side on the porch.

"'Lo, Big Brother," Casey said, then nodded at Burnett's gaping wife. "Amanda." Taking his sweet time about it, Casey backed off of Joanna, pushing himself to his knees.

Joanna scuttled to a sitting position. Then, taking her cue from Casey and realizing they'd done nothing at all to be ashamed of, she began casually plucking lawn burrs and grass from her shirt and hair.

"Well," Joanna said after a moment, when no one else seemed disposed to speak. "Did you two have a nice ride up? We took Highway 49. It was beautiful." She stood up, and brushed off her cutoff jeans. "Casey's already fixed us up with plenty of wood. Do you need some help toting things in from your car?" At that moment, Joanna noticed that the first button of her top had come undone. She decided not to button it up; that would only draw attention to it.

"Where is Mike?" Burnett said in a tone full of self-righteous reprimand.

Casey stood up, and went to the log at the edge of the yard to get his work gloves. "He went looking for Megan—his friend from last year."

"Alone?" Amanda asked.

"Yes. Alone." Casey slapped his gloves against his bluejeaned thigh, perhaps to rid them of slivers, but more likely to defuse his annoyance with his sister-in-law for her perennial attitude of pained reproach.

"My God," Burnett said, "That's the highway out there, not a hundred yards from the front door."

That was true, of course, but it was also Graeagle's main street, and as such hardly as dangerous as Burnett made it sound.

"Mike knows he's not to cross it alone," Casey said.

"He's six years old," Burnett accused.

"And very responsible." Casey pointed out.

The two brothers glared at each other. Then Burnett said with infinite patience. "It's simply not acceptable, Casey. You've completely ignored your obligations as a guardian while you..." He paused, as he presumably sought the most tactful way to describe what Joanna and Casey had been doing. "*Wrestled* with Joanna. What if Mike had seen you?"

Joanna looked down at her tennis shoes. Three whole days of this, she thought grimly, and then began casting about for some way to defuse the growing tension. She looked up at Burnett with a blinding smile.

"Well, Burnett," she said, "I guess if Mike had seen us he might have discovered that married people sometimes giggle and kiss each other. Then we'd have done our best to help him accept that.''

"This is no time to be glib, Joanna," Burnett intoned. Joanna faced him refusing to lose her smile.

Over by the log, Casey chuckled. "Ease off, Big Brother," he said. "Joey's got it exactly right."

Then Casey sauntered over to Joanna's side. He put his arm around her. She looked at him, and saw that he'd come to the same conclusion she had. If they were going to make it through the weekend, they'd need a sense of humor and a willingness to bend.

"Maybe we got a little carried away," Casey said, "but there's still nothing wrong with people who love each other kissing."

Joanna's heart expanded. *People who love each other...* What a lovely ring that had to it. Of course, she knew how Casey meant it. Nonetheless, it sounded wonderful.

Casey squeezed her shoulder. Joanna smiled at him—and at that moment, she had a dazzling insight. An insight that left everything exactly the same, and yet changed the world completely.

Joanna realized she would always remember this precise instant. It was the moment when all the confusions and pain of the last weeks suddenly made sense. The truth had come to her at last. She at last realized that she had fallen deeply, irrevocably in love with her best friend.

On the porch, Burnett went on complaining about the way his nephew was being raised, and Amanda interjected occasional breathless agreements with her husband's diatribe.

The hot September sun shone down. The warm

wind sighed gently around them, like the tender breath of a peaceable giant. From a nearby tree, a blue jay squawked, in counterpoint to Burnett's harangue.

Joanna memorized it all, and would remember the moment always.

The minute Joanna confessed her love to herself, she was assailed by conflicting impulses.

She longed to shout it out loud—shout it over the top of the tallest pine, out into the sky the color of Casey's eyes, beyond the clouds that were too beautiful to ever bring rain.

She wanted to be alone, and very quiet. She wanted to be in some secret place where no one would find her and where she could sit and savor what had happened to her. She longed to just turn the magic over and over in her mind and heart.

She wanted to go somewhere immediately with Casey, and make mad, passionate love to him until he swore he loved her back...

Until he loved her back...

Reality hit her like a physical blow.

Casey didn't love her, not in the way she realized she loved him. That was the problem.

And therein lay her pain.

One part of her mind commanded, *You must tell him at once.*

And another voice warned, *You must never tell him...*

Joanna stood there in the sun with Casey's arm around her and experienced a sense of both elation and despair.

Then a child's voice called from inside the house, "Hey, you guys, where are you? Grandma's here!"

Burnett hastily curtailed his tirade as Casey shouted, "We're out back!"

Mike burst through the screen. "Megan got braces. She'll be over later. Grandma's bringing her stuff in and we're s'posed to help."

Amanda knelt in front of Mike, the skirt of her summer dress pooling out around her like the petals of a flower in bloom. "Haven't you got a kiss for your Aunt Amanda?"

Dutifully, Mike complied. Casey's arm slipped off of Joanna's shoulder, and he took her hand. "Come on. We'll go around the side of the house." Joanna allowed herself to be tugged along, still half in shock from the awesome insight that she was madly, totally in love with her best friend.

Chapter Twelve

That night, they barbecued a huge flank steak that Amanda had carried, soaking in its savory marinade, on her lap through the whole trip to Graeagle. The au gratin potatoes, Amanda had had the foresight to make ahead of time; they only needed to be browned in the oven. The crisp green beans had been cut in advance, bagged and put in the picnic freezer so they'd stay fresh on the trip. Amanda simply put them on to steam when the time was right.

Joanna and Lillian were allowed to cut up the salad—for which Amanda had prepared a special dressing, of course.

For dessert, Amanda had baked a cake. Everyone praised the food. Amanda smiled modestly and said it was nothing, nothing at all. She'd always loved to cook.

Later, after Mike had taken his bath and been put to bed out on the screened-in side porch, time crawled for a while. There was no television or radio in the cabin. When Casey, Burnett and Emily were children, Lillian had forbidden such entertainments in Graeagle. She told them it was character building to have to entertain themselves for at least a few days out of the year. Somehow, the rule had become a tradition.

Sitting on the fat couch with the cabbage rose upholstery, lost in ruminations about her newfound love and still feeling unsure about how to deal with it, Joanna found herself longing for the reassuring sound of canned laughter; it would help her forget her confusion and provide a neutral focal point for a family that might otherwise end up at each other's throats.

But then Amanda discovered an ancient family album in the drawer of a pine desk.

"Oh, now, isn't this incredible," Amanda said with enthusiasm. She peeled back the cracked cardboard cover and looked down at the first page. "Oh, this is old, really old. Look at these *dresses,* Lillian."

"That was my Uncle Peter's album," Lillian said. "He gave it to me shortly before he died, and so I brought it up here, to the house that he left to me."

Amanda immediately squeezed herself between Lillian and Joanna on the couch. She turned the pages slowly, reverently, and Lillian explained that the stiff, stern people in the first yellowed photographs were her own grandparents and aunts and uncles, who had come to California at the turn of the century.

"That's Grandpa Lambert." Lillian pointed to an imposing, severe-looking man who bore a striking resemblance to Burnett. "Grandpa Lambert was a wanderer, always moving West and taking his family right along with him. Grandma used to say if the Pacific Ocean hadn't been in the way, Grandpa never would have stopped.''

Lillian pointed to the faces of her grandfather's children. ''There's my father, John Lambert. And here's Uncle Peter, the one who owned this cabin.'' She chuckled. ''Uncle Peter was a character. He never married because he said that a woman would have to be a damn fool to put up with him—and he wanted nothing to do with fools. He made his fortune in oil down in Bakersfield, and because Graeagle was famous for its golf courses, he bought this place so he could come up here to play golf. Uncle Peter loved music,'' Lillian went on, and her voice was dreamy. ''We used to visit him down south when I was growing up and I'd sit with him out on the porch of his great big house at sunset and he'd play gold rush songs on his harmonica—*My Darlin' Clementine* and *Oh, Susannah*... I loved those nights.''

Lillian's musing voice continued as Amanda turned the pages, and the sepia-toned photographs gave way to ones of black and white. Paul Lambert met and married Rose Adair. They had one child, Lillian, who then figured prominently throughout the next several pages. It was clear from the photographs that Uncle Peter, single and childless, had doted on his niece.

Hemlines rose, bathing costumes became swimsuits, and Lillian Lambert grew to womanhood.

Joanna felt Casey's hand brush her shoulder. She glanced up to see him leaning over the back of the couch behind her, looking at the photographs with them, just as Burnett was doing from down at the other end of the couch near Lillian.

Casey caught Joanna's eye when she turned. They shared a quick exchange of glances, a flash of a smile, and Joanna's heart picked up its rhythm. She wondered if everyone could see it beating so rapidly against the light cotton dress she'd changed into for dinner.

But no one was looking. They were all staring at the album and listening to Lillian. "This is the house in Bakersfield...That's me in my Easter dress when I was seven...Me learning how to play golf...My eighth-grade graduation...Christmas the year I finished high school..."

Joanna dragged her attention back to the photographs in time to see the picture of Casey. While it looked like Casey, clearly it couldn't be since it had been taken well over thirty years before. After a moment, Joanna realized it must have been Casey's father, standing out behind the cabin with a young, radiant Lillian at his side and a baby in his arms.

"Edward," Lillian said softly. She laid a hand on the picture, and touched the man's face. "Right after you were born, Burnett. He was so proud to be a father."

Burnett's voice burned with bitterness. "He had a hell of a way of showing it."

Lillian sighed. "We were very young."

"He deserted his family."

Lillian looked at her older son. "That was a long time ago. And he's been dead for seventeen years."

Joanna stared at the old picture of the man who smiled so rakishly into the camera. Just like Casey, she thought—in looks at least. And she understood a little better the age-old animosities between the staid Burnett and his reckless younger brother who looked so much like the father who had forsaken them.

Quickly, Amanda turned the page. "Oh, look," she said with contrived brightness, pointing to a picture of three children sitting on a rumpled chenille bedspread. "That's all three of you, I'll bet."

"Yes," Lillian pointed at each small face in turn. "Burnett and Casey and our Emily. That was right before Uncle Peter died and we moved to Sacramento to make a new start."

That was the last picture. Amanda closed the album and then stretched elaborately.

"Well, all this mountain air has just tired me out," she said. "I think it's time we turned in."

Nobody argued. Lillian was probably ready for bed, perhaps Burnett was, too. Casey and Joanna were being studiously agreeable. There were seventy-two hours to live through without incident, and they had survived approximately nine of them so far.

It took a half an hour for everyone to get their turn at the cabin's single bathroom, but it was still before ten when the house fell quiet for the night.

Casey and Joanna's small room had one lovely feature, a lace-curtained bow window that overlooked the backyard. Casey was standing, shirtless and barefoot, by the window, looking out at the moonlit clear space behind the cabin when Joanna returned from brushing her teeth.

She hung her robe on a peg behind the door. Then she went, without speaking, to the bedside lamp and switched it off. He glanced at her, then back out the window.

"Easier to see out in the dark," she explained.

Casey nodded. "It's so peaceful here," he said. "I've always liked that about this place."

Joanna stood by the darkened lamp, her love like a living thing wrapped around her heart, something tender and soft and very young. It was wonderful right at that moment, just to hold love inside her and know that it lived.

Casey turned from the window again. He stood looking at her. His back was to the pale spill of moonlight from outside, so that, as on the night he had convinced her to marry him, she couldn't see his features.

Faintly, below the window, she could hear the little peepings and chirpings of the night creatures in the grass and in the woods beyond.

"There's room at this window for two," Casey said, and though she couldn't see his smile, she could hear it in his voice.

Joanna walked around the foot of the old four-poster bed to reach his side. They faced each other, in front of the window, and he smoothed her hair back over her shoulder, the way he always did.

"This is pretty," he said of her soft cotton nightgown.

"I bought it for this weekend," she told him, her tongue suddenly feeling awkward in her mouth.

Soon they would climb beneath the old quilt on the four-poster bed. They would do all the wonderful things they'd been doing since the week after their wedding. But everything would be changed. Now there wouldn't be a single corner of her heart that the man standing in front of her didn't hold, unknowingly, in his hands.

Perhaps now would be a good time to tell him...

But, oh Lord, if he really wanted out of the marriage, telling him she was in love with him would only make things worse.

Unable to wrap her lips around the words *I love you,* but also unable to keep silent at that moment, Joanna began explaining what really didn't need to be explained at all. "I bought it two weeks ago." She smoothed the collar of the nightgown. "It seemed appropriate, with the whole family so close, to wear a real nightgown. Instead of just shirts and slips...you know?"

He nodded, his shadowed expression solemn, as if her stammered unnecessary words had been pearls of wisdom. "Well, it's very pretty."

"Thank you."

"You're welcome."

They looked at each other. Somewhere out in the woods, an owl hooted. Joanna jumped, then giggled nervously. "It's so quiet."

"Like I said, peaceful," Casey's voice held a teasing note.

"Yes. Peaceful."

Joanna wondered vaguely if being in love also made one incapable of intelligent conversation.

"I think it's going pretty well so far, don't you?" she tried bravely.

His eyebrows drew together. "It?"

"The weekend. Burnett. Amanda. Everything." The stilted words were out before she remembered that

Burnett and Amanda were a forbidden subject, one she'd been careful to avoid with Casey the past few weeks.

But, miraculously, Casey didn't shut her out or turn away. Instead, he chuckled. "You were incredible, out in the backyard."

Joanna gulped, her face flushing with pleasure at such praise. "I was?"

"Uh-huh. I'll never forget it. You, picking burrs from your hair and trying to button up your shirt without anyone noticing, chattering away about the scenery on the drive up."

"We didn't do anything wrong," Joanna said.

"Hey," he reminded her, "I'm on *your* side."

"Well, sometimes they just—" Joanna couldn't find the words.

"I know," Casey said, signaling that the subject was better left closed. He pulled her head to his shoulder, and put an arm around her, turning them both toward the window.

For a time, they just stood like that, looking out at the trees, while Joanna suffered—and gloried—in her unspoken love.

So many things cried out to be discussed. In those few short peaceful moments in front of the window, Joanna knew they could not go on forever with a tacit avoidance of forbidden subjects. Silence could not take the place of real communication.

Now was not the time to get everything out in the open, not when the primary objective for the weekend was simply to survive it without a major family fight. But the time for total honesty was coming. Perhaps next week while they readied her show in Los Angeles, or when they returned to Sacramento in the middle of the month. Perhaps then Joanna would tell Casey of her love.

And she would badger and berate and plead and do whatever was necessary to get him to open up about what was bothering him. Then together they'd face whatever ugly truth he revealed. They were bound together, for Mike's sake. And for Mike's sake, and their own, they deserved the best, most truthful relationship that two caring individuals could create.

"Are you dropping off on me?" Casey teased in her ear.

She turned, and slid her arms up his bare chest, hooking them around his neck. "Must be all the fresh air," she teased back, remembering Amanda's words earlier that evening.

As she stood with her chin tipped up to him, Casey kissed her. It was a slow, deep kiss. At the touch of his lips, Joanna forgot that there was anything but pleasure in the world.

It was even better when you knew you were in love, she thought giddily, as he walked her backwards and fell with her across the high old bed.

But then, beneath them, the old springs complained—loudly. Casey pulled away and looked down at her, a pained expression on his face that their lovemaking would be accompanied by squeaky springs. Both of them laughed like naughty children—until they heard something hit the floor in the room next door and both realized exactly whose room shared a wall with their own: Burnett's and Amanda's.

"Oh, no..." They mouthed the words in unison.

"We could try the floor," Joanna suggested helpfully, though the single small rag rug didn't look inviting at all.

Casey laughed. "Lord, you are a good sport," he said.

"That's me," she told him gamely, "good old Joey, willing to try anything—once." But both of them knew the mood was spoiled. They couldn't make love and enjoy it knowing they might be overheard.

"Come on." He pulled her to her feet, drew back the quilt and urged her to get in the bed. All the while, he was shaking his head. "How I ever let you talk me into this mess, I'll never know."

"It's for the sake of the family," she reminded him.

He took off his jeans and slid in beside her, "Isn't that what they said in *The Godfather?*"

She nudged him in the ribs. "Stop it. Think of Amanda's cooking."

He molded himself around her back. "I am. And it's great. But if she tells us all one more time how she carried that flank steak on her lap all the way up here, I'll—"

"You'll smile politely and listen, that's what you'll do."

"I'm trying, Joey. I really am," he breathed in her ear.

"I know." She turned her head and kissed him lightly on the chin. "And you're doing great. Just watch. It's going to be fine. We're going to have a pleasant family weekend and we'll all go home on Monday feeling good because not a single ugly word had been said."

Chapter Thirteen

The strained, uneasy truce between the Clinton brothers and their wives lasted through Saturday, primarily because Casey and Joanna ceaselessly conceded to the wishes of the other two.

Casey wanted to drive over to the nearby community of Blairsden for breakfast at the River Pines Inn—but Amanda had already planned her special Belgian waffles with sour cream and strawberries. They ate the waffles.

Casey and Joanna thought of taking Mike back to the Lakes Basin to swim at Sand Pond, near Lower Sardine Lake. Burnett thought the boy would learn more if they visited the gold mining museum at Plumas-Eureka State Park, just a few miles away. They visited the museum.

Later in the afternoon, Casey urged Joanna to go

for a swim with him in the Mill Pond. But Burnett wanted his brother's company on the golf course. Casey played golf.

A minor tiff between Joanna and Amanda occurred when Joanna decided to go swimming after all, and to take along Mike and his friend, Megan.

"What a lovely idea," Amanda remarked when Mike had dashed out to the side porch to pull on his swim trunks and Joanna was poised at the back stairwell. "I'd love to go myself, but there's just so *much* I have to do to get dinner prepared."

Joanna obediently picked up her cue and asked what she could do to help.

"Don't be silly, Joey, you know how you are in the kitchen."

Joanna thought a moment. Amanda's needling remark was just another in a never-ending series of similar remarks, but something in Joanna rose up this time and refused to simply let it pass. She said carefully, "No, Amanda. I don't know how I am in the kitchen. Why don't you tell me?"

At that moment, Lillian came in from the back porch where she'd been reading on the old Stickley couch beneath the kitchen window. Amanda blushed. "Oh, Joey, I've offended you. I forgot how sensitive you are."

"You haven't offended me," Joanna said. "How could you have offended me? You haven't said anything yet."

Lillian went to the ancient refrigerator and brought out a pitcher of iced tea. She busied herself pouring herself a glass.

While Lillian's back was turned, Amanda nodded

significantly in her mother-in-law's direction. "Now is not the time for an argument, Joey," she said.

Amanda had a point, Joanna silently admitted. It would be best just to let it go. But the strain of the past twenty-four hours was beginning to show. She heard herself saying instead, "Amanda, I simply asked you what you meant when you said 'you know how you are in the kitchen, Joey.' I'd just like an answer, that's all."

Amanda refused to give one. Instead, she shot Joanna an admonitory look, clearly telegraphing how insensitive it was of Joanna to make trouble in front of dear Lillian. Then she rushed to Lillian's side. "Here, Mother. Let me cut you a nice, fresh lemon slice to go with that."

Lillian said, "No, thank you, Amanda. I prefer it with sugar."

"But lemon is so much better for you."

Lillian nodded. "You're absolutely right. But I don't like lemon."

Amanda looked puzzled. "But how could you not like lemon?"

Lillian chuckled. "I don't know, Amanda. But it's not something I lie awake at night worrying about."

"Let me just cut you a slice. Just taste it, and I'm sure you'll find it much more to your liking than sugar."

Lillian said, very patiently, "Amanda, I'm fifty-nine years old. I have tasted lemon before, and I don't like it in my iced tea."

Amanda said, "Oh."

At that point, Lillian ladled two spoons of sugar into her glass and grinned at Joanna who remained by the stairwell. Joanna herself was realizing that the absurd exchange over the lemon had, at least temporarily, eliminated her urge to confront her sister-in-law.

"I hope I haven't interrupted anything," Lillian said, casting Joanna a quick look of understanding.

"Interrupted anything?" Amanda asked, innocent as a crafty child. "What in the world could you be interrupting? Joey was just on her way upstairs to put on her swimsuit. She's taking Mike and Megan over to the pond."

"That's right," Joanna said, thinking grimly, only forty-eight hours to go. "Want to come, Lillian?"

"No, no, you go ahead. I'll just go back outside and finish my thriller."

Because the water at the Mill Pond was too cold for real swimming, the children played in the shallows while Joanna chatted with a local artist who'd set up his easel not far from where Mike and Megan were splashing around in the water.

Dinnertime, once again, consisted of Amanda playing chef and Lillian and Joanna being allowed to help out. Tensions increased after Mike went to bed and the five adults were again left with the mountain silence and one another's company.

Later, when Casey and Joanna lay tucked beneath the quilt in the squeaky four-poster, Joanna asked Casey how the golf game had gone.

"Just more of the same," he said after a moment.

"Meaning?"

"Meaning Burnett is still waiting to hear about our divorce."

Joanna, who had been lying with her back against him, rolled over and canted up on an elbow. "He said that?'' The question came out sounding odd, because she'd started it at a normal volume and then had uttered the last word in a strained whisper when she realized who might possibly be listening on the other side of the wall.

''What's the matter?'' Casey asked, his voice suddenly sharp. Joanna realized the strain of having to put up with Burnett and Amanda on a round-the-clock basis was beginning to affect him, too. ''It's not as if that's news.''

''Keep your voice down.'' She said this in a whisper, but it came out as a low hiss.

For a moment, he just lay there. She thought he was watching her, but because it was dark in the room and his back was to the window, she couldn't be sure. Then, so fast it startled her a little, he threw back the covers. ''I've got to get out of here.''

''Casey, wait—''

He pulled on his jeans and buttoned them up. Then he slid his feet into a pair of slip-on canvas shoes.

''I'm sorry,'' she said.

''Don't be sorry,'' he told her. ''You didn't do anything.'' He was whispering now, too, his voice sounding as furtive and guilty in the darkness as her own.

''I spoke harshly. I didn't mean to.''

''It's not your fault,'' he told her, still whispering. ''None of this is your fault.'' He was already at the door.

''Don't leave.'' She was halfway out of the creaking bed. ''Running away isn't the answer.''

He threw out a hand to stop her from coming any closer. ''I'm not running away. I need a little time alone, that's all.''

"Yes, you are." Absurdly, Joanna felt the tears gather behind her eyes. "You're always running away. Ever since you married me, you've been running away any time things get too heavy for you."

"Joey, you don't understand," he said.

"Then *explain* it to me," she begged.

"I can't." His whisper held a pleading note in it, too. "Not here, Joey. Not now."

"Then when?"

There was a cavernous silence, then he murmured, "Soon."

She knew she should stop pushing him, but somehow she couldn't. "When? After this nightmare of a weekend is over? After my show opens in L.A.? After the holidays? After Mike's away in college? When?" Joanna felt the traitorous tears, pooling over, running down her cheeks.

"Oh, God, Joey," Casey said. He took a step toward her. "I'm sorry. I never meant—"

But Joanna knew if he touched her, it would be her undoing. She'd blurt out her love for him right then, in a tortured whisper, drowning in tears and pain. It would not be the way she had hoped to tell him.

She drew herself up. "No, please. Don't touch me." Casey froze where he was. Joanna swiped the tears away. "You're right. What we probably both need more than anything now is a little space."

He stood looking at her, a dark shape between the door and where she sat crouched at the foot of the bed. "You want me to go, then?" he said finally.

She forced a smile. "Nothing can be solved tonight, right?"

"Right."

"So you go on, take a walk...or whatever..."

"You're sure?"

"Yes, I'd like some time alone."

"All right." But then he didn't immediately leave. He added, "Joey, I'm sorry about this whole damn mess. You can't know how sorry."

"Don't be. It's no more your fault than mine."

"Yes it is. Us getting married was my idea—but we've been over this a thousand times."

"Exactly," Joanna said. "So go for a walk."

"I'll be back soon," he said.

"Take your time."

Joanna kept her brave smile until the door closed behind him. Then she wrapped her arms around the post at the foot of the bed and leaned her head against the smooth carved surface of the wood. She wanted to cry, but all her tears seemed to have deserted her. She felt only a bottomless weariness.

After a while, she slipped back beneath the covers and lay staring out the window at the moonwashed starry sky and the tall shadows of the pine trees on the surrounding mountains. She reassured herself that there was only Sunday and Monday till noon to get through now—they were halfway home. And as soon as they were away from the prying ears of Burnett and Amanda, she and Casey would get everything out in the open.

Joanna closed her eyes. Everything will be fine, she told herself. And then she felt the tears rising up again—because she didn't really believe that everything would be fine at all.

She had no idea what time Casey came back to bed, but when she awoke Sunday morning he was there.

When she opened her eyes, she found him watching her. He smiled at her.

"'Morning," he said, and the word was like a signal passing between them.

She repeated it to him and in doing so, without mentioning the night before, she was tacitly agreeing to his unspoken suggestion: they would leave what had happened between them last night unexamined—at least until they'd left Graeagle.

As they dressed to go downstairs, they were careful of each other, as if each considered the other in danger of breaking.

Joanna dressed in a sky-blue sleeveless shirt trimmed in eyelet lace, with a matching yoked skirt. Casey told her how pretty she looked. Joanna thanked him. Joanna looked out the window and noted that the day promised to be a warm one. Casey agreed.

They went downstairs to another of Amanda's gourmet breakfasts.

After the dishes had been cleared away, Mike begged to be taken to Sand Pond.

He said, "Yesterday we saw that old museum, today can't we please have some fun?"

Sounding slightly hurt, Burnett said, "I thought you enjoyed visiting the museum."

Mike, a sensitive boy, immediately corrected himself. "I did, Uncle Burnett, really. But today I want to go to the Lakes."

Burnett argued that it might be too late in the year for good swimming, but Casey, who saw how much Mike wanted to go, told his brother he was taking Mike to Sand Pond. Period.

"Excellent," Mike said. "Can I ask Megan?"

"You bet," Casey told him. Then added, "Now, who else is coming along?"

Burnett gave in at that point and then everyone decided to go. Mike ran over to Megan's, but her family had other plans. He resigned himself to having fun without her.

Lillian and Joanna threw sandwiches together while Amanda complained that she'd had something so much nicer planned. They were ready to go before noon and took two vehicles: Casey's Blazer as well as the old Jeep that Lillian kept in the cabin's garage. Lillian rode with Burnett and Amanda in the Jeep.

As Casey drove the Blazer back over the Gold Lake Forest Highway, and Mike sang an endless song Megan had taught him about finding a peanut with innumerable improbable things inside it, Joanna felt her spirits lifting. Perhaps the key to putting up with in-laws wasn't in always going along with them, but in doing exactly what one wanted to do—cheerfully.

Before they reached Bassetts Station, they turned off the highway, crossed a bridge and took the lower of two roads past the Sardine Lake Campgrounds to a blacktopped parking area. Casey parked his truck in the shadow of a cedar tree and Burnett pulled the old Jeep into the space beside him.

Sand Pond was several hundred yards away, along any of a number of trails that wound through the trees. Everyone pitched in to carry the big cooler, the folding chairs, the rubber rafts and all the picnic gear along a winding trail to a favored site on the west side of the pond not far from the larger Lower Sardine Lake.

They chose a picnic table in a sunny spot among the trees and marshy grass. Burnett's prediction proved false; the water was still warm enough for swimming. The pond, which was never too deep even at its center, and as sandy as its name implied, lay low in the ground and was surrounded by trees, which protected it from the cold mountain winds.

Mike had barely set down the bag he was toting before he had his shorts and T-shirt off and was splashing around in the shallows near the shore. Lillian, too, stripped down to her swimsuit, but then sat in a folding chair in the sun, absorbed in her thriller.

"Ouch!" Amanda yelped. "These hideous big flies bite!"

"Heads up," Casey advised her, and tossed her the insect repellent. He then finished shucking everything but his swim trunks.

Joanna swam for a while, but then she remembered the glimpse she'd had of Lower Sardine Lake from the top of the rise between the lake and the pond. The glimpse had promised a beautiful view, one that cried out to be sketched.

She dried off quickly, slipped on her shoes and took the canvas tote that contained her sketchbook and pastels.

Lillian was engrossed in her book and Amanda sat by the picnic table, presumably guarding the lunch from the flies and the yellow jackets. Burnett was nowhere in sight; he'd probably gone for a walk.

Casey, Mike and a few children from the nearby campground were playing King of the Mountain. Joanna smiled to herself as she left them behind. Casey, like all good uncles, had the grace to be easily unseated when he was king and to experience great difficulty pushing sixty-pound children off the rubber raft when it was his turn.

The cold mountain wind whipped her hair wildly about her face when Joanna topped the rise. Joanna threw her head back and drew a big, glorious breath of it into her eager lungs. The lake, rimmed by huge chalk-white rocks and sitting deep in a gorge of tall jewel-green pines, made her fingers itch with the need to start sketching.

She picked her way down among the sunbaked rocks, closer to the deep green surface of the lake, where the wind wasn't so fierce. But there, the sun was too bright, blinding her. So she moved toward Sardine Lake Lodge, on the northeast side, where the trees provided some sheltering cover. She sat beneath a fir tree, with a warm boulder at her back, and she began to draw.

For a while time had no meaning as Joanna lost herself in what she most loved doing. She'd filled several pages of her book with pastel strokes of color and images of the trees and the shimmering surface of the lake when she began to feel as if someone was watching her.

Slowly, she turned her head. Her brother-in-law stood not twenty feet away, outlined against the blinding brightness of the hot white rocks.

"Joanna," Burnett said, "I think it's time you and I had a little talk."

Chapter Fourteen

At first, Joanna didn't move. She looked at her brother-in-law without speaking, remembering all the promises she'd made to herself about this weekend— that her decision had been to avoid confrontations at all costs.

Then she thought that dodging showdowns just wasn't working. She and Casey were trying so hard to avoid family fights, that they'd ended up last night attacking each other, instead of their real targets.

There was too much hostility in the air. Throughout the weekend, they'd all been inhaling fuming resentment with every breath they took.

Maybe Burnett was right. It was time to confront a few things head-on.

Very deliberately, Joanna flipped the cover back over her sketchbook, then she put it and the pastels away in her tote bag.

"All right," she said. "We'll talk."

She had purposely chosen a sheltered spot, where the wind wouldn't tear at the pages of her sketchbook. The small, private indentation in the rocks was shaded by the fir overhead and a nearby pine: a beautiful spot. Joanna sighed. Too beautiful for what she suspected was going to occur between herself and Burnett.

She waited for Casey's brother to begin berating her. When he didn't, when he just stood there looking at her, Joanna began to feel impatient.

"Well, what is it?" she prompted.

He came closer, then, out of the blinding sun and beneath the haven of the trees. He sat down on a rock close to the one she was sitting on and he braced his forearms on his knees and folded his hands between them.

He looked at her intently. "What can I say to you, Joanna?" he asked, his voice low and controlled. "What can I do to make you see how wrong everything you're doing is? You're ripping this family apart."

Joanna's stomach tightened. It was unexpected, the tack he'd taken. Burnett sounded so *sincere*. His quiet intensity distressed her much more than his usual attitudes of hot rage or imperious command. It was clear that he firmly and passionately believed what he was saying. And the strength of his belief was convincing.

She had to consciously remind herself that there had been deeply rooted problems between Casey and Burnett even before she had ever met them.

"That's not true, Burnett," she said, careful to keep her tone calm and reasonable. "I am not and never have been the source of the problems in the Clinton family.''

He was silent for a moment. Then he actually conceded her point. "Maybe not," he said. "But you *have* continually aggravated those problems, always making them worse when they might have improved.''

"No, I—" Joanna started to protest, but Burnett didn't let her get the words out. He barreled on with his hurtful accusations, still in that low, troubled voice.

"You, Joanna, are a totally selfish person, only concerned with what you want at the moment, never thinking about the future, or about who might be hurt by the thoughtless things you do. You love yourself and yourself only, and you've been nothing but trouble for this family since the day we moved in next door to you all those years ago.''

"Burnett, that's not true—"

Burnett clenched his fists. "Let me finish, please. For years, I've wanted to tell you what I think of you. You will do me the courtesy of listening now. Please.''

Joanna drew in a long breath. "Burnett—"

"Please." It really wasn't a request, but for Burnett Clinton to utter that word—twice—was something Joanna had never expected to hear.

For a moment, she worried her lower lip between her teeth, thinking that listening to Burnett would do no one any good. But then, she thought that maybe it was only fair, maybe if he got it all off his chest, he would begin to let go of his anger toward her.

"All right, Burnett," she said at last. "But when you're done, you have to let me respond, to tell you what I think.''

"Agreed," he nodded, a short chopping motion of

his big head. For a moment, there was only the far-away laughter of the children in the pond over the rise, and the airy keening of the wind.

"Just like Casey, you are a person incapable of assuming adult responsibilities. And the two of you together are, and always have been, a disastrous combination. That's why I want you to admit that you've made another huge mistake in marrying my brother, and agree to return to Los Angeles where you belong."

Burnett paused, and for a moment Joanna hoped that he might actually be finished. It was a vain hope.

Burnett continued, "As I said at first, from the time you and Casey became friends, there has been nothing but trouble when you two got together. As children you egged each other on, from pulling fire alarms for fun to petty theft."

Joanna felt her face flushing. Once, when they were eleven, she and Casey had snitched a box of bubble gum from behind the counter at the corner store when the owner had turned away. They'd been caught an hour later when, having decided that robbery wasn't for them, they'd tried to return the box without getting caught. But guilt must have made them clumsy. When Joanna tried to slide the flimsy box back on the shelf, it had buckled in her hands, sending bubble gum raining all over the linoleum floor.

"We were kids," Joanna heard herself protesting. "Sometimes kids do things without thinking."

Burnett pinned her with a reproachful frown. "It's a habit you've never outgrown. As I was saying, you are bad for my brother. And you even played with *my* affections once upon a time."

Joanna drew in a breath. "Burnett, I was only eighteen when I said I'd marry you. My father had died. I was confused."

"Your mother told me you needed guidance," Burnett said. "And when I went to talk to you, you said you longed to be a different sort of girl than the one you were. I found myself asking you out—and you said yes. When I look back on it now, I remember that from our third date you were already hinting that you wanted to marry me."

"I was wrong," Joanna said.

"And then, out of the blue, you disappeared with my brother for two days and a night."

"I thought I could make my mother happy by marrying you," Joanna said. "It was all a mistake, that's all. People make mistakes, Burnett, no matter how hard you may find that to believe. We can't be dwelling on that for the rest of our lives. I regret any hurt I caused you, but it happened, and the best thing would be for both of us to let it go."

Burnett made a humphing sound, then he continued with his list of grievances. "You encouraged Casey to waste those years in the navy."

"It was what he wanted to do—and they were not wasted years."

Burnett went on as if he hadn't heard her. "I know you told him what a wonderful idea it was for him to throw his money away on that damned airfield."

"It was—and is—exactly what he wanted to spend his money on."

"Want, want, want. There is more to life, Joanna, than what you and my brother want." Burnett's face had grown flushed. He pounded a fist on his knee.

Then he restrained himself again, with visible effort, and spoke more quietly.

"You've maintained a..." he sought the precise words, "...questionable long-distance liaison with my brother for years, always keeping your hooks in him just enough that he never found a suitable young woman to settle down with."

Joanna felt the blood rush to her cheeks. A liaison, indeed. It was too much. It was a totally absurd accusation.

Or was it?

The awareness of her newly discovered love washed over her. Could there be a grain of truth in what Burnett said? Had she been in love with her best friend for years—and simply not admitted it to herself?

When Casey's serious relationships had ended, he had always come to her. Never had she advised him to go back and try again. She had listened—as a friend should, she had thought—and made no judgments. There was nothing wrong in that.

Or was there?

Joanna found she could no longer just sit there while Burnett lambasted her. She stood up. "We're best friends, Casey and I. We always have been. Naturally we kept in touch over the years." Her voice had a high, defensive edge to it.

Burnett lifted his head to accuse piercingly, "You kept him dangling."

Joanna had to swallow before she could insist, "That's absurd."

"I'd say you always wanted to get him to marry you, for the sake of that ego of yours, though you knew my brother was no more likely to marry you

than he was someone who might actually be good for
him. You were just waiting for your chance.''

''No. This is not true at all.'' Joanna put up her
hands, as if the protective gesture could shield her
from Burnett's farfetched assertions that somehow had
the awful ring of truth.

Burnett continued, relentless as an oncoming train.
''You waited for your chance, and when it came you
took it, becoming Mrs. Casey Clinton so that Casey
would keep Mike, not even considering it was bad for
Casey—and even worse for that poor little boy.''

''That's a lie,'' Joanna uttered the words with conviction at last. However cloudy her own motives were
beginning to seem to her, she remained absolutely certain that Casey was the one who should raise Mike.
''It was the best thing for Mike. Casey is an excellent
guardian. Emily made the right choice.''

''And both you and my brother were willing to do
anything, even marry each other, to see that Mike
wasn't raised by me.''

That was the brutal truth. Joanna opened her mouth
to utter a resounding yes, when she caught the glint
of triumph in Burnett's dark eyes.

He had set her up. This whole confrontation was a
trap to get her to admit that her marriage to Casey was
for one reason only.

Burnett stood. ''Say it,'' he commanded. ''Tell me
the truth, Joanna. Admit your marriage is a fake, a
put-up job to keep Amanda and me from giving little
Mike the happy childhood he deserves.''

Slowly, Joanna shook her head. ''I love Casey,'' she
said quietly. ''And even if Mike wasn't involved, I'd
marry him all over again. Maybe it's as you said, Bur-

nett. I've always wanted to marry him, and I took my chance when it came.''

Burnett's eyes grew stormy. ''That's not what you were going to say a minute ago,'' he shot back. ''You opened your mouth to say yes, to admit everything. I saw it, I saw it on your face.'' Joanna knew his anger was growing; he realized he had been thwarted.

''You saw wrong,'' she said, quiet and sure.

Something snapped in Burnett then, and he lost control. He reached out with punishing hands and took Joanna's shoulders.

''Damn you, Joanna!'' he hissed through clenched teeth. ''Admit the truth.''

''I've told you the truth. Let go of me.''

He gave her shoulders a shake. ''By God I'll—''

He was stopped from saying what by Casey's voice. ''Let her go, Big Brother.''

Joanna and Burnett whipped their heads around. Casey stood on a huge boulder above them.

Burnett dropped his hands from Joanna's shoulders as if she'd burned him. ''Go away, Casey. This is a private talk.''

Casey jumped down from the boulder, landing beside them. ''Whatever you want to call it, it's over.''

Absurdly, Joanna found herself staring at the damp denim at Casey's hips, thinking that he must have pulled on his jeans over his wet swim trunks before coming to search for them. It was much easier to look at Casey's wet jeans than to witness the heated looks that arced between the brothers.

''Joey,'' Casey said. She was forced to look up into his ice-blue eyes. She knew he wasn't angry at her, but that didn't make seeing the rage in him any more bearable. He'd picked up the tote with her things in it, and was handing it to her. "Take this and go on back to the pond."

Here it was again. Just like fourteen years ago. They'd end up trading blows.

Joanna raised her chin. Damned if she was just going to walk away and let the two of them behave like adolescent boys.

"No," she said.

Both men glared at her.

"Leave, Joanna," Burnett said.

"Go on, Joey," Casey said.

"No."

Then Burnett made the error of reaching toward her, giving her a little shove to send her on her way. That was all it took for Casey. He punched his brother in the jaw.

Burnett, taken off guard, went down on his back among the rocks. He sat up. "Why you—"

He got no further, because there was a strangled sob from the rock where Casey had been standing a moment before. The three adults looked up.

Mike stood there. His face was a portrait of confusion and distress. Lillian, who appeared to have been following a small distance behind him, reached his side just as he cried, "Stop it! I hate it, everybody's always hurting everybody all the time!" Then he turned and ran, vanishing into the trees above the rocks.

"Mike, wait!" Lillian called, but the boy was already gone. Lillian turned back to the three below her.

"Joanna," Lillian said in a tone of absolute command. "Go after him. I'm not as fast as I used to be."

Joanna obeyed instantly, leaving Lillian standing, glaring down at her two miscreant sons.

Chapter Fifteen

Joanna caught up with Mike near Sand Pond. He'd stopped to slump against a tree trunk and rest for a moment, taking large, sobbing breaths into his small chest. Joanna's instinct was to run to him, gather his body against her own and hold him until he'd cried out all his hurt.

But she knew the reserved side of Mike's nature well enough to realize that coming on too strong might force him to withdraw.

She slowed to a casual walk and approached more circumspectly.

Mike saw her. "Leave me alone, Joey!" he shouted between sobs. "I don't want you!"

Joanna shrugged. "Okay," she said, and sat down on a quartz boulder that lay half-buried beside the path.

"I mean go away, Joey!" Mike hiccuped.

Just then, three children that Mike had been playing with earlier appeared on the trail. They were trying to roll a huge, ancient inner tube ahead of them and giggling as the tube wobbled and bounced down the path.

"Hey, Mike!" one of the kids called. "Come with us! We're rollin' this thing to the parking lot and back."

Mike swiped away his tears and waved, but shook his head. "Can't now."

The sight of him bravely smiling and greeting his new friends moved Joanna. Realizing that staring at him would draw attention to him when what he probably wanted most at that point was to be invisible, Joanna looked down at her feet. She studied the ground between her shoes, watching an ant climb the length of a fallen pine needle.

Soon enough, the children were gone. All was silent from the tree where, she hoped, Mike still stood. The ant Joanna was watching reached the end of the pine needle, crawled over her toe and then under the rock she was sitting on.

Joanna dared to look up. Mike was staring at her, still leaning against the tree. His lower lip quivered. Joanna stood up and held out her arms, and then knelt as Mike ran into them.

For a moment, she just held him, and then she took him away from the trail, deeper into the trees where they could talk alone. In a more private spot, they leaned against a pair of tree trunks, neither saying anything for a while.

Not surprisingly, the first person Mike spoke about when he was ready to talk was his mother. Mike said

how much he missed her and how hard it was sometimes to think that she'd never be back.

"I do too, Mike," Joanna told him. "I miss her so
much. I loved her a lot. And I just keep reminding
myself that love is the one thing that never, ever dies."

"I loved her, too," Mike said, "so much. And if
she could have not died it would have been good."

"Yes," Joanna said.

"But she did die," Mike said.

"Yes, Mike. She did."

"And now Uncle Burnett and Uncle Casey are al-
ways fighting. And Uncle Burnett pushed you. And
Aunt Amanda is always mean to you. It isn't excellent,
Joey. You know what I mean?"

"Yes, Mike. I do. I know exactly what you mean."

"It's all because I asked you never to go, isn't it?"

Joanna crouched down in front of Mike, putting her
hands on his shoulders and waiting until he looked
into her eyes. "No, it's not because of that," she told
him. "It is honestly and truly not your fault at all.
When you asked me to stay, then it was up to me to
decide what I wanted to do. Staying was what *I* wanted
to do. Do you understand?"

Mike looked back at her solemnly. "You mean, if
things happened because you stayed, it's not my fault,
it's your fault?"

Joanna sighed, wishing she were wiser. The rote
answer would be that it was nobody's fault, but she
felt too guilty to say that convincingly. "Let me put
it this way: I stayed because *I* wanted to, so for you
to blame yourself makes no sense at all."

"You mean it is your fault?"

In his child's relentless search for clarity, Mike was

backing her into a corner. Joanna trotted out her rote answer after all. "Figuring out who's fault it is isn't going to solve anything, Mike."

Mike craned his head toward her and asked intensely, "But how can we make things better if we don't figure out what's wrong?"

Joanna could think of no immediate answer to that. She dropped her hands from Mike's shoulders and rocked back to a sitting position on the crunchy bed of dead pine needles that covered the ground. She decided to say what she felt. "I don't know, Mike."

Mike dropped to the ground and sat opposite Joanna, almost touching her, with his knees tucked against his chest, and his chin resting on them. His hazel eyes were piercing in their search for the truth. "Know what I really think?"

"What?"

"It's Uncle Burnett and Aunt Amanda's fault. I hate them."

Joanna had to look away. Hearing those ugly words from Mike was hard to take. Emily's dying wish was that her son, above all, be raised with love—and here he was talking of hate.

Joanna folded her legs Indian-fashion and found a pine needle to break apart, collecting herself before she spoke again. "That's sad, that you hate your Uncle Burnett and your Aunt Amanda," she said. "Because they love you very, very much."

Mike dismembered a pine needle of his own. "Okay, maybe I don't *hate* them."

Joanna said, "They sure do love you."

"Okay," Mike said. "Maybe I do love them, too."

He looked at Joanna, and she kept a neutral expression on her face. She was trying not to be judgmental. She'd decided to throw love in the face of hate and let the stronger win out.

"But they do bad things, and I don't like it," Mike added after a moment.

"Like what?"

"I told you already, Joey," he said, slightly miffed at her ostensible lack of attention.

"Tell me again, that way you can be sure I understand. Tell me the things they do that you don't like."

Mike said, very patiently, "Aunt Amanda does mean things to you. Uncle Burnett pushed you. And Uncle Burnett and Uncle Case are fighting all the time."

"Okay. Now what?"

He cast her an exasperated look. "That's all. Isn't that enough?"

"But what do you want to do about it?"

"I want them to stop."

"How would you make them stop?"

"Well, I could tell them." He thought for a moment, and then must have remembered what he'd said when he came upon the scene over the ridge at the lake. "Jeez," he added, "I guess I already did tell them."

Joanna smiled. "That's right. You sure did."

Mike said nothing for a moment as he broke another pine needle apart. Then he looked up. "I don't know what else to do, Joey."

"Well," Joanna shifted, curling her legs to the side and leaning on her hand. "Maybe you could wait and see if things change, now that you've told them."

"But what if they don't change?"

Joanna was grimly wondering exactly the same thing, but she didn't let Mike know it. She said, "*If* things don't change, *then* you worry about what you might do next. For right now, you've done all a six-year-old boy possibly could."

"I have?" He looked doubtful, but very eager.

"Absolutely. Besides that, you've realized that it is not your fault if Amanda and I don't get along, or if your uncles fight—right?"

"Right." He nodded, a quick, decisive gesture. Then he leaned back against the tree trunk and squinted up through the thick cover of pine branches over their heads, as if pondering what he'd just learned.

Joanna wondered if there was more she ought to say. It occurred to her then that raising children was a truly humbling experience. You were just never smart enough or wise enough or half as loving as you knew you ought to be.

"Joey?" Mike asked, when a few moments had passed with only the blue jays and the squirrels saying anything.

"Um?"

"I think we ought to go back now, don't you?"

"Yes," Joanna said. "I think that would be a good idea." They stood up and returned to the trail together.

When they reached the picnic spot by the pond, the others were all there. Amanda, the only one of the group who hadn't been involved decided it was her place to take things in hand.

"Well, it's about time we all got here," she announced as Mike and Joanna appeared. "It's getting late. It's after two o'clock. And no one's eaten lunch.'' Keeping up a steady stream of chatter, she urged them all to sit around the redwood table. Then she served up the sandwiches Joanna and Lillian had made.

For Mike's sake, Joanna assumed, everyone tried to make lunch as pleasant as possible. Casey and Burnett behaved toward each other with civility; Burnett even attempted one of his rare ponderous jokes. Amanda filled every silence with overly bright comments about nothing in particular. Joanna did her best to keep her end of the conversation going. And Mike was subdued but cheerful.

Of them all, Lillian was the silent one. As they drove back to Graeagle in the late afternoon, Joanna realized that Lillian had barely spoken two words since she'd curtly commanded her to go after the fleeing Mike.

It was the same over dinner. Lillian sat, barely touching her food, her gaze focused on each of the faces around the table in turn. It was as if she was studying each one of them, Joanna thought, as if she was evaluating them all through new eyes.

''Mother, that look!'' Amanda complained at one point. ''It's positively penetrating. Do I have spinach between my teeth?''

''No, not at all,'' Lillian said. It was the largest number of words she'd strung together all afternoon.

Amanda tittered, and then apparently decided the subject was better left alone.

After dinner, Mike paid his evening visit on Megan, and Casey asked Joanna to walk with him down by the Mill Pond. Joanna tugged on a sweater and went with him, her heart heavy with a sense of foreboding.

They strolled side by side, but not touching. The dragging sadness around her heart seemed to increase. Joanna knew that she only had to reach out to clasp Casey's hand, but somehow his manner discouraged such a gesture.

Casey seemed far away from her again. It was hard to remember that only the day before yesterday this same man had playfully tackled her to the sweet grass behind the cabin and wrestled with her there, finally kissing her into giggling submission.

When they stood by the water with the sun low in the sky behind them, Casey asked what had happened when she'd caught up with Mike. Joanna told him.

"You're good with him, Joey," he said when she was finished.

"You would have done as well—or better," she maintained.

He chuckled then, but without much humor. "Even a couple of confirmed bachelors can learn how to be parents, I guess—given the proper motivation and the necessary circumstances."

Joanna forced herself to chuckle, too. "I guess so."

They strolled on, past clumps of willow bushes to a place where they could stand right at the water's edge. Joanna thought of Lillian.

"What happened," she asked carefully, "after Lillian sent me to find Mike?"

Casey knelt, picked up a smooth, round stone and tossed it overhand out into the pond. When it dropped beneath the surface, the concentric ripples flowed toward the shore. Casey spoke just as the ripples, faint from traveling so far, reached their feet.

"Mother ordered Burnett to tell her what had happened.'' Casey's voice was flat, as if he wanted to give the information without injecting any of his feelings on the events. ''Burnett explained what happened more or less honestly, at least from the point where I came on the scene.''

''He didn't say what had happened between him and me?'' Joanna asked.

''He said you were having a *little talk*.''

''Oh.''

Still in a crouch, Casey tossed another stone. ''Then Mother asked him what your talk was about.''

''And?''

Casey looked up at her. His light eyes were shadowed, his mouth a grim line. ''Burnett said that that was between you and him.''

Joanna said, ''He was trying to get me to admit that I only married you so that he wouldn't get Mike.''

''I figured that,'' Casey said.

Joanna longed to tell Casey everything that had passed between herself and Burnett. But that would hit too close to the tender subject of her newfound love, and this was a bad time to get into that.

Furthermore, Burnett's cruel accusations had put a new and harsh light on her own actions. She needed time to think about the hard things Burnett had said, to face them or to reject them before confessing them to Casey.

Casey continued, ''I know my big brother. He thinks he's protecting Mother, by not telling her what he and Amanda have been up to since you and I got married.''

''But, earlier, he told her he was going to sue you for custody,'' Joanna said.

Casey explained patiently, "That was before we married, when he at least had his two-parent argument to make him sound somewhat reasonable. If he told her now that he's still after custody, he'd have to upset her by saying he thinks our marriage is phony. And who knows how she'd react to that.

"No, he thinks it's better to get us to break up first, and then tactfully let her know that he's taking Mike away from me—for Mike's sake, of course."

Joanna couldn't restrain a disgusted groan. "Does he think that Lillian's an idiot? She knows as well as anyone else does what's going on."

Casey's voice was flat. "Burnett knows exactly what he's doing. Mother plays ostrich about the problems between him and me; Burnett's just making it easy for her. He's careful never to give her any direct information that she might feel she has to actually do something about."

Joanna shook her head in frustration at the whole situation. Then she told Casey, "I didn't admit anything to Burnett."

"I never thought you did." Casey threw several stones in succession, so that the tiny ripples at their feet came at a faster rate.

"What happened next?" Joanna asked.

Casey stood up. "Nothing." Joanna looked at him, perplexed. He went on. "Nobody said anything for what seemed about a century. Then Mother said 'all right, let's go back.' And she left. Burnett and I stood there for a minute, feeling like a couple of prize jerks—or at least, *I* felt like a jerk—then I picked up your bag with your sketchbook in it and went back to Sand Pond. He followed after me."

Out on the Mill Pond the fish had begun to feed. Joanna caught a glimpse of a shimmering white belly, surging up, twisting, and then flopping back beneath the smooth water. Soon the swallows would come.

"Casey," she said. "We just can't keep on like this. It's terrible for Mike—and for all of us, really."

"I know," Casey said. "I think it's come to a parting of the ways."

Joanna swallowed; she thought for a moment that he was telling her their marriage was over.

But then he continued, "I'm through with these family events. I'm through pretending I can get along with my brother and his wife. It's been nothing but disaster every time we've tried. I brought you out here to say I want to leave tonight, and to tell you that seeing either Burnett or Amanda again is off unless things somehow really change."

"But Casey..." Despite everything, Joanna hated to see the break happening. The love between Burnett and Casey was steeped in conflict, but they *were* brothers. "Cutting them out of our lives isn't any kind of solution."

"Maybe not, but right now it's the only thing we can do, I'm afraid. Mike's had enough pain in his six years on this earth. Damned if I'll see him suffer any more than he has to." He took a deep breath, then added with a sad quirking of one eyebrow. "Maybe someday..."

"Yes," Joanna nodded, forcing a smile. "Maybe someday."

The first swallows soared above when they turned away from the pond and strolled back toward the cabin, side by side, but not touching.

* * *

Lillian was waiting for them on the porch. "I've done some thinking. And I'd like to talk to everyone. Right now. Burnett and Amanda are waiting in the kitchen."

Casey said, "There's no point, Mother. Let it be. We're going home."

"That's up to you," Lillian told him. "But there's something I'd like to say to all of you first."

Casey drew a long breath. "I'm tired of it, Mother. I'm fed up to here. Can't you understand that?"

"Completely," Lillian said.

"Good. Is Mike still at Megan's?"

Lillian nodded. "He came back and asked if he could stay overnight. I said I thought it would be all right, so he took his pajamas over there. But I know he'll understand if you've decided to leave. He's an incredibly reasonable child."

"All right," Casey said. "Joey, you start getting things together and I'll go get Mike."

Rather than do as he'd said, she murmured his name.

"What is it?" He glanced at her absently, eager to collect his nephew and be on his way. "What?" A frown creased his forehead. Then, reading her expression, he knew what she wanted.

He said, "No, Joey. Just let it be."

Lillian left them alone, silently passing back into the house.

Joanna said, "Casey, let your mother have her say."

"Nothing anybody says ever makes things any different."

"Yes, but Lillian's never spoken up before. She has a right to speak, and it's our place to listen."

He shook his head, his eyes showing a bottomless weariness. "I want to go."

"I understand," Joanna said. "And I know that I should stop pushing you."

Casey smiled then, a smile that would have made her lose her heart to him, if it hadn't already been entirely his. "But you're not going to stop pushing me, is that it?" he said.

She nodded, smiling in return. "That's it. I'm hoping you won't make me beg."

He looked at her, a deep look that made her stomach flutter. "Would you beg me, Joey?"

"Absolutely. In this situation."

"I owe you. A hell of a lot," he said.

She didn't want him to owe her. She wanted him to love her. But this wasn't the time to talk about that. She wondered, miserably, if the time would ever come.

"Does that mean we'll hear Lillian out, then?" she finally asked.

"Only because you asked me," he said.

"Fine. Whatever it takes."

She went up the steps. He followed reluctantly, but he did follow, nonetheless.

They all took chairs at the big rectangular pine table in the kitchen, each of them armed with a cup of coffee and a wary, vigilant expression.

Burnett sat at the head of the table, but it was Lillian who held firm control.

She began by saying that she had always tried her best to stay out of the conflicts between her sons. Not until this afternoon, had she seen the extent of her error—at least when it came to the question of Mike.

"It is time," Lillian announced, "that I made it clear where I stand."

Joanna looked around the table. Burnett was doing his best to look unruffled, though the tightness around his eyes gave his anxiety away. He seemed a little too quiet, actually, Joanna thought. Then she realized that he was feeling badly about what Mike had witnessed that afternoon.

In spite of his overbearing nature, Burnett was not evil. However misguided his methods, he loved his family and wanted the best for them. To have been caught behaving so shamefully by the boy he sought to protect was probably weighing on his conscience.

Amanda, sitting to Burnett's left and across from Joanna, displayed her nervousness with every move she made. She kept taking tiny sips from her coffee, setting the cup down, and then immediately picking it back up again. Lillian sat next to her, her handsome face set in determined lines. Casey, opposite Burnett, had turned his chair and leaned his chin on the back-rest. He looked comfortable and relaxed, as he always did—revealing nothing of the turmoil Joanna knew must be going on inside him.

Joanna herself rested her arms on the table, her cup between them. Her coffee was untouched.

Lillian continued, "What Mike was forced to wit-ness this afternoon must never be allowed to happen again. We all—" she paused, to glance piercingly at each of them in turn "—are *adults*. That means it is our responsibility to behave as such in the presence of children."

Amanda set down her cup with a little clink and complained, "I still don't quite understand what exactly happened. I stayed behind to guard our lunch, and—"

Burnett said flatly, "Joanna and I had words, Amanda. Casey interrupted us. We asked Joanna to leave and when she wouldn't, I pushed her. Then Casey punched me. Mike saw that and ran."

"Why, that's terrible," Amanda said. She aimed a withering look across the table at Joanna and then asked her husband, "What kind of words did you and Joey have?"

Lillian cut in, her voice icy. "You may ask him that later, Amanda. As far as this meeting goes, that's a side issue."

"Well," Amanda said. "Pardon me." She grabbed her cup again and gulped down another sip.

"The main issue," Lillian went on, "is that somehow Mike's guardianship seems to still be in dispute."

Burnett made a sharp sound in his throat, and Amanda's cup hit the table again.

"I can't see why you're so surprised that I'm aware of what's going on in my own family, Burnett," Lillian pointed out. "You did, after all, tell me you planned to take Casey to court for custody before he married Joanna. And I'm not blind, you know. It's been obvious that you and Amanda have done everything short of breaking the law to drive a wedge between Casey and Joanna since the day they exchanged vows."

"That's unfair and uncalled for, Mother," Burnett said in his most impressively imperial tone.

"Is it?" Lillian challenged.

"Yes."

For a long moment, Lillian just stared at her oldest son. And then Burnett seemed to come to a decision.

He said, "All right. Do you want to get it all out in the open, Mother? Is that what you're asking for?"

"This is precisely what I want." Joanna thought that Lillian had never sounded so resolute.

"Fine, then," Burnett said. "Let's deal first with that so-called *marriage* that Casey and Joanna are involved in."

Casey said, "No, let's not." Although his voice was low, soft as velvet, it brought a moment of charged silence in its wake. He went on. "My marriage to Joanna is *our* business and our business alone."

Burnett stood up and accused blankly, "Not if it's a farce—a fake you engineered to keep the boy away from me."

The two men glared at each other, down the length of the table.

Then Casey stood up, too. "There's no point in continuing this," he said. "Joanna, we're leaving."

Lillian reached out. She put her hand on Casey's arm. "Please, just let me finish." She turned to Burnett. "Will you please sit down."

Slowly, both brothers dropped back into their seats.

Then Lillian spoke again. "Casey is absolutely right. His marriage with Joanna is none of your business, Burnett." Burnett drew an outraged breath. "I'm not finished," Lillian said, before Burnett could speak. "It was Emily's wish that Casey raise Mike. And I thoroughly agreed with her."

Amanda gasped, a wounded sound.

"You what?" Burnett's voice was hollow, shocked.

"I agreed with her," Lillian repeated, slowly drilling each word home. "You are a good man," she said, facing Burnett squarely. "And you have been the backbone of this family since Edward left us. But you lack essential qualities that Mike needs—patience, tolerance, a sense of humor. I am sure that you could have learned to develop these qualities, were you the only choice as guardian. But you were not the only choice. There was also Casey, and he possesses these qualities already. Moreover, since he returned home from overseas, he has found himself work that fulfills him and is happy here at home. So along with the other qualities I've mentioned, he is stable and satisfied with his life. He is absolutely the superior choice to raise Mike, and I never intended to allow it to be otherwise."

Amanda, whose lovely face had grown crimson, could no longer contain herself. "But what about me? Didn't you even consider me? *I'm* a better choice as a mother than—"

Lillian cut her off with a look. "I know you want a child, Amanda," she said. "And someday, I'm sure you will have one. But Mike is not that child. Accept it."

Amanda withdrew with a small, stricken sob. Very slowly, Lillian let her gaze sweep the table, making sure she had everyone's undivided attention. The gesture was a formality only. She held them all riveted.

"*Single or married,*" Lillian said at last, placing a slow, meaningful stress on each of the words, "*Casey will raise Mike.* And I will stand behind him one-hundred percent." Once more she turned a penetrating look on Burnett. "If you take Casey to court, you'll be taking me, too. By the time you have finished, you will have driven away both of us, and you will have done damage to an innocent child.''

Burnett sat very still gazing back at his mother. And then his big shoulders seemed to visibly slump.

Joanna glanced at Lillian, and caught the look of sympathetic anguish that flashed briefly in the older woman's eyes. This was her own son Lillian was being forced to hurt, and it caused her great agony to do so.

Burnett seemed unable to speak, and no one else could bear to.

Then Lillian spoke, keeping her voice low and even. ''Have I made myself clear at last?''

Burnett coughed into his fist, and forced his shoulders to straighten. He said, with great and quiet dignity, ''Yes, perfectly clear.''

Lillian sat very straight in her chair. She folded her hands on the table. ''Does that mean there will be no more harassment of Casey and Joanna? And no more talk of lawsuits?''

Burnett said, ''Yes. It's over. I can't fight you both.''

Amanda, who had been gripping her coffee cup in a stranglehold, suddenly burst into tears and stood up, knocking her chair over with a loud crash. ''That boy needs a home!'' she cried between sobs. ''A real home! I could give him that, but instead, you're going to let her raise him!'' She cast Joanna a quick, vicious look and fled from the room, trailing sobs.

Burnett quietly rose. ''Forgive her,'' he said. ''You have no idea how badly she wants a child.'' He went up the stairs after his wife.

When Burnett was gone, the silence lay over the bright kitchen like a pall. Joanna sat looking at her cold coffee, wishing that what had just been accomplished could have been done in a gentler, less hurtful way.

Lillian's words, when she spoke, echoed Joanna's thoughts. "I didn't want to have to do it," she said. Outside, the shadows thickened as night approached. "I hated to do it. And it doesn't really make things any better, does it?"

"It makes them clearer," Casey said. "And it's the right thing for Mike. That's what counts."

Lillian patted his hand. "You're right, of course." Then she asked him again to stay the night.

Casey looked at Joanna, who nodded. Then he said they would.

It was full dark when Burnett came down the stairs alone. Amanda, he explained, was already in bed. They wanted to get an early start for home tomorrow.

Then he asked Casey to go for a walk with him. Casey agreed.

When the two men were gone, Joanna and Lillian found themselves looking at each other across the knotty surface of the old table.

Lillian smiled. "Come out to the back porch with me."

Joanna stood up, and carried her cold coffee to the sink. "I don't know, Lillian. I was thinking of going up to bed."

"Please?"

The word was said to Joanna's back, and she thought of Burnett that afternoon, saying *please* before he told her all the ugly things he'd been storing up for years. Lillian, of course, had really meant the word. It was a request, not a command.

And Joanna never could say no to a request from Lillian. She turned, and gave Lillian a smile in return. "All right."

Outside, they sat together under the kitchen window, on the wooden couch with the cracked canvas cushion. The trees that rimmed the yard looked ghostly in the moonlight, like the shadows of mythical night creatures crouching just beyond the circle of silvered grass.

"The stars are so much brighter up here," Lillian said.

Joanna gave a small noise of agreement, and rested her head against the window frame. She closed her eyes.

Lillian's next question took her totally by surprise, "Joey, do you love my son?"

Perhaps the dramatic events of the day had made her numb. She heard herself asking, "Which son, what kind of love?"

Lillian chuckled. "Casey. Are you in love with Casey?"

Without turning her head to her mother-in-law, or opening her eyes she said, "Yes."

"But you weren't in love with him when you married him?"

It didn't even occur to Joanna to obscure the truth. And keeping the true nature of their marriage a secret was no longer necessary, not after tonight anyway.

"No," she said. And then she thought of Burnett's accusations that had hurt too much not to have some truth to them. "Or if I was in love with him then," she amended, "I didn't know it."

"Have you told him how you feel?"

"No."

"When are you going to tell him?"

"I don't know. Soon."

The two women were silent for a while. "I'm so happy, Joey," Lillian said.

Joanna suddenly wanted to cry. "Why?"

"Because I think you two have been in love forever, but you just haven't realized it."

"Lillian, I don't think Casey's in love with me," Joanna said, this time turning to seek out the older woman's eyes in the darkness.

"Oh, certainly he is. Of course he is. Emily and I have always known it."

Hope, like something so hot it burned, flared in Joanna's heart. "Did Casey tell you that?"

"Well," Lillian looked away. "No, he never said it in so many words, but—"

Joanna didn't want to hear anymore. "Don't," she said. "Let's drop it, and please don't say anything to Casey."

"Of course not. That's for you to tell him." Lillian leaned a little closer. "You *will* tell him, though?"

Joanna rubbed her eyes. "Let it go, Lillian. Please."

Lillian sank back to her side of the couch. "I'm sorry. I've done so much interfering today, it's becoming a habit, I'm afraid."

"You were brave and wonderful," Joanna said.

Lillian grunted. "I kept putting off the confrontation, hoping I could save us all the pain. As a result,

I ended up causing everybody more pain than was necessary.''

''It's settled now,'' Joanna said.

''That's what happens when you don't do what needs to be done,'' Lillian elaborated somewhat archly. ''Things only get worse.''

Joanna took Lillian's meaning and turned it in her mind. It was true, she knew. That was why, right now, it hurt to hear it said.

''Oh Lillian,'' Joanna said very low. ''Since we got married, I've lost my best friend.''

Joanna felt the soft, dry touch of Lillian's hand on hers. ''Tell him,'' Lillian said.

Lillian was right, Joanna admitted to herself. They couldn't continue like this: talking but not talking—together but miles apart. Joanna needed to get the truth out in the open right away.

But not tonight, she hedged silently. Not upstairs in that room with Burnett and Amanda on the other side of the wall from us. I need absolute privacy to tell him how I feel...

But then she realized that there would always be one excuse or another to keep her from revealing the secret of her heart. Tonight, it would be lack of privacy. Tomorrow, that she had to get ready for the flight to Los Angeles. And then, all this week would be taken up with preparing for the show. And then she'd need to focus on the bank commission...

Joanna almost chuckled aloud. If she planned it right, she could keep from telling Casey she loved him until both of them were old and gray—or at least, she thought wryly, remembering her words to Casey the night before—until Mike was in college.

　　"When will you tell him?" Lillian prodded gently from the other end of the couch.

　　"Tonight," Joanna answered. "I'll tell him tonight, as soon as we're alone."

Chapter Sixteen

When Joanna and Casey were alone in their upstairs room, Joanna asked first about how things had gone between Casey and his brother. Casey told her that he and Burnett had walked to the Graeagle Meadows Golf Course and back. Nothing of significance had been said.

"But it was better between you, wasn't it?" Joanna asked. She wanted to hear that it was. She wanted to hear some good news before she told Casey she was in love with him. That way, if her confession brought on rejection, she could console herself with the knowledge that something good had still come of all this: two brothers had made the first hesitant steps toward healing the wounds of a lifetime.

Casey, however, refused to be too optimistic. He said, "Joey, it's going to take a lot more than an evening stroll to fix what's wrong between Burnett and me."

"But it's the first step."

"I suppose."

"That's wonderful."

Joanna thought of Amanda, with whom she would probably never make real peace. The thought made her sad. But, then, if she and Casey split up, it probably didn't matter at all how she got along with Amanda Clinton. Her relationship to Burnett's wife would be terminated—no marriage, no sister-in-law.

That thought made her sadder still, so she ordered her mind to stop dwelling on the negative.

Joanna had perched on the edge of the bed when she entered the room. Casey was standing near the door. Both of them were still fully clothed. The space between them seemed to vibrate with uneasiness—as if all of the things unsaid bounced and swirled in the air, invisible, but nonetheless profoundly disturbing.

"Well," Casey said, leaving the other side of the room and walking to the bow window, which was behind her. Joanna had to turn around to look at him as he finished, "I guess we should get ready for bed."

"Right," Joanna said, standing up. She felt a coward's sense of temporary relief. She would get ready for bed—and *then* she'd tell him she loved him.

Taking comfort in having something to do, she pulled the T-shirt she was wearing over her head, tossed her bra on the bed and shimmied out of her jeans. She took her nightgown off of the peg behind the door and stuck her arms through the sleeves, gathering the material, before she stuck her head through the collar. She glanced up at Casey watching her.

Reflexively, she smiled, and pulled the wad of nightgown against her bare breasts.

"Think I'll go downstairs for a cup of hot chocolate," he said.

Joanna blinked. "But, Casey, I—"

He came toward her quickly, and was around her and out the door before she could say any more.

"You go ahead and turn off the light," he said just before he shut the door between them. "I'll be a while."

Joanna dropped the nightgown over her head and went back to the bed. She slumped down upon it.

I should follow him downstairs, she thought glumly. But her nerve was gone.

Alone, she crawled between the covers of the bed.

The next morning, Burnett and Amanda left before Mike returned from Megan's. Amanda wore dark glasses and said little as they carried their luggage out to their car. Once the suitcases were stowed in the trunk, she got in on the passenger side and waited for her husband to be ready to leave.

It was Burnett who surprised Joanna. He hugged his mother and his brother. They were rather formal, stiff hugs—but they were hugs nonetheless.

Most amazingly, before he climbed in behind the wheel he looked up to where Joanna stood a few feet away.

He said, "Joey, we'll see you at home."

Joanna knew that that was as close to a request for a truce as she'd ever get from Burnett Clinton.

She nodded. "Yes, see you soon, Burnett," she said.

Burnett got in his car and backed out of the wide gravel driveway.

Mike returned soon after that, and Casey and Joanna were ready to go. Lillian stayed on for a few hours. The caretaker was due to stop by and Lillian needed to give him a few added instructions.

Casey took them home by the route along the Feather River and through Quincy. They reached Sacramento before noon. They unpacked, ate lunch and swam. Then one of Mike's friends, who lived across the street, called and asked him over for hotdogs. Mike was given permission, but told to return by seven sharp.

Joanna went upstairs and began packing again for the trip to Los Angeles the next day. As she packed, she rehearsed her declaration of love.

She would make that declaration tonight, she'd decided, if she had to tie Casey to the bed to get him to listen to her.

Most of her clothes were still in the studio room, so she was riffling through the closet in there when Casey came to talk to her.

He sat on the end of her supply table. "I've been thinking about L.A.," he said.

Joanna hooked a blouse she'd been considering back onto the closet rod and glanced over her shoulder at him. Her heart seemed to have lifted and paused in her chest. She waited for it to start pounding again, before she said, studiously casual, "Oh? What about it?"

"Well, maybe you'd rather go on down by yourself," he said.

Joanna just looked at him. The phrases she'd been rehearsing played in her mind:

Casey, it has become clear to me over the past few weeks that I love you in a much deeper, more profound sense than I had previously realized…

Casey, I feel more for you than I've told you…

Casey, I not only love you, I'm in love with you…

"It *is* Mike's first day of school tomorrow," Casey was saying.

The plan had been that Casey would go with Joanna, and that Lillian could come stay with Mike. Then Casey would fly back to collect Mike on Friday afternoon so Mike could be there for the party at the gallery that opened Joanna's one-woman show.

The two of them at last spending some time without their ready-made family had been an intimate joke between them; they'd finally be able to explore all the erotic possibilities of her apartment.

"I kind of feel I should be here for Mike's first day of school," Casey continued. Then he laughed, an utterly false laugh. "What good am I going to be to you anyway down there, right? You'll be busy getting things set up with Althea, and all that."

Of course, that was true. Setting up a gallery for an art show could be a hectic, demanding process. Everybody from the program printer to the caterer always considered himself an artist in his own right. It could end up being three days of tempers and temperaments. Maybe that was the last thing Casey wanted right now. Perhaps he needed a little more time to himself after the mess at Graeagle. Joanna could understand that, however much it might hurt.

Joanna reached for the blouse that she'd already decided not to take, and concluded that she needed it after all. She carried it over and slid it into the garment bag that lay on the daybed.

The litany of her unspoken declarations kept playing in her mind.

I love you, maybe I always have...

And not only as friends...

But as a woman loves a man...

Casey was fiddling with some of her brushes that were standing handles down in a coffee can. "And I've been thinking that maybe we could both use the space."

Space. At the mention of that word, something snapped inside Joanna. She whirled on Casey.

"Space," she said, planting her hands on her hips. "That's what you think we need? More *space?*"

Casey looked stunned. "Yeah," he said rather dumbly. "What's wrong with space?"

"Space," she repeated, injecting all her frustration into the single word.

His expression wasn't so confident now. "That's what we need—isn't it?"

"Is it?"

He looked as befuddled as a game show contestant who just can't seem to find the correct answer to the sixty-four thousand dollar question. "It isn't?"

"Not as far as I'm concerned," she said. "As far as I'm concerned, all we've got is space. We've got so much space, we don't talk to each other, so much space, we don't touch each other. And you think we need *more* of it?"

"Joey," he said, still nonplussed at the sudden change in her. "Settle down..."

"Space," she said the words again, as if it left a disgusting taste in her mouth, "is the last damn thing we need."

"Joey, I thought you wanted—"

"You thought I wanted?" She stopped, halfway across the room, spun on her heel and faced him directly. "How could you possibly have the slightest idea what I wanted, Casey Clinton? For weeks now, you've been either making love to me or leaving the room the minute it looks like I might actually *say* anything!"

They stared at each other. Finally, Casey stood up. "All right," he said grimly. "Tell me. Go ahead and tell me."

She narrowed her eyes at him. "You won't suddenly decide you have log sheets to take care of?" she said, wary now—and frightened. The moment was upon her. Lord help her, she didn't want to blow it.

"I'm not moving from this spot," he told her.

"All right," she said.

"Fine," he said.

They stared at each other.

Then she said, "Casey, I—"

And he said, "Joey, listen—"

Both fell silent.

After endless seconds, they said simultaneously, "What?"

They looked at each other again.

Joanna began to feel foolish poised in the middle of the floor. She went to the daybed, pushed the garment bag aside and sat down. Then she slipped off the sandals and drew her legs up under the hem of the drop-waisted sundress she wore.

Oddly, she was conscious, even within her apprehension, of a new feeling of relief. At least it was going to all be said. By the time they left this room, they would know where things were.

Across from her, Casey had stood up. He looked confused and uncomfortable, totally at a loss for what to do or say next.

Joanna said, "It's not easy anymore, is it?"

"What?" He sounded defiant, even angry.

"Talking to each other. We've gotten so out of practice."

"There are things," he said, still defiant, "that I just have trouble talking about. It's all too new. It confuses the hell out of me."

"What things?"

He looked away. "I thought you wanted to say something."

"But so do you, am I right?"

He looked back at her. "Yes."

"Go ahead," she told him. "You go first."

He went to the bay window over the side yard. He looked out. Then he seemed to force himself to face her again, to say what he was going to say while looking into her eyes.

"All right," he said. "Something really strange has happened, something I never thought would happen to me. Something I'm not very comfortable with, something that's hard for me to talk about."

"My Lord, what?" she asked, aching for him, because he looked so absolutely miserable.

"I love you, Joey," he said. "And I don't mean only as a friend. But as a man loves a woman."

Chapter Seventeen

Joanna stared at Casey. "Could you say that again?" she finally asked.

"I'm in love with you. Maybe I always have been, I don't know about that for sure."

Her heart had stopped—this time with joy. "Oh, I see," she heard herself murmur idiotically.

"When Emily was dying…"

"Yes?"

"She told me I was in love with you," Casey said. "She said that we should be together, and that together we could make a home for Mike. I humored her, saying I'd do what I could about that."

In Joanna's mind, Lillian's words echoed. *Of course he's in love with you. Emily and I have always known it…*

Casey went on, "You know how Emily was, so

frail, almost…transparent at the end. You could see the blood in her veins through her skin."

"I remember," Joanna said.

Casey went on, "I would have agreed to just about anything she asked for then, and not thought twice about it."

"I can understand that."

"But the strange thing was, after she was gone, I couldn't quit thinking about it, about what she'd said. That I was in love with you. And when you insisted on coming here to help out, and I was around you every day, I thought about it more and more." He sat down on the window seat, and stuck his hands in the pockets of his slacks. He looked down at his feet, then back up at Joanna. "But I kept telling myself it wasn't true. I'd always thought of myself as someone who didn't want any forever kind of commitments. I accepted myself that way. And then, to start having these…" he had to search for the words, "…forever kind of thoughts, about you, well, I pushed them from my mind.

"And it worked," he went on, "for those first few weeks you were here. We had had so many years of practice in relating to each other in a certain way. I could keep it friendly and affectionate, and my own dangerous thoughts never came up." He looked at her narrowly. "You never guessed, did you? At first, when you came here to stay?"

"No," she told him honestly. "I didn't have a clue."

He laughed, a dry sound. "But then, Burnett decided to take me to court, and I heard myself announcing that we were getting married—and it hit me. Marrying you was *exactly* what I wanted. Because Emily was right. I am in love with you.''

Joanna said, ''You mean you've known for sure since the night you announced we were getting married?''

He nodded. ''I came to your room that night to tell you, to get it all out in the open. But you were so beautiful, and I thought...'' he paused, then he pulled his thoughts together. ''I thought that if I scared you away by telling you too soon, I'd blow my chances for making you love me back.''

Joanna tipped her head to him, knowing he wasn't telling the whole truth, but having no idea what he was leaving out.

''All right,'' he said, reading her expression as he always could. ''Maybe right then it was a little more basic than that. I wanted to make love to you. What I really thought that night was that we'd never make love if I spilled everything too soon and scared you off.

''So I took advantage of the situation with Mike to get you to marry me,'' Casey's voice was steeped in self-disgust. ''I thought I could make you love me, eventually. I didn't realize what should have been obvious.''

''And that is?''

''That starting the whole thing on a lie would eat at me. That it would get harder and harder to tell you how I felt.'' He shook his head, his expression one of sad wonder. ''My own idiocy amazes me. I wanted you so badly, so I tried not to rush you.''

''By not making love to me on our wedding night, you mean?''

"Right. And then later, when we finally made love in L.A., and you told me you'd been ready all along, I could see that you must have felt I didn't want you then. But somehow, I couldn't tell you the truth about that without telling you *everything*. By then I'd convinced myself that if I told you everything, it would only make things worse. So I started making love to you whenever it looked as though we might be getting too close to the truth. I believed I was *showing* you how I felt, rather than actually saying it. But it was really just another excuse for not taking the risk of losing you altogether.

"And then," he said grimly, "there was Burnett and Amanda. Naturally, they made you their prime target. It became like some never-ending nightmare. I wanted to make you love me—and what I did was push you away and set you up to be victimized by my family."

"Nobody victimized me," Joanna said. "I chose to marry you and I accepted the consequences."

Casey waved his hand in front of his face, indicating that he didn't buy her interpretation. "Whatever."

"There's no *whatever* about it, Casey. That's how it was—and is. I'm willing to accept responsibility for my own actions. Believe it. Mike does, and he's only six."

He stood up. "Anyway, I thought after this weekend you'd want to get as far away as possible from me and the rest of the Clintons. So that's why I suggested you could have your week in L.A. alone."

"I see."

"And," he continued. "We have to face the fact

that what Mother did this weekend changes everything.''

''It does?''

He glared at her. ''It's obvious that it does. You don't have to stay married to me anymore. Mike stays with me, whether we're married or not.''

''Yes,'' Joanna smiled at him. ''It's wonderful, isn't it?''

''You do want your freedom, then?'' Casey asked, his voice flat.

''Are you asking me or telling me?''

He looked angry again. ''Isn't that what this is all about?''

''No.''

''What do you mean, no?''

''No, it isn't about freedom, if by that you mean another word for space. I don't want space, I want my best friend back. And I want to keep the marriage we've made together.''

''Damn it, Joey,'' he said. ''Don't be kind to me. I think I could take just about anything right now, but you being kind.''

Joanna stood up. ''Don't worry, I'm not.''

''Not what?''

''Being kind.''

''Then what?''

Slowly, she approached him. ''I'm trying to find a way to tell you.''

''What?''

''What I've been longing to tell you.'' She felt like her bare feet weren't even touching the floor. She felt she floated toward him.

''So do it. Tell me,'' he said.

She stopped before him. "I love you."

"You *what?*"

"I love you. And as much more than a friend. As a woman loves a man."

"But—"

"Yes?"

"How long have you known that?"

"At least since last Friday, when Burnett and Amanda caught us kissing on the back lawn. But maybe longer. Maybe years. Burnett thinks I've always been lying in wait for you..." She paused for a moment, just to breathe in his nearness. Slowly, she took the collar of his sport shirt and pulled him even closer than he already was. "...Like a spider in her web," she said in a sinister tone.

Casey's lips were so close, she could have reached out and kissed them. And she intended to, very soon.

He said, "Burnett said that?"

She nodded. "Yesterday. He said I had kept you from ever finding a suitable woman to marry. And you know what?"

"I'm listening." He was watching her lips with extreme concentration.

"He might be right," she confessed. "I never wanted you to marry anyone else, not really. I think, deep down, I was always a little jealous of the other women you cared for. But we both had so many things we wanted to do in life. It took a little boy who needed us to be together to make us see what the other people we loved knew all along."

"And that is?"

"Didn't I just say it?"

"I wouldn't mind at all if you say it again. It's not

the kind of thing a man gets tired of hearing from the woman he loves.''

''Okay, I'll say it again. We were meant to be together. I'm in love with you, and now that I've got you, Casey Clinton, I'm never letting you go. Understand?''

He was quiet. He gave her one quick, tempting kiss. ''Well, I don't know,'' he said.

''What?''

''Maybe you should explain more thoroughly...''

''Maybe you should tell me you're going to L.A. with me, like my best friend would.''

''All right. I'm going to L.A. with you.''

''Good. And maybe we should also agree that, from now on, whatever happens, no matter how hard it is to talk about—we *will* talk about it, like best friends should.''

''Agreed,'' he told her, kissing her once more, pulling her close to his heart, so that something inside her kindled and then flamed.

His lips moved over hers, tender and seeking—then hungry and demanding. And Joanna responded in kind.

And once he had kissed her so thoroughly that her whole body had turned to molten desire in his arms, he kissed her some more, waltzing her across the room as he did it, until he could close and lock the door to the landing.

At that point Joanna opened her eyes and asked drowsily, ''Why, Casey Clinton, what is going on?''

His answer came against her lips as he began kissing her again. ''We're about to explore the erotic possibilities of this very room—starting with that drawing board over there.''

She pushed at his chest. ''What? You're nuts.'' She eyed the drawing board. ''Uh-uh, no way. Not on that...''

''Joey...'' he was kissing her ear. ''Let's just try it.''

''No way,'' she said firmly.

But then he said, ''I dare you...''

She pulled back to meet his eyes.

He looked at her; she looked at him.

''You dare me?'' she asked.

''I double dare you,'' he said then.

Joanna laughed, a woman's laugh, full of knowing and promise and just a touch of coyness. Then she opened her arms to him—her best friend, her lover, and the companion of her heart.

* * * * *

Dear Reader,

Some books that I read are dearer to my heart than others. The same is true of the ones I write. *Molly Darling* was one of those, and I am delighted with this new edition of the story… and an excuse to read it again.

Molly Clelland is just the sort of person I'd like to have for a friend—rock steady, loyal and kind. Okay, she can get angry, but only upon extreme provocation—for instance, in the case of a hardheaded rancher who's having a problem with his former in-laws and needs a wife to prove he's a stable father for that winsome baby, Lass. Who wouldn't get mad at being seen only as a "solution" to a man's troubles! However, Sam finds out there's a lot more to his new wife than he'd ever dreamed.

Don't you just love it when these stubborn heroes finally see the light?

Laurie Paige

Molly Darling
Laurie Paige

To Mary-Theresa Hussey

Chapter One

Molly Clelland flicked the curtain aside and frowned at the empty driveway. Sam Frazier was late. Again.

She studied the clouds. Thunderheads clashed like medieval knights decked out in gray plumes as they raced over Roswell, twelve miles west of her, and charged across the winter sky.

The huge cloud masses had hovered over the landscape all day, ominous and dreary, threatening anyone who ventured out. She sighed. She really wanted to get home before it rained for the third day in a row.

Turning from the window, she put the dust cloth away and finished straightening the basement room of the church, then stretched and yawned. It had been a long day.

She'd opened the nursery school at seven that morning and had hardly sat down a moment since then.

By now—six-thirty at night—she should have been safe at home, snug in the adobe cottage across the street from the church, sipping a cup of hot tea and catching up on the world news on television. The cats were probably howling for their supper.

Where the heck was Sam Frazier?

He knew the rules. He should. She'd had to remind him of them often enough during the past four months. Worry wound its way through the irritation as thunder pealed overhead.

Torrential rains had fallen all that week. Here in the southeastern corner of New Mexico, they occasionally got the edge of a fierce storm blowing in from the Gulf of Mexico.

Llano Estacado. The Staked Plain. A plateau of desert hues and formations with mountain peaks thrusting upward as if the land sought the caress of the sky. However, this land, beautiful as it was, could be treacherous. A dry wash could become a raging river without warning.

She'd fallen in love with New Mexico ten years ago when she'd arrived as a summer teaching volunteer in a federal program—the proverbial do-gooder—and had vowed to stay.

So here she was at thirty-two, spinning out her modest dreams in this land of enchantment with her own nursery school and a cozy little house where she lived with two cats.

The proverbial spinster.

Her parents called her their "changeling." She was unlike the rest of her family. Where they were laughing and witty, she was serious, given to lectures on nutrition, the value of hard work and the cultivation of sober habits. She found them fascinating but exhausting. They found her prim but amusing.

A gurgle interrupted her thoughts. She crossed to the crib in the corner and peered down at the six-month-old baby.

Lass Frazier let go of the bright booties covering her feet and grinned up at Molly, waving her arms in the air and making her little sounds of welcome.

"Hello, darling," Molly murmured. "Do you need a change?"

Lecturing about the weather, the lateness of the hour and the thoughtlessness of men, she put a fresh diaper on the tiny girl and lifted the child into her arms.

Lass touched Molly's lips, then her nose, then clutched a handful of hair and tried to taste it.

Molly gently tugged the lock from the child's hold and gave her a rabbit teething ring to chew on.

"Where is your father?" she asked.

Lass gave her a big grin, then clicked her tongue against the roof of her mouth several times, evidently liking the sound, while Molly walked to the window and peered outside again.

The church was built on the side of a hill, its front door opening on a circular driveway. The nursery was accessible from a winding lane that led down the hill and behind the building. A stand of junipers interrupted the rocky ground that sloped off toward a dry wash, now running in muddy torrents.

Headlights appeared on the lane. A truck slowed and stopped at the end of the sidewalk leading to the basement door. The driver jumped out and strode up the walkway with his usual long-legged stride and preoccupied air.

He fascinated her, this silent, unsmiling man with a forebidding presence. Like the land, he had an aura of vastness, of limitless distances and a toughness that had to do with survival and determination and other facets of being that she couldn't define.

The local gossip painted him black. While still a teenager, he'd been caught rustling cattle from his own family's ranch. The charges had been dropped, but where there was smoke…

After a significant look, the storyteller would continue. The Frazier boy had fought constantly with his stepfather…had left home as soon as he got out of high school…had been a trial to his poor mother, bless her soul. Yes, he was a bad one, that Sam Frazier. As wild as a mustang, you know.

Molly thought of what she knew of Sam Frazier. One, he was a man, not a boy. His boyhood had disappeared long ago. Two, he took better care of his daughter than many mothers she'd known.

She fixed a smile on her face when the door opened, then closed behind him. He filled the room, bringing the fresh scent of the outdoors with him. Sam Frazier wasn't a brawny man, nor unusually tall, but he dominated the space around him. When he removed his hat, drops of water fell to the floor.

"Good evening. Looks like it's raining out your way," she said, determined to be pleasant. Ill manners didn't win friends or solve problems. "Were the roads bad?"

He answered her greeting with a nod. "Yes, it's raining. The roads aren't bad yet. I had a cow that was down with a calf," he explained his tardiness.

It was as close to an apology as she was going to

get from him. She instinctively knew he was a man who didn't like having to explain himself to others, nor was he given to small talk. In four months of twice daily meetings, five days a week, they hadn't exchanged more than the most cursory of comments, and not one of them personal.

For a second, she tried to think of something personal he might say to her, then gave up when nothing came to mind except a dash of poetry—*come be my love*. She frowned at her musing.

He raked a hand through his black, curly hair while his eyes, the color of dark, clear molasses, fastened on his daughter as if to make certain she'd made it through the day without mishap.

Molly sometimes felt insulted by his manner. However, she was sure it was an unconscious gesture on his part. And there was the look in his eyes when he gazed at Lass.

Sometimes in those intense depths, in a flash before he hid his feelings, she saw the love he had for his daughter—a fierce, protective love that was utterly sweet and filled with such tenderness, it brought a lump to her throat.

The way it did now.

For that look, she could forgive him anything. At times, she even dreamed he'd look at her that way someday.

Mentally shaking her head at her extravagant fantasies, she nodded toward the clock. "Lass just woke up. I think she's hungry. Perhaps we should feed her before you make the trip back to your place?"

He paused after picking up the bag of Lass's be-

longings and considered the suggestion as if it were
of world importance.

Molly had to smile. Here was a person who evidently took life even more seriously than she did. Her
parents would marvel over that.

"Would you like to go out to dinner?" he asked.

She tried to figure out what he'd said. It sounded as
if he'd invited her out to dinner. She must have mis-
understood.

"I beg your pardon?" She removed a tendril of her
hair from Lass's fist and substituted a rattle.

Lass shook the rattle, then settled happily to chew-
ing on the bright red handle.

"It's late. I've kept you from your supper. I thought
we could go somewhere and eat."

"Oh." Her heart kicked up a bit before common
sense reasserted itself. "That's all right. You don't
have to do that. Lass was a perfect angel. I didn't mind
keeping her."

He gave her an impatient frown. "I'm as hungry as
a bear. I've been working since before dawn, and I'd
like to sit down and relax a bit."

"Oh." She cleared her throat. "Well, of course.
That would be nice." She peered down at her slacks
and blouse, which were wrinkled from a day of tending children under four years of age. "I'd better stop
by the house and change."

"You'll do," he said, giving her an impersonal
once-over with his quick, restless gaze.

After shifting Lass to one side, Molly picked her
purse and coat up from the desk, slung them over her
shoulder and turned to him. "Then I'm ready."

She bestowed a sweet smile on him. It was one of

her tactics for handling obstreperous people. They didn't know what to do in the face of such gentle forgiveness for their churlish ways. It was very effective.

He gave a sort of surprised snort under his breath and followed her out, turning off the lights and making sure the lock clicked into place behind them at her request. Outside, he held the door to the pickup open, took the baby while she climbed inside, then strapped the baby into her seat.

Molly tucked a light blanket around the child. It wasn't until Sam climbed in that she realized there might be a problem.

The front seat was distressingly intimate with her stuck between him and the baby's car seat. She could feel his body heat all the way down her left side. Once in a while his shoulder brushed hers as they rounded a curve.

Keeping her feet to one side so he wouldn't touch her leg when he shifted gears, she asked, "How is the cow?"

"What?" He roused out of his deep, dark thoughts long enough to glare at her, making her wonder why he'd bothered to invite her out. He certainly wasn't in the mood for company.

"The cow that had trouble calving. Is she all right?"

"Yes." He dropped back into the brooding silence.

She forebode to give him a lecture on manners. If he hadn't wanted her to come, why had he invited her?

Well, that was easy to answer. Guilt.

He'd kept her waiting four times in the past ten days. She'd let him know the last time that she expected him to be on time to pick Lass up. After all, she had a life, too.

Right. She'd been late for the monthly meeting of her literary club. Big deal.

However, the sharing of thoughts and ideas and conversation with friends was important, she reminded herself. Reading gave one entry into another mind, sometimes into a life so different from one's own a person was startled by it.

"I beg your pardon?" She realized she'd missed some mumbled message from him.

"The truck stop. Is it all right?"

The dining room at the truck stop was a popular place. Most of the people in the surrounding ranching community ate there at least once a week. It would be crowded on Friday night. Everyone would see them together.

For a briefest instant, she wondered what the local citizens would think—the local nursery schoolteacher with the local black sheep. "The truck stop is fine."

He pulled into the driveway and parked. "Wait," he said in a commanding tone and slid out.

He came around and removed the infant car seat from its straps, keeping Lass in it. The baby made noises to her father and smiled widely at him, eliciting another of those brief, but fiercely loving glances.

Molly slipped past the car seat base and jumped to the ground. To her surprise, Sam took her arm and escorted her inside. Several heads turned when they entered the dining room.

Nearly every table was full, and two of them were occupied by parents whose children came to her nursery school. She gave them a smile that said she had everything under control and this was a perfectly normal outing of the schoolmarm with the rancher and his baby. It was a good thing they couldn't see the flutters taking place inside her.

The waitress, a young woman in tight jeans, led them to a booth. Sam and Lass took one side. Molly took the other. She laid her coat beside her. He looked around for a place to put his hat. She indicated the seat beside her. He handed it over and she placed it on her coat, feeling the Stetson had been given into her guardianship just as Lass was each morning.

They studied the menus in silence, then ordered when the waitress indicated she was ready. When the girl walked away, a vacuum surrounded the table. It filled with uneasy silence. Molly waited for her companion to speak.

"I'd better feed her before she realizes she's starving," he said, indicating Lass. He reached into the side pocket of the diaper bag and fished out a spoon and a jar of cereal with fruit.

Molly watched in perfect fascination as Sam Frazier, tough, rarely smiling rancher, fed his baby with the utmost gentleness and care. When he wanted Lass to open her mouth, he opened his and said, "Ahh."

Lass imitated him.

He used the opportunity to stick another spoonful of food into her mouth. Then he smiled at the trick he'd played on her. She smiled back, nearly losing the bite. He caught it on the spoon and scooped it back into her mouth with the touch of an expert.

Molly's heart melted. "The doctor's office called today. It's time for Lass's six-month checkup."

He flicked her a glance, then nodded.

"You could come in and have lunch with us the
day of the appointment," she suggested. She liked for
parents to take part in their child's life as much as
possible. "It would be good for Lass," she added at
his unreadable glance.

"We'll see."

Not exactly a promise, but she knew he would. He'd
do anything for his daughter. The baby had him
wrapped right around her finger. Molly had known
that the moment he brought the infant to the nursery
school.

Normally she didn't take children under six months,
but Lass's mother had died in childbirth. Sam had
taken sole care of his tiny daughter for two months,
then asked if Molly would take her during the day.
She wasn't sure why she'd broken her own rule and
agreed.

"Why don't you hire someone to stay at the house
with Lass while you do your work?" she'd asked.

"I don't have anyone I'd trust with her," he'd answered in his blunt, but honest way. "Everyone knows
you run the best nursery school around and that your
reputation is spotless."

She'd preened a bit at the time. And from such moments, fantasies were born. For the first month, she'd
gotten shaky whenever he came for Lass, knowing
he'd never give her a glance.

Time and lack of nourishment had starved those
dreams into thin, pale images barely remembered now.
She wondered if he was still mourning the loss of his
wife.

Their food came. He finished with Lass and gave
her the rabbit to chew on while they ate.

"This is very good." Molly was determined to make pleasant conversation. A relaxed atmosphere aided the digestion.

He glanced at the cashew chicken dish she'd ordered and nodded. He continued with his steak.

A half a pound of red meat. She hoped he didn't eat that way all the time. Ranchers worked very hard and burned a lot of calories, but all that fat and cholesterol wasn't good. However, she wasn't going to expound on that. Dinner should be enjoyable.

"I wonder if the weather pattern is going to hold another week." Ranchers were always concerned about the weather so she knew it was a topic Sam would be interested in.

He gave a noncommittal grunt.

She felt her hackles begin to rise. She really hated to lose her temper. It was so uncivilized.

"Someone said the Pecos was near the top of its banks in several places south of us," she continued.

He paused and frowned. A shrug of his shoulders indicated there was nothing he could do about the river if it flooded.

Molly chewed, swallowed and patted her mouth with the napkin before she spoke. "Mr. Frazier, it is considered polite to respond when someone is talking to you." She gave him a sterling smile that, combined with the reprimand, usually brought about the desired change in behavior.

He gave her a long perusal, studying her as thoroughly as a horse buyer looking over stock that was being touted as prime and suspecting it wasn't. He had a way of gazing at a person from under those dark, imposing eyebrows that was intimidating.

She hadn't studied motivational psychology for nothing. "It is also considered correct to engage in conversation during a meal. We are not primitives, are we?"

A flash of emotion went through his eyes. She thought perhaps she'd gone too far, that he was furious. Then he smiled.

His teeth were startling white against the duskiness of his skin. His father had had some Mexican and Indian blood, she'd heard. Certainly he didn't look as Anglo as his name implied.

Except his eyes had tiny flecks of gold mixed with the brown, she noticed for the first time. Like hidden treasure.

"No, ma'am, we're not," he replied solemnly.

She stiffened, wondering if he was making fun of her. She did tend to be a little...stuffy. Inhibited was the term her parents had used when she frowned upon their hedonistic behavior. Prudish was the teasing way her brother had put it.

However, she decided her companion was no more prone to uncalled-for levity than she was. "Good," she said approvingly, drawing a sardonic glance from him.

"It was raining when I left the house, but I think we're getting the dying gasp of the storm," he said, picking up her conversational tidbit. "I rode the river today, checking for erosion along the banks, but everything looked fine."

"I'm sure that was a relief. We've had so many floods the past few years. The ranchers must worry each time a cloud appears on the horizon."

He laughed suddenly, unexpectedly. She stared at

the tanned column of his throat. He'd bathed and shaved before coming to pick up Lass. His face was smooth, and she got a whiff of his after-shave once in a while. His jeans and white shirt were fresh. He'd rolled his sleeves up, exposing tanned forearms with fine black hairs sprinkled generously over them.

For a second, she had the oddest sensation…as if she'd like to kiss him, right where his neck joined his shoulder. And perhaps along those strong cords running up his throat. The impulse to do so was almost irresistible.

She cleared her throat. "Do share the humor, Mr. Frazier."

His laughter was brief, but a smile lingered at the corners of his mouth like the promise in a rainbow. "I was thinking of clouds. That seems to be all that's on my horizon these days."

"I see." She instilled the proper amount of sympathy in her tone, indicating a willingness to listen if he wished to talk.

"Please, call me Sam."

A definite change of subject. She followed his lead. "Is that short for Samuel?"

"No. It's just Sam. Sam Watson Frazier."

"Is Watson a family name?"

He shot her a glance from under the dark slash of his eyebrows that made her heart jump erratically. "It was my mother's maiden name."

"How nice. I think names are so important. They convey a sense of continuity, handed down from one family member to another like that. I'm named after my grandmothers, Millicent Dorothea."

"I thought you were called Molly."

"I am. I chose Molly when I was four and refused to answer to Millicent thereafter. My parents thought the name suited, so Molly I've been ever since."

"You must have understanding parents."

"They're very liberal, one might say."

"Might one?"

There was the slightest sarcastic edge to the question. She ignored it. "Yes, indeed. Interesting, too. In fact, most people find my parents fascinating. Actually I do, too."

He nodded, but said nothing as he concentrated on his meal once more. Sam. She mentally tried the name, picturing herself saying it to him. After months of thinking of him as Lass's father, it sounded odd, much too personal.

"Your accent is Eastern. Where are you from?" he asked after a bit.

"A tiny hamlet in Virginia."

"Did your folks object when you moved out here?" He seemed sincerely interested in her answer.

"Actually they were horrified, but then they said it was like me."

"How's that?"

"Contrary." She smiled nostalgically. "My parents said I was born to be their conscience."

His eyebrows rose fractionally. "Were you?"

"Not really." She was never less than truthful. "However, I was rather a sober child and I worried about things…"

"What things?"

"Starving children and…and things like that. I used to send my allowance to a fund for feeding the children until the counselor at school called my parents in to ask if I needed to be on the free lunch program. They were pretty angry with me over that one.''

''What else did you do?''

She tried not to feel flattered at his obvious interest. After all, this wasn't a date, merely a recompense on his part for keeping her late. ''I fed a starving dog once. It followed me home, so I took it to my room and let it sleep with me. It had some kind of seizure the next day. My father had to shoot it. Then I had to take rabies shots.''

''Dangerous,'' he murmured. ''What else?''

''Another time I brought home a kitten from the woods. I was so disappointed when my mother told me to take it back at once.''

''Your parents wouldn't let you have pets?''

''Not this one.'' She looked down as if saddened by the memory. ''It was the prettiest kitten, too—black with a silver line on its head that divided into two lines along its back.''

When she looked up, she saw comprehension and amusement flash into his eyes, followed by a low, genuine chuckle, unlike that earlier hollow parody of a laugh. She smiled, enchanted by two surprising dimples at each side of his mouth. She hadn't noticed those before.

''I think you were a trial to your folks,'' he commented.

''I'm afraid so.'' She paused. ''Were you?''

He was silent so long she didn't think he was going to answer. Instead he gazed into her eyes as if looking into her soul. It unnerved her. When the waitress stopped and poured more coffee in Sam's cup, Molly was relieved.

When they were alone again, he studied Lass, who had fallen asleep, before glancing back at Molly. "My dad died when I was twelve. I hated my stepfather."

"That's sad," she said quietly. She had very firm ideas of how families should support and love each other. "I adore my parents and my brother. They love me, too, although they find me as perplexing as I find them."

"Because you're quiet and they're flamboyant?"

His insight was startling. "Something like that," she murmured. "Um, this is quite good." She indicated her chicken dish. "How's your steak?"

"Great. I rarely get steak. My cooking tends toward the quick and easy."

"I thought all ranches had an irascible old cook who dribbled ashes into the pots and shot anyone who complained about the food."

He shook his head. "I can't afford one."

The hardness crept into his voice. She guessed his pride was pricked at having to admit he didn't have a lot of money. His life had been hard, it appeared, then to lose his wife and have a baby to take care of... Her heart went out to him.

She tried to stifle the feeling, knowing herself to be the softest of soft touches when it came to another's pain. If ever there was anyone less needy of her pity it was Sam Frazier.

During the rest of the meal, she was aware of the glances directed their way and wondered if others saw their being there as a date. The spinster and the cowboy. It was almost a parody of every dime novel ever written.

Except she was real, and so was he.

After he cleaned up every bite on his plate, he ordered more coffee and settled back in the booth with a tired but satisfied sigh. "I could go to sleep right here," he told her.

"Please don't. You're too big for me to carry."

His eyebrows jerked upward in surprise. He studied her for a long minute before asking, "Would you take me home and tuck me into bed the way you do Lass when I bring her to your nursery?"

Chills tumbled down Molly's spine at his sexy question. He probably didn't realize how provocative he'd sounded, his voice dropping into a deeper, quieter register while he spoke.

She glanced into his eyes. The dark intensity of his gaze stalled any answer she might have made. Words went flying out of her head. Then the expression disappeared, leaving her to wonder if she'd imagined it.

"You're not a baby," she finally said.

"No, I'm not." He frowned suddenly, as if realizing he'd said too much. "How did you happen to start a nursery school?"

She relaxed. The nursery was dear to her heart. She had definite ideas about the learning experiences of young children.

"Most adults have very little conception of the learning capacity of children," she said, launching into one of her favorite topics. "For instance, Lass already knows to push a blue button when she wants to hear music, a red one when she wants food and a yellow one when she wants to play with a mobile over her crib."

"Is this learning or training them like Pavlov's dogs?"

"Oh, no. Babies know what they want. Lass won't ask for food if she isn't hungry. If you offer to push the red button for her after she's eaten, she pushes your hand to one of the others, then smiles when the music plays or the mobile lowers."

"So maybe my kid's a genius?" The hard-edged question was skeptical of her conclusions.

"Lass is very bright," she informed him. He didn't seem to be taking her research seriously. However, she'd already had several articles published in various parenting magazines. "Most people don't realize how much children absorb before they're able to talk and express themselves coherently."

He nodded and looked again at his sleeping daughter. Molly realized she was lecturing him on the subject. Heat crept up the back of her neck, and she shut up.

Really, she didn't know why she always had this propensity to expound upon a topic until she bored everyone into a stupor. That had been one of her problems in high school and college, her mother had told her.

Her serious nature coupled with strictly average looks hadn't garnered her many boyfriends, although both males and females had regarded her as a friend. People had always come to her for advice. Her teachers had complimented her on being levelheaded.

Glancing at the man seated opposite her, she wished she wasn't quite so pedestrian. If she were more... exotic...maybe he wouldn't be sitting there with his head resting against the back of the booth and his eyes half-closed, studying her as if she were from another planet.

Oh, well. She finished her tea and laid the napkin aside. "I think it's time to go home. I'm tired, too."

He nodded and sat up straighter. He signaled for the check, paid it, then lifted the car seat with the sleeping Lass.

Molly spoke to several couples on the way out, people she recognized from the local church. Sam nodded but spoke to no one. She wasn't surprised.

The local people viewed him with suspicion and, as far as she could see, he made no effort to change their minds about his character.

Some folks said he'd married his wife for her money. Molly didn't believe the rumors. He was too straightforward, too bluntly honest in his dealings with her to be conniving.

Of course she did tend to take the side of the underdog...or outcast, in this case. She didn't tell him that. He wouldn't appreciate the gesture.

Chapter Two

Sam leaned against the window frame, his stance deceptively calm compared to the frustrated rage he felt inside.

"Marriage. That's my best advice," Chuck Nader said.

Sam glanced at the attorney, then back at the busy street below. "What's your second best?"

"Take the kid, leave the area, change your name and go into hiding until she's eighteen."

Sam dismissed the suggestion with an angry snort. This was his and Lass's home. They weren't leaving.

He'd been a drifter for a few years after getting out of school. He'd left the ranch that had been his heritage because of his stepfather. He wasn't about to take to the road again.

When his mother had died, the land had passed to

Sam. He'd returned home and fought his stepfather for possession of the ranch that was rightfully his.

For the past two years, he'd worked hard to pay the taxes and mortgage and get the place back on its feet after his stepfather had drained all the cash he could, using the ranch's money to set himself up in an easy life-style down in Texas. Sam clenched his fists in useless anger.

This land represented his past and his future. He would guard and nurture it. Someday he would pass it on to Lass. He wanted her to grow up on Frazier land, to know her heritage and love it with the same intensity he experienced when he rode over its broad mesas and hidden arroyos.

He cursed aloud, but it didn't relieve the rage.

"Tisdale isn't going to give up easily," the lawyer said. "He needs the money. If he has custody of his grandchild—"

"And the two hundred grand that goes with her," Sam added.

"Right. With that money, he'd be sitting pretty."

"Until he ran through it the way he did with his wife's inheritance." Sam ran a hand over his face, feeling the utter frustration of trying to deal with the situation.

It looked as if he was going to be involved in another legal battle. He was in charge of Lass and her trust fund. He'd set up the blasted thing for her.

His former father-in-law fancied himself as a wheeler-dealer. Mostly he was a loser. He'd gone through all the money he could get his hands on. Now he wanted Lass's fortune.

Over Sam's dead body.

Sometimes he worried it might come to that. William Tisdale was getting desperate. Two hundred thousand dollars would go a long way toward relieving his worries. The Tisdale land was mortgaged to the hilt. Tisdale assumed the Frazier ranch was, too. It wasn't, thanks to Sam's depleted savings.

Sam cursed again. "I feel so damned trapped."

"Marriage is the best way out," Chuck reminded him. "My sister said she saw you and the nursery schoolteacher at the truck stop Friday night. The woman is perfect. I couldn't have picked a better candidate if you'd asked me."

"Molly," Sam said.

"What?"

"Her name is Molly."

The attorney hooked a leg over the arm of his executive chair and grinned. "Yeah. Molly Clelland. As I said—she's one hundred percent perfect. The minute you're married to her, Tisdale won't have a leg to stand on if he takes this to court. Her reputation is impeccable. Half the county would testify on her behalf. And yours...if you're married to her."

"I haven't touched a penny of Lass's money, not a red cent. There's no way he can say I'm a fortune hunter...or an unfit father. I don't even look at women, much less bring any home. Tisdale hasn't a chance of winning, not based on the truth."

Sam paced the narrow space between window and the chair he'd sat in briefly when he'd arrived to discuss the charges being threatened against him by his wife's father.

His father-in-law had accused him of wasting Lass's inheritance. An out-and-out lie. The old man had also implied he had evidence that Sam was an "unfit father."

Such talk had scared him. While he knew he loved Lass and would defend her from harm with every drop of blood in his body, he also knew evidence to the contrary could be fabricated against him. He remembered reading about a case in which a man had been convicted of child abuse and imprisoned for three years before it was found to be a false charge by a vengeful ex-wife.

That was one of the reasons he'd put Lass in Molly Clelland's nursery school at his attorney's urging. The respected teacher could see that Lass was a healthy, happy baby who showed no signs of abuse or neglect. He intended to see that she stayed that way. Give Lass to his lying s.o.b. of a father-in-law? No way.

"All right," he said as if facing the firing squad.

Chuck looked amazed. "You'll marry her?"

Sam set his hat on his head grimly. "I'll think about it," he said, mainly to get the attorney off his case.

"Listen, I'll have my wife invite the two of you over for dinner so you can see what married life is all about." The attorney paused to laugh. "I'll tell Janice she can't nag or scold me while you and the teacher are there."

"Sounds like real married bliss," Sam scoffed.

Chuck grinned secretively. "Oh, it is. You'll find out." He became serious. "Call me before you do anything drastic. We'll have to work out the prenuptial agreement first. Okay?"

"Sure." When he thought about marriage, Sam got a smothery feeling in his chest.

He'd thought he was in love with Elise, but it wasn't

long after their marriage that he'd realized she'd married him to spite her father. Marriage to him had been her final rebellion against the old man. Within six months, she'd been restless and ready to move on... until she'd found out she was pregnant. Then she'd been as mad as hell at *him*.

When he'd reminded her it took two to produce a child and she sure as hell had been a willing partner in their marriage bed, she'd screeched like a fury. Six months later, she'd died during the birth—a stroke induced by the high blood pressure caused by the birthing process. He'd watched helplessly during the ordeal.

The doctor had explained about the weakness in the wall of the blood vessel, that the stroke could have happened at anytime and, in fact, would have happened sooner or later without the pregnancy. The explanation hadn't relieved Sam's guilt. He'd been the one who'd insisted she go ahead and have the child.

And now his father-in-law was out for his blood. And his child. Lordy, how complicated life got.

He was tired of hassles and legal wrangling. He was tired of people looking at him suspiciously as Tisdale spread lies about his marrying Elise for her money. He was tired of worrying all the time.

He had placed all of his wife's money, including the life insurance, into an irrevocable trust for Lass. However, irrevocable trusts could be broken if a person knew the right lawyers and judges. And Tisdale knew them all.

With that rustling episode from his past, Sam figured the odds were against him. If his father-in-law had his way, he would be in prison for his wife's death. As it was, the man was doing everything in his power to make life miserable.

Sam clenched a fist. Let Tisdale get his hands on sweet, innocent Lass? Never.

Marriage wasn't something he looked forward to, not even for Lass and God knows, he'd do anything for his child, short of murder. Marriage might be the only way.

"Think about it," Chuck advised, sympathy in his gaze, his manner serious once more.

That his attorney looked upon the threat from his father-in-law with misgivings scared Sam even more than the scenarios he'd already formed in his own mind. To lose Lass, the one good thing in his life… It didn't bear thinking about.

"Yeah, right." Sam headed for the door after giving his lawyer and friend a wave.

Downstairs, he sat in his truck, his brain in a whirl of half thoughts and plans. It was Wednesday. He'd called Molly and told her he was coming in for lunch today and would take Lass for her doctor's appointment afterward. She'd sounded pleased.

He tried to picture marriage to her. The image wouldn't come. She was Lass's teacher, a nice, neat, sort of preachy little woman, but not his type.

Although she did have the most marvelous eyes— gray and lucid, like a mist off the mountain.

He paused and envisioned those cool eyes gazing up at him in the heat of passion. To his surprise, his body stirred. Well, hell, he wasn't dead, after all, but…marriage?

It was the last thing he wanted to think about. Besides, why would she want a down-at-the-heels rancher and another woman's kid to take care of? Shaking his head, he turned the key and headed for the church.

Marriage? Surely there was another way.

"I couldn't believe it when my mother told me you were there with Sam Frazier," Tiffany said. She rolled her big blue eyes heavenward before focusing on her boss once more.

Molly and Tiffany were resting while the children ate their lunch. It was one of the few quiet times they had during the day and a welcome break for them.

Molly swallowed a bite of turkey sandwich, then turned to her helper. "What's so odd about it? He took me to dinner because he was late again and wanted to get back in my good graces. After all, we run the best nursery school in the state."

Her smile was composed and calm. Over the past five days, she'd reasoned away the fantasies induced by the dinner...and the strange desire to kiss his neck and snuggle her face in the black springy hairs showing above the V of his shirt collar.

"Well, of course we do," Tiffany said in a "that goes without saying" tone. "It's just that...well, watch out for him is all I can tell you. I've heard things..." Her voice trailed off in warning.

"What things?" Molly took another bite of sandwich.

"About him and his wife." Tiffany stared into the middle distance with a frown of concentration. "I went to school with Elise Tisdale."

Molly wanted to ask a hundred questions about the

woman, but she refrained. It wasn't any of her business.

"She was very popular. You know how some girls have this way about them, as if they were born knowing everything? She was like that—knowing and sexy and beautiful."

She would be, Molly thought, refusing to let the information send her into the doldrums.

"In a wild sort of way." Tiffany finished her comments thoughtfully.

"Oh?"

"She skipped school a lot and was sort of, like radical, if you know what I mean."

"Actually I don't," Molly said, avid with curiosity about the woman he'd married. She imagined him looking at his wife in that sweet, fierce, loving way he showed only to his child.

"She hated anyone telling her what to do. Sometimes she'd do things—chew gum in class, smoke in the rest room—just to show the teachers she could. And she always drove like the devil was on her heels. The rest of us admired and envied her. We wanted to be like her, but few of us had her daring."

"I always obeyed the rules," Molly admitted.

"Me, too." Tiffany sighed. "I guess we were a couple of stick-in-the-muds. Or is it sticks-in-the-mud?"

"Either way you're probably right." Molly met her friend's eyes, and they both laughed. "There are worse things to be, I'm sure."

"Yeah, but nobody's thought of 'em yet. I would have given my eyeteeth to be the daring, devil-may-care person Elise was. It was such a shock when I heard she'd died. She wasn't even my friend, but it was like a light going out. I mean, she'd been so vibrant and all. I couldn't imagine anything snuffing out that spark of...of wildness she possessed.''

''I understand,'' Molly said, remembering the girls like that in her own high school and college classes. They were self-assured, their stride confident as they whizzed through life and love, doing what they wanted, often getting by on charm.

Molly'd been smart, but then she'd always loved books and reading. She was a natural as a student, given her quiet, reserved ways. She wasn't a great beauty and wit like her mother, who'd been the most popular girl in her class.

''We all have different talents and virtues,'' she added for Tiffany's sake. ''You're wonderful with the children.''

''Because you've taught me so much. Every child we accept seems to be a genius after six months under your care. I don't know how you do it.''

''It isn't me. I merely try to bring out the child's natural curiosity and channel it.'' She stopped and sighed. ''Don't get me started. You know how I am.''

Tiffany nodded and rolled her eyes again. ''Do I ever!''

They were still smiling when Sam Frazier walked in the door. ''I came for lunch,'' he announced.

Sam felt like a fool. It was obvious he was way too late for the meal. The kids had eaten and were napping now. The two teachers were finished, too.

''Looks like I'm too late,'' he muttered, trying to get himself out of this gracefully. ''Actually I came to take Lass to the doctor.''

Molly stood. "You're not too late. We're having turkey sandwiches today. Would you like one or two?"

"Uh, one." He took his hat off and stood in front of the door, not sure what to do.

"Join us," the other woman invited, indicating a seat at the desk.

"Thanks, Tiffany." He glanced toward the swing where Lass slept peacefully, then looked at Molly.

"I'll only be a minute," she told him, giving him a pleasant smile. She hurried to a little alcove at the side of the room and began preparing a lunch for him.

He hung his hat on a hook and took the regular-size chair behind the desk. The rest of the chairs in the room were scaled for the children, including the two Molly and the other teacher used. He was glad he didn't have to sit in one of those. He'd have probably broken it.

Feeling like an oversize Goldilocks, he settled into the chair and watched Molly's efficient moves. She wore calf-length gray slacks that were full like a skirt and a red sweater. She looked as chipper as a robin.

With the overhead light shining on her face, he noticed how smooth and delicate her complexion was. A man would have to be careful not to mar that skin when they made love. He looked away.

The other teacher was watching him with open curiosity. He felt the heat creep up his neck. She frowned as she glanced from Molly to him. A subtle shifting of her features indicated her suspicions of his motives.

Ha, if she only knew what his attorney had proposed, she'd probably be warning Molly away from him at that very moment!

He gave the woman a slow, deliberately bland smile that didn't tell her a thing. He didn't care what the people of the town thought of him. He'd written them off years ago when no one, including his mother, had believed his stepfather was stealing from the ranch.

No, he wasn't going to marry again. He couldn't believe he'd even considered it. He'd tried once and it had been pure hell for the most part.

However, he figured if he was seen with Molly, if people realized they were friends and she trusted him, well, that ought to be as good as marrying, but without the complications.

When Molly returned, he thanked her for the meal as she set a plate containing a turkey sandwich and various vegetable sticks before him. There were also three potato chips.

"That's all that were left," she said apologetically.

"It's plenty. Sorry to barge in on you so late."

"No problem. I'm delighted that you could join us. We usually eat around eleven-thirty since the children are hungry by then." She placed a paper cup of lemonade by his plate.

He was reminded of his elementary days at a country school near the ranch. They'd had to carry their lunches since the school didn't have a cafeteria.

Glancing at Molly, his thoughts traveled far from his own school days. He'd caught a whiff of some light cologne when she'd leaned forward to place his meal on the desk. Suddenly he wanted to nuzzle along her neck and discover exactly where she dabbed the floral scent.

Damn Chuck for his crazy ideas!

He forced his attention to the sandwich, which had

cranberry sauce rather than mayonnaise spread over the bread. It moistened the turkey and added a tangy taste to the meal.

"This is good," he told Molly.

"I'm glad you like it."

Her smile was one of approval, and he experienced a surge of pride as if he'd done something especially nice in complimenting her on the food.

He noticed her teeth were very straight. Probably braces as a kid. Everything about her bespoke neatness and wholesomeness, of the mind as well as the body. She'd probably be shocked at some of his thoughts.

"Lass was very good this morning, but she'll probably be cranky this afternoon," Molly told him.

He looked at her in question.

"She'll have the last of her shots today and may run a fever as a result. Ask the doctor about giving her some baby acetaminophen when you put her to bed tonight."

"I will," he promised. He cleared his throat, then glanced at Tiffany.

She immediately rose. "I've...um, got things to do." She disappeared into a room at the back of the school.

Sam finished the lemonade and cleared his throat. "Would you like to go to a movie Friday night?"

Molly gave him a blank look and didn't answer.

He tried again. "Over in Roswell there's a movie that got good reviews. It's about a teacher in Australia. I thought you might like it."

"Well, actually I have plans. The literary club is having a potluck dinner at my house. A local writer is going to be our speaker. Would you like to attend?"

"Yes."

She seemed taken aback at his quick acceptance. He was a little shocked, too, he realized. But if they were to become friends, it was a beginning. Satisfied that his plan was in progress, he smiled.

So did she.

Her mouth trembled a bit at the corners. He noticed her lips were evenly balanced between the upper and lower one and that her mouth was a little wide. Her face reminded him of a cat with its small, pointed chin and flaring cheekbones.

He wanted to taste her, to see if her lips were as soft as they looked…

"It's at six-thirty. You don't have to bring anything. I mean, I'll have plenty. I'm going to bake a ham."

"That sounds good." He stood. "I guess I'd better get Lass on down to the doctor's office. I hate to wake her, though."

He retrieved his daughter from the swing. She opened her eyes, grinned at him, then laid her head on his shoulder and went back to sleep. He felt the familiar tug in his chest at her trust in him.

Molly held the door for him to go out. "Are you going to bring Lass back this afternoon?"

"If you don't mind. I have some errands in town. I thought I would do those this afternoon, then pick her up when I finish."

"That will be fine."

She closed the door after him. After strapping Lass into her seat, he glanced back at the nursery. Molly stood at the door, watching him with a curious expression on her face. He wondered what she was thinking. Probably questioning his motives in asking her out Friday night.

He leapt into the truck and drove off. For the first time in months, he felt something like peace inside. With Molly as his friend, he and Lass would be okay. Friday night he would start a campaign to become the very best friend she'd ever had.

Molly frowned at the empty road. Sam Frazier was late. She sighed and settled into the rocking chair.

"This little piggy went to market," she said, wiggling Lass's fingers as she quoted the nursery rhyme.

The baby gurgled with laughter when she finished with an exaggerated "wee-wee-wee all the way home."

"Ah, what a doll you are," she murmured.

Sometimes when she thought of being thirty-two and not being married, regret would set in. She felt a flutter of it now. She might never have a child, never hold a baby of her own, never have the warm companionship her parents shared so joyfully.

She hadn't thought of the future in those terms in a long time. Until recently. Until Sam and Lass Frazier had come into her life.

Recalling Tiffany's description of Sam's late wife, she smiled at her musings. While she wasn't a knock-out, a couple of men had been interested in her in college, but there'd been no spark. No male had ever enticed her into the mating dance.

She wasn't the only one. Twenty-two percent of the American population never married, if she remembered the statistics correctly. Wedded bliss didn't appeal to everyone. She'd chosen her own path, and most of the time she was content.

The wind blew around the corner of the building, a mournful sound that brought the hair up on the back of her neck.

Where *was* Sam Frazier?

He arrived at ten to six, rushing in on a gust of wind, looking handsomely disheveled. He removed his hat and smoothed his hair. "Sorry. My errands took longer than I expected. I brought Chinese." He held out a white bag.

His grin was so engaging, Molly found she couldn't stay mad at him. "If that's an apology, I accept. I'm starved."

"Me, too." He spread the feast on the desk, then took Lass while Molly washed her hands and was seated.

"I fed Lass her supper at five-thirty," she told him. She spread a "busy" mat on the floor that had mirrors and rattles attached to it. "Put her on the mat. She likes to play there."

He put the baby on her stomach and watched her tug at a huge button before putting it in her mouth for a taste. Molly watched the play of emotion in his eyes before he turned to her.

She let him have the teacher's chair while she sat on a tall stool. He loaded up a paper plate with chow mein, fried rice and a chicken dish, then handed it to her.

"No sweet-and-sour pork or Mandarin beef," he said pointedly. "I remember you ate chicken last week and frowned upon my steak."

She was embarrassed at being so obvious. "I didn't realize I looked so disapproving."

"Very schoolmarmish," he told her solemnly. His eyes filled with amusement, and she realized he was teasing.

It was so startling, like standing by a statue that suddenly started speaking. "You have a sense of humor," she exclaimed.

He nodded and swallowed before speaking. "I guess I haven't been very cheerful lately. Things have been tough."

"On the ranch?"

"Well, there, too, but mostly with my father-in-law."

Molly shifted uncomfortably, recalling Tiffany's gossip about his deceased wife. She gave him a sympathetic smile.

He seemed to take that as encouragement. "He thinks he'd be better at taking care of Lass than I am."

She was shocked. "I don't. Lass is one of the happiest, healthiest babies I've ever seen."

"I'm glad to hear you say that." He ate in silence for a minute, then looked up at her from under the dark slashes of his eyebrows in that intriguing way he had. "Would you say it in court if we needed you to?"

She stared at him, wondering if there was trouble here that she didn't know about. Slowly she nodded.

"Would you?" He pressed on, his gaze intensifying.

"I wouldn't have said it if I didn't think it true."

He heaved a sigh of relief. "It won't come to court,

not if I can prevent it, but my attorney suggested I line up my best shots. Just in case."

"Of course."

His eyes took on a warmth she'd never seen in them. They seemed to deepen as he stared into her eyes as if looking into the farthest recesses of her soul. She sat very still.

"Has Mr. Tisdale tried to take Lass from you?" she asked.

"He's working on it. He has a private detective following me around." Sam shook his head. "As if I wouldn't realize it. Around here, the man stands out like a crow among sparrows."

She laughed at his comparison. "Both of which are nuisance birds," she said pointedly. "Is that your opinion of people in general or the ones around here in particular?"

He smiled, and she was enchanted.

"Not all people," he murmured. "Some people are okay." He looked straight at her. "Very much okay."

Flutters raced from her throat to her stomach and back. Heavens, if she felt this way at an implied compliment, she'd probably faint if he so much as touched her...if he kissed her.

She drew back from the idea. A couple of dinners together did not constitute a raging affair. At best, maybe a tepid friendship. All right, a growing friendship, she decided, liking the way his eyes kept going to her lips when she spoke.

He wanted to kiss her. She was certain of it. Well, almost certain. He was staring at her mouth.

Which meant she probably had a grain of rice sticking to her lip. She wiped her mouth with a napkin.

"The groundhog saw his shadow, so we'll have six more weeks of winter," he told her. "Personally I'm ready for some sun and balmy skies. I've been mending fences so I can move the cattle to new pasture. It's hell working outside in a cold rain."

"You need a warmer coat. I've noticed you never wear anything heavier than that denim jacket." She pressed her lips firmly together and shut up. She didn't need to lecture him as if she were his mother.

"I wear a ski jacket and a rain slicker on the ranch. They're too bulky in the truck, so I switch to come to town."

"That's good." Oh, heavens, she sounded so stuffy. Her family was right. She was a throwback to some other era.

He spooned out another plate of food for himself after offering her seconds, which she refused.

"Tell me about your ranch," she said invitingly. "Does it have a name?"

"It's called Diablo Mesa Ranch." He studied her for a moment before he continued. "It's on the El Camino del Diablo."

"The Devil's Highway?" she mused. "What's it like?" She pictured a barren, hardscrabble place.

"It's the most beautiful place on earth." His expression softened the way it did when he looked at his daughter. "The ranch lies along the Pecos, so we have running water all year."

She altered her image to a lush, green valley.

"We're on a high, flat mesa—"

"What is a mesa?" she interrupted him to ask. "I mean, is it a mountain or what? Some people have said it is. Others told me it isn't."

"It's the flat-topped part that's left when the rest of a plateau erodes." He made a broad, sweeping gesture with one hand. "This area was once a tableland that was shoved into a tilt sloping from the northwest to the southeast when the Rockies thrust their way up through the earth's crust. Erosion has cut gullies and ravines through it. Mesas form where a harder layer, such as cap rock, protects that section of the plateau from the weathering effects of rain and wind."

"Ah," she murmured in understanding.

"The ranch house sits on a rise above the mesa. From it, you can see eternity—" He halted abruptly, as if he'd said too much.

He had shared part of himself with her, she realized. He knew and understood the land as keenly as any geologist. More than that, he had a vision within himself of the land, with him a part of it. This place was home to him as it was to her.

"Do you have gullies and ravines?" she asked softly.

"Yes. They're mostly dry washes—arroyos, the Spanish settlers called them. I've dammed some of them on my land to form ponds, but they go dry a couple of times a year, so it isn't a dependable source of water."

"I see."

At her interest, he expounded on the land and what he'd like to do someday "when I strike oil or a gold mine."

She smiled at his wry crack.

"You have a nice smile," he said, startling her.

"Thank you."

"You should smile more."

"So should you," she responded in her usual tart way. She clamped down on the inside of her lip. A lecture wasn't the way to a man's heart.

A stillness came over her while she contemplated the question that leapt into her mind. Was she aiming for his heart?

No, of course not. It was just a thought.

Chapter Three

Molly pushed the cat out of the way with her foot and checked off the items on her mental list—ham, rolls from a local bakery, freshly made cookies. All was ready for the potluck dinner honoring the local author.

"You've had your dinner," Molly reminded Persnickety, who pressed against her leg and made cat sounds of starvation. "Be nice like your sister. She's not begging for a bite of ham."

Porsche snoozed on the throw rug by the back door.

Molly heard a vehicle in the driveway. She glanced at the ham on the table, then at the black cat with three white whiskers. "I don't trust you," she declared. She ushered both cats out the back, then rushed to the front door.

"Am I too early?" Sam called, climbing out of his truck.

He looked very presentable in dark wool slacks, his usual white shirt—open at the collar, the sleeves rolled up. He carried a bouquet as he came up the flagstone walk.

"No, of course not. Lass will be glad to see you." She'd brought the child home with her after the nursery school closed.

He handed over the gift at the door, then took off his hat as he stepped inside. She watched his gaze take in the small house with its spit-polish shine.

She'd worked all last evening to make sure it was perfect. As if she'd wanted to impress him. For a second, while they stood there, suspended between one moment and the next, she tried to analyze her feelings. She shook her head hopelessly.

"Lass is in the kitchen," she told him, leading the way.

She was aware of him following close behind. His after-shave drifted on the air, mingling with the tiny dabs of perfume she'd put behind her ears.

All her senses seemed heightened. She felt the silky swish of her dress against her stockings. Her friends from high school and college had all told her she had nice legs...really nice legs. The blue silk dress, a gift from her mother, cleared her knees by an inch or more.

Spinster tries to seduce cowboy, she mocked. As if that would be possible. She hadn't a sexy bone in her body.

Sam hung his hat on an old-fashioned highboy and followed her into the kitchen. "Smells good in here," he murmured.

Soaking up the flavor of the place—the aroma of home-cooked food, the lemony scent that bespoke cleanliness and a tantalizing whiff of mingled cologne, soap and powder that shouted *woman* to his starved senses, he realized how bare his own life had grown.

For a second, he imagined this was his home, all clean and shining, his dinner, hot on the stove, his wife and child, eager to welcome him with smiles and kisses.

He took a step forward... A babble of sound from Lass kept him from making a fool of himself. He changed his direction and headed for the playpen.

"Hello, sweetheart," he said, scooping Lass up and tossing her toward the sky.

She squealed in delight. "Da, Da, Da, Da," she said.

"Da-da," he encouraged. "That's me, your old man. I'm the boss and don't you forget it, young lady."

Lass pulled his nose.

"Hey," he scolded and dodged the moist tug.

He glanced across the tiny kitchen. Molly was watching them, a gleam of approval in her eyes. A smile glazed her lips.

Her mouth looked soft and inviting. A rosy pink shine indicated lipstick. He realized she'd rarely worn any on the days when he dropped Lass off at school. Odd, he'd never missed it on her.

His wife had used a lot of makeup and had looked pale without it. She hadn't liked for him to "muss" her up. The sure knowledge came to him that Molly didn't have those vanities. His glance strayed down her slender curves.

Molly was aware of his perusal with every nerve

ending in her body. She busied herself with the flowers.

She knew he was looking at the sheer black stockings she'd worn with three-inch evening pumps. Somewhat irritated by her own vanity, she wondered if women teetered around on high heels to indicate they'd like to be swept off their feet.

That was obviously the last thought on her guest's mind. He hugged his child to his chest with a protective arm under her bottom and a hand on her back and continued talking to her.

"Hi, how's my girl?" he questioned in a soft voice.

Lass clicked her tongue at him. He laughed and clicked back at her. When he glanced up and saw Molly watching, he looked sort of sheepish.

"I took her riding with me a couple of weeks ago," he said. "She heard me click my tongue to the mare and has been doing it ever since then."

"Yes, babies are great mimics."

"Guess I'd better tell the spring roundup crew to watch their language from now on."

"I thought roundups were in the fall when ranchers sold their cattle."

"I hire on a couple of extra men to help with the branding and all. They usually stay until after the cattle are sold."

"I see. Then you're alone the rest of the year?" She thought of him on the ranch, alone during one of the blizzards they occasionally had.

"Yes."

"I'm sure it's beautiful, but isn't it lonely?"

"No."

Her eyes met his at the quick, harsh denial. Their

gazes locked and wouldn't let go as they engaged in some primal clash that shifted her equilibrium. A knotty sensation settled in her throat as she wondered wildly what he was thinking.

Lass's head, with its soft wisps of cottony curls, bobbed against Sam's chin, severing the unexpected tension that had leapt to life between them.

Full of nervous energy, Molly busied herself filling a vase half-full of water, adding two tablets as a preservative and poking the bouquet of daisies into it. She placed the flowers on the table behind the platter of ham.

The bright yellow blossoms looked nice against the earthy red of the tablecloth.

"Still life with ham," she said, standing back so Sam could admire the effect. She glanced at him. The moment of awareness between them when she'd mentioned the loneliness of the ranch might never have been.

She drew a calming breath. "I think I hear the others arriving. Shall we go into the living room?" She glanced back over her shoulder. "Lass has had her supper, so she should be okay until bedtime. Do you give her a bottle then?"

"Uh, yes." He looked up.

His attention had been on her legs. A light fluttering invaded her middle. She was intensely aware of her short skirt, the silky dress...the heat that tumbled out of some place inside her as if the door to a furnace had been opened.

Most of the literary club arrived together. "Come in," she invited the preacher and his wife.

Mrs. Liscomb checked on the threshold, causing her

husband to stumble over her. The knot of people behind them halted.

"Do all of you know Sam Frazier?" Molly asked, standing back so her guests could get a clear view of him standing behind her.

Aubry Liscomb's jaw actually dropped open. "Sam Frazier," she echoed.

Sam watched surprise segue into animosity from several of the locals, the ones who'd lived in the community when he'd left and had still been there when he returned. Old resentment welled up in him, hot and churning. The residents had always been a bunch of sanctimonious hypocrites as far as he was concerned. They hadn't changed a damn bit—

Molly took his hand, forcing him to step forward and acknowledge her guests. He sliced her a glance and saw the expectation in her eyes.

He sighed internally. The prissy little teacher expected her guests to be on their best behavior... including him. He clasped her hand tightly when she would have removed it. He'd be nice if it killed him, but he deserved a reward for the effort. Touching her was it.

"Evening, Mrs. Liscomb, Reverend," he said.

"Evening, Sam," the preacher said. He gave his wife a gentle push from behind. She mumbled a greeting and stepped into the room. Sidled was more like it, as if she'd be attacked if she got too close.

Sam forced a smile on his face. He wanted Molly for a friend. That meant he'd have to accept these people, too. He let go of her hand reluctantly so she could perform her duties as hostess. When the guest of honor arrived, he moved back to her side, standing close so that she was aware of him. He smiled at her startled glance, then spoke to the man whose book had won some prize or other; he remembered reading about it in the paper. He laid his hand at the back of her waist.

Molly felt warm the rest of the evening and didn't catch more than one word in three of the guest speaker's lecture on the terrible state of American art and government funding for it. Sam's eyes were often on her, a quiet watchfulness in the rich dark depths.

A quietness grew in her, too, as if she were waiting...

Lass slept peacefully in the playpen in the study off Molly's living room. Sam stood watching her from the doorway, his thoughts on other matters.

He couldn't believe the evening had gone so quickly. He'd actually enjoyed some of it. Except when that windbag writer had held Molly's hand for a long time at the door while he told her what a delightful time he'd had. The man was interested in Molly. That much was clear.

Sam frowned in irritation. His carefully constructed plans didn't allow for outside interference.

Another problem was Molly herself.

She'd thrown him for a loop when she'd opened the door and invited him inside. Gone was the schoolteacher who handed out advice on child rearing or one's manners. In her place...God, in her place was a stunning woman.

He closed his eyes. Soft. That was the impression she gave—a delicate softness that made a man want to reach out and stroke that smooth skin, those flyaway wisps of hair.

Yeah, but he knew only too well how fast a woman could change from a sweet, ethereal creature—loving and clinging and making a man want her so bad he'd forsake the world—and turn into a shouting fury that made him want to crawl into a hole and not come out till hell froze over.

"Well, that was the last of them." Molly's voice cut into his musing. "It went well, didn't it?"

"Yes."

She bent over the makeshift crib. "Ah, the sleep of the innocent. Lass is such a good baby, not a peep out of her about sleeping in a strange place."

Her soft voice whispered over him like a caress. Her light brown hair fell over her shoulders in a silky cloud. Her skirt hiked up to expose an enticing bit of black-clad thigh as she gazed down at the sleeping child.

He looked away and stared out the window until his blood settled down again. It had been over a year since he'd made love with a woman. His marriage had gone from wild passion to cold fury in a few short months. Abstinence had to be what had sparked this crazy desire he had for his daughter's teacher.

That and his attorney's urging him to marry her. Molly, the intelligent little prude, would probably be shocked at the thoughts that had run through his mind all evening.

She straightened and turned to him. "Would you like to leave her for the night? I have enough diapers. There's an extra outfit in the diaper bag and I can run over to the nursery for more food."

"No, I'd rather take her home."

He doubted he would sleep a wink if Lass wasn't snug in her own bed. He had a need to know she was nearby, safe and sound. The problems with his former father-in-law had made him paranoid where his daughter was concerned.

"But thanks for offering," he added belatedly, realizing how harsh he'd sounded.

She smiled graciously. "Here, wrap her in the blanket. You can return it Monday when you bring her in."

He nodded in thanks, the sense of well-being he'd experienced at odd moments all evening returning. He liked Molly Clelland, he realized.

She was a bossy woman, like most teachers, and yet she wasn't. She gave choices and coupled them with instructions in such a way that a person automatically did what she said. He found her presence soothing…for the most part, except when his libido kicked up.

They walked down the hall. He retrieved his hat and jammed it onto his head. At the door, he paused. "Listen, my attorney wanted to know if we'd like to have dinner with him and his wife sometime. How about tomorrow night?"

"I'm busy then," she said and looked regretful.

He wondered if she was saying that to make it seem as if she had lots of dates. His wife had done that. Molly's next words assured him she wasn't playing a game with him.

"Perhaps next weekend? I have both Friday and Saturday free." Her eyes held no hint of subterfuge.

"Right," he said, relieved that she hadn't turned

him down. "I'll check on the day and time and get back to you."

"Fine." She stood by the door and held it open for him.

He shifted Lass from one shoulder to the other. A moment dragged by. A question appeared in her eyes.

"I had a nice time tonight," he finally said. "Thanks for having me." He stepped out into the night.

"It was a pleasure," she called after him. He heard the smile in her voice, then she closed the door against the chilly night air, and he was left out in the cold.

In the truck, after fastening Lass in her seat, he drove off quickly, feeling like an utter fool. For a moment there, he'd considered kissing Molly good-night.

She would have probably fainted or slapped him. No, she would have given him a lecture on propriety or manners or some such fool thing.

He smiled, a soft feeling stealing over him. Lass stirred and clicked her tongue in her sleep and settled again. The smile evaporated, and his thoughts returned to practicalities.

He wanted Molly for his friend, not his lover, he reminded himself. Once the sex wore off, men and women didn't remain friends—at least not in his experience. He needed her friendship.

The idea gave him pause. He didn't think he'd ever been friends with a woman before. It was a different concept.

Sure, he'd been friendly with girls while growing up and with some women he'd known. But being friendly and being friends seemed two different things.

A friend, he repeated. For some reason, it made him feel good deep inside.

Molly stifled a yawn. "Janice and Chuck are nice," she said. She and Sam had met the other couple in Roswell where they'd gone to dinner and a movie. "Have you known him long?"

She rested her head on the back of the seat and observed Sam's face from the glow of the pickup's dashlights. A terrible clenching in the vicinity of her heart worried her. She felt it each time she saw Sam, which was to say, every day.

"Only for a couple of years."

"Since you've been back home?"

"Yes. He was new in the area and an outsider." Sam cast her a glance before concentrating on the road once more.

"Like me."

"Like me," he corrected. "He's from back east. He married a local girl and settled here about the same time I returned."

"You were born here," she said pointedly.

"But I was gone for twelve years. Before that, I had a reputation for wildness."

"Did you deserve it?"

"Maybe. I drove fast. I acted tough. And I didn't like taking orders."

"Especially from your stepfather."

She saw his hands tighten on the steering wheel, then relax. "Yeah, especially from him. He waltzed into our lives six months after my father died and took over. Thought he was J. R. Ewing."

"You resented his taking your father's place. That's

natural. Obviously he didn't win your trust or friendship."

"He was eight years younger than my mother and looking for the main chance. I hear he's courting a rich oil widow in her sixties down in Texas. Should I warn her he has a way of moving money from a joint account to one in his name only?" His tone was hard and cynical.

Molly made a sympathetic sound. She knew more about his past now, thanks to Tiffany and the pastor's wife. They had both warned her about becoming involved with Sam.

The preacher's wife had taught Sam in high school. "A smart boy, sailed through school making *A*'s and *B*'s without cracking a book. But he had an attitude. Very independent. Hated taking orders from anyone. Caused trouble at home."

Molly knew it was gossip, but she'd listened anyway.

"He hated his stepfather, who was a charming man by all accounts. However, I didn't know him. They weren't churchgoing people, you know. The ranch belonged to Sam, but his mother had the use of it for her lifetime. That might have caused trouble. Gives a young person too much sense of his own self to come into an inheritance too early."

"Sam isn't like that," Molly had said.

"There wasn't much money, I understand. The Tisdale girl had money from her grandmother. He married her within a few months of moving back to these parts."

"Because he loved her," Molly said softly, knowing it was true. "He married her for love."

The preacher's wife sniffed in disdain. "All the men wanted her. She was like a cat, a wild one, racing around in a little red car like she owned the road. She and the Frazier boy were two of a kind. Some say he didn't want the baby and tried to make her get rid of it."

Molly was shocked and furious, but she didn't show it. She assumed an innocent expression. "But we know Sam better than that, don't we? Isn't it amazing how gossip gets started and spreads without any base whatsoever?" she asked.

Mrs. Liscomb had had the grace to blush.

As well she should, Molly thought indignantly. No wonder it was so easy to plant suspicion about a person when people who should know better perpetuated the stories.

"Something bothering you?" he asked. "You huffed as if you'd just thought of something that made you mad," he added when she looked at him in surprise.

Molly relaxed. During the time she'd been seeing Sam, she'd often been amazed by his perceptiveness. "I was thinking about how gossip gets started and how it lingers."

"People been telling you to stay away from me?"

She straightened. "Sometimes you scare me. You seem to read my mind."

"You're very open and honest in your relationships and emotions. Sometimes that scares *me*."

Laughter bubbled out of her at the thought of this man being scared of anything, much less her.

"I like it when you laugh," he murmured. "It makes me think that all is right with the world."

Her world was very much all right. She'd been happy these past four weeks. She loved her work, a handsome man was interested in her, what more could she want?

"The world can be a nice place."

"Maybe."

"If we don't let our troubles overwhelm us."

"A little pep talk, teacher?"

She smiled. A deep contentment pervaded her. The inside of the truck was comfortable and cozy. The evening had been pleasant. More than pleasant.

When they'd left the movie and stood talking to the attorney and his wife beside their car, Sam had laid his arm casually across her shoulders. She'd linked her hand in his while they finished their conversation and said good-night.

The warmth of his body alongside hers lingered in her memory, causing tingles along her throat and down her chest.

They were growing close, she thought. Sam was more relaxed in her presence. During the four weeks since that first dinner, they'd gone to the truck stop twice more, then to the café in town once for lunch.

Sam hadn't been able to go to the literary meeting this month because of Lass, but he'd brought dinner to the nursery school this past Wednesday. He'd waited at her desk while the other parents picked up their children.

When she'd locked up, they'd gone to her cottage, fed Lass and eaten the roasted chicken dinners he'd brought. He'd left immediately afterward. He hadn't once tried to kiss her. Not ever. Although she'd thought he was thinking strongly about it a couple of times.

It was very confusing.

Sometimes he seemed to be…interested, but at others, it was as if his mind were far away, in another world.

They arrived back at her house shortly before midnight. Tiffany let them in. "Lass is asleep."

"Was she any trouble?" Sam asked.

"Not a bit. She's a doll." She patted back a yawn. "Did you have a good time?"

"Yes, it was a wonderful evening," Molly replied.

Tiffany gave her an assessing look, then flicked her gaze over to Sam. Molly could sense the reservations her friend had about her seeing the rancher outside of school hours, but she said nothing.

Molly would not tolerate any insults to Sam. He had been a perfect gentleman each time they'd been out. Of course, until tonight, Lass had always been with them.

"Good." Tiffany grabbed her coat and purse. "Well, I'll be on my way. Good night."

"I'll walk you out." Sam saw her to her car and on her way.

Molly hung her coat in the hall closet. When Sam returned, she smoothed her sweater down over her slacks, feeling like a teenager whose mother might walk in any minute and find a young man in the house.

"I'll put on some coffee while you check on Lass," she said. "If you'd like."

He nodded and strolled into her bedroom where the playpen was located. Molly hurried to the kitchen. Her hands trembled ever so little while she measured out coffee and water.

Tension gathered in her like a coiled whip. She'd felt it in the air while at dinner. Sam had watched her during the evening with an intensity she hadn't seen since the first time they'd gone to dinner.

She had noticed Chuck Nader, Sam's attorney as well as his friend, giving him a couple of sardonic glances that seemed filled with hidden meaning. Sam had frowned at the man and sent him a warning look.

Footsteps behind her sent a nervous tingle along her throat again. She spun around.

Sam stood a few feet from her. His eyes were almost black in the dim light of the lamp over the table.

She sensed strength in him, and the emotions that he kept clamped inside. She wished she had the key to free them, to let him love again the way he'd once loved.

There was no way she could give him back a happy past, to make his boyhood days the carefree, happy ones he should have had, but his future...

A tremor rushed through her when she realizéd what she was thinking. "The coffee is about ready." She sounded breathless.

He reached out and touched a strand of her hair. "Did you have a good time tonight like you said?"

"Of course."

"Of course," he repeated. "You always tell the truth, don't you?"

She was intensely aware of his hand close to her face, of the way he smoothed the curling strand over and over between his finger and thumb as if judging its quality for some purpose of his own.

"I try."

A ghost of a smile touched his lips and was gone. He released her hair and sighed. "Let's have that coffee, then I have to get home. The day starts early on a ranch."

She poured them each a cup and went to the table. Sam sat opposite her and blew across the hot surface before taking a drink. "You make good coffee."

"Thank you."

"But then, you do everything well."

"Thanks again. I think." She wasn't sure that was a compliment or not. "Do you get tired of tending the ranch? There seems to be so many problems, so many things you can't control, such as the weather, farm prices and all."

"There are times during the winter when I think an inside job would be a good idea." He grinned, then continued in a softer tone. "But when the sage is sweet and the air is balmy, when the sun shines and all the world seems right, then I wouldn't trade it for anything."

She pictured him astride a horse on a high mesa…king of the mountain…and envied him.

It was a curious emotion, envy. She realized it was the sense of oneness he shared with the land that she wanted.

Maybe dating this handsome rancher wasn't the best thing for her. He made her think of things she shouldn't. For example, she wasn't a sensuous person, yet she often thought of touching him. Worse, she couldn't seem to control the longing to do so. It was disconcerting to say the least.

She didn't think Sam was looking for a romantic

attachment. However, the world must be a lonely place after having someone to share it with. A soul could wither and die from the loneliness.

A meow at the door diverted her thoughts. She reached out and turned the kitchen doorknob, letting Porsche, long, black and sleek, into the house. The cat went at once to her food bowl.

"If there's reincarnation, I hope to come back as a cat in your house," Sam told her. "Food, shelter and nary a worry."

"How long would you be satisfied as a pet?" she teased.

"Forever, if I were a cat. Not long as a man. I wouldn't fancy being kept on a leash."

"Perish the thought." She cupped her chin in her hand and leaned her elbow on the table. "I can't see you as a pet."

A flash of emotion appeared and disappeared in his eyes. "No, neither could I."

Chills chased along Molly's arm. He seemed to be speaking of something in his past. She wondered if she dared question him on it, but decided against it. He would tell her what he wanted her to know and nothing more. She'd learned that in the past four weeks.

Porsche finished her meal and leapt into Molly's lap, her purr turned up full blast. Molly stroked the smooth black fur. "Where's your playmate?" she asked the cat.

"There's two of them?" Sam asked.

"Yes. Someone dropped them near here last summer. They were mere babies. I fed them by hand for a few days until they learned to eat on their own.

They're shy and tend to stay out of sight when some-one is in the house.'' She looked up with a smile. ''They've gotten used to you and Lass.''

Sam watched her rub the cat and thought of that pale, slender hand stroking through his hair. His body went on red alert, and heat pooled low in his abdomen. He'd tried not to think of Molly that way this past month. It had been hard.

His adult relationships with women had been based mainly on physical attraction and the need of the mo-ment. Since meeting Molly he'd learned the value of friendship with the opposite sex.

Her viewpoint, her opinions, her understanding of life were different from his. It had been a new expe-rience to explore her sharp, agile mind. Glancing at the clock on the wall, he saw the hour was well past midnight.

He finished the coffee, reluctant to leave this warm, peaceful place. Maybe Molly would invite him as well as Lass to stay the night... He cursed at his wayward libido and stood.

Molly, startled, stood, too. The cat jumped to the floor, meowed with annoyance and walked out of the kitchen with a stately gait.

''I'd better go,'' he said.

She nodded. Her expression was as innocent as Lass's. Molly, for all her degrees in learning, never seemed to realize the times when he was gritting his teeth to control his reactions to her warmth, her scent, her womanly nature.

Tonight she wore dark slacks and a red sweater that hugged her delicate shape like the black nylons had defined her legs at the literary meeting. He wondered how he could ever have thought she was plain.

She wasn't an attention-getter the way his wife had been, but she had a muted vibrancy about her that reminded him of wildflowers in a spring meadow.

"Molly," he said. He heard the deeper register of his voice, the shift into the husky tones of desire. Since he'd stood close to her, his arm over her shoulders while they said good-night to the other couple, he'd wanted to touch her.

Really touch her.

She looked up at him, her eyes shining like a mist backlighted by the sun. The sure knowledge came to him that he was going to kiss her.

For a second his breath hung in his throat. He didn't trust his control with her, and he didn't want to frighten her. Molly was a lady; all his experience had been with a different kind of woman.

He took hold of her shoulders. His hands looked big and rough on her slender form. Her candid gaze, slightly questioning but trusting, affected him in ways he couldn't explain.

Instantly he knew without a doubt the opinionated little schoolmarm had never had a man. She had no idea what he wanted from her, of the mindless lust that could drive a person into equally mindless acts... like marriage.

It almost unnerved him.

He hesitated to pull her close, afraid that he wasn't reading her right. With Elise, it had been no problem. They'd met at a bar in Roswell. One look, one dance and they'd left the place. Elise had been all over him the minute they'd arrived at the ranch. They'd married two months later.

But this was a different time, a different woman. Molly wasn't ruled by her senses or a childish greed for pleasure and fun all the time. He watched in fascination as her tongue stole out and moistened her lips. She was nervous.

A quick kiss, just a taste, that was all he'd take, he assured himself, nothing to alarm the most circumspect of maiden schoolmarms.

He slid his arms around her, carefully, slowly drawing her close. He lowered his head, his gaze on those soft lips that now showed a tendency to tremble. The tenderness he often felt toward Lass washed over him.

To his surprise, he felt her arms lift and come around his shoulders, felt her warmth plaster itself down the length of his body, felt the richness of her generous nature as she accepted his touch.

Heat burst outward in a shower of red sparks behind his closed eyelids. Heaven. This was pure heaven. He didn't want to stop.

Chapter Four

Molly couldn't believe this was happening, that Sam was really going to kiss her, that she was going to let him.

Her eyes widened as he bent toward her and his arms gathered her closer and closer. For a second, during that endless time it took for him to span the distance to her lips, she remembered the kisses she'd experienced in the past.

Her brother had foisted dates on her a few times, buddies who came home from college with him. She generally liked people, and things usually went well until the evening ended.

Those awkward endings. The problem of where the nose went and should she breathe or not. The general sloppiness of kissing, of someone else's moisture on her lips, of sweaty hands raking at her clothing.

She'd found the whole process distasteful and had refused any further help with her love life. She grimaced at the memory.

At her frown, Sam paused. She tensed, afraid all of a sudden that he wasn't going to kiss her, but knowing she wanted him to. She just didn't know why.

After that hesitation, his lips settled on hers as lightly as a butterfly on a thistle. He closed his eyes, and she was left staring at the dark lashes that outlined his eyes. She closed her eyes, too.

She found kissing didn't have to be awkward at all. His kiss was incredibly tender, his lips barely touching hers. He moved from one corner of her mouth to the other. It was so unbearably sweet.

To her surprise, she found herself on tiptoe, wanting to do something more. She wasn't sure what. Those funny tingles that started in her throat and worked their way down her chest whenever she thought of him in a certain way, now slid hotly past her breasts and stomach until they lodged deep in her abdomen.

Her skin became hot, too. And her bones. She melted right into him, needing his arms to keep her standing upright.

Was this the passion of song and poem?

She heard his slight grunt of surprise, then his arms tightened even more. His tongue swept over her lips in a circle, making them tingle in the most delicious way. Her breath moved in and out of her lungs.

Breathing. She realized she was breathing and it felt quite normal. Except she was also quite dizzy.

Lifting her arms, she clung to his broad shoulders. The movement shifted her breasts against him. They beaded up hard and…yes, they tingled, too, like her lips, but different.

So many sensations assaulted her at once—the wonderful strength in his body as he wrapped his arms around her and held her closer than she'd ever been held before, the heady scent of his after-shave mingling with her own perfume that intensified as she became heated, the tantalizing knowledge that there was more to be learned.

''Open your mouth,'' he murmured against her mouth.

She'd seen couples in movies do that. It had embarrassed her, all that ravenous mouthing, as if they were trying to take a bite out of the other person. She crimped her lips together.

He continued to stroke her lips with his tongue, very, very lightly. It tickled. She felt a grin coming on.

He lifted his head and gazed at her from only an inch away. His stare was fathoms deep, but amusement lurked at the corners of his mouth. She felt silly. Really, this was ridiculous.

Finally she couldn't stand it any longer. Her lips softened and parted into a smile. He took advantage. His lips swooped on hers, startling her.

With sure aim, his tongue delved into her mouth.

The effect was shocking. The tingly sensation dipped all the way down into her body. A shiver attacked her as if she had a chill. At the same time, she'd never felt so hot in her life. And her heart was racing, banging away like an engine gone berserk.

His hands stroked down her back, cupped her bottom and lifted her into the cradle of his thighs as he spread his legs. A new awareness attacked her. Of him and the changes in his masculine body. Very, very masculine.

He released her mouth just in time.

"I think I'm going to faint," she managed to whisper.

"No, you're not." He kissed her eyes, her temples, her ears, then down her throat. "It just feels that way."

"For you, too?" She was amazed.

He smiled. "Not quite, teach, but close."

He shifted her slightly, setting the tingles to surging again. She thought the sensations were too strong to be called so simple a name. She just didn't know any other. Then he was kissing her mouth again, and she could no longer keep up with all the things happening to her.

She moaned and cupped his face in her hands, taking the kiss to unbearable depths of pleasure as she answered every thrust of his tongue with hers. She knew this wasn't the ultimate pleasure and wanted more. She squirmed against him.

"Easy," he said. He moved slightly, brushing against her again and again in that throbbing place she had known existed in a clinical way and now discovered in all the carnal joy of the human body.

His hands moved over her back, then one caressed along her side. They weren't sweaty or grabby at all. His every movement gave her pleasure and increased her awareness of delight. It seemed so strange to find this…like a secret garden that had existed right under her nose.

But only this man had opened the gate and invited

her inside. That was the key, she realized vaguely. He coaxed and and teased and playfully guided her along pleasure's path.

It was incredibly wonderful.

Sam fought his own needs. He knew himself to be a physical person. He enjoyed using his body, whether for ranch work or other, more intimate labors. Right now, her needs were more important than satisfying an appetite of his.

He knew he could take her to bed. She was filled with the hunger of their kisses. Every caress of his had been designed to bring her maximum tactile pleasure. He wanted desperately to give her the total fireworks—the explosion of passion that would leave her sated and wondrous as she shared her first experience with a man. It was an odd feeling, one he couldn't recall ever having before. And he couldn't do it. It wouldn't be fair.

Knowing he wouldn't, couldn't take this all the way didn't stop him from wanting to, or from taking a little more of her before he was forced to stop.

He caressed the lean line of her torso, moving up and up…a bit more…ah, the perfection of it.

Her breast fit his hand. It was fuller than he'd expected, but then she didn't wear her clothing so snug that every curve was visible. With this woman, there were surprises. He wanted to discover all of them.

Only half-conscious of what he was doing, he skimmed down the red sweater, under it and back up to that perfect mound.

When she gasped, he drew back a little. She opened her eyes and stared at him, dazed, limpid and aflame with the passion he'd given her. He waited, wondering if she'd tell him to back off. It was even odds she'd never let a man touch her this way.

She didn't speak, but stood there as if waiting for him to guide her. Passion was new to her, and she didn't know what he expected. She didn't even know exactly what she wanted.

He did.

With a groan, he shoved the soft knit of the sweater out of the way and dipped his head to her breast. Through the satiny material of her bra, he found the hard peak and rubbed it with his lips, then took the succulent tip into his mouth.

He felt the passion claim her once more. She locked her arms around his neck and ran her fingers through his hair. Her breath came quickly as he sucked her.

With one hand, he unfastened the back clasp and the material slid upward. He pushed it out of the way and his mouth met flesh—warm, sweet, woman flesh. He nibbled hungrily at the delicate pink tip.

When she arched against him, they nearly lost their balance. He turned and braced against the wall, using its support to keep them upright for he, too, was as far gone in passion as he'd ever been without being in bed. Opening his legs to a wider stance, he urged her to step inside.

He laved attention on each breast until he was nearly crazy with the need to explore more of her. Her skin was delicate, and he could see the tracings of veins that disappeared under the dark pink aureole that surrounded the rosy nipple.

She would be soft and delicate in other places, too. He wanted to go lower, to stroke her into bliss while he held her and kissed her mouth and her breasts.

"Kiss me back," he said on a groan, returning to her lips.

She did what he said, raising her face to his in mindless obedience to the attraction. He was more than surprised by the passion between them. He was almost overpowered by it.

A white-hot surge of need hit him. He realized she had pressed herself solidly against him and was instinctively rubbing that part of him that wanted to bury itself in the hot welcoming center of her.

It would be sweet. It would be like heaven...

A screech from hell brought him back to earth.

"What the devil?" Sam said.

Molly clutched his shirtfront in fright. Then she realized what the scream was. "The cat. Something's hurt it."

She started for the door, then stopped and looked down in shock. Her bra and sweater were scrunched up almost to her neck. A tide of hot pink flowed over her face and neck. She had nearly gone outside half-unclothed!

"Stay here." Sam was out the door in a flash, leaving her to fumble with her bra clasp, which suddenly wouldn't close...oh, there, she had it.

She jerked her sweater down, then headed out the door as fast as her trembling legs would take her, her mind a welter of confusion. "Do you see her? Is she hurt? Is it a coyote?"

"No," Sam called. "Stay inside while I look around."

"I'll get a flashlight." She ran inside and searched through a drawer, throwing half a ball of twine, a pack of mailing labels, a box of matches and two clothes-pins on the floor before she found it.

She ran back out into the cold night air. The first day of spring had occurred that week, but the weather hadn't caught on yet. It was still cold and rainy. She flicked the light around the backyard and saw Sam.

A black streak materialized beside her and disappeared into the kitchen through the open door.

"There she is. She's inside. I think she's okay."

"Give me the light. I'll look around a bit more."

Molly glanced at the dark shadows of bushes and trees. The wind had risen in the last hour or so. The shadows danced eerily. Sam removed the light from her hand and headed back toward the gardening shed. She stood in the doorway and watched as he knelt and looked around.

When he finally returned, she asked what he'd been looking at or for.

"Whatever I might find" was his terse reply.

She studied his tense stance and frowning face. "You suspect something. Do you think someone was out there?"

He shrugged. "Probably a fox or a coyote," he said without answering her question.

She peered anxiously out the window, but couldn't see any signs of anything wrong.

"I have to go." He locked the back door and made sure it was secure. "I should have left an hour ago, then we wouldn't have gotten into...what we did."

"Are you sorry?" she blurted. She realized she wasn't.

"I..." He rubbed a hand over his face. "I'd like to

remain friends with you. You're the only one I have.''
His smile was filled with irony.

''That's not true. What about Chuck Nader and his
wife? Others around here would open up if you'd
make the first move.'' She crossed her arms over her
chest and gave him a stern look. ''You might try smiling and saying hello to people.''

''Yeah, I might.'' He looked down at his shirt,
looked grim for a second, then began tucking it into
his pants.

She must have pulled it loose. She could remember
running her hands over his back, liking the feel of his
firm flesh and the flex of muscles she could feel under
the skin.

Heat rose to her face again. She'd never known she
had the capacity to be a wanton. But perhaps every
woman had. With the right man.

''I'm going.'' He hesitated. ''Is it okay if Lass
stays?''

''Yes.'' She nodded several times as if the answer
wasn't enough to convince him.

''Lock up after me.'' He headed for the front door.

She followed and turned the dead bolt securely after
him. He paused at the truck, raised a hand in goodbye
and left a minute later. She watched until he was out
of sight.

Sam attached the wire to the connector and made
sure it was secure, then leaned on the corner post and
looked at the sky. Not a cloud to be seen. Well, a few
horsetails floating above the Pecos, but nothing to
worry about.

Spring had painted the pastures in shades of vibrant

green. The grama grass sprouted lush new growth. Actually the rains had arrived at just the right time that year.

Calves cavorted beside their placid cud-chewing mamas in several sections. It was time to move them to new ground. He twanged the electric wire once more to be sure it was firm, then went to connect the battery.

This was something new he was trying—moving the cattle across the pasture in blocks of heavy grazing, then "resting" the grass until it recovered. An electric fence provided a simple and cheap method to keep the cattle in the right section.

Down at the county road, he saw the postman stop at the mailbox. He decided to ride down and pick up the bills. He smiled a bit grimly. His mail rarely contained anything else.

Swinging up on a big-boned roan gelding that had a gait like a rocking horse, he headed down the ranch road, one eye on the stock fence as he went. A sense of accomplishment brought a lightness to his heart that had been missing for years.

The ranch's affairs and his personal affairs were in good order. He'd paid off all debts to his attorney and the bank and had enough money to make it through the year. If the Good Lord was willing and the creeks didn't rise... And if the rains kept coming so the pastures would grow. And if no one started a prairie fire. And... Well, the list could be endless, but today, he didn't care.

His friendship with Molly was paying off. The owner of the local general store had actually smiled at him when he walked in the other day.

He grinned at that and whistled the rest of the trip. At the end of the road, the gelding sidled close to the mailbox so that Sam could lean down and collect the mail and the newspaper.

Feeling the friskiness in his mount, Sam chuckled as they wheeled around for the return trip. "Yeah," he agreed, "I've got a touch of spring fever, too."

He patted the horse's neck in sympathy. "Poor chum, you don't even know what it's all about, do you? You just feel the urge without knowing how to take care of it."

With a subtle shift of his body, he gave the gelding tacit permission to run. The big horse took off toward the barn and the oats he knew would be there for him.

Sandy, one of the two men he'd recently hired, waited by the stable door for them. "Somethin' after you?" he asked when Sam swung down and handed the reins over.

Sam laughed. "Only kicking up our heels a bit. Must be spring fever."

The young man grinned in understanding. "Come Saturday night, I'm heading for town. Come on, you bag o' coyote bait," he muttered to the horse. "Stop prancing around like a derby winner. You ain't worth..."

Sam flicked through the mail while he crossed the unmowed patch of grass that constituted the lawn around the ranch house.

Nothing but bills, he noted as he leapt onto the porch without making use of the two steps hewn from giant cottonwoods and went into the kitchen. One letter was from the bank.

He opened it, expecting an advertisement for an investment opportunity the bank advised him not to miss. Instead he found one of his checks had been returned for insufficient funds.

Cursing under his breath, he called his attorney from the wall phone in the kitchen. "The bank says my check to you was returned. I don't know why. I made a deposit last week from the spring sell-off."

"I knew it was okay. Call the bank," Chuck advised. "They probably credited it to someone else. Let me know when to send it through again. By the way, are congratulations in order?"

Sam was instantly on guard. "What for?"

"You and the schoolmarm. I've heard from three different sources that things are pretty hot between you two. One of them was my wife, so the women are speculating about you, too."

Sam cursed aloud. "What exactly have you heard?"

"Well, you had your arm around her outside the movie the other night. Lots of folks saw that. Then there's talk that you didn't go to your house after you took her home that night." The attorney's voice took on a cautionary tone. "Don't forget those prenuptials. You need an agreement before you take the final plunge. You don't want to put the ranch in jeopardy in case the marriage doesn't work out."

Sam gripped the phone, recalling scenes from Saturday night. Him with Molly locked in his arms. Kissing. Touching. His hands on her breasts. Her hands under his shirt, her eyes closed, her teeth clamped on her bottom lip as he kissed and sucked at her bare nipples. The wonder and confusion in her eyes when they'd finally come up for air.

Some friend he was. Because of him, people were

talking about her, questioning her virtue. Because of his inability to control his baser impulses, she was the center of gossip.

After hanging up, he called the bank.

"That was an out-of-town check," the woman in accounting explained. "It takes three business days to clear."

With any of the other local ranchers, the bank would have held the check until the deposit cleared, but no one trusted him. Except Chuck. And Molly.

From the bank teller's disapproving tone, Sam was sure the older woman had heard the gossip, too.

And he knew exactly where those rumors had started. He'd found footprints out by Molly's shed. The detective he'd forgotten about in the blaze of passion had lost no time in letting Tisdale know.

"Is the money in my account now?" he asked, reining in the sarcastic remarks on the tip of his tongue. Molly would have told him such tactics only alienated people. Not that he gave a damn. At least, not for himself. But for her...

"Yes," came the snooty reply.

"Thanks." He hung up the phone none too gently, anger getting the better of him.

Grabbing the truck keys, he went outside and took off in a shower of dust and gravel. In fifteen minutes flat, he stomped the brakes in front of a two-story Tudor-style mansion and came to a screeching, skidding stop.

He leapt to the ground, slamming the door behind him so hard the truck trembled on its shock absorbers. Elsie Tisdale opened the door before he had time to knock.

"He isn't here," she lied, wringing her hands together at her waist. She was a short, skinny woman who reminded Sam of a plucked chicken. "William isn't home."

"Excuse me, ma'am." Sam stepped by her and walked into the study, done up in the manner of an English gentleman's club, to the right of the hallway.

William Tisdale, his former father-in-law, glanced at him, then screwed his face up as if he smelled something rotten. "What the hell are you doing here?"

"I came to see you about a small matter." Sam rocked back on his heels. "Such as the rumor floating around town about me spending the night with Molly Clelland."

Triumph flashed through the older man's eyes before he tried to assume an expression of righteous distaste. "Your prurient activities don't interest me in the least."

Sam strained to keep his temper under control. Tisdale was a bastard, he'd known that for two years, but he couldn't afford to let the man get the best of him. Lass depended on him.

He carefully unfolded his hands from fists and tucked his thumbs into his back pockets and assumed a relaxed stance. He smiled, and for the first time alarm flashed through the gray eyes across the desk.

Briefly he wondered how gray eyes that looked like mist in sunlight when they were Molly's eyes only reminded him of vermin when they belonged to his former father-in-law.

"Maybe this will interest you," Sam said softly. "A check in the amount of two thousand dollars paid to a certain fleabag detective from a, shall we say? somewhat shady law firm who also happened to receive a check for a like amount the same day from a certain rancher from hereabouts.''

"Oh, William, what have you done?" Elsie Tisdale had come into the room unnoticed by the two males. She hovered by the desk, her thin legs trembling like a tired roadrunner's.

Tisdale's face turned an interesting shade of purple. His eyes shifted from his wife to Sam, then away from both of them. "You can't prove anything," he blustered.

"I can prove invasion of privacy. That's a felony." Sam felt no triumph in winning a battle against his former father-in-law. He wanted peace and quiet and the opportunity to raise his child without fearing for her future. That's all he wanted.

Elsie gasped and made little sounds as if she were a chicken with a piece of corn stuck in its craw.

Tisdale stood and leaned over the desk. "Get out of my house. You're not welcome here. You never were. You never will be. And don't think that goody-goody teacher can help you. She's as much a part of this as you are. If that dolt of a detective had had a camera, I could prove it."

Sam straightened from his don't-give-a-damn slouch. "Leave Molly out of this. If I hear one more word about her…"

He let the thought trail off, realizing he'd left himself open when a gleam appeared in the older man's eyes. Tisdale now knew Sam had a vulnerable spot besides Lass.

"You'll what? Sue me?" The older man thought he had the upper hand. His smile was full of malice.

"You bring that baby here where she belongs and Saturday night will be forgotten."

"Lass," Sam said tersely. "Her name is Lass. Or Elizabeth Gail if you prefer to be more formal."

"How is she?" Elsie asked.

She wore such a pathetically eager expression that Sam felt sorry for her. The woman hadn't seen her granddaughter since Sam had taken Lass home from the hospital. He hadn't thought to invite the woman over to the ranch.

"You can come see her." He gave William a warning glance, then spoke again to the timid woman. "But come alone. You can visit with Lass, but no one else."

William leaned across the desk with a roar. "She's not going to visit anywhere. You seduced my daughter and sweet-talked her into marrying you, but you're not going to ruin my granddaughter's life the way you ruined my girl's. If she'd come home to us, she'd be alive today."

Tisdale knew how to kick a man where it hurt the most. Sam flinched inwardly, but showed no emotion.

"She left this house because you made her life miserable," he said, interrupting the tirade. "Whatever else was between us, she trusted me. She left me in charge of her inheritance, not you. And every penny of it is in an irrevocable trust for Lass."

"An irrevocable trust!" Tisdale exclaimed. His face turned pale. He slumped into the richly padded leather of the executive chair. "I don't believe you."

"It's true. And in case you get any ideas about my dying soon, my attorney and the bank are the alternate trustees. I've made provisions for Lass's care as well."

Tisdale assumed an aggrieved air. "The child needs

her own family. No court in the world would give her to someone who isn't blood kin, and I know you don't have living relatives.''

''But they would give her to her mother.''

''Her mother,'' Elsie echoed. She swayed as if a wind whipped around her frail body, as if she might snap right into pieces. ''Elise…Elise is dead. Lass has no mother.''

Sam took the woman's arm and led her to a chair. She collapsed into it, uncontrollable tremors running over her.

''Yes,'' he said gently, ''Elise is gone.''

''Thanks to you,'' William snarled behind him.

Sam faced the man and his unreasoning hatred and greed. ''But I'm not. I'm alive. I can marry again and give Lass the family you say she needs. My wife would be her mother.'' He smiled at this winning thrust.

''Wife?'' Tisdale taunted. ''What decent woman is going to take a man everyone knows married his first wife for her money, then forced her to have the child that killed her?''

Sam took a deep breath. ''My fiancée,'' he replied calmly. ''Molly Clelland.''

Chapter Five

Molly clapped her hands and led the singing while Tiffany banged away on the old upright piano in the corner. The twenty preschoolers marched around in a snaky circle, some with drums and triangles, which they clanged with great enthusiasm while the rest sang.

It wasn't until the door opened and Sam entered that she realized he was on the place. Tiffany had opened the nursery that morning while Molly ran errands. She hadn't seen Sam when he'd brought Lass.

Heat rushed into her face and neck. She hoped she wasn't as bright red as she felt.

The morning after. Although this was a couple of days later, she understood that expression perfectly now and wondered if she would be less or more embarrassed if they had consummated that torrid session in her kitchen.

Smiling with a calmness she was far from feeling, she left the children and crossed to Sam's side.

"Hello," she said above the din. She bravely met his eyes, then as quickly looked away. She didn't know how to handle the fact that this man had seen more of her than any living person. Except her doctor, who was also female, and of course her mother had taken care of her when she was little.

But no one knew her body the way he did.

Saturday night, with her blood hot—another expression she could now fully appreciate—and her mind in a whirl, her wanton conduct had seemed natural and right. But in the cold light of day...

Oh, heavens, those clichés...they were all too true.

"I need to talk to you," Sam said, leaning near her ear so he wouldn't have to shout. "It's important."

Misgivings churned like a whirlpool in Molly's stomach. Something was terribly wrong. She'd never seen him look so grim. Or angry. She nodded.

Looking across the room, she caught Tiffany's eye and motioned that she was going to step outside. Tiffany nodded and, not missing a beat, took over the singing, adding her voice to the children's boisterous trebles.

In the crib, Lass slept through the racket without a twitch. Molly saw Sam's eyes on his daughter. She recognized the fierce vulnerability he tried to hide.

Grabbing her jacket, she led the way outside. Sam followed and walked with her along the path. She headed for the creek, which had calmed into a gurgling, fast-running brook.

He stood by her without speaking for a couple of minutes. Instead he looked into the clear water as if seeking answers to questions he couldn't speak aloud. She waited.

Finally, he turned to her. "Saturday night," he began. He took off his hat and ran his hand through his hair. "Something's come up..."

Her gaze flew to the snug-fitting jeans and the point where his zipper started.

His snort of laughter was harsh. "Besides that."

A wild blush erupted. This time she didn't have to wonder. She knew she was as red as the proverbial beet. Her knowledge of the male anatomy wasn't as clinical as it had once been, and her dreams of late had been shocking. She folded her arms across her waist and waited for the bad news.

"Molly." His eyes searched hers.

She saw supplication in those lucid depths, but she didn't know what he wanted from her.

"Ah, God, Molly, I'm sorry," he murmured and surprised her by taking her into his arms.

She didn't know if he was trying to comfort her or be comforted, but whatever, it was obvious something was troubling him.

"Sam, what is it?" She put her arms around his waist. He'd been working and hadn't stopped to change clothes. His scent reminded her of sunshine and hay fields and of...um, yes, of horses. She breathed deeply.

"How can I help?" she asked, leaning her head back to gaze into his troubled expression.

"Would you consider marrying me?"

She waited for the words to make sense. It had sounded as if he'd asked her to marry him. "I beg your pardon?"

His grin was brittle. ''Yeah, I know. I've probably shocked your logical little brain, but after Saturday night…we have to get married.'' He finished the sentence in a rush.

She still couldn't figure this out. ''My brain is full-size, I'll have you know,'' she informed him, convinced he was making a joke and she was the brunt of it. She hadn't thought he was a cruel man, but now she wondered.

Sam touched her forehead, then lifted a strand of hair that blew to and fro in the mild March breeze. The air was crisp but balmy, the sky was clear, the sun was shining. All should have been right with the world.

When Molly peered into his eyes, her own lucid gray ones confused and somewhat wary, he experienced a desire to gather her close and protect her from all the hateful things in the world. She would be mortified if she heard the rumors flying around the county about them.

At the gas station, when he'd stopped to fill the truck, he'd nearly gotten in a fight with a ranch hand from the spread east of his place. Sam had gone to school with the man. The cowboy said he hadn't realized the nursery schoolteacher was such a sexy dish until Sam started taking her out.

''Let me know when you get tired of her,'' the lout had said.

Sam had informed him in deadly tones that Molly was his fiancée. By now, that statement was all over town. He had to let her know before she heard it from someone else.

He didn't give a damn what anyone thought of him,

but he couldn't let her be hurt. He hated Tisdale for forcing them into this position. He hated the gossip-mongers of the town. Most of all, he hated himself for having put Molly into it.

Molly, the sweet and innocent. Molly, the virgin.

She hadn't really known how to kiss. That had nearly blown his mind. But she caught on quickly. By the time they came up for air, she was giving as well as taking.

He could still remember the feel of her hands running over his back, the sweet scent of her clean, delicate body, the sight of her translucent skin with the veins tracing faint blue paths on her breasts. He broke out in a sweat.

Dammit, he was marrying her for her sake, not his. He'd not let sex come between them again. Not until she was sure she wanted the marriage.

Marriage. The smothery feeling settled in his chest. His first marriage had been a disaster, once the passion wore off. But this was the only way he knew to protect Molly. The honor of his name, such as it was, was all he had to offer her.

"I hate to rush you, but I have to have an answer," he said, prodding her when she remained silent.

"Now?"

The word came out a startled croak. He had to smile. For once, the mouthy little schoolmarm was without the proper advice and reprimands, it seemed.

He nodded. Pushing his hat off his forehead, he took her by the shoulders and faced her squarely. "After the other night, we both know it's inevitable."

He looked away, unable to face the clear honesty of her gaze. He didn't want to see the hurt in those eyes when she heard the rumors. He had to protect her.

A hollow feeling hit him in the gut. Marriage. The thought of it weighed on his chest. He'd never had a friend like Molly before. He wondered if they could continue the same way after marriage as before—as friends.

Maybe without the confusing issue of sex between them, they could. He'd give her that choice.

She took a deep breath and forced herself to meet his gaze. "Yes, I know. It was…"

"Yeah," he agreed, feeling like the lowest snake in the world. He was using her, her friendship, the passion that had grown so unexpectedly between them. He had to tell the truth. "However, there's another problem. Lass's grandfather is giving me a hard time." Well, that was part of the truth.

Molly nodded. Others, as well as Sam, had told her of the troubles between him and his former father-in-law.

"With us married, it'll solve several problems. I need someone I can trust to take care of Lass. In case something happens to me," he added.

Her mouth puckered into its disapproving mode. She frowned at him. "I don't want to hear that kind of talk. Nothing is going to happen to you."

"Not if I can help it," he agreed with a grim smile. "But I have to be prepared. I have to know Lass is in good hands."

"I understand." She stepped into his arms and hugged him fiercely, proud that he'd come to her. He hadn't said the words, but none were really necessary.

She knew his heart. And her own. "Of course I'll marry you."

His embrace tightened into a bone-crunching hug. He lifted her from the ground and swung her around.

"Help," she cried, laughing with the joy that invaded her like a shining light. "You're squeezing me to death."

He put her down at once and lightened his hold. "You won't be sorry," he murmured huskily, pressing his face into her hair. "I swear. You won't be sorry."

"I know."

She snuggled against his shoulder, then with a daring she'd never had, she kissed along the base of his throat and up the cords of his neck.

He laughed, and for the first time since he'd arrived and called her outside, she sensed the easing of anger in him.

"We'll get a license right away. Today."

"We have to get blood tests first."

His gaze was tender. "Ever the practical one. Okay, let's go do it."

"Wait!" she pleaded when he started off for his truck, towing her along like a startled heifer.

He stopped. "Make it fast."

She folded her arms and gave him the teacher's stare, which didn't daunt his good humor at all. He winked at her and waited.

"First of all, a marriage is a partnership," she began when she recovered from the charming grin he bestowed on her. "I intend to be a full partner, so don't think you can boss me around."

"I am the boss. And I'm bigger than you." He folded his arms across his chest, mimicking her and obviously enjoying himself now that he had her agreement to his mad plan.

A delicious shiver splashed down her spine. Marriage. She hadn't dared let herself dream of anything coming from their friendship. And now *this*.

Of course she'd known how she felt, that she was falling in love and trying very hard not to. But now she didn't have to hide her feelings anymore.

Oh, love was wonderful! It was just like the songs said.

"Second, I'm not going to have a hurry-scurry wedding like some kid in trouble." Her neck grew warm, but she persevered. "The people at church will expect a decent wedding. My parents will fly out. My brother." She totted the numbers up on her fingers as she counted. "And I want an engagement ring."

"My mother's is in the strongbox at the ranch. I thought you might like it...you know, continuity and all that stuff."

She was pleased and touched that he remembered her little sermon about that and family names. "I'll be a good mother to Lass," she promised. "I already love her."

He heaved a deep sigh. "I know. That's what makes this so much easier."

Easier? A strange word.

"That and the fact that you're such a good sport about it all. I'll be a good husband to you," he said. He hesitated as if unsure of his next words, then added, "I won't rush you or anything. I promise. I know marriage will be new to you. We'll take things slow and see how they work out."

She hadn't the foggiest notion what he was talking

about. A thought came to her. "Sam, how old are you?"

"Thirty-two."

"When was your birthday?"

"A couple of months ago. My doctor can give you a written report on my health if you're worried—"

"No, no. It's just…I'm thirty-two, and I wasn't sure if you were a couple of years younger." She peeked at him through her lashes. "I'm almost six months older than you are."

"That much?" He looked amazed. "You're remarkably well preserved for an old lady." Then he laughed before she could get more than moderately indignant. "We'll have a proper wedding, but let's hurry. It's important to me that we get things settled as soon as possible. I'll feel a lot better about Lass and the ranch when we're married."

"Oh, Sam." She hesitated, then flung herself into his arms, teary-eyed at his trust in her.

"Let's go get the blood tests. The nurse said she could take care of it whenever we stopped by."

"You've already asked?" Molly thought of people all over the county speculating about Sam's plans.

"Yeah. Can you leave now?"

"Let me help Tiffany serve lunch. We can go during nap time." She held his hand as they walked back up the hill.

Marriage. She couldn't believe it. She, who had made up her mind long ago that she was destined to spend her life alone and had actually been content with the idea, was marrying the most exciting man in the county!

"Shall I tell Tiffany?" she asked before they entered the nursery. She felt shy all of a sudden.

"The more the merrier," he told her.

A slight cloud appeared on her horizon of happiness at the grim determination in her fiancé's eyes.

"Is there something more you're worried about?" she asked.

Sam looked into Molly's beautiful gray eyes and saw her soul. Honest, trusting, candid. Molly thought everyone was as kind and decent as she was. She appeared happy about their marriage. He wondered if she thought she was in love with him.

He shied from the thought. Love was just another name for lust, an insanity that made a man make mistakes. He and Molly were friends. Friendship was good. It would form the basis of a solid marriage. He would have to control his wayward instincts and forget the way she went wild in his arms.

"Have another," Mrs. Liscomb urged.

Molly declined another cookie. "That was delicious."

The preacher's wife fluffed the ruffles over her ample bosom. She served ornate teas at the parsonage on Sunday afternoons. Molly had been invited for the last serving. No one else was there. She braced herself.

"It was certainly a surprise about your engagement," Mrs. Liscomb told her.

She gazed at the ring on her finger. The diamond flashed brilliantly in the light from the window. Everyone in town wondered if she knew what she was doing. All the old rumors regarding Sam and his first marriage had been dusted off and brought to her attention.

"To me, too," she admitted. "I mean, I knew how I felt, but I wasn't sure about Sam." Her tone said she was now and nothing could change her mind.

"One doesn't want to be hasty."

"No, one doesn't," Molly agreed. "Sam and I are both over thirty, so we're old enough to know what we want. It wasn't a snap decision." After all, they'd been dating for a month before he'd kissed her.

And what kisses they had been. She could hardly wait to try some more of them. When he had sucked and stroked her breasts, it had stirred the wildest sensations. She wished he would do that again.

Heat rushed through her, and she was embarrassed at her own wayward thoughts. She would never think of her body in quite the same way as she had before that tender assault.

Her most womanly assets were places of joy and pleasure, she'd learned, not mere physical representations that she was a female. She was still amazed at the potential for response that lived in her. She'd had no idea—

"You've led a sheltered life." Mrs. Liscomb was determined to carry through no matter how difficult the subject. "Sometimes a person can be overwhelmed by a man." Two red spots erupted in her plump cheeks.

Molly sighed quietly and nodded. She was going to get a lecture whether she wanted one or not.

Mrs. Liscomb mentioned hormones and the temptations of a handsome face and the perils of physical attraction. She gave a summary of male behavior. She brought in fear of being alone and growing old. She concluded that someday Molly would meet a man who'd be exactly right for her.

"I've never been afraid of being alone," Molly said. "My life has been very pleasant. I'm sure it's going to be more so. Lass is a wonderful child, and Sam is a wonderful man."

Mrs. Liscomb glared at her as if she were being particularly dim-witted about the whole thing. Molly smiled serenely.

She knew she was doing the right thing. Sam needed her. Together they'd make a home for Lass.

Flutters dived from her throat down into her chest. She wondered if she'd have any other children. A brother or sister for Lass would be nice.

She stood. "Thank you for tea. I'd better be going. It will be time for the evening service before you know it."

The minister's wife accompanied her to the door, put out by her guest's refusal to take her sage advice, her concern giving way to irritation in the face of Molly's stubborn complacency.

Molly walked out the door and across the road to her own snug cottage with a happy step.

She quickly changed clothes and jumped into her car to go to Sam's house. He'd invited her out for a cookout and to look the place over so she could plan what changes she wanted to make. Sam had told her to do whatever she wanted about the furniture.

The drive took forty minutes. She thought of him driving back and forth twice a day to leave Lass at the school, then pick her up. A devoted father.

He and Lass waited on the broad Spanish-tiled

patio. She parked and went up the path, noticing he'd used Southwest plantings in the garden. An unmowed patch of bunch grass formed the lawn.

"This is delightful," she told him after they'd exchanged greetings. They were almost formal with each other.

"I don't have time to mow," he explained about the grass.

"It doesn't need it. This looks lovely and natural, like a small meadow. The dry creek is a lovely touch."

She was aware of his eyes on her. In jeans and a loose shirt, with her hair in a clip at the back of her head, she probably looked more like a teenage babysitter than the woman he would marry the second Saturday in April. Only a bit more than two weeks away.

"Did you talk to your folks?" he asked.

A flush seeped into her face. "Yes. They'll be here in time for the wedding."

She didn't tell him that after a stunned silence, her mother had declared the news "wonderful!" and followed by asking if she were "in the family way?"

"Sam is a gentleman," she'd reprimanded her erring parent.

"Yes, but you're getting married so soon. I always thought you'd insist on a year's engagement at the very least," her mother had teased, "just to be sure you were suited."

Right now, Molly was wondering if she and Sam were suited. He was often distant around her, his mind preoccupied with other things. He'd made no move to kiss her again.

She'd observed him for over six months. Sometimes

she thought she wasn't any closer to knowing the real man than she'd been the first time they'd met.

"Good," he said in answer to her news.

She'd insisted on waiting until her parents could join them for the occasion. Sam had no one. He'd suggested going to a judge's chambers. Her friends from church wouldn't hear of it.

"Molly must have a big wedding," Tiffany had informed him. "Everyone will want to come."

Molly remembered the way he'd gazed at her, a smile at the corners of his mouth and a look in his eyes…it had been almost as tender as the way he looked at his child. It had given her goose bumps.

She wished he could express what he felt in words. Or kisses.

Heavens, she was getting so bold, she worried about herself!

"I've got the grill going. It's around this way." He led her along the porch that wrapped from the front to the back of the house.

She admired the peachy-beige stucco that glowed in the setting sun. Sam told her he had recently painted it.

While the charcoal turned gray with ash, he told her about the ranch. His great-great-grandfather had settled on the land over a hundred years ago. He'd been a land agent for the federal government, sent out to check on some conflicting claims.

She told him of her past. "My ancestors were whalers. They settled first in Boston, then on Long Island. Later, they moved to Virginia." She took Lass while Sam spread the coals. They went inside.

The kitchen was modern. His mother had had it remodeled shortly before her death. The cabinets were light oak. The counters and walls under the cabinets were tiled with white ceramic squares. Some tiles had paintings of desert wildflowers on them and were interspersed among the others.

"Oh, I love this," she said, turning all around.

"Do you?"

"It's lovely. All that counter space. My kitchen is so tiny." She stopped, coloring when she remembered what had happened in her kitchen.

"Molly, about that night," he began slowly.

Her lungs constricted at the seriousness of his tone. "Yes?" she managed to say.

"Do you have any regrets?"

She shook her head. Lass grabbed a flyaway curl and tugged. She removed the lock. "None. Do you?"

"Only that it forced a decision you might not have been ready to make. Some people will wonder about us and our marriage." His smile was cynical. "There's already talk that I seduced you into marrying me. People think I need money."

"You had a check bounce." Molly had to smile at the startled, then exasperated expression on his face. "Tiffany has a cousin who works at the bank. Do you need money?"

"No. Well, yes, but I have enough to get by."

He put Lass in a playpen and gave Molly a quick tour of the house. "You keep a very neat house," she complimented him. She glanced around the master suite. "I've never been in a man's bedroom before. It makes me feel odd."

"Odd?"

"Like I might get scolded for meddling any minute.'' She turned to him with a smile. ''Doesn't that sound like a nervous spinster?'' Her smile wilted under his keen appraisal.

''Why haven't you married?''

She'd been asked that question before. She usually replied that Brad Pitt, or whatever movie star was currently popular, had never asked her. They walked down the hallway.

''I never really had any desire to,'' she said truthfully. ''I thought about it some when all my friends were anxious about boys calling for dates, but it never really interested me. I'm afraid I much preferred books over boys.''

''Yes, you would.'' He nodded toward the baby from the kitchen doorway. ''She's ready for dinner.''

Molly noticed that Lass was sucking noisily on her fingers, a sign that she was hungry. She watched while Sam got out jars of food, warmed them in the microwave, stirred them and tested the temperature before bringing the meat and pasta combination to the table. He opened a can of pureed pears.

Molly strapped Lass into the high chair. ''I'll feed her.''

''Molly, about our marriage…''

''Yes?'' She glanced at him after feeding Lass the first bite. He looked so worried.

''I care about you, about our friendship,'' he said, then he hurried outside to put their steaks on the grill.

Molly sighed in confusion. Something was troubling Sam. Maybe he'd tell her later. She fed Lass, then gave her a quick wash. Going to Lass's bedroom, she put a clean diaper, then pajamas on the sleepy baby.

After winding up a music box and turning out the light, she left the room and went to find Sam. It was time they had a talk.

She found him on the back porch, tending the steaks. He also had vegetable shish kebabs sizzling over the coals.

"Mmm, that makes my mouth water," she commented. She sat on the porch railing and watched for a few minutes. "What's bothering you?" she finally asked, turning her attention from the sunset to the silent man.

He placed the meat and vegetables on a platter and placed it on the warming shelf beside the four dinner rolls. "I've heard talk in town," he began. "About us."

She nodded. "I've heard the rumors. People think you've charmed me." She believed in getting things out in the open. "That you need money and that's why you want me. I've also been told the same rumors about your first marriage."

"I would never marry for money. My stepfather did that to my mother. She thought he was wonderful. Fortunately she never knew he was skimming money from the ranch and putting it in his own account. I had enough savings to pay off the ranch mortgage, so it's in the clear. I don't have a lot of cash, but I don't owe anyone, either."

"I didn't believe the rumors, Sam."

A tinge of color seeped into his face. "There's one more thing. I have some papers. My attorney thinks we should sign them. Just in case."

"Just in case of what?"

"In case the marriage doesn't work. If you want out—"

Sam stopped speaking and watched the transformation. The girlish look disappeared as Molly assumed her teacher's stance—arms crossed, feet firmly planted, eyes like spear points.

"It hardly bodes well for our future if you're already thinking of the ending before the marriage starts," she lectured sternly. "A marriage isn't an on-again, off-again thing. It's something that people work at."

"I rushed you—"

"No, you didn't. I made up my own mind."

"You've never said what you expect from marriage."

"My wants are simple. Respect and common courtesy will do for a start. I've seen people treat family members worse than they treat strangers on the street. I disapprove of that. No one deserves kindness more than the people you live with. They're the ones who will stand by you."

Molly realized she was sermonizing and shut up. A vague alarm hummed through her mind. She felt threatened by outside forces she didn't understand.

Sam, like the preacher's wife, was determined to have his say. "I want you to be happy." He gave an odd half smile. "You're the only friend I've ever had."

"I'm very pleased with our plans," she said solemnly. "Now, where're the prenuptial agreements? I suppose he wants us to list all our assets so I won't claim any part of the ranch if we wind up divorced."

She grinned as Sam turned a becoming shade of red

and mumbled about lawyers and their distrust and all that. He hadn't learned to trust many people, but he would learn to trust her.

Laughing, she leaned close and nibbled his ear, startling him. "I'm not your only friend, but I intend to be your very best friend for life," she whispered, happy that they understood each other.

Chapter Six

"**Y**ou've certainly found your soul mate." Molly's mother observed Sam across the crowded reception room at the church. "He's as quiet and serious as you."

"Not all the time. You should see him playing with Lass. He's wonderful with her."

"And with you?" Her mother gave her a shrewd appraisal.

"Oh, yes," she said, so earnest and heartfelt that she blushed at being so obviously and foolishly in love with her husband.

"My darling changeling, I'm so glad for you." Her mother hugged her tightly. "I want you to have the happiness I've had with your father. Establishing a home and being true to one's vows is important. Children need constancy, but few people realize it today.

They think their own temporary happiness takes precedence over the good of their family. It's so sad.''

Since Molly was the one who usually delivered mini lectures on family life and children's needs, she was pleased when her mother expressed the same views.

"Feeling sentimental, old gal?" Mr. Clelland inquired, dropping an arm across his wife's and daughter's shoulders and giving them both a hug. "Actually, she's felt rather a failure. Here we presented the perfect marriage for our children to follow and we thought neither of you were ever going to marry.''

Molly kissed her father's cheek, catching a whiff of his after-shave, a scent as familiar and comforting to her as a child's favorite blanket. "And now you not only get a son-in-law, but a granddaughter to boot.''

"That Lass," her father said in loving approval.

The baby had already stolen their hearts. She had taken to them as they'd taken to her. It had been endearing to watch them *ooh* and *ah* over the child. Lass had accepted the admiration as her due and given back smiles and tongue clicks and her own mode of conversation.

At that moment, Sam looked at Molly. Her heart lurched. He was so incredibly handsome in his suit and tie, his hair freshly trimmed, his face smoothly shaved. She couldn't tear her gaze from his as he made his way across the room.

Her father released her when Sam came up and put his hand on the small of her back. "Lass is getting fussy," he said. "Shall we go?"

She nodded, unable to speak past the emotion blocking her throat. Her mother gave her one more hug. "Be happy.''

"Yes, I will," Molly said, looking at Sam.

The two men shook hands. Her brother, Gareth, joined them. "Be good to her," he said as he shook hands with Sam. An implicit threat underlined the words. She frowned at him.

He hooked a hand behind her neck and gave her a kiss on the cheek. "Be happy, little sister."

Tears swam into her eyes. She and Gareth, who had been two years ahead of her, had been close during their high school and college years. He'd once been in love, but his fiancée had died in a car wreck, the victim of a drunk driver one rainy evening on her way to meet him. His grief had been deep and silent.

"You, too." She tried to think of someone she knew who might suit a high-powered attorney who argued cases before the Supreme Court. No one came to mind.

A whimper alerted her to Lass's distress. She kissed her brother and leaned into Sam. "Let's go home."

A light flared in his eyes and was gone. He let her mother kiss his cheek, then, his hand on Molly's back, he guided them to where Tiffany bounced Lass on her knee. When Molly appeared, Lass held her arms out to her. Molly hefted her new daughter into her arms. Lass settled sleepily on her shoulder.

"She'll drool on your dress," Sam cautioned. He slipped a folded diaper under Lass's head. "Let's go."

Amid wishes of a happy future, muted in respect for the sleeping child, the newlyweds made their way out to Molly's compact car. Sam strapped Lass into the car seat.

They were ready to leave. He sighed in relief.

Birdseed rained on them from the laughing crowd

as he ushered Molly into the front seat. Everyone for miles around had come to wish the beloved nursery schoolteacher, who also taught Sunday school, he'd learned, good luck in her marriage.

His smile became somewhat sardonic. Molly's friends thought she would need all the luck she could get. He'd seen the concern on their faces during the hectic days before the ceremony.

He fastened his seat belt, checked to make sure his two girls were okay, then drove up the winding lane to the road and out toward the ranch. Other drivers blew their horns upon seeing the ribbons attached to the car and the writing on the windows.

On the way home, he thought of the difference between this second wedding and his first. He and Elise had had no friends to see them off. They'd been married by a justice of the peace in Roswell with no one but the old woman's husband and a friend who happened to be visiting as witnesses. It had been a spur-of-the-moment thing, performed the day after the final quarrel between Elise and her father. They'd both worn jeans.

Glancing at Molly's white dress, he struggled with a sudden ache. He wished he could offer her the same nervous eagerness he'd felt as a first-time bridegroom. He wished he could offer her his heart, pure and unsullied by reality. For some reason, he felt she deserved it.

Molly, the good, the kindhearted.

He made another vow. If, after a reasonable time of marriage to him, if she decided she wanted it to be real, he would be the best husband a woman could want. He'd cherish her. He'd be gentle. He'd never take his frustration or anger out on her. He'd remember the little things women were supposed to like, flowers and little surprises and all. He'd...

There wasn't a snowball's chance that he could be that saintly. He sighed. He'd do his best not to hurt her, by deed or word.

Molly's heart lurched again when Sam turned onto the ranch road. She'd been having a lot of trouble with that organ during the past few days. Whenever she thought of Sam, it would leap around like a bronco in a rodeo.

She hadn't seen much of him during the preparations for the wedding. He'd been busy at the ranch. She'd volunteered to take Lass home with her the nights his work kept him late.

Now they were a family.

Smoothing the satin skirt of her dress, she thought of the night ahead. The sun was setting. Soon it would be dark.

"Here we are," Sam said, bringing her out of her mood.

Tension knotted her stomach.

"I'll pull into the garage later. You might snag your dress." He paused, then added, "You were very beautiful today. You are beautiful. I know you don't think so, but...you are."

His words warmed her clear through. "Thank you," she managed to murmur. Honestly, she'd never get through the evening if every little thing got her all choked up.

She fumbled with the door and finally got out. Sam lifted Lass, car seat and all, and carried her into the house, motioning for Molly to go first.

The ranch house seemed warm and welcoming. She hadn't moved any of her things from her house yet, but she had plans.

Sam had surprised her by inviting her family out for a dinner of grilled chicken and a bakery pie for dessert the previous night. She'd made a salad and twice-baked potatoes to complete the meal.

Her suitcases were stored in the trunk of the car. Next week she would get the rest of her clothing and decide exactly what furniture she wanted to move. And there were all her dishes, linens, pots and pans plus the collected treasures of ten years to consider.

The church had already asked to rent her cottage for their caretaker and grounds keeper. She'd agreed, but asked for a month to sort through her stuff. At the moment, following Sam into her new home, her thoughts were too distracted to consider the furnishings.

"Let's get Lass settled, then I'd like to change," she told him. She wondered what brides wore in the interim between the wedding and preparing for bed. A going-away suit hardly seemed appropriate since she was already at her destination.

The new sports outfit she'd bought last month, she decided. It was a soft knit the color of spring grass with eyelets embroidered in gold and rust-colored satin thread.

"Right. I'll bring your luggage in."

She watched as he headed back outside in a long stride. She wondered if he felt as awkward as she did. There'd been no more torrid sessions like the night in her kitchen. Sam had been almost rigidly circumspect after that.

A niggling fear that she expected more of this marriage than she was going to get nagged her. No words of love had been spoken by either of them. Kisses had been brief and very few.

Had he married her only to protect Lass and save his land from his father-in-law? No. She couldn't believe that after the passionate interlude they'd shared.

Memories of those kisses had haunted her dreams. This moment might have been easier if they'd already become lovers, she thought, standing awkwardly in the middle of the living room.

Lass stirred and whimpered slightly. Molly carried her to the bedroom and put her in the crib. Lass smiled up at her, then promptly closed her eyes, pulled a corner of the blanket around her thumb and stuck it in her mouth.

The sleep of the innocent, Molly mused, gazing at the child with a heart filled with love. Hearing Sam's footsteps in the hall, she stiffened. Clutching the billowing skirt of her dress, which had been her mother's and grandmother's before her, she rushed out and closed the nursery door behind her.

"Lass asleep?" he asked.

She nodded.

"She'll probably be out for the night. It was a long day, and she didn't have a nap this afternoon."

They stood there for a minute. The silence intensified. Only the night-lights were on in the hall. They were a foot from the polished stone floor, shaded by a clever adobe awning that was part of the wall. The effect was one of semicircles of light along the hallway.

"Your room is this way," Sam finally said. Heat

slid down and pooled in the lower part of his body.
He wasn't sure he could keep his vow to give her time
to adjust to him and decide if she really wanted this
marriage. But he had to. He had to play fair with
Molly.

She followed behind him. He opened a door at the
end of the hall and on the opposite side from Lass's
room. It was a neat room with Spanish oak furniture—
an ornate bedstead and matching dresser. Two chairs
and a table formed a sitting area.

"This is a guest room," she said.

He saw the puzzlement on her face. He set her two
pieces of luggage on a bench at the end of the bed and
rubbed his hands down his thighs. He felt sweaty-
palmed and as awkward as an adolescent on his first
date.

"Molly," he began. The room was lit only by the
sunset. It felt too dark, too intimate. He flicked the
wall switch and two lamps beamed pools of light, one
on the bed, the other on the table. "Listen, we don't
have to begin our marriage right away. I realize I sort
of forced you into it."

He stopped, unable to explain that he valued her
friendship, that he was afraid she'd dislike his lovemaking. She was a lady, and sex was...well, it could
be sort of wild.

She said nothing. Just stood there watching him.

He felt a prickle of misgivings, but having started
he had to finish. "Later, if you want an annulment, if
you find ranch life boring, well, it would be easier all
around if things were kept...simple."

"Simple," she repeated.

"Yeah." He didn't like the look in her eye. The

satin moved over her breasts, then stopped. He realized she'd taken a deep breath and was holding it. He stared, fascinated, until the material moved again, slowly, deeply…again, then again.

"And in the meantime, I'm to be a guest here?" Her voice was deadly quiet.

Sweat popped out on his forehead. "For your sake, I thought it would be best."

"Because you think I'll grow bored and want to leave." She finished the thought for him. "Is that what your first wife did?"

"Yes."

He was pretty sure he'd made a bad mistake in not explaining all this before the wedding. Molly's mouth primmed up and her stance subtly shifted. Flags of color flew in her cheeks.

If he didn't know her better—that she was a sensible, levelheaded woman—he'd have thought she was furious.

"So we're to have a trial run before we commit ourselves?"

Put like that, it sounded pretty silly. "Well, yes. I think that would be reasonable."

He tried to explain, to show her he was being gallant about it, that he wouldn't expect more than she wanted to give—

She gave him a look that would have stopped a charging buffalo, much less his stumbling, rambling explanation, and walked to the door.

"How long do you think it will take before everyone in the county knows we're sleeping in separate rooms?" she questioned. "Then they'll really have something to talk about."

She left the room. He heard a door slam. She'd left the house. He hurried after her, wondering how to make things right when every word he'd uttered had made them more and more wrong.

Molly gripped the top rail of the fence with both hands. Anger burned hot and bright within her. She couldn't figure anything out, not Sam, not their hasty marriage, nothing.

Except he didn't really want her.

He had made her think they were in love. Those kisses in her kitchen, he had wanted her then. However, she was old enough to know that sex didn't mean love. As of this moment, she hadn't a notion of what it *did* mean.

Across the paddock, a big red horse eyed her, then snorted a couple of times. He threw up his head and neighed.

Molly gave him her teacher's stare. His racket interfered with her thinking. She pressed a hand to her temple, causing the ruffles of Brussels lace at her sleeve to cascade down to her elbow. Thunder rumbled. She glanced up in surprise.

The horse charged toward her. She moved back a step and watched it in a disinterested fashion. It came right up to the fence and stopped, then, arching its neck over the rail, it tried to bite her!

She slapped it on the nose, then was appalled. She'd never touched another living thing in anger before.

It threw up its head and screamed, then ran around the paddock kicking its rear legs up in the air like a ninny.

Molly leaned on the rail. "Stop that," she ordered.

"You look silly." She snatched a clump of succulent grass from beside a boulder and held it over the rail. "Here, you spoilt bully."

The big red monster quit its act and watched her from a distance. Finally it began to sidle over that way.

From the shadows of the back patio, Sam shook his head at the two cowhands who'd come out of the barn to see what the ruckus was about. One held a lariat in his hand. The other held a pitchfork ready to drive the stallion back if necessary.

Sam watched as the stallion, known as a man hater, edged closer to Molly's outstretched hand. He wanted to grab her and shield her from danger, but was afraid to move, afraid he'd startle the red into more of a fury.

"Molly," he called softly. "Move back. That horse is dangerous. He hates people."

She didn't show that she'd heard his words, just continued to stand there. On the night air, he heard her murmuring voice calming the big horse. To his amazement, the horse reached out and took the tuft of grass. Then Molly stroked its neck and ran her fingers through its forelock.

When the stallion snorted and galloped to the far side of the paddock, Sam ran across the yard and grabbed Molly away from the fence. "Don't ever disobey me again," he ordered.

"What will you do—beat me?" And she smiled up at him with all the insolence of the boy he'd once been, bent on defying his stepfather and running the ranch the way his father had.

"Don't tempt me," he advised and knew from the flare of anger in her eyes that she'd drawn a battle line between them.

"Ah, hell," he said and hoisted her into his arms.

Startled, she clutched his shoulders. "What are you doing?"

"Taking you to bed."

Molly burned with humiliation as Sam carted her toward the house. Behind them, she could hear laughter as well as shouts of encouragement from the two cowboys who were helping out on the ranch that summer.

She felt utterly ridiculous—the plain-Jane who had naively thought this dashing, handsome man was in love with her. How could she have been so stupid?

Her foolish heart had read more into the situation than had been there. She'd been too inexperienced to understand.

"Put me down at once," she ordered in a voice sure to bring the desired action in the classroom.

He ignored her. Sam Frazier wasn't a four-year-old used to obeying the teacher. He carried her into the house and into a suite of rooms that opened off the living room.

After setting her down on the carpet beside the bed, he caught her arms. When she struggled, he simply held on, his thumb and fingers encircling her wrist, not hurting, but holding her securely.

She realized the futility of trying to break his hold. "If you think I'll…I'll…*cohabitate* with you after that insult, I can tell you right now—I won't."

"What insult?" He looked thoroughly puzzled.

He didn't even know! She certainly wasn't about to enlighten him on her lovelorn expectations.

"I was thinking of you and your comfort," he said impatiently. "I know you haven't slept with a man—"

She couldn't control the gasp, nor the heat that rushed into her face. "You can't tell," she began, then stopped, uncertain.

His knowledge of the female body exceeded hers on certain subjects. Another humiliation. She gave him a fulminating glance, crossed her arms over her chest and stared out the window at the cactus and sage growing on a nearby hill.

Sediments of the multicolored silt that had once covered the floor of an inland sea were exposed by erosion, forming layered hues of rusty red and ocher and tan over the terrain. She stared at the hill until the colors blurred and she had to blink.

"Look, I'm not asking you to cohabitate." His very tone mocked the word and her use of it. He knew very well what she meant. "You were the one who brought up what people would think about us having separate rooms. You're right. No matter how careful we are, things have a way of getting out."

She rounded on him, words rushing so sharply to her tongue she had to bite them back. To say them would be to admit her fantasy that he'd fallen in love as she had. Pride wouldn't allow her to concede that much to him. "I'd rather sleep with a rattlesnake," she said instead.

"You'll sleep with me," he snapped. "And like it."

"I will not!"

A weary smile hovered at the corners of his mouth. "Well, maybe you won't like it, but you'll sleep in this bed. And I probably won't sleep at all," he added with a smile dipped in acid and stalked out the door.

She stood in the too-silent room and wondered what she should do now. Going to the window, she watched the long shadows of evening color the mesa lavender and magenta and purple.

Diablo Mesa. The Devil's land. And she was going to be sleeping in his bed!

A thump outside the door brought her heart to her throat. Sam brought her bags in, placed them none too gently on the floor and walked out without saying a word.

She pushed the door closed and laid her hand on the lock.

Sam's headache rose a notch at the slam of the door behind him. He sighed. There were chores to be done. He grimaced at his suit. Damn. He went out to the barn anyway.

Sandy and Tom were mucking out the stables. He nodded to them and grabbed a bucket. After putting it in the stallion's manger, he eased the outside door open, then quickly retreated, getting the stall door closed before the big horse could come inside and try to kick him into oblivion.

Although he could use a little oblivion right now.

He leaned on the stall gate and watched the red come tearing inside and dip his nose into the oats.

It was a fact, he'd never understand women. Here he'd tried to be gentle and patient with Molly, considerate of her feelings and all, and what had happened? She'd gotten huffed up like a puff adder and nearly taken his head off.

Hell, he should have just taken her to bed and done

all the things he wanted to do to her. That would show her.

But, he reasoned, he was trying to be fair to her. Dammit, he was trying to act like an honorable man rather than a rutting stag crazy with lust.

He knew Molly wasn't the spoiled prima donna his wife had been, but she might not like ranch living. She might not like *him* once she got to know him. However, he had to convince her to stay with him for a year. Maybe by then everyone would forget or disregard any rumors spread by Tisdale.

The big red threw up his head and whickered for more oats when he finished. Sam glared at the animal.

"Hey, boss, watch out for that man hater," Sandy called, stopping work to lean on the pitchfork and toss a grin his way.

"Yeah. He's a mean'un all right," Tom agreed, coming out of a stall after spreading clean straw. "Won't let a man within a hundred feet, but now gals is a different story. B'lieve the red has a soft spot for pretty little fillies."

"Yep," Sandy chimed in. "She walked right in and wrapped the meanest bronco this side of the Pecos around her finger. Think the boss eats out of her hand, too?"

The two cowboys laughed uproariously at their humor. Sam gave them a narrow-eyed glare, then grinned, too. An idea came to him. "Hey, you may be right. The red might take to a human female."

The rope burns on the mustang's neck testified to his misuse at the hands of the men who'd tried to catch and tame him. It had been a stroke of pure luck that the red had entered an open paddock when the men were moving the remuda. The big mustang had been after his mares.

Sam saw the men had the chores well in hand. He headed for the house. He had other fences to mend.

He entered the kitchen cautiously. No pot hurled past his head the way it once had.

Molly wasn't there. He hurried down the hall, worried that his bride might decide she didn't want to stay even one night on the ranch. After checking on Lass, who was out for the night, he silently tried the doorknob to his room. It turned.

He was grateful for small favors. At least she hadn't locked him out. ''Molly?''

No answer.

She wasn't in the room. Her luggage was gone. He whirled around, intending to go down the hall and get her. A noise from the adjoining room stopped him. Opening the door, he saw her.

As if he weren't there, she calmly hung a dress in the closet. She had changed from the wedding gown to a pants and top outfit. He couldn't help but notice how nicely curved she was.

''What are you doing?'' he asked after clearing his throat.

''Unpacking.'' Her face, usually so open, was closed.

''In here?''

''Yes.''

The room reflected the tradition of the past century when a smaller room commonly adjoined the master suite. It had been used as a nursery in the past. His mother had used it as a sitting room where she read and sometimes entertained close friends.

It had a daybed against one wall. A Greek recliner and two comfortable rockers along with a dressing table and three smaller tables completed the furnishings.

"Then you're going to stay?"

She gave him that drop-dead glance again. "Of course. Our marriage has hardly begun." She placed the hanger in the closet, closed her empty suitcase and placed it inside before closing the closet door.

For a second, she stood there as if thinking, then she looked him square in the face. "Did I tell you I don't believe in divorce?"

Relief washed over him. "No."

"I don't."

"All right." Whatever she wanted, he was agreeable. If she'd left before the first day was over...God, he wouldn't live that down in two lifetimes.

He didn't like the idea of marriage, but he liked Molly. If ever a marriage had a chance, it should be this one. Without the confusing issue of love, which was a nice name for lust, they'd get along fine. They'd be friends, then they could be lovers.

But he wouldn't rush her. He'd control his impulses. He'd show her how much fun life on the ranch could be.

A sinking sensation hit his middle. He'd tried that once. But Molly was different. She was interested in all kinds of things—the land, history, people, weather, everything. She was a woman a man could talk to.

Except she didn't seem to be speaking to him at the present.

She walked across the room. He moved aside, then followed her down the hall to the kitchen. She opened the refrigerator.

"I'm hungry. Do you want a sandwich?" she asked.

"Yes." A question burned in the back of his mind. "If you don't believe in divorce, how long are you going to stay in the other room?"

"Until the time is right."

Chapter Seven

Sam turned on his side, lay there, then flipped over to the other side. He settled on his back and stared at the patterns of moonlight on the ceiling.

He'd go for a hell-for-leather ride, but sure as he did, the ranch hands would wake and think it was a rustling operation. That's all he needed—for them to come running out, loaded for bear, and find him restless and unable to sleep.

Hell.

He'd never been in a fix like this before. He was acutely aware that through the door separating the bedroom from the sitting room was his wife. Once he'd heard her cough. That had been soon after they'd eaten their sandwiches—their wedding supper—and she'd gone to her room, saying she was tired.

After that, he'd heard her in the bathroom, then

she'd disappeared for the rest of the evening. He'd watched TV until ten, then he'd gone to bed. And here he lay.

One o'clock.

Dawn came early on the ranch. They had a bunch of calves to brand, the one part of the operation he didn't like. But it had to be done before he turned them loose on the hilly range that formed the backside of the ranch. If his cattle strayed over on Tisdale land or vice versa, he didn't want any questions about which ones belonged to whose ranch.

He wondered what Molly had meant by that "until the time is right" remark. When would that be?

Marriage. It made him nervous. The female mind was beyond him. Elise had claimed to love him, but she'd hated being tied down, being pregnant. In the end, she'd hated him.

He didn't want the same to happen to him and Molly.

His body reared up at a sound…no, it was a coyote baying at the moon. Molly wasn't going to come waltzing in and climb into bed and…

Gritting his teeth, he forced himself to count backward from a hundred. Finally he fell thankfully into slumber.

Sunlight and the rush of running water awakened him the next morning. He lay there and listened while Molly took a shower. He wondered how she'd react if he joined her.

The pure pleasure of the thought entertained and tortured him until she finished. When he heard the door open, he didn't know whether to pretend to be asleep or not. Too late. She was in the room. Her eyes met his.

She paused. "Sorry, I didn't mean to awaken you."

She wore a robe of pink silky looking stuff with pink scuffs on her feet. Her hair was twigged on top of her head. She walked through the bedroom and into her room as if she were out for a Sunday stroll.

A grin pushed its way onto his mouth. Bet if he checked her pulse, the little schoolmarm's heart was beating like sixty. The way it had Saturday night three weeks ago...

At the clenching in his lower body, he dropped the thought and flung out of bed. In the bathroom, he paused before stepping into the shower.

Her scent lingered on the warm, steamy air. Two new toothbrushes had joined his in the toothbrush holder. A box of curlers, the kind that plugged in and heated up, sat at the end of the counter next to the wall.

A damp towel and washcloth hung neatly across the bath towel rack. A new bar of clear soap was in the soap dish. He lifted it and took a sniff. It had that fresh, clean scent he associated with her.

For the first time in days, he relaxed. They'd work their way through this marriage business. Molly was sensible. As soon as she got used to the idea, things would settle down. Then, when the time was right...

Molly prepared biscuits, ham and country gravy, which she'd learned to make since living in the west. It was an odd dish that cowboys, whether they were real or urban, seemed to relish. Made of bacon, sausage or ham drippings, thickened with flour like a white sauce, and milk, it was easy enough to prepare.

Except she replaced half the grease with vegetable oil to cut down on the saturated fat.

When Sam entered the kitchen, she ignored her wildly pounding heart and assumed a serene expression. She'd be so calm, so sweet, it would drive him nuts. "Breakfast will be ready in about ten minutes. Tell the men not to be late. I don't want the gravy to get cold."

"Uh, sure." He fairly rushed out the door.

She smiled grimly. Marriage was going to take some getting used to...for both of them. She'd learned the men usually ate together, taking turns with the cooking. She had some ideas along those lines to share with them.

Begin as you mean to go on.

Good advice for anyone starting on a new adventure. And marriage was surely that. Thus far it had been full of twists and surprises. She had a few twists of her own.

When she heard a cry from the baby's room, she turned off the burner, checked the biscuits in the oven, then hurried down the hall. Lass had pulled herself up at the side of the crib and was hollering for attention. She hushed as soon as Molly came in. Holding her arms up, she demanded to be held.

Molly cuddled her new daughter for a moment, the anger inside her softening slightly, then changed the baby's clothing before returning to the kitchen. After placing the child in the high chair with a toast triangle to chew on, she poured up the gravy and finished preparing breakfast.

When the men shuffled into the kitchen, she welcomed them with a cheery, "Good morning. Have you washed up?"

She saw that they had. The two ranch hands, whom she'd met briefly the previous week, had wet and slicked back their hair. The tooth marks from the comb were visible. They carried their hats in front of them like shields. She could see the dip in their hair where the hats usually rested.

Like Sam, they dressed in jeans, scuffed boots and work shirts. Their wiry grace fascinated her. Two stereotypical characteristics impressed her. They were as tough as whip leather, and they were shy.

"Please take your seats, gentlemen. Breakfast is ready." She moved Lass closer to the table.

After placing the basket of biscuits on the table, she took her place at one end and looked over the table with a critical eye. Frankly it looked delightful. Her mother would have been proud of her.

A green vase held some dried seed heads of a lovely golden hue. She'd found them along the fence row near the stable. The green-and-white striped place mats went well with the dishes, which were white with a dried wheat pattern along the edge.

The bowl of scrambled eggs, the platter of ham and the dish of gravy provided a nice contrast in color and texture. She took a biscuit and passed the basket along, then spooned some egg onto her plate. The men sat after she did and dug in.

For several minutes the muted sounds of forks against plates were the only noise. Molly observed with mounting awe the amount of food three men could put away in a short time. Amazement gave way to irritation when they ate without speaking.

"The past week has been lovely," she remarked to no one in particular. "I hope it bodes well for the rest of spring." She waited for a response.

The cowboy named Sandy broke open another biscuit—his third—and spooned gravy over the two halves. He forked another slice of ham onto his plate.

Tom sprinkled a generous helping of pepper over a second mound of perfectly cooked eggs. He slathered margarine on a biscuit, added a thick layer of jam, heaped a fluffy clump of egg on the edge of the biscuit and chomped it off with a look of pure delight on his face. His jaws worked vigorously.

Both men were in their mid to late twenties. Old enough to have manners.

Down the length of the table, Sam ate as silently, although not as voraciously, as his men. Her irritation doubled.

"Do you get to rest on Sundays, or do you have work that can't wait a day?" she inquired, maintaining an even tone.

Chomp, chomp.

She took a deep breath—

"Gentlemen, my wife expects people to answer when spoken to," Sam informed them. "We are civilized folks, aren't we?"

She saw the sardonic humor in his eyes before she quickly looked away. Was he making fun of her?

Anger and confusion roiled in her. She intensely disliked both feelings.

The two men stopped stuffing their faces and stared at her in the manner of startled bucks, not sure whether to bolt or not in the face of this possible, but unknown, danger.

Molly crimped her lips together to keep from saying something hateful. She reminded herself that indeed civilized people did not resort to shouting and insults.

Sandy's ears turned red. "Uh, we have some chores."

"But we have most of the day off," Tom offered. He held a half-eaten biscuit in his hand. He looked at it in longing.

Molly thought if he ever looked at a girl that way, he'd melt her heart like sun on snow. Her own heart softened. She'd tame these wild broncos in time.

All of them, she vowed, looking at her husband, who watched her with a moody stare while he ate.

Nodding, she ate her meal, allowing the men to do the same.

Lass clicked her tongue and waved her hand toward the table, wanting the adult food. Before Molly could rise, Sam was on his feet. He prepared jars of cereal and fruit.

"I'll feed her," he said.

Lifting the high chair, he placed Lass close to him and began feeding her, his expression serious as he concentrated on the task. Lass ate until her hunger was satisfied, then she started flirting with her father.

After getting no more than a preoccupied smile from him, she enlarged her scope to include the other two men. Sandy winked at her when she clicked at him.

"Ah, Lass has made a conquest," Molly teased, detecting a soft spot in the men's hearts.

"She's a heartbreaker, this one," Sandy agreed. He nodded his head toward his plate. "Appreciate the grub. I ain't had nothing this good since I got out of the army five years ago." His ears turned red again.

"It's kind of you to say so." She gave him her teacher smile that complimented a student who'd done well.

Sam wiped Lass's hands and face. "Last week he said my beef stew was the best he'd ever eaten."

"Well, it was pretty good," Sandy admitted. "First time you hadn't burned it."

The two cowhands laughed. Sam smiled.

Molly thawed somewhat. Her husband was a very handsome man when he stopped scowling at the world. She'd see that he smiled more often. It was one of several changes she intended to make in his life.

She struggled with anger while she wondered at the real reasons for their marriage. To protect her good name?

He'd been furious at the gossip about them and felt he'd caused it he'd said in that insulting explanation he'd made.

He had, but it took two to tango, as the saying went. If she'd been seen in his arms, she was as much to blame as he was. She had been as lost in that kiss as he had. More so, if the truth be known. She hadn't wanted to stop.

She wanted that mad, breathless passion again. She also wanted declarations of undying love. But it was obvious she wasn't going to get either of her wishes.

All night she'd tried to sort through things, but it had been hopeless. She didn't feel calm and logical. For one of the few times in her life, she wanted to shout and throw things. It was an insight into herself that wasn't pretty. It even shocked her a little.

Most of all, she felt cheated. She'd waited for years for the right man, well, not exactly waited…

Actually she hadn't thought much about marriage at all—she'd been busy establishing her school—then to have all these strange longings awakened by this one man was humiliating. He was her husband, but he didn't want to be.

There. That was the one insulting, inescapable fact she'd had to face during the long, black night.

It made her angry. It made her want to scream at him and demand to know why they'd married.

Protect her name? As if she needed someone to do that for her. She was a responsible human being and a darn good nursery schoolteacher. Her reputation was impeccable. Those who didn't think so were welcome to think whatever they liked.

She hadn't asked to fall in love, hadn't dreamed of finding someone she'd want to share the intimacies of marriage with. It was patentedly unfair.

Noticing Sam staring at her over his coffee cup as he drank, she jerked and nearly dropped her own cup. She glared at him.

He continued to study her. He looked as perplexed as she'd been when he'd taken her to the guest room.

The oaf. He hadn't a clue as to why she'd felt insulted by his supposed reason for wedding her.

To have one's dreams flung back in one's face, to find a love she hadn't expected, hadn't asked for, and realize it meant nothing, to be rushed into a marriage and find it wasn't a marriage… She couldn't bear thinking about it.

She clenched the cup as anger rolled through her once more. Maybe she didn't understand all the mo-

tives behind this ill-conceived merger, but she wasn't
going to walk out.

Sam had married his first wife in the heat of the
moment, so to speak. It had not turned into a happy
union. Now he was married again, forced into it by
his strong protective instincts, which no one seemed
to notice but her.

However, she wasn't completely naive about the
male-female relationship. There was a physical attraction between them. She suspected he was a sensuous,
earthy man. To her amazement, she'd found she was
something of the same.

With his first marriage, there had been nothing behind the passion. With her, Sam had a friend.

They both loved Lass and this harsh, beautiful country. Sam had seemed to enjoy her company during the
month prior to his proposal. Having seen his love for
his daughter, she knew he was a good man, capable
of deep caring.

A flicker of hope overlapped the doubts. Maybe,
just maybe, this marriage had a chance after all.

But on her terms, not his.

She lifted her gaze from her cup and gave him stare
for stare. Luckily the two cowhands kept eating and
didn't notice the tension between the boss and his
lady...partner, she corrected. She took a deep breath.
It was wise to have a plan.

Molly, the ever sensible.

"That was very good," her husband said when he
finished.

He looked every inch the boss of the outfit. He'd
been wearing a denim jacket when he came in. He'd
hung it on a hook by the back door along with his hat.

The other men had done the same. All three were at home on this rugged land.

She was the outsider here. She'd have to make a place for herself on the ranch as she had in the town. Summoning a smile, she responded to the compliment. "Thank you."

"Let's go, you guys. If you eat much more, you won't be worth a plug nickel the rest of the day."

He stood. So did Tom. Sandy wolfed down a last bite of biscuit with jam, then joined them.

"Be sure to rinse your plates before you put them in the dishwasher," she reminded them, starting her *begin as you mean to go on* plan with a sweet smile. "I'll clean up the rest of the kitchen this time. Next weekend, we'll take turns as usual."

There was a beat of hesitation, then Sam took his plate to the sink, rinsed it and put it in the dishwasher. The two cowboys followed his lead.

Finished, the three men grabbed their jackets and hats and left the kitchen.

"Good thing Sunday is a light day," Molly heard Tom say, loosening up once he was away from her inhibiting influence. "Did'ya notice Sam was moving kind'a slow this morning, Sandy? Half the chores were done before he showed up."

Molly felt a blush highlight her face. Sam's ears turned red. "Get on with it," he ordered gruffly, pausing before stepping off the porch. He returned to the kitchen. "Will you be okay here for a while?"

"Of course."

"I'll get the sides on the hay truck. We'll pick up some of the things at your house if you know what you want moved."

"I do." She laid her napkin aside and crossed the room. "What time will you be ready to go?"

"Around one." He glanced at the kitchen. "About lunch—"

"I have a roast started. On weekends, I usually prepare something that will last the first part of the week for leftovers and sandwiches."

"We can hire someone to help," he told her. "Someone could do the housework."

"I was thinking along those lines, too." She forced herself to nod agreeably. "I think we can work it out, don't you?"

Her question seemed to confuse him. "Uh, yes."

"I have a high school girl helping at the nursery in the afternoons. She has a friend who's interested, too. I think I'll hire them and ask Tiffany to close at night, so I'll get to the ranch earlier."

Sam stood there by the door, not wanting to leave the warmth and brightness of the house. He felt funny inside, sort of squeezed and anxious.

His new wife watched him without speaking. Her eyes were like curtains of mist this morning, obscuring her thoughts from him. He didn't like it. He wanted things as they'd been last month. All the world had seemed right then, as if things were finally going to go his way.

She seemed to be waiting for him to finish and leave. It irritated him—that wall of calm she'd erected between them. He stalked toward her.

Her eyes opened wider, but she stood her ground when he came near. He recognized defiance in her stance. It surprised him.

But then, so had her fury yesterday. Maybe she wasn't as open and easy to read as he'd thought.

She lifted her chin and waited for him to speak. Talking wasn't what was on his mind. Gone were his good intentions, his restraint. In their place was a burning need to remind her she hadn't found him all that repulsive in the past. He took hold of her upper arms and pulled her toward him.

Then his conscience kicked in.

He tried to ignore it, but couldn't. With a sigh, he gave up and loosened his hold on Molly. Truthfully he wasn't certain what she thought of touching and all that.

However, she had been caught up in a sensual daze that night in her kitchen. Still, he didn't want to shock her. He'd have to keep a tight rein on things.

He bent down slowly, carefully, giving her time to withdraw. She stiffened, but she didn't move away. He brushed her lips with his.

Her mouth was warm and sweet. Longings that he hadn't felt since he'd left home to make his way in the world stirred in him. He wasn't sure what they were.

He lingered, wanting a response from her, but she simply stood still, as if waiting for him to finish so she could get on with her chores. He pressed harder. Her lips moved slightly.

Fighting the urge to haul her into his arms, he jerked his hat down firmly on his head and headed outside. A friend, he reminded himself. Not a lover. A friend.

"No, no, I'm sorry, but this isn't right. Let's move it back." Molly lifted her end of the table.

Sam hefted the other. They moved the heavy drop-
leaf table back to its original position. He waited for
her next command.

She realized what the problem was. The sitting
room in the master suite was the perfect place for
Sam's desk, not the formal dining room. The modern
computer furniture didn't fit in with the carved walnut
set.

However, until she moved out of the room, Sam
could hardly claim it for an office. And she wasn't
moving out, not until something changed between
them.

Until he wanted her for herself.

"Okay, that's it. You can escape back into the great
outdoors," she said, maintaining the light tone she'd
managed for the past six days.

She hesitated, then went to him, unsure of what she
was going to do. The week had been a tense one. Even
the two cowboys had sensed it as they helped move
furniture from her cottage to the ranch house.

It was difficult to maintain a facade of happiness in
the face of Tiffany's probing interest. And the pastor's
wife. They were keeping an eye on her, watching for
signs of trouble.

She wasn't going to confess her marriage was on
the rocks before it had even sailed out of the harbor.

But one thing she'd resolved. Her husband was going to know she was there, a part of his life whether
he wanted her or not. He'd tried to avoid her all week,
getting up and out of the house before the sun rose
each morning, appearing only for meals, then again at
bedtime. It was like being married to a ghost.

That had to change. Going to him, she put a hand

on his shoulder and leaned against his arm companionably, making no demands one way or another. Under the cambric shirt, she felt his muscles tense and hold.

There was an attraction, and she was going to make the most of it. She liked touching, she'd discovered. It hadn't been a momentary madness. She was more sensual than she'd known.

And if it drove him crazy, so much the better.

She took pleasure in the strength and warmth of his body. She liked his bigness and no longer felt intimidated by it. A man who could handle a child the way he handled Lass was no threat to a woman.

In their six days of marriage, she'd learned more about herself than Sam. One thing—she wasn't the patient person she'd thought she was. A second thing—she wasn't above using those feminine wiles she'd read about on him.

Leaning into him, she let him take a bit of her weight, knowing he could also feel the warmth of her body along his side as she did his. Then she moved away and let him go.

When he walked out without saying a word, she followed him. She went over to the paddock where the red mustang munched on the few blades of grass that pushed through the compacted soil. After gathering several handfuls of grass, she leaned over the railing and held it out to him. He lifted his head and tweaked his ears toward her.

They stayed that way several minutes.

At last the stallion couldn't stand it. He ambled over and sniffed at the offering. Finally he decided to eat it.

Molly held her hand flat so the horse didn't accidentally chomp on a finger. When the grass was gone, she wiped her hand on the side of her jeans.

"Here's a bucket of feed," Sam said, coming out of the stable. "Hold it and let him eat from it." He handed it to her and stepped back from the fence.

She did as directed. The big horse stuck his head in the container and *whuffled* in delight. The sound of corn and oats being cracked between strong teeth made her a bit nervous.

The bucket was awkward and too heavy to hold over the railing for long. Finally she climbed up two rails and was able to lower her arms to a more comfortable position.

"Hang the bucket over the post and stroke his neck," Sam called softly.

She hung the wire handle over the support post. The stallion followed as if he were a trained pet. She gingerly touched its neck. The powerful muscles twitched. She flinched in nervous reaction, then tried again.

The horse hadn't allowed her to touch it since she'd swatted it on the nose, then fed it the grass to say she was sorry. The mustang had galloped to the far side each time she'd paused by the fence and talked to it. Now it stood still, listening to her voice while it ate.

Laying her hand flat on the beast's neck, she rubbed down to the shoulder, then did it again. Feeling bolder, she ran her fingers under the heavy mane and through the rough hair, smoothing out some of the tangles.

The stallion shook his head and rolled his eyes.

"That's enough," Sam told her. "He's getting nervous. The bucket's empty. Move slowly and bring it with you."

She unhooked the handle and lifted it to her side of the fence. She climbed down to the ground, then walked toward Sam. He was grinning as if she'd done something great. She did feel a bit cocky about her success.

When she stopped in front of him, he hooked an arm around her shoulders and took the bucket from her. "You're going to tame him yet," he exclaimed exultantly.

Their eyes met. The smiles of triumph disappeared.

They stopped outside the stable door. Around them, tree frogs and crickets sang to the coming night. To her, it seemed like a love song. A shiver chased over her.

"It's getting cold," Sam murmured, his gaze on her mouth. "You'd better go in. We'll be ready to eat in a half hour."

She nodded. They lingered in the twilight.

Slowly he bent his head. Her breath came out in a shaky sigh. *Begin as you mean to go on.* She raised one hand and touched his cheek. Very gently. As if he were the stallion that needed taming.

She saw desire flame in his eyes and felt an answer in herself, that slow-fast buildup of heat and longing. His muscles bunched and she waited for him to take action.

For a heart-stopping moment, she thought he might overrule caution and carry her inside as he'd done that first night, but he simply heaved a deep breath and let her go.

It was extremely frustrating. If he wanted her, why had he insisted they needed time to get to know each other?

She went inside to see if Lass was awake. She was.

"Hi, fussy thing," she said with a sympathetic smile at the child when she went into the bedroom and flicked on the light.

The baby was teething. Top and bottom teeth were erupting almost simultaneously. Lass was irritable. Her sleeping habits had become unpredictable. They had hardly slept two hours in a single span for the last four nights.

Molly decided she'd give the child some baby pain reliever when she went to bed for the night. "Come on, we'll have some dinner before Da-da and the men have theirs." She lifted Lass from the crib and carried her to the kitchen.

When Sam and the cowboys came in, Lass had more food on her and the high chair than in her tummy. She whimpered and waved her arms on seeing her father, knocking the spoon from Molly's hand and sending pureed apples across Molly's shirt and the floor, which had already been mopped twice that day.

Her success with the horse wasn't being repeated with the child. Lass was as cross as a sore-tailed coyote and didn't want anything to do with her.

"I'll take care of it," Sam said. He swiped up the floor with a damp paper towel. He handed another one to Molly after glancing at the apples sprayed across her chest.

While she wiped her shirt, Sam worked on Lass, getting most of her supper down her by teasing and playing with her.

Molly felt the foolish press of tears. She had set the table when the two ranch hands came in, washed and

ready for the meal. Five minutes later, they sat down
to eat.

When Lass started crying, she sprang to her feet,
but Sam was already up. He held Lass and paced the
floor while Molly and the men ate.

"Getting hot now," Tom told her. "The hay is
coming along. We'll be able to cut the first lot by the
end of May if the weather stays this warm."

She'd asked so many questions about ranching that
the men, especially Tom, who she suspected was a
little sweet on her, automatically filled her in on what
they were doing and what was coming up. Sam
scowled and said nothing.

When Sandy finished his meal, he took Lass and
walked up and down the kitchen floor with her, keeping her quiet. When Molly finished, she took her turn.

Sam cleaned up the kitchen after sending the men
to the bunkhouse for the night. Molly gave Lass a
teething ring and put her in the high chair.

"You look tired," Sam commented.

She pushed a strand of loose hair out of her face.
"I never realized what a blessing it is to send children
home with their parents at the end of the day."

He nodded. "I thought I was going to lose my mind
that first couple of months with Lass. She seemed to
cry all the time. One night I couldn't stay awake any
longer. I fell asleep in front of the TV. When I woke
at dawn, I realized Lass had either slept all night or
cried herself back to sleep if she woke up. At any rate,
she slept all night from then on. It was a relief."

"I can imagine."

"She's been a good baby, otherwise."

"She's adorable, but it does make me anxious when

she cries. I feel I have to do something for her right away. Being a parent isn't as easy as it sounds in the books."

"Ah," he drawled, "the wisdom of experience."

She smiled. Between rearranging her time and running the nursery school, getting herself and her personal items settled in the ranch house, and taking over some of the care of Lass and the house, she felt as tired as a new parent.

"I've found someone to do the housework," she told him.

"Who?"

"A Mrs. Stevens. She helps in the nursery at church sometimes. She's a widow."

"I don't know her." His face hardened. "You're not to let anyone around Lass without my approval."

She was dumbfounded by this order.

"Her grandfather—" He stopped abruptly.

"Surely you don't think Mr. Tisdale would try to kidnap her, do you? He couldn't possibly get away with it."

"I don't trust him. Lass isn't to be left alone with anyone at any time."

"I leave her with Tiffany at school when I have errands." She reminded him rather stiffly.

He frowned. "I guess that's all right. Make sure Tiffany knows not to go off and leave those teenagers in charge."

"The nursery is my responsibility. I'll handle my staff."

He started to say something more, something harsh she was sure, but he refrained. "Just make sure they know about Lass. No one, but no one, takes her anywhere but me or you.''

"I'll see that they understand the rules.''

"I…'' He raked a hand through his hair, which was developing lighter streaks from his days in the sun. She'd often seen him with his hat and shirt hanging on a post while he worked at branding the calves, a task she couldn't watch.

"Yes?'' she asked, coolness in her tone.

He sighed. "I'm sorry. I didn't mean…I know you'll watch over Lass.''

"Did you ever think that you might win your former father-in-law to your side if you tried a different tactic with him?''

His scowl returned. "Like what?''

"Inviting him over to see Lass. Acting friendly. Making the first move. The flies and honey trick.'' She ended on a lighter note, seeing his frown deepen.

"There are some things that can't be changed,'' he told her in a voice like ice shards. "I don't want him near Lass.'' He caught her arm. "Don't try any of your schoolteacher tricks on him. They won't work.''

She didn't say anything. His distrust of people rose like a wall between them.

Chapter Eight

"Are you sure you want to sign this?"

Sam nodded. He had no choice. "Yes."

His attorney gave a resigned shrug and pushed the document across the desk.

Picking up a pen, Sam flipped to the second page and signed his name on the line. Of all the uncertainties in his life, this wasn't one of them.

If anything happened to him, his wife, Molly Clelland Frazier, would inherit the ranch free and clear. She would also become a cotrustee of Lass's fortune, along with the lawyer and the bank.

He'd also given Molly his living power of attorney in case he became incapacitated for some reason.

"Are you going to let Molly adopt Lass?" Chuck asked.

Sam looked at him blankly.

"If she becomes Lass's legal mother and you two get a divorce, she'll have equal rights to custody." The attorney looked worried. "She might anyway."

"Molly doesn't believe in divorce."

"Yeah, and lightning doesn't strike twice in the same place." Chuck gave him a sharp glance, then picked up the will, looked it over and replaced it in the file folder. "Does she know she's your chief beneficiary, and that she holds the power of life and death over you?"

"Not yet."

"Maybe you'd better not tell her until you see how things go. You might change your mind. I've seen more than one man make serious mistakes in the throes of…uh, early marriage."

Sam didn't care for the cynical remarks. Besides, Chuck didn't know the half of it. Since there was no sex between them, he wasn't in danger of losing his mind because of it.

However, he might due to the lack of it.

Something had changed, but he didn't know what it was. If he hadn't known her better, he would swear Molly was acting the temptress. Only she was more subtle about it than any woman he'd ever known. There was something so naturally innocent about her. She couldn't have a conniving bone in her body.

But sometimes, when she looked at him in a certain way… Well, it stirred the blood and made him dream of nights with her in his arms. Sometimes he thought she did it deliberately.

No, he knew Molly. She wasn't a vamp. Neither was she out for the main chance. She had a comfortable nest egg put away, and her nursery earned a darn decent living. She didn't need anything from him.

"You were the one who told me to marry her," he reminded the other man.

Chuck gave him a severe look. "Yeah, but I didn't tell you to put your life and fortune in her hands."

"Who else have I got?" Sam pushed up from the chair and headed for the door. He paused before leaving and gave his friend a cynical grin. "My lawyer and banker? Most people would tell me to watch out for you two, not my wife."

Chuck snorted in disdain.

With a laugh, Sam went out, closing the door before the paper clip the attorney threw at him could land. He heard it plink against the wood. He nodded at the secretary, who was on the phone, and stepped out into the mild spring afternoon. The streets of Roswell were crowded with going-home traffic.

Hurrying now, he drove out the road toward the ranch, but that wasn't his destination. He'd decided to stop by the nursery and see if his girls were there.

His girls. Molly would probably deliver a lecture about the male possessive attitude and the reference to her as a girl, but that's the way he thought of her and Lass. They were his, and he dared anyone to try to take them from him.

Loosening his grip on the steering wheel, he considered the past seven days. It still gave him a pleasurable shock to come in at the end of a hard day and see the lights on at the house, to know they were there, waiting for him.

Molly and Lass and the two cats. His girls.

He turned off in front of the church and drove down

the winding road to the nursery. Through the open curtains, he could see the children inside, all as busy as bees in a clover patch.

Molly was there, too. She was reading a book to several children gathered around her on the floor. Lass lay on a mat beside Molly. Another group of kids worked on some project with the other teacher at the back of the room.

As he watched, a knot formed in his chest. Breathing became difficult. The problem happened frequently of late. It worried him. He wasn't sure what it meant.

Shaking off the feeling, he climbed down from the truck and went into the colorful room. There were pictures of flowers everywhere, plus some real ones growing in pots around the room.

"Hello. Come join us," his wife invited. She moved over a space so he could sit on the cushion beside her. "We're almost finished with this story. Can someone tell Sam what has happened so far?"

Sam folded his legs in front of him and plopped down. He listened while six kids tried to tell him about the story.

"Okay, I got it," he said, recalling the story from his childhood days.

Molly called for quiet and began reading again.

Sam smiled at Lass. His daughter gave him a drooling grin, turned over on her stomach, bunched her knees under her and crawled into his lap.

"Oh, look, children," Molly exclaimed. "Lass has learned to crawl. Good girl, Lass."

The kids cheered and offered encouragement. Sam felt the squeezing sensation in his chest again. Inhaling deeply, he caught a whiff of Molly's soap and cologne. It was as familiar to him as the smell of his shaving soap.

She took a shower in the morning. He took one at night when he came in from the ranch work. He looked forward to Sunday. He'd like to linger in bed and listen to the sound of running water, his imagination steaming up his thoughts as he pictured her in the shower, which was roomy enough for two.

Fighting back the images this called forth, he lifted his daughter into a comfortable position. Lass made gurgling noises while Molly resumed reading.

When the story was over, Molly and the children talked about the tough choices the young hero of the tale had had to make. Sam realized the reading session was also a lesson on ethics.

"I'm ready to go. Are you heading for the ranch?" she asked him after she stood and dismissed the kids for a play period.

"I thought we might eat out tonight."

Her gaze drifted over him. He'd cleaned up before coming to town. Instead of jeans, he wore dress slacks. He'd even put on a tie with his white shirt. However, he'd drawn the line at adding a coat. The temperature was in the seventies, although the air would cool with the coming of night.

"That would be nice. I'll tell Tiffany I'm going."

While she told her assistant goodbye, he walked outside with Lass. They looked at a yellow lupine growing near the driveway.

"Da-da," Lass said and touched his face.

"She knows who you are," Molly said, coming up behind them, her purse and jacket in her hands.

She looked trim and stylish in green slacks with a white blouse striped in the same green. He'd noticed she wore pearl studs in her ears. She'd explained she didn't wear dangly earrings around the children. It was too easy to get one yanked out by accident.

On her left hand, she wore the wedding band and pearl ring that had been his mother's engagement ring. Tiny diamonds formed arcs around the pearl. It was an old-fashioned design. He'd offered to have it reset or to get something different, but Molly had been delighted with it.

Nine days and she still seemed pleased and interested in everything at the ranch. She and the cats. They, too, were curious about everything. Now that Molly let them outside—she hadn't the first week—they were as likely to appear in the stable as the house. One of them had taken a shine to Sandy.

Things were working out. He'd give Molly a couple more months, then see how she liked it. A cold, wet winter like the last one, slogging through the mud and muck to check on five hundred hungry cows, could change a person's romantic views real fast.

But there was no way he could wait until winter. She'd have to make up her mind about staying before then. He forgot the cynical advice when she stooped and studied the lupine with them.

"It's a pea flower," she said.

"Yes." He drew in the sweet essence of her. This close, he noticed the texture of her lips and the tiny scar that marred the perfect outline of one.

"Does that mean it's a legume?"

He didn't really hear the question. "Yes."

She stood. "I need to stop by the grocery store.

Would you rather take Lass to the truck stop and wait there or go to the market with me?''

Standing, he lifted Lass into the air a couple of times while she squealed with delight. ''We'll save you a seat at the restaurant.''

''Now why did I think that would be your choice?'' She smiled, gave Lass a kiss on the cheek, then left.

Sam watched her for a second before buckling Lass into the truck and heading toward the truck stop. It would be crowded on Friday night, which was good.

The few times he'd gone to town since the wedding, everyone from the bank teller to the guy at the gas station had asked how Molly was. He wanted the townsfolk, especially the gossips, to see their darling teacher so they'd know she'd survived the first seven days of marriage to him.

Molly squeezed into the parking place next to Sam's truck and hurried inside the restaurant. She spotted Sam and the baby easily. He was the best-looking man in the place.

She admitted she might be a little prejudiced in his favor, but he really was handsome. She slid into the other side of the booth. ''Hi. I made it. Have you ordered?''

''No, I was waiting for you.'' He signaled the waitress after Molly looked over the menu.

The girl brought a cup of coffee for Molly and refreshed his cup. They gave their orders, then Molly suggested he give Lass some crackers and juice.

''Damn,'' Sam muttered under his breath.

She looked up in surprise. She'd rarely heard him

use any swear words. She twisted around to see who he was watching.

It took a couple of seconds, but she connected a name with the faces. The older couple taking a seat at the one empty table in the place was Mr. and Mrs. Tisdale, Sam's former in-laws.

She observed Sam while he watched them. A grim frown etched a furrow between his eyebrows. He nodded his head toward them.

Glancing around, she saw the other two had seen them. It didn't take a genius to recognize the animosity between the two men. Mr. Tisdale was a large, beefy man, probably handsome in his younger days but running to fat now.

His wife was a tiny woman, so scrawny she reminded Molly of a wet cat. The woman was gazing their way like a starving person left out of a banquet. Molly realized it was Lass that held Mrs. Tisdale's gaze while her husband glared at Sam.

Her heart went out to the older woman. She settled in her seat. "You should take Lass to visit them," she told Sam. "Mrs. Tisdale is dying to know her granddaughter."

Sam flicked her a glance that warned her off.

She wasn't a person who could sit back and do nothing when she saw a situation that needed attention. "We could invite them over for dinner one night."

"Let it go, Molly. Tisdale better not set a foot on my land. He's liable to get it shot off. He feels the same about me, and I sure as hell am not going over there."

His tone was so cold, she was taken aback. "My gosh, I can't believe two men can be so stubborn."

"You don't know the half of it," he said with a sarcastic edge.

"That poor woman," Molly said in heartfelt sympathy, feeling a kinship with Sam's former mother-in-law.

Sam's snort mocked her feelings. She glared at him.

"I told her she could visit Lass at my place, but she has to come alone." He glared at her.

Lass made a snubbing sound, a sign that she was getting ready to wail to the high heavens.

"Now see what you've done. You've upset the baby." Molly crooned to Lass and played pat-a-cake until the tears dried up.

Sam prayed for patience. He didn't want to quarrel with Molly over his former in-laws. A quiet dinner with his wife and kid. Was that too much to ask?

Over Molly's head, he could see Tisdale glance his way once in a while. Besides marrying Elise and turning down an offer to merge the ranches into one operation with Tisdale the boss, Sam wondered what else he'd done to make Tisdale hate him.

The man reminded him of a trapped fox he'd once seen, its eyes cunning and desperate. He looked at Molly and Lass, worry eating at his insides. He'd do whatever was necessary to protect them. A fierce tenderness rushed over him. They were his, and he'd not let anyone hurt them.

When their food came, he tried to follow his wife's dictum for table manners. "How did things go today?"

She glanced at him with a preoccupied air, her

thoughts obviously miles away. She was a quiet person, introspective and reflective in her nature. He wondered what she did alone in her room at night. She usually retired early.

"Fine," she said. "We're going to put on a play next weekend. We could use a hand with the props."

He'd never been much of a social mixer, but with her gaze on him, fully expecting him to volunteer and, more than that, to *enjoy* it, he couldn't refuse. "What do you need done?"

They talked about the play for the rest of the meal. He found himself agreeing to make a gingerbread house out of plywood for Hansel and Gretel to find. Watching Molly's face while she talked about the project, he wondered why he'd ever thought she was plain or prudish.

Enthusiasm sparkled in her eyes as they talked. Her smile was frequent and natural the way it had been before they married. A flush highlighted her cheeks.

He watched her lips move while she explained her plans for the event. He barely listened as she spoke of the social hour that would follow the play.

With those eyes like moonstones, that delicate complexion and little cat face, she was really very pretty. The difference between her and other women was that she didn't *act* pretty. She wasn't impressed by her own or other people's looks. She expected courtesy and decorum from people. And usually got it.

They finished just as Lass was getting cranky. He was relieved to be going. A squalling kid could make a nervous wreck out of a Tibetan monk.

Molly held Lass while he paid at the register. Car-

rying the baby seat, he took his wife's arm to guide
her out. They had to go past the Tisdale table.

He knew what was going to happen. Molly dug in
her heels and wouldn't be urged forward no matter
how he tried to ease her past the older couple.

"Mr. and Mrs. Tisdale," she said cordially. She
could drip honey when she wanted to, he noted. "I'm
Molly Frazier, Sam's wife. Sam," she said sweetly,
"look who's here."

She gave him one of her bright looks. He nodded.
Her mouth screwed up. He forced out a "good evening," but she wasn't going to coax a smile out of
him.

"And this is Lass," she continued as if they were
all the best of friends. "I hope you'll come visit her
soon."

"Oh, yes," Elsie said. She reached out. Lass
grabbed her finger. "Oh, my, she's strong."

Sam was aware of the other diners avidly listening
while pretending to eat their dinners.

"You can bring the child to visit us," Tisdale spoke
up.

The light seeped out of his wife's eyes. She moved
her hand away when Lass let go. "Perhaps we will
visit," she said in a squeaky but stubborn voice. "One
day."

Sam was surprised at the woman's spunk.

Molly beamed at them. "Good. We'll plan on it. If
you have time, stop by the nursery. We're putting on
a play next Friday. Hansel and Gretel. Do come if you
have time. The children love to have guests to show
off for."

With her usual warm manner, she said good-night

to both the Tisdales and walked out. Sam heaved a sigh of relief. Tisdale was a dangerous man.

In the truck, he waited until Molly and Lass had pulled out onto the road, then followed behind them at a safe distance. He felt like a sheriff from the Old West, riding shotgun for a stagecoach of important passengers.

So he was. Molly and Lass were the two most important people in his life.

Molly drove in her usual careful manner, staying right on the speed limit. Sam usually drove about ten miles over, but fifty-five was fast enough on the highway. It was too fast when she turned off on the ranch road. She slowed to forty.

At the house, she parked in the garage while Sam left the pickup outside. He helped her carry in Lass and the groceries.

The two cowboys had been in and had supper, she assumed. She'd left a bag of homemade cookies on the counter with a note to take them to the bunkhouse with them. The bag was gone.

"I'll give Lass her bath," Sam volunteered when she started putting the groceries away.

She nodded. Her mind stayed on the scene at the restaurant. For some reason, she felt sorry for the Tisdales. She'd sensed resentment in the grandfather. Some people couldn't accept growing old. She thought he was one of them.

Elsie Tisdale had once been a very pretty woman, probably something like her daughter, but now she was as crinkly and dried as an oat husk. The longing in her eyes when she'd gazed at Lass had wrung Molly's heart.

Something was going to have to be done about that. It wasn't fair for Lass to miss out on having grandparents who lived practically next door.

She finished putting things away. Yawning, she stretched wearily and tried to decide what to do next. She should wash a load of clothes so they wouldn't pile up, but she was too tired.

Tomorrow, she thought. She'd get home early and do it then. Thank goodness Mrs. Stevens had agreed to take care of the house. With Lass fussy and not sleeping well, Molly didn't have the energy to think about the house, much less clean it.

There was something to be said for a tiny cottage, she continued the line of thought as she went to the bedroom.

Without thinking, she opened the door and walked in. She stopped on the threshold and stared.

Sam stood by the closet.

Naked.

She'd never seen a naked man before.

Not in person, only movies. And never like this.

Her mind had switched to slow motion. She could only think of one word or phrase at a time. She clutched her throat while tingles cascaded down her skin like spilled champagne.

He turned slowly and faced her. She couldn't tear her gaze from his magnificent form. He was fully, flagrantly erect.

A man for all seasons, she thought, forcing her gaze upward. She swallowed as her nerves knotted into a ball and lodged in her chest. Meeting Sam's eyes, she could only stand still while his eyes searched hers as if looking for something that only he knew.

"Excuse me," she said and lit out for her room, scooting inside and closing the door like a rabbit leaping into its hole.

She fell onto the Greek lounge, her legs trembling, her breath uneven and harsh, like a runner's at the finish line.

If she lived to be a hundred, she'd never forget. That powerful masculine image burned behind her eyelids. She couldn't close her eyes without seeing it...

Pressing her hands against her eyes, she tried to block out the shock and, she admitted, the pleasurable awe of seeing her husband without his clothes. She didn't think she could face him again. She'd blush, and he'd know what a ninny she was.

She heard his step outside the door and froze.

"I'm going to watch a program on TV," he called out. "If you need the bathroom, it's free."

"Thank you," she replied, sounding as stuffy as her mother had once said she was when she hadn't laughed at a guest's risqué story about the time he'd visited a nudist camp.

When she heard the outer door close, she changed to her pajamas and pulled on the matching robe and scuffs. As quick as a cat burglar, she finished her ablutions and returned to the safety of her room.

Once inside, she paced restlessly, then picked up a favorite novel she'd started reading over the weekend. She'd read it several times over the years. The story was a beautiful romance, one involving a teacher and a tough rancher. Two hours later, she finished the book and laid it on the table.

She compared her circumstances to those of the hero and heroine in the book. They'd known practically from the first moment that they loved each other. They'd stood by each other through all their troubles. That was the way love should be.

She didn't know what Sam wanted from her. He was her husband. She'd seen desire in his eyes that past week, but he held himself aloof, refusing even physical gratification.

He said they should wait until she was sure this was what she wanted, but she thought he was afraid of involvement.

Had his first marriage been awful?

Guiltily she repressed the surge of hope this thought produced. She'd never wish for happiness at another's expense.

She surveyed the titles of her beloved romance books. Some of them were marriage of convenience stories. She realized that was what she and Sam had. A marriage of convenience. It sounded feudal, medieval...Victorian at the very least.

And it was damn inconvenient as far as she was concerned!

This waiting was ridiculous. Making love was one of the most bonding of human endeavors. If more people realized that and paid attention to it in their marriages, the divorce rate would drop drastically.

Her mother had explained it. "A woman needs to feel loved to make love," she'd said. "A man needs to make love to feel loved. Make sure he feels loved. Tell him that you need to feel the same. Marriage is about two people giving and taking equally, not one doing all the giving while the other takes."

Molly believed that. It was the basis for friendship, too. Both had to get something from the relationship for it to last.

Now all she had to do was figure out a plan to make her husband overcome his scruples, or something like that.

Tomorrow she'd study on how to become a femme fatale.

Removing the many throw pillows from the daybed, she turned back the covers and slipped between the sheets. Every bone in her body sighed wearily. She fell asleep.

The wail seemed a part of her dream at first, then Molly realized it was Lass. She flicked on the lamp, leapt out of bed and dashed for the door. Sam had his light on when she entered his room. He paused by the bed and looked up.

This time she could only register his nakedness. She hadn't time to dwell on it. "I heard Lass," she said.

She went to the crying infant and lifted her into her arms. "There, darling, there now. Are those ol' teeth bothering you again? Poor baby."

Wiping the tears and runny nose with a tissue, she sat in the rocker and began to hum. Lass quietened and finally stuck her thumb in her mouth and laid her head on Molly's shoulder.

Sam entered carrying the medicine dropper. "Let's give her some of this. The pediatrician said it would help."

She held still while he gave the medicine to Lass, then began to rock again. Lass settled down, an occasional snuffle catching her breath.

Sam left with the medicine dropper. Molly heard him washing it in the kitchen. He returned in a minute and watched while she rocked and hummed to the baby, his shoulders propped against the doorframe.

After a while he pushed upright and crossed the room. "She's asleep now," he murmured.

He lifted the sleeping baby and deposited her in the crib. After covering her with a blanket, he patted her back, then motioned for Molly to leave when he went to the door.

Going down the hall, she realized she was in her pajamas, her feet bare. Sam was also barefoot. He'd pulled on a pair of jeans. The zipper hung open partway down his abdomen. She was acutely aware of this fact all at once.

"After midnight," he murmured. "Maybe she'll sleep until dawn. Do you have to go in early tomorrow?"

"Yes." It was hard to speak past the tightness in her throat. Their footsteps made hardly any sound on the Spanish tiles in the hall.

The entire house seemed to be holding its breath, waiting to see what would happen.

She wondered what Sam would do if she crawled into his bed. She regretted that she hadn't slept there when he'd carried her into the house on their wedding night. By now, their marriage would have been bonded in the most elemental way.

Sam was a sensual man, a man who took pleasure in using his body in his work. From his perceptiveness and gentleness, she knew he would be a considerate lover.

Her pride wouldn't let her stay with him that first

time. Nor was she forward enough to suggest it now. Somehow he had to come to her, or at least meet her halfway, before this marriage would work. She'd have to make him see that.

In the meantime, there were those feminine wiles she needed to practice on.

Chapter Nine

Molly stirred the jar of baby food and set it on the desk before picking up Lass and putting her in the high chair. The other children were eating while they listened to a story being read by Tiffany.

After strapping Lass in and putting the tray across the chair, Molly took her seat and lifted the first bite toward Lass. The door to the nursery opened a crack.

A slice of face—an eye, part of a nose, mouth and chin—appeared in the one-inch opening.

"Come in," Molly called in a soft voice.

The door closed.

Puzzled, she went over and opened it. A woman stood on the other side. She looked so nervous, Molly was afraid she'd fall right over if someone said "boo" to her.

"Mrs. Tisdale," she said, putting extra warmth in

her tone. "Please come in. We're having lunch. Won't you join us?"

While she chatted, she laid a hand on the other woman's arm and drew her inside. She closed the door behind them. "Come."

Mrs. Tisdale followed her to the desk at the side of the room. Lass waved her arms at the jars of food.

Molly had an inspiration. "She's hungry. Would you mind feeding her while I take care of our lunch?" She made this sound like a great favor.

As if in a daze, Mrs. Tisdale nodded her head. In less than a minute, Molly had the timid grandmother out of her suit jacket, an apron over her blouse and the spoon in her hand.

Molly headed for the kitchen. She prepared a plate of pasta salad and sliced vegetables for their guest. When she finished, she lingered and watched Mrs. Tisdale feed Lass.

The woman's hand shook noticeably at first, but she settled down after the first few bites. Lass, who hadn't yet entered her bashful phase around strangers, smiled and clicked while she ate the vegetables and fruit.

When the story was over, Molly helped Tiffany and the kids clean up the lunch debris, then it was quiet time. The children pushed the chairs out of the way and lay on their floor mats. The two teachers brought plates and drinks to the desk when the children were settled.

"It's time for Lass's nap," Molly said. "Tiffany, have you met Mrs. Tisdale?"

"Uh, no, I don't think so. That is, I don't think we were ever introduced." Tiffany cast Molly an uncertain glance before greeting the older woman.

"Please, call me Elsie."

"Sit here, Elsie," Molly invited, indicating the desk chair. "I'll tuck Lass in—"

"Oh, may I?"

Molly hesitated, recalling her husband's warning. Well, the woman was hardly going to grab the child and run off with her. "Of course. Do you want to change her diaper, or shall I?"

She led the way to the crib in the corner of the room, the sleepy Lass in her arms. After placing the baby in the bed, she laid the clean diaper out, along with a damp washcloth, and left Elsie Tisdale to do the work.

"I can't believe she's here," Tiffany whispered when Molly joined her at the desk. "I didn't know she knew how to drive."

"Maybe she had someone drop her off." Molly casually peered out the front window. "A late-model car is parked in the driveway."

"I've never seen her without her husband." Tiffany studied the woman as she fussed over her granddaughter. "He's a strange man. Elise used to fight with him something terrible. My dad said Mr. Tisdale has to control everyone around him. He hates anyone who doesn't agree with him."

"Maybe that's why he hates Sam," Molly mused aloud.

"Their quarrel was no secret. Mr. Tisdale wanted to combine the ranch operations after Sam and Elise were married, with himself giving the orders, of course. Sam declined the offer. Rumor has it Tisdale blew his stack and ordered Sam off his place after calling him a few choice names, ingrate the nicest among them, I understand.''

"How foolish to alienate your family like that."

"Yeah. Apparently Tisdale suggested it in front of some men from the bank. I guess he was humiliated when Sam said no.''

When Elsie finally finished with the baby, Molly told her she was delighted she'd decided to stop by. "A baby needs a sense of family," she told the woman. "I hope this won't be the last we see of you."

"It won't be," Elsie promised, her smile shy but pleased.

Molly's heart went out to the older woman. She wondered what her life had been like. Surely whatever love had been in it had disappeared when her daughter died. It wasn't right that Elsie be deprived of Lass because of her husband.

She was pretty sure that Mr. Tisdale didn't know his wife was visiting her granddaughter. Well, she and Tiffany were certainly not going to tell.

On the heels of that resolution came a question. How would Sam feel about it when he found out?

He said he'd given Elsie permission to visit her granddaughter. What if he'd changed his mind and didn't want Elsie around Lass, what would she do?

She'd see how things went. Maybe Elsie wouldn't get up the courage to return. If she did, Molly could explain it to Sam when she saw how grandmother and granddaughter got along.

Coward. She didn't want to deprive the woman of the baby, but she didn't want to face Sam's wrath when she defied him in case he said no to Elsie's visits. For defy him she would.

Elsie Tisdale needed something to nourish her soul, or the poor woman was going to dry up and blow away like a skinny tumbleweed during one of the wind storms. Lass, with her infinite supply of love, would be good for her grandmother.

A picture of her own dear grandmother, who'd given her a thousand shares of private family stock when she'd graduated from college, came to mind. Right now, Nana was on a cruise around the world or some such thing. Eighty-four and off on a lark.

Molly hoped she was as active and daring at that age. At any age, she added.

After they ate, Elsie quickly left, reminding the two teachers of a student who was afraid of missing the class bell.

"She's so timid," Tiffany said in a pitying tone.

"Do you think so?" Molly watched the car back, then pull forward and disappear up the winding driveway. "She came here even though her husband said she couldn't."

"When did he say that?"

Molly explained about the restaurant scene.

"He scares me." Tiffany shivered. "Anyone who hates that much and that long over something so silly, well, it scares me."

"Sam has left the ranch to me."

"He didn't!"

Molly nodded. "And the care of Lass."

Tiffany's mouth gaped. "He must really trust you to give you everything like that. It was said he put his lawyer in control of the ranch instead of Elise when they married and that the ranch was willed to the baby in case of his death. Elise supposedly threw a fit over it. I heard she'd already planned on divorcing him and taking him for all she could after the baby was born.''

Molly couldn't hide her shock. What kind of people were these? She didn't want to know. The talk was making her uneasy, even though it was gossip.

''Well, let's see, we need to run through the play this afternoon. Can you work with Krissie on the song she's supposed to sing while I teach the bluebirds their dance?''

''Sure.''

Molly put the problem of the Tisdales out of her mind.

Sam parked the truck near the barn. From the back, he hefted a calf and carried it inside. After putting it in a stall with clean straw to snuggle in, he trudged across the wide gravel driveway to his house.

The windows glowed like beacons. He'd seen them miles away and had followed them through the dark until he'd arrived home safe and sound.

Home.

Once he'd reached a point where he'd rather sleep in the stable than return to the house. No more.

Opening the back door, he inhaled the scent of stew, left on the back burner to cook slowly through the night. Molly was a miracle of organization. She planned and posted the weekly menus so he and the hands knew what to prepare if she didn't get home in time to start supper during the week.

The house looked nice in a sort of cluttered way. Molly might be organized, but she wasn't exceptionally neat. There were books and magazines on nearly every surface. Lists of things she'd planned were tacked all over the bulletin board.

He took off his boots and left them by the kitchen door. In sock feet, he went to his bedroom and shed his clothes, which were both muddy and bloody from birthing the calf he'd left in the barn. The mother hadn't made it.

He'd left the carcass in the field. The mountain cat living in the hills east of the ranch would find it. If not, the coyotes would. He wondered what Molly would think. She'd probably want to hold a wake and a formal funeral.

Grinning, almost groaning with weariness, he turned the shower on full blast and as hot as he could stand it. When he stepped out a few minutes later, he felt rejuvenated.

After drying and hanging up his towel—the school-marm didn't approve of wet towels left on the floor—he headed for bed.

The clock struck eleven. He paused by the window, yawning and stretching, and peered at the nightscape. The moon hung low and cast sooty shadows through the mesquite onto the rocks of the dry creek. A breeze flirted with the tree. The tree tossed its branches in a provocative response.

He thought of Molly's hair. It was softer than the down from the cottonwood trees that grew along the river. He tried not to, but sometimes he had to touch it...and then he'd think about how soft she would be all over.

Whew. That wasn't something to dwell on. Heat rippled through him, driving the fatigue from his muscles and bringing the clamor for relief from the fantasies he'd been having since their rushed marriage.

He couldn't deny it—he was on fire for his wife. Her scent, an article of clothing left in the bath, hell, anything and everything that was hers sent him into instant arousal. The way he was now.

Sighing, he folded the bedspread neatly at the end of the bed and pulled the sheet and blanket back. When he lay down, every muscle groaned. Except one. It was ready for action.

She'd been ready for him on their wedding night. He'd realized that later. He should have carried her to bed in the first place rather than trying to be so damn noble about rushing her.

God, he'd messed up. She'd been starry-eyed then and filled with expectations for their marriage.

He who hesitates is lost.

Yeah, well, he'd had good reasons to hesitate. He just couldn't remember what they were. Molly was the same person after marriage that she'd been before. She was still a lady and every inch a schoolmarm. With her disapproving stare and bright smiles, she could control an army.

Most important, she was still a friend. Other than those glances that sometimes made his blood heat up, she acted the same, listening and questioning until she understood all about the ranch and his concerns.

She told him about her school and her concerns, too. That reminded him, he had to load the gingerbread house on the truck and take it to town in the morning for the play tomorrow afternoon. He and the hands had worked on it every spare minute during the past two weeks. It looked nice, if he did say so.

He turned restlessly, then realized he hadn't eaten supper. He'd been too tired to think about it, wanting only a shower and bed. The aroma of the stew in the Crock-Pot had awakened his hunger. He tossed aside the cover, pulled on a pair of white briefs and headed for the kitchen.

Passing Lass's bedroom, he stopped and went in to take a quick peek at her. She was certainly happy with the new living arrangements. He paused on the threshold.

Molly was there.

She and Lass were asleep in the recliner-rocker she'd brought from her house in town. It was Molly-size, just right for her to snuggle in.

That odd, fierce tenderness he'd felt only for his child before Molly came into their lives clutched his chest. He couldn't put a name to it, but Molly invoked it just as Lass did.

It confused him to feel this way about a woman. He couldn't figure out what caused it. She wasn't a child needing his care and protection.

Bending, he lifted the baby and put her to bed. Molly didn't stir. She was probably as tired as he was. She was up at dawn and off to the school. She'd taken over the care of the house. She'd been getting up at night with Lass for the past week, a relief for him since they were so busy with the cattle.

He slipped a hand behind her and one under her legs and lifted her into his arms. She weighed less than some of the calves they'd been roping and branding.

She laid her head on his shoulder and murmured against his neck. "It's late."

"I know." He carried her down the hall. Pushing

the door closed behind him with his shoulder, he hesitated. The moonlight threw a square of light on the covers, all turned back and ready.

If he laid her there, would she notice?

Without giving himself time to answer the question, he walked to the bed and laid her on it. She sighed without opening her eyes. He reached down to pull the covers over her. Instead he touched her hair and smoothed it on the pillow.

"Molly," he said.

She opened her eyes.

The moonlight cast the room into silver-edged shadows. It created a halo of light around Sam as he bent toward her. It made the night magic.

Slowly, so very slowly, he moved beside her. She felt his weight on the mattress, then the contact of his thigh against hers. In the stillness that followed, she heard the beat of her heart, loud and insistent in her ears.

"Molly," he said, a husky whisper in the dark.

She heard the longing in him. An answering need suffused her whole body. He hadn't said the words, but she didn't think they were necessary. She knew his heart.

With a sureness borne of love, she touched him, letting her fingers meander over his chest. Her senses heightened, she was acutely aware of the crisp feel of his body hair and the warmth of his skin.

The world condensed into this moment, this place.

"Is the time right?" he murmured, his lips only a few inches from hers.

"Yes."

His chest touched hers as he drew in a deep breath, then let it out slowly. A current of sensation flowed into her breasts. Her nipples contracted almost painfully.

He placed his left hand on the bed beside her and shifted his weight to it. With his right hand, he smoothed the strands of hair from her temple, then he cupped her chin.

She held her breath as his mouth descended. Through an eternity of waiting, his lips finally touched her. It was the sweetest thing imaginable.

There was no need to think about her reactions. Her body acted on its own, knowing instinctively the right moves.

She reached for him, circling his broad shoulders with her arms, running her fingers into his hair, which was cool and damp on top, but warm in the underlayers.

His arms slipped under her, bringing her upright and deepening the kiss at the same time. He held her tightly, and she felt the *th-thump* of his heart against her, the beats fast and powerful.

Light-headed with happiness, she skimmed her hands down his back, loving the smooth ripple of muscle under his skin, exulting in his masculine strength, secure in the knowledge that he would never use it against her.

He moved his lips over hers. She opened hers, inviting him inside. He dipped lightly, the merest butterfly of a touch, again and again, then drew back to study her.

A demand pushed its way to her throat, a soft moan of need greater than the other time she'd been in his arms. She knew what to expect. She knew what she wanted. And she wanted it now, this moment.

"Easy," he murmured when she stirred restlessly in his arms.

"I want you," she confessed.

"You'll have me," he promised, a heated avowal that stirred new longing in her. He laid her against the pillow.

She'd never felt so wild, so abandoned to her senses, so very, very right in her instincts. This was her man, her mate, and she was his. This was right.

"Sam," she whispered on a shaky breath as he kissed along her neck. At the neckline to her satin pajamas, he paused.

"May I?" he asked, his fingers on the top button.

"Yes." She hardly recognized her own voice, it was so choked with love and the passion he invoked in her.

He flicked the buttons open...one, then another...another...and the last one. Pausing, he looked into her eyes, his handsome face serious and filled with purpose.

Sam ran his fingers inside the edge of the material and slowly pushed it to each side.

A tremor glided through him, as if his world had tilted on its axis. Molly looked up at him with complete trust in her eyes. She waited for him to complete the task he'd begun. He wasn't sure if he could go slow for her.

The moment was breathtakingly beautiful. He didn't want it to end. But the rush of anticipation burned in his blood, and he couldn't ignore the need to see her, to touch her, any longer.

Sliding the material completely off her breasts, he gazed at her, feeling like a starving man at a feast. "You're beautiful," he said, the words inadequate, but he couldn't think of any others to express how he felt.

She laid a hand in the center of his chest. "We both are. We're beautiful together."

It made perfect sense to him.

Like him, she understood, even without words, the beauty of the moment. A need to cherish her, to softly and reverently kiss every inch of her, stole over him.

The words came of their own volition. "Ah, Molly," he said, fighting for control. "Molly, darling."

He needed to be inside, buried in her warmth, in the sweet, welcoming center of her. He needed...her.

Moving carefully so as not to frighten her with the lust that raged through him, he slipped his thumbs under the elastic waistband of her pajamas. "Lift your hips."

She did as he wished.

With one liquid motion, he peeled the material from her. His breath caught in his throat. She lay still under the siege of his gaze and permitted him to look his fill.

"Beautiful." It was the only word he could find.

He leaned over her, letting his body skim hers ever so lightly. Her breasts beaded again, drawing into tiny buds of passion he had to taste.

Molly couldn't seem to get enough air. She gasped when his lips opened and gently sucked one nipple into his mouth. With his tongue, he teased and stroked until she writhed against him in increasing demand, wanting more...more...

"Come to me." She panted with need. "Now. Please, now." She wasn't sure what she wanted, only that he held the key.

"Not yet. I wouldn't last a second. One stroke and…" He smiled down at her, then nuzzled her nose with his. "I want to make love to you for hours."

"I don't think I can last that long."

His chest moved against hers as he chuckled. "I'll make sure you do." He paused. "Molly, I want to lie beside you."

She ran her hands over his back, urging him closer. "Oh, yes, please do."

He stood. With one swift movement, he stripped out of his briefs. The moonlight from the window outlined his powerful body. She vaguely wondered if she should be alarmed, but oddly, she wasn't. Her faith in her husband was absolute. He would know what to do.

With the same care as before, he lifted her and slipped the satin top off her shoulders and down her arms. It pooled on the floor with the other items of clothing.

She shivered.

He must have felt it. "Don't be afraid."

"I'm not. I'm just…anxious."

His smile flashed briefly, then his mouth was on hers again. She felt his chest, the brush of his thigh as he changed position on the bed, then…then the sheer wonder of his flesh all along hers, a hot, powerful presence that registered in every cell in her body.

For a second she was unsure about what to do next. Nature took over. She moved against him. The thrust of his body on her thigh both shocked and thrilled her.

His tongue stroked hers, coaxing her into joining

his sensual play. She responded joyfully, filled with the most wonderful sensations, pressing and retreating, loving the pressure of his lips on hers.

With a knee, he nudged her legs apart. Without breaking the kiss, he moved over her, his body fitting into the grooves and angles of hers as if they'd been designed for each other.

She sucked in a quick breath when he touched the most intimate part of her. Still maintaining the kiss, he thrust gently at the jointure of her legs.

Sam didn't try to penetrate the tight closure of her body. First he wanted to get her used to his touch and to assure her he was in control. He was...barely.

He ignored the fierce need to thrust inside and find the peace that only she could give him. He wanted to make this first time a time to remember for her. He wanted to give her so much pleasure she'd never regret coming to him or giving him this gift of herself.

Between him and Molly, there was respect as well as passion. He could never tell her how much it meant to him. He wanted to shower her with the most exquisite pleasure she'd ever known.

That would be his gift to her for her trust.

He stroked gently at the portals of her womanhood. He kissed her breasts. A deep sense of satisfaction raced through him when she lifted to his touch, clearly indicating her desire for more.

"Yes," he encouraged. "Show me what you want."

Molly hardly heard the words. She was whirling in the haze of desire he stirred in her. It was like that night at her cottage, but better.

She loved the feel of his body on hers and was

momentarily dismayed when he pulled away. But only for a second. The next instant, his mouth was on her breasts again, first one, then the other, suckling, kissing them with the heated passion they shared.

With trembling hands, she stroked through his hair and down his back. She found the small protrusions of his nipples in his chest hair and toyed with them. She glided down his torso to his abdomen. He sucked in a harsh breath when she touched him more intimately. She hesitated, then closed her hand around him.

He lifted his head and gazed at her. Motionless, they watched each other.

"We'll take this as far as you want to go," he told her. "I can stop at anytime. You only have to say the word."

She nodded. Yes, she'd known all that without him saying it. She smiled at him, deliriously happy. "If you stop, I'll bite you," she promised and pulled his chest hair with her teeth to show him.

Sam laughed and gave her a bear hug, then turned them over so she was on top. "Okay, you can explore now."

Her eyes opened wide, then narrowed as she studied him, taking her time in deciding where she wanted to go first. He gritted his teeth, determined to wait out the exquisite torture.

Curiosity got the better of her. Shifting to one side, she stroked down his stomach until she reached the destination she'd chosen.

He held his breath as she touched him, gingerly at first, with uncertain glances at his face to see how he was reacting. He remained still, a smile kicking up the corners of his mouth as she became bolder.

Hooking his hands under the headboard, he reveled in her earnest exploration. Mixed with the passion she aroused was that odd tenderness she induced. He'd never felt exactly this way about a woman before.

The moment came when she grew too bold for his self-control. Bending down, she kissed the tip of his shaft, then drew back and looked at him, her eyes dancing with seductive mischief.

He uttered an expletive as heat exploded inside him like a rocket. Turning with her in his arms, he slid between her legs and pressed the full length of his body on hers. He began to move in a smooth cadence, rubbing intimately until she moved with each motion of his.

The moonlight had shifted, and he couldn't see her face as clearly. He didn't need to. Her panting gasps and soft moans told him she was as caught in desire's net as he was.

He could feel the moisture where they met, the sweet dew of passion a woman couldn't hide. The need to take her all the way swept over him in a tidal wave of possessive tenderness.

Moving his hand between them, he stroked gently, intimately, urgently. She hesitated, but he wouldn't give her time to think about this new strategy. He kissed her mouth until they were breathless, then he kissed her some more.

Suddenly she went totally still beneath him. He gritted his teeth together and kept up the same rhythmic movements.

When she stopped breathing, he moved faster, feeling his own control slip as he sensed the coming climax.

"Sam," she whispered. "Oh…yes…oh…yes. Oh, Sam…oh, darling…oh…*yes.*"

His own breathing grew more and more ragged while she clutched his shoulders and murmured his name in a passionate delirium. He brought her down gently.

Molly couldn't lift a finger. Her bones had dissolved, and her body floated in a warm, sloshing liquid that rose and fell in gentle waves with each breath.

Sam kissed her closed eyes, then moved away.

"Don't go," she managed to murmur.

"I'm not going far."

She heard the rasp of a drawer. Opening her eyes, she saw him remove a packet from the bedside table.

"You're not on birth control, are you?" he asked, sitting up beside her.

"No." She frowned. "Sam, I'd like a baby."

He paused. "Now?" He sounded hoarse.

She wished she could see his face better. The moon had disappeared behind a hill, and the room was darker than when they'd started. "Soon. It would be nice to have a brother or sister for Lass." She sounded defensive, but couldn't help it.

"Would you mind waiting awhile?" he asked, almost formally.

"No, of course not. I didn't mean we had to start tonight, but in a few months. It's important to me."

He finished his task and returned to her. Lying beside her, he stroked her body, fondling each part as if she were the most precious thing in his world. He made her feel special.

"Is it?" he asked, more as if he were talking to himself than her, as if he were checking the idea from all angles.

"Yes. I love children. That's the one thing I wanted and thought I could never have. And now...well, it would round out our family."

"Our family," he repeated, his tone low and hoarse again. He peered into her face intently. "You mean it, don't you? You really mean it."

"Of course." She couldn't figure out why he found that a thing to marvel at. It seemed natural to want children.

"Molly," he said.

That was all, but she heard more. For some reason, her desire for children had touched him. She reached for him and pulled his mouth to hers, telling him without words how she felt.

This time when he moved between her thighs, she knew they could find completion together. He touched her as he had before, with feather strokes over her breasts and abdomen, her thighs and finally that very sensitive place that welcomed him so greedily.

She opened to him, taking him inside. They both trembled when the complete journey was made, then he lay still over her for a moment before he began the journey all over again.

Once, when she cried out and clung to him, she thought she heard him laugh, but she wasn't sure. The roar of the blood through her ears was like a gale in the cottonwoods. She was caught up, swept away, overjoyed by it.

"I love you," she told him. "I love you, love you, love you." Over and over again. Those were the only words that came close to describing the magic.

Chapter Ten

Molly watched the dawn creep across the eastern sky in tendrils of color. She lay beside her husband, happiness a core of bubbling warmth inside her. Sam slept with one arm over her waist, his face pressed into her hair.

It was nearly time for her to be up and about. The play was on for that afternoon. There was a ton of work to be done before then. Ah, but she didn't want to move. If she could stay there forever, just like that, she'd be content.

Resting her hand on his arm, she relived the moments of the night. The sense of being one with him lingered like a melody in her mind—one body, one soul, one love.

A touch on her neck followed by the coolness of moisture told her that her husband was awake.

"You taste good," he murmured, drawing a moist line up to her earlobe. He nibbled there, sending little currents of electricity down into her chest.

"It's easier," she said.

"Is that the answer?"

"Yes."

"What's the question?"

"After the night at the cottage, I wondered if it would have been easier to face you the next morning if we'd slept together that night. It would have."

He raised his head and propped up on an elbow. He peered into her face, then smiled when she held his gaze. Odd, she didn't feel embarrassed at all after sharing the most intimate of experiences with him, yet she'd dreaded her next encounter with him after that night in the kitchen.

"We're married now. We can cohabitate all we want to with everyone's blessings."

His teasing reminder of their wedding night did bring a flush to her cheeks. He laughed, then nuzzled her ear again.

"I thought you didn't want me," she said, defending herself.

"I can't believe you thought that after that first session. I nearly lost it. I was envious of Lass getting to spend the night at your house, and I couldn't."

She stroked his face and found his beard rasped against her finger when she rubbed upward. "But you could have. That was why I was embarrassed. I did lose it."

He moved suddenly, swinging his long, lean body over hers. After making love, he'd put her pajama top back on to keep her from getting cold, but the bottoms were still on the floor. From the waist down, flesh touched flesh.

She felt the nudge of his body against her. A pleasurable flash of anticipation shot through her. "Do we have time?" she asked, uncertain. It seemed they'd made love for hours during the night.

"Yes," he said. "If we concentrate."

She discovered that things could move very quickly when one concentrated. Later, she made another discovery—that showering together could be fun.

"I love you," she said, laughing helplessly as he dried her off, but mostly rubbed the places he liked best.

He stilled for a moment, then dropped the towel over her head and rubbed her hair. She wished he could say the words.

Not that it mattered. Whatever his past had been, the future was theirs to shape together. She'd work with him to see that it was as wonderful as it could be.

And he was going to have to get used to her loving him. She intended to tell him often.

A half hour later, she was ready to leave the house. Sam followed her out to the car, Lass in his arms. When the child was strapped into her seat, he paused by her door.

"Take care." His eyes caressed her, giving the words extra meaning.

"You, too." She lifted her face.

He bent down until he could kiss her.

"I love you," she murmured when he straightened. "See you at one. Don't be late." She gave him a stern glance.

Waving, she drove off. Halfway to town, she remembered what she'd been going to tell him last night. She'd call him when she arrived in town. He might still be at the house.

No one answered the phone. On the tenth ring, Molly hung up and started to work.

"Why are you crying, Krissie?" Molly lifted the four-year-old onto her lap and wiped the tears with a tissue.

"Zack said I sounded funny," the girl said. "He said my song was *stoopid*."

"Why did you believe him? Didn't Miss Tiffany and I say your song was very nice?"

"Y-yes," Krissie said with a snuffle. Her blue eyes were filled with doubts.

"We're your teachers. We know how the song is supposed to sound. You sing it perfectly. I would have said if you'd gotten it wrong. Your mother and grandmother are going to be very proud when they hear it."

"You think so? My brother said it was a silly song."

"Well, he is simply wrong. I wouldn't have a silly song in our play. It's a *fun* song, and our guests will like it."

"Oh."

"Let's dry those tears. We don't want you to have red eyes instead of blue ones when the parents arrive, do we?"

Molly gave Krissie an ice cube wrapped in a paper towel to hold to her eyes for a few minutes, then went to solve the next crisis. Blowing a strand of hair out of her face, she separated two trees who were fighting

over their position at the front of the stage. "You stand
here on the blue X, Zack. Tony goes on the red one."
She gave them a stern look, which settled them down
for about a tenth of a second.

Plopping into her chair, she wondered why she'd
thought it would be a good idea to put on a play. The
whole production was falling apart right before her
eyes.

With one eye on the kids and one on the clock, she
ate a square of lasagna, some vegetable sticks wrapped
in a cabbage leaf and gulped down a glass of tea.

"I'm going to hang Sam from the church bell tower
if he doesn't get here within the next five minutes,"
she muttered to Tiffany as they helped the children
clean up their lunch trays.

"Did he get the house done?"

"Yes. It's adorable. I can't imagine why he's late."

"Well, he was late a lot in picking up Lass."

"Yes, but that was before..." She trailed off, thinking of her marriage and that morning and the night
before. She felt married now, a part of him as he was
a part of her.

"You're blushing," Tiffany said pointedly, her grin
an equal mixture of envy and irony. "Marriage seems
to agree with you. One month and you're blossoming.
Or are you increasing, as my grandmother used to
say?"

Molly fixed a stern eye on her friend. "That's between my husband and me."

Tiffany smothered a giggle. "We'll soon know. All
the old biddies at church have been trying to decide
if you and Sam had to get married."

"Honestly," Molly mumbled, irritated that her life

and her affairs were on the tongues of the local gossips.

She heard the sound of an engine. Rushing to the window, she saw the ranch truck park and the two hands climb down. "Here they are," she called to Tiffany and went out to help.

"Where's Sam?" she asked, going behind the truck.

"Uh, something came up that he had to take care of. He'll probably be by later," Tom told her.

She ignored the disappointment and directed the men in getting the gingerbread house inside and set up for the play.

"Thirty minutes," she reminded everyone as they scurried into costumes. She pulled the sheets, which were strung on wires, across the room to hide the riser that formed the stage.

Tiffany ran to the store for ice to go in the punch that would be served during the social hour after the play. The first parents and neighbors arrived. Molly supervised her "greeters" at the door. The guests were escorted to their seats.

Finally it was time. The folding chairs, borrowed from the church, were filled. Sandy and Tom stayed for the drama. She wished Sam could have come and wondered what he was doing that was so important.

Just as she and Tiffany were about to pull the curtains, the door opened again, blowing the sheets inward. She peeked out and saw Elsie Tisdale slip inside. Molly smiled at the woman. When she had time, she'd find out what had happened to Sam.

"Ready?" Tiffany whispered loudly. There was a titter of laughter from the guests.

Molly nodded. The play was on.

An hour later, they closed the sheets on a happy family reunion as the father of the children held their hands and they all danced around in a circle while the trees and bluebirds of the enchanted forest sang the closing song. Krissie's voice soared above the others in a sweet, true treble.

The applause was tremendous.

"Wonderful, children," she told them. "That was a very successful play. I am so proud of us all."

She had to help the children out of their costumes before she could find out about Sam. She hoped the men didn't leave before she could get to them. She'd told them to stay for cookies and punch, then they could take the gingerbread house back to the ranch.

She had a feeling there was trouble. What it could be, she had no idea. A heaviness settled in her stomach.

At last, the sheets were pulled back for the last time, and the actors mingled with the guests.

Molly went to the kitchen alcove to check on Lass, who'd shown how she felt about the play by sleeping right through it.

The baby was gone.

Startled, she glanced around, but didn't see the child with Tiffany or anyone. She looked under the crib just to be sure Lass hadn't slipped out of the bed, landed on the floor and rolled out of sight. Panic began to flutter through her, making it hard to breathe.

"Elsie," she said and whirled around.

The woman wasn't in the room. Molly, smiling at parents and trying to appear calm, hurried to the door and out onto the sidewalk. She went limp with relief.

Elsie and Lass were in the Tisdale ranch vehicle. A

sharp rebuke sprang to Molly's lips, but when she stopped by the car, it died. The older woman had tears running down her face.

"Elsie, what is it?"

Elsie wiped her eyes and turned to Molly. Lass, sitting in her grandmother's lap, was exploring a new toy.

Molly knelt by the open car door, perplexed and concerned by Mrs. Tisdale's ravaged face.

"I was supposed to steal her," she said.

Molly jerked in shock. "Why? You couldn't possibly get away with it. That would be kidnapping."

"William thought it would prove you weren't good parents. He thought we could show the judge you didn't keep a watch on Lass, that anybody could have taken her."

"Why didn't you leave?" Molly asked gently.

Elsie shook her head. "I couldn't." Her lips trembled. "Lass is a happy baby. You and Sam have made a good home for her. I couldn't snatch her away from a happy home and bring her to ours."

Molly shoved her hair back from her face. "Why does he hate Sam? It's like an obsession."

"Sam's a success. That's reason enough." Her eyes beseeched Molly to understand. "Once William was handsome. He had money and looks and a fast car. All the girls were crazy about him. His father died when he was little, and his mother spoiled him. So did I. We thought, his mother and I, that the sun rose and set with him. But money...none of us knew how to make it, only spend it. Now we're about to lose everything."

"And William is too proud to ask Sam for help," Molly concluded.

"Yes. He asked Sam to join operations, but Sam wouldn't." She hesitated. "Sam said Lass's money was in an irrevocable trust."

"It is. Sam has made me the trustee in case of his death. Did William think he would get the use of the money if Lass were put in his custody?"

"I think so. We stopped telling each other our plans and dreams long ago." She sighed. "I no longer have any, and I don't care about his."

"Oh, but you must," Molly protested. "It's most often the woman who carries the dreams for the whole family, who sees everyone's potential and encourages them. If the mother gives up, the entire family can be lost."

Elsie looked at her as if she were speaking a foreign language. Molly stopped her sermonizing. "You didn't take Lass away," she said softly. "That proves you care about something. Lass loves you, too. She watches for you each day."

"Don't spoil her the way William and I did with Elise. She was a terror—defiant and rude and self-centered." She handed the child to Molly. "But you won't ruin Lass. I can see that already. Your love is the good kind."

Lass patted Molly's cheek, then leaned forward to give her a sloppy kiss. Molly's heart squeezed into a tight knot. That often happened around Lass and Sam. She had so much love she felt her body wasn't big enough to hold all of it.

"All love is good, but it has to be tempered with discipline and the expectation of good manners.

Speaking of which, I need to find out what happened to Sam. He was supposed to be here for the play. He made the gingerbread house.''

"It was lovely. Everything was. The little girl who sang was very good. She reminded me of Elise at that age.''

Molly stood and laid a hand on Elsie's shoulder. "Will you come back?"

Their eyes met in wordless questions and answers. Elsie nodded. "Nothing can keep me away. You don't have to worry. I won't do anything to hurt Lass.''

"I know that. That's why I trust you.''

Pleased surprise appeared on Elsie's face. "Do you? Even though I tried to leave with her?''

"You didn't. That's what counts. Do come back. Lass needs you. Her grandfather, too.''

Elsie shook her head. "I don't think anyone can reach William now. He's let things go too far—'' She broke off.

Uneasiness traveled the bumpy road of Molly's spine. "What has he done?''

"Nothing. So far. I'll talk to him.'' Her lips firmed with purpose, and she looked younger, almost prettier as she sat up straight and started the car.

"Wave bye-bye, Lass,'' Molly encouraged. "Wave bye-bye to Nana.'' She watched Elsie leave with a sense of foreboding. Then she headed back inside to find out what had delayed Sam.

Probably a cow with the sniffles. He practically hand-raised the whole herd. It was one of the best outfits in those parts according to the cowhands. She'd been so proud of Sam when they'd told her. She headed back inside.

* * *

Molly parked at the sheriff's office. It was the first time she'd had an occasion to go there in the ten years she'd lived in the area. A frown, perplexed and concerned, etched itself on her forehead. The men said a deputy sheriff had come out to the ranch. He'd asked Sam to come in to town for questioning.

Questioning for what?

It sounded ominous, like something out of one of those police shows on television.

Inside she asked for Deputy Merritt and was directed to a room down a long corridor painted institutional green. She instantly disliked the place.

She knocked at the door. A burly command to "Come in" made her tense even more. Inside her gaze flew to Sam, sitting in a straight-back chair, his face giving nothing away.

"Molly," he said in surprise. He was displeased.

She went to him, dropping into a squat to study him and make sure he hadn't been hurt. "Are you all right?"

His grin, tough and cynical, kicked up the corners of his mouth. "Sure. They haven't got out the rubber hoses yet." He smoothed her hair from her temple. "I told the guys not to tell you."

"They had to. I was threatening to turn the kids loose on them." She tried a smile, and found she could hold it.

"That would convince them."

"Excuse me?"

Molly looked around.

"You Ms. Frazier?"

"Yes. Molly Frazier. Why are you holding my husband? Has he been charged with anything?"

"It hasn't got to that."

"He's been here for over an hour," she reminded the officer. She knew something about the law from helping her brother study when they were both college students. "Did they read you your rights?" she asked Sam.

"No."

She turned on the deputy, ready to read him the riot act. Sam clasped her hand and tugged on it. "Sit down and relax, Molly. They just wanted to ask a few questions."

"They can't charge you with anything without reading the Miranda Act rights to you, and they can't hold you indefinitely without telling you your crime."

"Thanks," Sam said dryly. "When I need a defense attorney, I'll call you."

She didn't think Sam was taking this with the seriousness it deserved. She knew how people's minds worked. No matter how innocent Sam was—and she knew he hadn't done anything wrong—there were those who thought, because he'd been picked up for questioning, that he must be guilty of something. The old *where there's smoke, there's fire* syndrome.

"Could I see you outside?" the deputy asked.

Her eyes darted to Sam, a question in them. He shrugged, his face as blank as a stone wall.

Facing the deputy detective, she shook her head. "You can ask me whatever you like, but in front of Sam." She held out her hand. "I don't think we've met."

Sam almost laughed as the deputy and Molly shook hands and exchanged greetings as if they were at a damn tea party.

"Bill Merritt, Ms. Frazier. My niece was in your school before she started kindergarten this year. My sister says you helped Dottie a lot. She used to be sort of difficult."

"Oh, Dottie," Molly exclaimed affectionately. "She's a lovely child. She needed a bit of help in learning to finish her tasks and perhaps a few social skills. I'm sure she's going to be a fine student. She was very bright."

Sam felt the familiar tenderness swell like a spring blossom waiting to burst forth. No wonder her students loved her. Molly looked on the bright side and saw the good in everyone.

Uneasiness washed over him. He hoped she kept faith with him after this episode with the law. Anger burned in him at the turn of events that afternoon. He'd been hauled down to the county sheriff's office for questioning about a rustling incident.

Legally he had no "priors." His youthful escapade, done to prevent his stepfather from stealing and selling off any more of the ranch's cattle, had backfired. He'd been arrested for rustling when he tried to hide a small herd.

The charges had been dropped, but no one had believed in his motives or innocence, not even his own mother. As a man, he'd forgiven her for that, but it had been hard.

He glanced at Molly and away. Would she believe in him? He steeled himself for the opposite, for the disappointment that would darken her eyes to stormy gray when she realized the charges being investigated.

"What's happened?" Molly asked the deputy in a quiet tone. Her manner implied that she understood there was a problem and she was equipped to handle it. The schoolmarm in control.

Bill shifted uncomfortably. "There was some trouble last night. A man got shot—he's going to be fine," he added quickly at her expression of concern. "It was out near your place, on a spread east of the Pecos. A rancher found his fence had been cut out by the county road. Some cattle were missing. He followed the tracks of a truck and found one man standing guard with the herd. Instead of going home and calling in the law, he decided to play hero and arrest the man. Got himself shot in the shoulder."

"That's terrible." Molly looked from the officer to Sam and back. "But I don't understand. What has Sam to do with this?"

"Well, uh, he was involved in a rustling operation once before, so I had to bring him in for questioning."

"Questioning for what?"

"For the rustling."

Sam knew the minute Molly realized that *he* was being questioned as the culprit. Her eyes flew open, then narrowed into spear points. She crossed her arms, shifted her weight to one hip and thrust the other out as if she might start patting her foot any minute.

"Sam didn't do any rustling. It's ludicrous that you think he would. He runs a very successful ranch."

The deputy's ears turned a dull red. "Well, there was that other time—"

"He was sixteen years old. The charges were dropped. Even if they hadn't been, his record would have been wiped clean when he became eighteen. That's the law." She gave poor Bill her I'm-really-disappointed-in-you look.

Sam felt sorry for the man as he hemmed and hawed, trying to explain why he had to do his job. "Can you vouch for Frazier last night?" he finally asked.

"Of course I can." She was in fine form now—indignant and hot on the trail of justice. "Sam was with me last night." She looked at him. A red tide swept up her face.

Sam grew hot, too, but not from embarrassment at remembering what had happened between them. Every time he thought of last night, a fiery arrow shot straight through him, lodging in his groin where he became hard and throbbing.

"Can you give me some idea of the time you were together?" The deputy got out his notepad.

"Yes. He came in at eleven. I know because Lass has been cranky of late. She's cutting teeth."

Molly and the officer exchanged glances of understanding and sympathy. Sam mentally shook his head at how easily she could bring a person over to her side.

She continued. "Lass and I'd gone to sleep in the rocker in her room. Sam came in and put Lass to bed and—" she lifted her chin "—and carried me to our bed and tucked me in. We were together the rest of the night and this morning until Lass and I left for school shortly after seven."

"You sure it was eleven when he came in?"

"Yes. I heard the kitchen clock strike the hour and looked at the clock on Lass's wall. It was eleven."

"And he stayed in bed the rest of the night?"

"Yes. I'm a light sleeper. I'd have known if he got up."

"There was blood on his truck."

She nodded. "He helped birth a calf last night.
That's why he was late getting in. I put his shirt and
pants in cold water to soak out the bloodstains. You
probably saw them if you went out to the ranch."

Sam gave the man a sardonic smile. Her story
agreed with his. The rustling had taken place in the
wee hours of the morning. It had been pure luck that
the rancher had seen the cut wires when he came in
from a late poker game.

Fortunately for Sam, there wasn't enough time for
him to do the dirty deed between the time he was last
seen by his two hands and the time he arrived home
and found Molly asleep in the chair.

Bill asked a few more perfunctory questions, but it
was clear the deputy considered Sam off the hook.

The detective hadn't believed him, but Molly's
word was as good as gold in the bank. His attorney
had been right about marrying her.

However, it didn't set well with Sam to hide behind
a woman's skirts. His word ought to count for something.

The lawman let him go with a promise to keep them
informed of future developments. Molly beamed her
approval. The deputy beamed back. Sam shook his
head in resignation.

Outside, he walked her to her car. "How about
some lunch? I missed it during the excitement."

"Well, I should get back to school." She grinned
up at him, looking for all the world like a teenager
about to play hooky. "I'll keep you company while
you eat." She paused and studied him before getting
in the compact sedan.

He tensed and waited for the accusations to come. His mother had had the charges dropped against him, but only to protect the family name. She hadn't believed his tale of saving the ranch. He steeled himself for the suspicion that would show up in Molly's face.

He'd been an outcast before. He could take it.

Her eyes searched his, then she surprised him by throwing her arms around his shoulders and giving him a fierce hug. "Are you very angry?"

"For what?" He hesitated, then put his arms around her.

"For being questioned. Anyone who knows you should know you're not a thief. You're one of the most honorable people I've ever met. And the gentlest. With Lass and with me. Last night, you were wonderful, simply wonderful."

A ball of emotion leapt into his chest. For a moment, he couldn't speak. His throat clogged up, and a terrible pressure built behind his eyes. All because this woman believed in him…really believed in him.

"You're one of a kind, Molly," he managed to whisper. "One of a kind."

And she was his. *His.*

Chapter Eleven

"You said you could ride," Sam reminded Molly at noon on Saturday. "I thought we might take a lunch and ride up the Pecos a ways. There's a pretty spot for a picnic by the river."

"I'd love it." Worry nicked a frown between her brows. "What about Lass? It's almost nap time."

"I have a carrier."

Fifteen minutes later, they set off, Lass strapped into a baby harness in front of Sam. He was mounted on a big, bony gelding that Molly had discovered was a prince of a horse, good-natured and easygoing. Her own steed, also a gelding, was smaller and quite feisty.

"Painter's got a rough gait," Sam had told her, "but he's as surefooted as they come."

She didn't know about the surefooted part, but she could vouch for the rough gait. When Painter trotted, it was like sitting astride a jackhammer going full blast. She mentioned this fact to Sam after they galloped across a broad meadow. He merely grinned. The brute.

"Look, Sam, tire tracks," she called at one point. "Were you up here in the truck recently?"

He circled back and studied the tracks when she pointed them out. They formed a faint trail through the dust and sage.

"One of the boys might have been. I don't remember."

She took a deep breath of the sage-scented air. "I can see why you love this place. Look at the view."

He studied her instead, making her self-conscious about her windblown appearance. Although she wore a hat, freckles tended to pop out on her nose at the least hint of sun on her face.

Sam glanced at the tracks again, then clicked to his mount. Lass clicked, too, drawing a laugh from Molly. She clicked and her horse fell into step behind Sam's mount.

The day was beautiful, perfect for dancing around the Maypole as folks used to do in olden times. She could recall doing it herself in elementary school.

"Maybe next year we'll plan a Maypole Dance for the students," she said, sharing her idea.

"Do I have to build it?"

"Of course."

"It'll cost you," he warned. "Be careful along here. We have to climb a ridge."

Molly discovered the little gelding was adept at getting between a rock and a hard place. By the time they came out on a rocky ledge overlooking the river, she was holding on to the saddle horn and being careful not to look down.

Once up, she discovered they then had to go down. She gritted her teeth and stared at Sam's back until they stopped.

Sam dismounted and came to her. "At least you didn't close your eyes," he commented.

"I was too scared. I didn't want to miss something to grab hold of in case Painter went over the bluff."

Her husband laughed as he swung the saddlebags off his horse. He untied a blanket and spread it over a grassy patch of ground under the cottonwood trees. He placed Lass on it.

"You going to get down?" he asked, giving her a quizzical look.

"I can't. My legs are numb."

He shook his head and held up his arms to her. She fell into them and moaned when she tried to stand on her own. Sam looked concerned.

"I'm okay. It's just that…after all that riding last night, and then today…" The thought trailed off, and heat climbed her face. She wasn't as bold in speaking of their lovemaking as she'd thought she could be.

Understanding dawned. He touched her hair. "I should have realized you'd be—"

She placed a hand over his mouth. "Actually I was hoping you'd brought me up here to ravish me where my cries for help wouldn't be heard."

He wound the strand of hair around and around his finger, bringing her closer and closer to his mouth. "They didn't sound like cries for help last night. It sounded to me like cries for more. I seem to remember a *don't stop* in there...and *please*...'' His lips were very near hers.

"Well, whatever." She shrugged nonchalantly.

Suddenly she was caught up against a broad chest, her mouth definitely ravished by his in a long kiss of leashed emotion.

When he let her go, they were both breathing hard.

"We'd better feed Lass before she realizes she hasn't had lunch yet," she suggested, shaken by the intensity of the kiss.

He'd kissed her that way last night, too, with a desperate silence that sliced right down to her soul. She wasn't sure what he felt, but whatever the emotion, it was powerful, driving him to hold and kiss her for hours, to make love until they were sated and exhausted, and still he'd held her...all night...as if he'd never let her go.

They settled on the blanket with their daughter. She laid out their sandwiches while Sam fed Lass. She poured them each a cup of lemonade from a canteen. Sipping hers, she watched her husband—in every sense of the word—as he lifted the spoon.

Her heart contracted painfully. She loved Lass as her own, but she wanted to have a baby with Sam, too. Watching him with the child, thinking of his care of the animals on the ranch, his respect for his two ranch hands, his kindness toward her, she knew this man was special, so very special.

"I love you," she said softly, compelled by the urging of her heart to say the words.

"How do you know?" he asked, giving her an odd glance as he wiped Lass's sticky fingers after finishing the jars of baby food. "Was it love or a satisfying of the senses that we shared last night?"

She ignored the hurt his question caused. "Lust?" she mused aloud. "Well, there is that. It's usually the beginning between a man and a woman, but there has to be more to form a lasting bond. I think we have that."

He was silent for a long time. "So do I."

Her gaze flew to his. He gave her an earnest smile. She searched the rich darkness of his eyes and wondered if he was telling her he loved her.

"We were friends before we were lovers," he continued softly. Lass had crawled into his lap and was snuggling down like a fawn in a bed of leaves. "That we're friends afterward seems like a miracle to me. I've never known a woman like you, one that a man can share things with."

She knew if she didn't lighten the mood, she might cry. And she didn't know why or whether they'd be happy tears or sad ones.

Because he was glad of their friendship? Because he couldn't call it love? Because they did share something special between them? She didn't know.

Adopting a teasing grin, she informed him they were going to be friends and lovers for a long time. "You can have other friends," she told him generously, "but there'd better not be any other lovers besides me. I'm quite firm on that, Sam."

"You'll never have to worry." He leaned over—carefully because of the sleeping baby—and kissed her. "You're the best lover I've ever had."

That surprised her. It must have shown on her face.

"The very best," he said with quiet sincerity.

She felt beautiful and desirable and lots of other nice things. "Thank you," she said with deliberate primness. "We aim to please."

Sam chuckled and accepted the sandwich she handed him. Together they ate and watched the play of sunlight on the river. The water, golden-hued from the silt it carried, flowed with a swift rush to the Rio Grande.

Sam rearranged Lass, then settled with his head in Molly's lap. She was aware of him watching her before his eyes drifted closed. Leaning against the cottonwood tree, she watched a hawk soar in the sky. A deer appeared on the other side of the river, drank from it and cautiously slipped away. A squirrel made sleepy noises above her.

The peace of the afternoon settled around her as if it were a comforting blanket. She, too, went to sleep.

A patrol car was parked in the shade next to the house when they returned at five.

Sam frowned, then forced himself to relax when he saw the worried glances Molly cast his way. For her sake, he'd be polite no matter what developed.

Bill Merritt stepped out of the light shade of the mesquites and returned Molly's friendly wave.

"Hello," she called. "We've been on a picnic up on the river. It was simply marvelous."

Merritt nodded and looked slightly ashamed.

Sam swung down, one hand holding Lass securely against him. "What brings you out this way?"

He helped Molly dismount, catching her discreet grimace as she swung her leg free of the saddle. A pang of regret as well as amusement coursed through him. He realized he'd have to play the gentleman and let her rest tonight. She wasn't used to being a wife.

"Problems," the deputy answered his question.

"The same ones?"

"Yeah."

Sam nodded. "Why don't you take Lass in?" he suggested to Molly. "I'll take care of the horses."

She wore a troubled look but she didn't argue. "Would you like a glass of iced tea?" she asked the deputy.

"Not now, but thanks for asking. I'll talk to Sam for a minute before I mosey along home."

She took Lass and went into the house. Sam let out a breath of relief. He had some things to discuss with Merritt.

Bill followed him into the stable, lingering by the door while he removed the saddles and brushed down the horses before giving them a pail of oats.

"More rustling?" he asked when the man didn't speak.

"Yeah, south of your place this time. Thought I would warn you. There're rumors in the county. Ranchers are arming their hands, although the sheriff warned them not to."

"You worried that I'll get shot?" The question was sardonic. "Think I should give myself up now?"

Bill pushed his hat back. "Don't be a fool, Frazier. I'm not after you, but...I think someone is."

Sam looked questioningly at the deputy.

"Your name is being linked with the rumors. I suppose you were with the missus last night and today?"

"Yeah, I was with Molly."

"Well, I think someone is using your place as a

staging area. You got some wild country back of your ranch, easy to hide a herd on it.''

''You told anybody else your suspicions?''

''Only the sheriff.''

A smile crooked Sam's mouth. The sheriff was the same person who'd arrested him years ago. ''Well, he was probably impressed with your deductions. How come he didn't send you out to arrest me?''

''I talked him out of it.''

Sam studied the detective, who was around his age. ''Because of Molly?'' he asked, a tightening in his gut.

''Partly,'' the man admitted, meeting his gaze. ''Also, I don't convict a man before I have evidence.''

''But someone has.'' Sam thrust his hands into his back pockets and walked outside the dim stable with the deputy.

''By the way, Molly spotted some tire tracks in the pasture near Deer Ridge today. The tracks veered off toward the ravine.''

''The one that drops down to the river on your side?''

''Yes. I thought I'd head over that way in the morning and see if I could find out who was sightseeing on my land.''

''Don't go taking the law in your own hands,'' Bill advised.

''Then you'd better come with me.''

''Yeah, maybe I'd better 'cause you sure as hell aren't going to listen to reason.''

Sam laughed. ''You can talk reason all you want on the way over there. Let's meet at that old trailhead at the south end of the ridge. Seems like a good starting place.''

"Right. Nine o'clock?"

Sam gave him a pained look. "This is a ranch, not a banker's office. We start at six."

Merritt muttered an expletive, then grinned. "I'll see you there. Keep this under your hat, okay?"

"Sure. Is this an official investigation?"

Merritt gave him an irritated frown. "Yes, but it's on my own time, so don't give me any grief. Or make me regret including you in on it."

Sam nodded in reply to the steely-eyed stare he got from the lawman before Merritt strode to his patrol car and left.

He helped the men with the evening chores before going to the house and facing Molly's curiosity. He didn't want to worry her about rustling operations carried out on his...*their* place.

When they went to the kitchen for supper, he saw she had bathed and changed into pink cotton slacks and a matching knit top. Lass, clean and smiling, played in her high chair.

While the men were hanging up their hats and taking their places, Sam went over to his wife. He had a feeling he was about to make a fool of himself over her, but it didn't matter.

She glanced at him with a smile. "Could you bring that platter? Be careful. It's hot."

"Sure, but first..." He leaned over and kissed her solidly on the mouth.

She was surprised, but pleased. "What was that for?"

"Because," he said. "Just because."

"That's an excellent reason."

He found, later that night, that Molly didn't want

him to be a gentleman and let her rest. She turned to him, restless with need as soon as they were alone in their room.

"Love me," she whispered. "Love me now."

"I will," he promised, his head swimming with the passion she induced in him. "Always."

Molly pushed the flying tendrils of hair back from her face. "You heard what?"

Tiffany repeated the rumor. "It's all over town. About Sam being arrested last Friday."

"He was not arrested," Molly stated flatly, but softly. The children were napping. She and Tiffany were having lunch.

Indignation welled in her, a rising pool of anger on Sam's behalf. She huffed with annoyance at how ready people were to believe the worst of another person.

"Well, he was brought in," her assistant reminded her in an apologetic tone.

"He drove in voluntarily and talked to Bill Merritt at the sheriff's office."

"Did they have any evidence?"

"No." Molly bit the word off, then was ashamed for her shortness. "The only reason they had for questioning Sam was that episode when he was a teenager."

"Oh, yes, I remember." Tiffany looked away. "People are talking about that, too."

"I can imagine—*that Frazier boy, always knew he'd turn out bad,*" she parodied the gossip going around. "They're jealous that he came back and turned the ranch around. Instead of picking up his land cheap in a bankruptcy sale, they had to watch while he made good.''

She stopped when she realized the other teacher was staring at her with a curious expression.

''You really love him, don't you?'' Tiffany said, not really a question, but a realization on her part.

''Of course. Why would I marry him otherwise?''

''I wasn't sure. You were both so…calm about it. I never even saw him steal a kiss when he dropped Lass off, either before or after you were engaged.''

Molly took another bite of the soup she'd made when she first arrived at the nursery school. Chicken noodle was one of her favorites, but she hardly noticed what she was eating.

Sam had ridden out at first light yesterday and today. She'd spent Sunday with Lass, staying close to the house, waiting for Sam to return. It had been dark when he came in.

She recalled the grim weariness on his face when he'd returned in the truck and the horse trailer with two horses in it that he pulled behind the truck. She'd held Lass and watched while he groomed and fed the animals.

''Who was with you?'' she'd asked.

''Merritt.''

''What were you looking for?''

''Whatever we found.''

''Did you find anything?''

''No.''

This morning he'd done the same, leaving with two horses in the trailer, heading for parts unknown. She hadn't said anything to him about being careful. She'd simply put her arms around his waist and snuggled against him. He'd let her hold him for a minute, then he'd gently moved her aside and left.

Molly sighed. They hadn't made love last night.

Tiffany touched her arm. "Don't worry. I'm sure it's going to be all right."

It wasn't.

As the month crept by, as the mesa bloomed and hummed with life, the situation grew worse. The parents of Molly's students wouldn't meet her eyes when they left their children or picked them up. If they did, she saw sympathy or pity in their gazes before they glanced away. The locals thought Sam was guilty.

On Friday night, she was ready when Sam came in. She followed him from the kitchen, where he left his boots, to their bedroom. Dust boiled off him like vapor with every step. He looked as if he'd been riding drag on a monthlong cattle drive and had just hit town. He headed for the shower.

When he returned to the bedroom, Molly had clean jeans, briefs and a white shirt laid out on the bed. She couldn't help watching as he finished towel-drying his hair. She liked him best as he was, without a stitch on his hard, lean frame.

The desire to caress him all over almost overpowered her earlier decision. She forced it into abeyance.

"Get dressed," she said. "We're going to town."

He tossed the towel over the back of a chair and gave her a look she couldn't decipher...sort of belligerent. He'd never given her a cross glance before. It briefly unnerved her.

"What for?"

"I want to go dancing. Tom will watch Lass," she said to waylay any protests. "I thought we'd have dinner at the truck stop, too. It's been a while since we were there.''

"No."

"Yes."

"Dammit, Molly—"

"Yes," she reiterated. She gave him glare for glare, determined to have her way in this one thing. She hadn't said a word all week about him searching for the thieves all alone.

"Why?" he finally asked after a tense silence.

"Because I want to."

He frowned at her. A smile popped on her face. He eyed it suspiciously, but he was wavering.

She removed the slippers she wore at home and put on a sexy pair of sling-back high-heel evening shoes. After refreshing her lipstick, she ran a brush through her hair.

He watched her the whole time, although he'd managed to pull on the briefs during the interval. She finished and turned to face him.

"I want you to do this for me," she said, putting it quite simply. Her body stopped functioning while she waited.

He nodded and picked up the jeans.

Molly let out a relieved sigh. She didn't have a backup plan in case he'd refused. "I'll check on Lass." She hurried down the hall. Lass was asleep.

She closed the door and went to the kitchen. There, she rang Tom on the intercom and told him they were ready to leave.

Sam joined her, his face grim. She lifted her chin. No one would hurt Sam while she was present. No one.

* * *

The first person Sam saw when they entered the truck stop was the minister and his wife. "There's Mr. and Mrs. Liscomb," Molly said pointedly and waved at them across the crowded room. "Let's say hello."

The reason for the trip came to him. His wife—his do-gooder, determined-to-do-her-part-for-him wife—was showing the world what a jewel he was. Molly took his hand and tugged him along in her wake. She tossed out greetings left and right.

He muttered a curse.

She gave him her behave-yourself look.

For his own part, he didn't give a damn what the rest of the world thought of him. But he did care what Molly thought.

They stopped by the preacher's table. "Hello," Molly said cheerfully. She chatted about the weather they'd been having recently and declared spring in New Mexico was the most beautiful time and place in the world. "Don't you agree, Sam?" she asked, forcing him into the farce of friendliness.

Mrs. Liscomb eyed him with the same interest she'd give a scorpion who climbed in her lap. Molly looked at him, her heart in her eyes. He swallowed. There was no way in hell he could disappoint Molly. She was just so damn *kindhearted*. To hurt her...well, a man had to live with himself and his conscience.

"Yes, darling, I do," he dutifully responded.

Her eyes widened at the endearment, then she beamed at him as if he'd given her a wonderful gift. Her hand squeezed his.

He wished they were home so he could make love to her. Only when he was lost in her magic did he forget the world and that it thought he was a thief and a liar. Only with Molly did he find ease from a pain deep inside at a place he hadn't realized contained a sore spot. Only since she'd married him, or maybe since she'd told him of her love did he look forward to a future for them. Only with Molly.

He didn't know whether she loved him or not. He was no longer sure what love was. But if it was loyalty, she loved him. If it was faith, she loved him. If it was everything true and good, then she loved him. Because she'd given him all those.

"I'm glad the rain slacked off," he continued casually. "I've been riding the back ridges, looking for clues to the thieving that's been going on for the past month or so and keeping an eye on my herd."

A bubble of silence surrounded them at his words. He glanced around, meeting the eyes of neighboring ranchers, letting them know he knew the gossip about him and that his place hadn't been hit because he was taking care it didn't.

"There's Tiffany and Bill," Molly said. "We're joining them." She wished the reverend and his lady a good evening and pulled Sam over to another table, where she took a seat. "Well, this is nice," she remarked.

"Right," he said sardonically. He arched an eyebrow at the deputy, who smiled widely.

The man had been in on the conspiracy to get him into town and have him seen with friends whose reputations were as solid as a brass door knocker. Instead of making him rebellious as it once might have, the experience gave him that tight, squeezed feeling inside he often got around Molly and Lass.

He'd been a loner for years. For a few months, six

in all, there'd been a sexual, mindless joy in his first
marriage. That hadn't lasted long. With Molly, he'd
found the true pleasure of friendship. It was nice. Real
nice.

Even Tiffany had come over to his side. She smiled
and chatted without one wary glance his way. He wondered how much the deputy had to do with her change
of heart.

Love. It was in the air.

He was intensely aware of Molly beside him. She
looked especially pretty tonight in a pair of black
slacks and a black-and-gold top. The black high heels
were so damn sexy he wanted to kiss her toes...and
work up from there.

"Right, darling?" she asked.

"Uh, right."

The other three laughed.

He grinned. "What was the question?"

"I asked if dancing wasn't your favorite pastime."

Hardly. His favorite pastime was making love to his
wife. "As long as it isn't more complicated than the
two-step."

"I don't know how to do the two-step," she admitted.

"I'll teach you."

She smiled with delight at her husband. With Molly,
no task was impossible. Look at the headway she was
making with the mustang. He would stand for hours
while she brushed him, which she liked to do. She
was spoiling the horse.

After the meal, the four of them went to a night
spot that featured Western music. Sam ordered a
pitcher of margaritas.

"I'll go to sleep," Molly warned, lifting her glass for the first sip.

Sam leaned close. "Not for long," he promised.

She laughed and tried a sultry glance from under her lashes.

"Keep that up and we'll go home now." He took her hand and swung up from his chair. "There's our song."

He showed her how to do the basics of the Texas Two-step. After she had that down, he taught her several variations. By the third dance, she was trying out her own steps.

"Hey, wait for me," he called, catching up when she spun off on her own. He caught her in his arms.

She wrapped her arms around his neck and danced in close, her body plastered all along his. She sighed happily. "I love dancing," she told him.

"It has its moments." His voice was husky as he tightened his arms around her.

Leaning back, she gazed into his eyes. She shook her head so her hair fell back behind her shoulders and swung out when he spun them around. "I feel incredibly sexy."

His chest lifted against hers. "You are, darling."

"You called me that earlier. At the restaurant. It was the first time—"

"Not the first." He corrected her.

"I meant, in front of other people, not just when we're making love."

"Shh," he cautioned, but he was smiling. "Okay, here we go." He twirled her around, then into a dip as the song ended.

Molly laughed happily. The night was magic. She

was soaring. She could touch the moon…but touching her husband was so much nicer. She nibbled on his ear when she had the chance.

"Stop that, or we'll have to go home now."

By midnight, she'd learned the Electric Slide plus two other line dances. "You're really good," Tiffany said. "It took me ages to remember the steps."

"After all the reels and folk dances we've taught at school, these are a snap."

"It took me ages to remember those, too," Tiffany complained with a mock sigh. "Fortunately we rehearsed a lot."

Molly sipped her margarita. She looked at her glass in surprise. It was full. "Is this glass magic? I was sure I'd drunk half of it."

"The waiter refills them when he comes by. Don't worry. I'm keeping an eye on you," Sam said with a lazy grin.

She gazed at him solemnly. "I'll try not to embarrass you."

"You couldn't." He met her gaze.

She became lost in the compelling depths of his eyes while love consumed her in its gentle flames. She'd be glad when they were alone so she could touch him completely. Thinking of his hands on her, stroking and coaxing her to greater heights of bliss, her breath caught in a rapturous sigh.

"Come on, let's dance," Bill invited Tiffany. "These two need to be alone."

Molly straightened. A blush climbed her face.

Sam touched her cheek. "I like it when you look at me that way," he murmured for her ears alone. "As if I'm the only man in the world you see."

"You are."

He swallowed hard. "I know. Come on. One more dance, and then we'll mosey along."

When she came into his arms, so sweetly willing, he fought a losing battle with his conscience. He no longer cared if it was lust that drew her to him. Whatever they shared, it was good, and that was all that mattered.

Tenderness stole over him. It reached right down to that sore place in his soul, pressing hard so that it was both painful and satisfying. He couldn't explain the sensation, only knew that it was there and it was because of the woman in his arms.

His wife.

"One more song," he murmured before they sat down. "Wait."

Molly watched him go to the band leader. Money exchanged hands. Sam had requested a song. She smiled dreamily when he came back to her. They were the only couple on the floor.

When the music started, Sam reached for her. They danced, alone on the floor, alone in the world as far as she was concerned. Tears filled her eyes as love filled her heart.

"Do you love me, Molly darlin'? Let your answer be a kiss," Sam sang softly to her.

Cupping his face in her hands, she kissed him.

Whistles and thunderous clapping brought her out of her daze. She looked around the dim room. Everyone was laughing and applauding them. She smiled and blew kisses.

"Come on, dream girl. It's time to go home."

Chapter Twelve

"Easy, boy," Sam said to the gelding.

The big horse flicked one ear toward Sam. He shook his head, showing his impatience at being reined in.

Sam pulled firmly, stopping the horse under the shadows of a juniper where it would be harder to spot them, in case anyone was looking. Lifting binoculars, he searched the area thoroughly.

Nothing.

But something had the big gelding excited. Could be a herd of wild horses, of course. Or maybe there was someone else on his land, such as cattle thieves. They would have to be on horses in this country. It was too rough for vehicles.

He rode on after a spell of sitting and watching. Ahead of him was the big arroyo. It was a quarter-mile long, dropping down to the river from the mesa.

During hard storms, water rushed along its rocky seams so fast it could kill a man. One of the wild horses that roamed the area had been found in the bottom last year. It had drowned.

He checked the sky. Not a cloud in sight.

Some cautionary instinct caused him to dismount before he showed himself at the rim. There, backlighted by the sky, he'd be an easy target, if someone was in the mood for practice.

After tying his mount to a young mesquite, he walked to the edge of the dry wash, keeping a heap of boulders between him and the rim. Climbing over and between the rocks, keeping his head low, he eased out onto the ledge and peered over.

His eyes widened in surprise. The arroyo, which should have been lush with grass from the spring rains, was trampled, the grass eaten down to the ground.

Someone had kept a herd of cattle in there.

There was only one way out—up the sloping end of the arroyo itself. Unless they swam the Pecos. Cattle weren't inclined to swim a river any more than they were inclined to climb a rocky slope unless driven to it.

Anger boiled in him. The deputy had been right. The cattle thieves were using his land for their staging area. But how the hell had they taken the cattle out?

Backing from the edge, he mounted and scouted the land until he found what he was looking for. An old cattle chute down in a pine thicket told of days past when some dreamer had tried to made a profitable ranch out of the rough tract.

His father had bought the land for back taxes, afraid that a shifty land developer would come along and put in a resort. Next thing they knew, his dad had told him, the Pecos would be dammed and people would be water-skiing on it and complaining about the cattle polluting it and scaring the tourists who picnicked or hiked along its banks.

A resort might help his cash flow. He smiled. His dad was probably turning over in his grave at the idea.

Leaving the gelding ground-hitched in a shady patch of grass, he inspected the ground around the chute. Pine needles littered the area, but they didn't obliterate the signs of trespassing. He found a boot print, several cow patties, which weren't all that old, and a tire mark where a truck had backed and turned. The rustlers were using his land.

All he had to do was figure out who they were, then catch them in the act. He retrieved a camera from his saddlebag and snapped several shots of the prints and the chute.

Finished, he settled on a log in the shade and ate an egg sandwich he prepared that morning and washed it down with a cup of black coffee. He'd take some pictures of the arroyo, then head home and call Bill Merritt with the information.

Home reminded him of Molly. He'd left her asleep that morning. She deserved a break.

Peace settled over him like a warm blanket. He'd been out on the range for hours last week, not getting in until his wife was in bed and asleep. Until last night, he hadn't made love with her in five days.

His body stirred in memory. His wife—prim schoolteacher that she was—had gotten tipsy at the dance. She'd declared she wasn't when he mentioned the fact to her. Okay, she'd been very happy, he'd conceded.

She'd agreed to that. Then she had proceeded to attack him in the most erotic manner. It had blown his mind...and his control. They'd made love in one of the bedroom chairs, on the floor and finally in bed.

He'd been a little tipsy himself. Not on alcohol—he'd watched his intake carefully—but from Molly. When she'd asked him to sing to her again, he had.

"My song," she'd whispered, caressing him all over as if she couldn't get enough of touching. "Sing my song."

When he'd gotten to the part where he'd asked if she loved him, she kissed him as if there was no tomorrow.

He let out a ragged breath. He'd thought life's greatest moments had come with his daughter, and they had. However, Molly had brought her own special joy to his life. Long after Lass was grown and on her own, he would have Molly.

He liked that idea—him and Molly, growing old together. They'd have their grandkids out to the ranch for summers and holidays. With Molly, life would be good.

He trusted her as he had no other person since his father had died. He'd come to think of her as a friend. He wanted her as a woman. She seemed to like him, too.

Tossing down the rest of the coffee, he rose, repacked and mounted, eager to finish and go home so he could see his wife, and maybe make love when Lass had her nap. Remembering the photos, he headed the gelding toward the arroyo once more.

He smiled. Everything was working out—his life, his problems on the ranch. He was even willing to see

what he could do to help his former father-in-law.
Molly would give him a gold star when he told her
that.

Arriving at the ledge, he reached back to unfasten
the saddlebag and retrieve the camera. Before he
could, a rattle warned him of another's presence. The
gelding screamed, then reared and spun in a tight circle, lashing out with his forelegs.

Taken unawares, Sam fell backward from the saddle. When he hit the ground, pain spread through his
side, his head and his shoulder. The startled snake
slithered off into the safety of the rocky crevices.

The gelding, reins flapping behind him, took off.
Sam watched the world grow dark and knew he was
on the brink of passing out. He fought the blackness.
He had to catch the gelding. Standing, he gave a piercing whistle. He clutched at air as he lost his balance
and pitched over the ledge.

His last thought was of Molly. He wished he'd said
the words...

Molly watched the two cowhands moving around
the stable and outbuildings. She'd already fed the mustang. While it was eating, she'd laid a saddle blanket
on its back. It hadn't moved a muscle.

She'd put a halter on it two weeks ago. It had accepted the bit after a few snorts and tosses of its head.
Later the stallion had let her lift its hooves and check
them. At the present, it had its head over the railing
while it watched the men, too. Probably hoping for
another bucket of feed.

She finished setting the table and removed the corn
bread from the oven. Tonight she'd grilled a pork loin

along with kabobs of peppers, onions and potatoes. After slicing the corn bread into wedges, she placed it in a cloth-lined basket and put it on the table.

"Where is your father?" she asked Lass, who had crawled off her blanket and was inspecting the legs of her high chair.

"Da-da."

"Right." She scooped the child into her arms and placed her in the high chair. Although Lass preferred table food, Molly prepared her a plate of baby food. "Nothing you can eat but potato tonight, my girl."

The men came in shortly thereafter. They helped themselves while Molly finished with Lass, who had four teeth now and liked to bite on the spoon.

"Did you see any signs of Sam?" She cast a worried glance at the darkening sky. She liked him home in the evening.

"No. He lit out on the gelding right after first light this morning. Didn't take the truck and trailer this time."

She gave Lass a cracker to chew on. Lass smiled and clicked her tongue, then settled down to eating.

"He went alone?" She didn't like that. Usually he and Bill worked together for a few hours each day, then Sam returned to the house and the ranch work.

"Guess so," Tom said.

Sandy, as usual, didn't say much of anything. He kept his eyes on his plate as he helped himself to butter and corn bread and another slice of meat.

Molly stifled her irritation with the men. Sam would be in when he got there. He could take care of himself.

This evening she didn't ask questions about the men's plans for the next day. They didn't volunteer their work schedule. The meal passed in an uneasy silence.

She glanced up once and caught Tom watching her. A funny sensation crawled over her back. He smiled and went back to eating. She listened for hoofbeats.

"We thought we might go to town," Tom said while rinsing and putting his plate in the dishwasher.

She nodded. They usually went to town on Saturday night. It was a big night out for cowboys from all the ranches while Friday was the entertainment night of choice for the townsfolk. She wondered briefly how the tradition got started.

After cleaning up the kitchen, she gave Lass a bath, then played and read to her until it was time for bed. Later, after getting into her pajamas, she roamed the house, lonely for Sam and unable to sleep.

Where was that man?

Sam woke to the cold ache of the night. He tested his side but didn't find any ribs sticking out. They were cracked maybe, but they weren't broken into pieces. He examined his shoulder.

A gash there, but not too bad. A trace of blood had dried to a crusty patch on his shirt. He was lucky the rattler hadn't sunk his fangs into him.

He'd live, he concluded. As a kid, he'd had a bite from a rattler. *That* had been a real pain.

His head hurt, but he didn't have any trouble focusing. No concussion. Thank God for small favors. He checked the sky.

Evening was coming on. Molly would worry.

He'd roused a couple of times during the afternoon, but he hadn't had the energy to try to make it out.

Since no one had found him, he'd better make an effort to get home.

In fact, he had to get home. He had to protect his girls from the polecats who'd been hiding cattle on his land.

He knew who they were.

His mouth went dry at the thought of them at the ranch with Molly and Lass. Fear lent him strength and he pushed to his feet. He'd make it back if he had to crawl.

Setting his teeth against a groan, he climbed and clawed his way out of the arroyo. At the rim, he rested against a boulder, which was still warm from the sun. His breath rushed from him in harsh rasps of sound. He hoped the snake wasn't near.

Across the river, he could hear the lowing of cattle as they settled in for the night. Tisdale cattle. He wondered how many the rustlers had stolen so far.

Rising, he opened a button on his shirt and slipped his left hand inside. It wasn't much of a sling, but it was the best he could do. He had a five-hour walk ahead of him before he'd get home to his family.

His girls. Molly and Lass.

Molly couldn't settle. She surfed through the channels until she couldn't stand the noise. She stopped on a nature show, then muted the sound.

For a long minute, she listened to the night wind blowing around the house. Tonight it seemed especially lonesome.

Recalling last night, she felt the ready heat rush to her skin. She couldn't believe it was possible to love someone so much. She'd told him again and again during the hours before they fell asleep.

A smile briefly touched her lips. She couldn't believe Sam would actually sing to a woman, either, but he had. To her.

She hugged the memory to her. He had so many endearing traits...

A noise had her springing to her feet. No, it was just the nightly serenade from the coyotes beginning. She went into the kitchen and made a pot of tea. Going to the door, she peered into the dark.

The moon was bright and almost full, although the light was far from being as bright as day, as some folks said. Shadows lay over the land in sooty blackness. Daylight shadows were blue or lavender, sometimes purple, but not night shadows. They were stark in their absence of color.

She shivered and folded her arms across her waist. Come home, she silently demanded. Come home now.

The pickup the men owned was gone from its usual place next to the bunkhouse. A feeling of being utterly alone washed over her. Something felt wrong. She hesitated, then opened the door.

In her slippers, she silently crossed the gravel, feeling sharp edges through the soles of her shoes. She went into the bunkhouse and flipped on the light.

It was empty. Not just empty of the men, but bare. They'd taken their things with them, including their saddles, which usually hung from sawhorses in the corner.

That's what had bothered her. Their saddles had been under the tarp that covered their pickup bed. The saddle horns had formed identical humps, which she hadn't recognized at the time.

They didn't intend to return.

She ran back to the house and called Bill Merritt. No answer. She tried the sheriff's office. The dispatcher said he was on night duty and out on patrol. Molly left a voice mail for him to call her whenever he returned, no matter what time.

She put on a pot of strong coffee and dressed in jeans and a black shirt. If Sam didn't come in soon, she was going to start a search. Fear caught her by the throat.

Oh, Sam, please make it...

Who could she call to take care of Lass? Tiffany. No. She was forty minutes away. Lass's grandmother was closer.

She went to the phone, knowing Sam would be probably be furious with her for calling. "Elsie? This is Molly," she said when the phone was answered. "Could you come over, please? I need your help."

Elsie Tisdale arrived in less than thirty minutes. Her husband drove her over. "What's happened?" he asked.

"Sam hasn't come home. I'm worried about him." She offered them coffee and refilled her own cup. "I'm going to try Bill again and see if he's in."

She left another voice mail for the deputy, reminding him to call as soon as he came in. She knew the sheriff wouldn't mount a search without evidence of something wrong until Sam had been gone for twenty-four hours. She doubted a gut feeling would be considered valid evidence.

"It's only a little after nine," William Tisdale

noted, glancing at the kitchen clock. "Or does he keep banker's hours?"

She rounded on him. "I don't want to hear that kind of talk. If you don't have anything important to say, then keep it to yourself. I invited Elsie here in case I decide to go look for Sam or have to take him to the hospital when I find him. You can leave at any time."

Mr. Tisdale's eyes widened at the reprimand. A flush colored his face. Molly didn't care if she'd made him angry. She was damn angry herself.

"Why do you think something's wrong?" Elsie asked. She took a seat at the table and cupped her hands around the warm mug.

"The hands have left. Cleared out," she clarified. "I think they were the ones behind the rustling. If Sam caught them, he could have been hurt."

Her imagination provided pictures of him lying alone and bleeding someplace where they would never think to look. He could be dead…

No, not Sam. He was too vital, too dear to her heart. She couldn't lose him. Their marriage had hardly begun.

"He can't be dead," she repeated in a hoarse whisper.

Mr. Tisdale sank heavily into a chair. He licked his lips, opened his mouth, closed it, then tried again. "It's my fault. If he's dead, it's my fault."

"Were you in with the rustlers…with Tom and Sandy?" It hurt to say their names. She had trusted them. Tom had kept Lass for them the night before. Surely they weren't guilty.

So why would they leave without a word of farewell?

They hadn't looked at her at supper. They'd been silent. She'd thought the tension was from her, because of Sam. Now she thought they had contributed. They must have known Sam wasn't coming in. Oh, dear God...

"No," Mr. Tisdale answered her. "But I started it. I paid one of my men to spread the rumors about Sam."

"Why?" she asked. Her voice shook, she was so angry. She reined her emotions in. "Why do you want to ruin him?"

"Because he had everything and I had nothing. He'd saved his money and paid off the mortgage on his ranch. We're going to lose the land." He raised haunted eyes to her. "Land that's been in my family for generations."

"So has Sam's." She refused to heed the pity that formed in her. People made choices. They had to live with the results.

"Yes. I hated it that he could come back, take over and pull this place out of the fire. I was losing out no matter what I did. I thought he would help me, but he refused. I thought, when he and Elise married, he'd be like a son, but he wasn't."

Molly stared at the older man. He seemed to be talking to himself, and the voice was one of defeat. He was giving up...on his ranch...on life...

"Sam would have helped," she said, totally certain in her estimation of her husband, "if you'd been honest with him. You tried to make it sound as if you were doing him a favor. He knew you weren't. Trust has to be earned."

He nodded his head. Elsie reached out and touched

her husband's hand, lying idle on the table. She looked at him in sorrow. Molly spared a moment's pity for both of them. They'd made a lot of mistakes.

She paced to the window. Across the meadow she saw a horse silhouetted in the moonlight. It walked toward the stable. She realized something was on its back. A saddle, perhaps. No, larger than that. A man, lying over the horse's neck.

She rushed outside to meet the gelding at the paddock gate.

The big roan stopped by Molly and nuzzled her shoulder. He seemed to be asking for help. On his back, Sam clutched a handful of mane as if it were a lifeline.

"Sam, can you hear me?" she asked, laying a hand on his shoulder. She felt the dampness on his shirt and rubbed her fingers together. Sniffing, she detected the salty tang of blood. Her heart lurched painfully and started pounding.

"Molly," he gasped. "Watch out. Rustlers... here."

"They've gone," she assured him, her tone dry. "They took off right after supper. Can you get down?"

He slid from the gelding with a groan of pain. She put her arms around him and held him upright.

"I'm all right. Let's get to the house."

"Hold on to me," she ordered, fearing he'd topple over.

"Yes, darling," he said meekly.

Relief made her dizzy. "Now I know you're going to be all right. You're making fun of me."

She guided him across the gravel driveway to the

back door. Elsie held the door open for them and closed it after they were safely inside. Mr. Tisdale was on the phone.

"I don't give a damn if he's entertaining the president. I want to talk to the sheriff. Where is he?"

Molly guessed he was trying to rouse the sheriff into going after the two thieves. She led Sam down the hall to their room.

After he was seated on the chair, she unfastened his shirt and examined him. There was a bloody slash along the fleshy part of his shoulder.

"What caused this?" she asked.

"Snake," he said, grimacing as she probed the spot. "I fell off my horse." He explained briefly.

"The skin is torn." The anger burned as keen-edged as a sword in her. Because of the rustling, her man had been hurt, and she wasn't going to forget it. "The wound looks clean."

"Yeah. Help me get out of these clothes. I need a shower. Then you can bandage it," he added at her protest.

"We have to get you to the hospital. You might need a couple of stitches."

"I think we have some butterfly bandages." He gestured toward his feet. "Help me with these boots."

She pulled them off as gently as she could. She saw bruises along his side. "You're black-and-blue."

He quirked a sardonic grin her way. "Yeah, living color." He pushed to his feet and tried to unfasten his jeans with one hand. "I was lucky to catch up with the gelding later. He'd stayed close. Where are the hands?"

"Gone," she informed him. "They lit out after supper with all their gear."

"Good. I won't have to shoot them."

"You knew it was them?"

"Suspected it when you found those tire marks. Today I found the place where they worked."

"Here, let me." She pulled the snap and tugged the zipper down. "I trusted them. Tom stayed with Lass. She loved him."

"Yeah, well, just goes to show you—you can't trust your best friend nowadays."

"Why did they hang around here until after supper? They must have known you knew about them. Why didn't they take off as soon as they got back to the house?"

"They didn't want to arouse your suspicions, I assume. Maybe they were waiting to see if I'd caught on, then chickened out and decided to leave. Maybe they wanted your company and a home-cooked meal one more time. Tom was sweet on you and Lass." He smiled as if he found the idea amusing.

"I know," she said sadly. After pushing the pants down, she told him to step out.

He did, laying one hand on her head for balance. "I'll have to watch you. Always trying to get a man out of his pants."

She looked up at him. Something in his eyes gave her pause. She shook her head. He was hurt and vulnerable right now. What she saw was gratitude for her help.

"I'll get the shower started." She dashed into the bathroom and adjusted the spray to a comfortable warmth.

Sam followed her. He'd finished undressing. A sigh escaped him when he stepped under the water.

"Wait. I'll come in with you." She stripped as quickly as she could and stepped into the shower.

Sam leaned against the tile wall, his eyes closed. He looked so utterly weary. A wave of tenderness washed over her with the cascading of the water down her back. Along with it grew a fierce protective anger on his behalf.

Soaping her hands, she washed him carefully, checking his body for scrapes and bruises as she did. Other than the graze on his shoulder and the bruise on his side, he didn't appear to have any other injuries. She found the bump on his head when she washed his hair. The anger rekindled.

Sam touched the frown lines between her eyes. "Don't look so fierce. You make me nervous."

"It makes me angry that you were hurt."

"Make me feel better," he suggested. He pulled her against him and kissed her.

The passion surprised her. "You...we can't," she whispered when he kissed down her neck. "The Tisdales are here. You're injured." Otherwise, she'd have taken everything he offered.

He gave a brief laugh. "Don't I know it. But I'm not dead. Tomorrow I'll be as good as new. Right now, you'd better get me to bed before I fall on my face."

She dried him off, then wrapped a towel around her and led him to bed. She rubbed antibiotic ointment on his wound and taped a gauze square over it. He ran a finger along her skin just above the towel. "Stop that," she ordered, smiling.

After tucking him in, she dressed again, combed her hair and, after checking him one more time, headed for the kitchen.

Bill Merritt had arrived. "Tisdale told me an interesting tale. He thinks your ranch hands saw the main chance when he spread the rumors about Sam rustling cattle. They decided to make the story true, thinking they'd get the benefit and Sam would get the blame."

She sank into a chair and pushed her damp hair back from her face. "It looks that way. They left tonight with all their gear in their truck, so I don't guess they mean to come back."

"How's Sam? What happened to him?"

She repeated the story she'd pieced together while she'd washed her husband and taken care of his injuries.

"A rattlesnake?" Bill whistled at her nod. "He's lucky to be alive. By the way, we have an all-points bulletin out on the pickup, also your cattle truck."

She looked questioningly at him.

"It's missing. I figure one of them is driving it, loaded with the cattle they stole. If it's spotted, we want to follow them and see who's buying."

"Catch the source, huh?" Tisdale chipped in. He looked pretty grim.

Molly glanced at the clock. After eleven.

Elsie followed her gaze. "I suppose there's nothing more we can do tonight. It's time we were getting home." She stood and looked expectantly at her husband.

William seemed startled by her decisive manner.

To Molly, Elsie seemed younger and more energetic than when they'd first met. Tonight she'd dressed in blue slacks and a white shirt with a blue scarf around her neck. She wore sapphires in her ears and a matching ring on her right hand.

Perhaps the woman had recovered her spirit. Love could do that to a person, and Elsie certainly loved Lass.

"We'll need a statement from you," Bill told the older man, "on your part in all this."

Tisdale started to argue, then stopped at a look from Elsie. "I'll come down to the station tomorrow."

"Some of your men might be involved," the deputy went on, thinking aloud about the case. "We'll have to check that out."

Again William appeared to want to argue. He heaved a deep breath, his mouth settling into grim lines. He may have been handsome once, but now he looked tired and frayed around the edges. His anger at Sam had disappeared in the face of the problems he'd caused. She wondered if he'd be arrested as the instigator of the crime.

Molly walked them to the door. She kissed Elsie's cheek. "Thank you for coming."

"I'd like to come back. Anytime you need a babysitter, I'm only a phone call away. I hope you'll let me."

"Of course." She looked at Mr. Tisdale. "Thank you for coming tonight."

He flushed. "I'm a damn fool," he said. "You can tell Sam I said that."

She smiled. "You can count on it."

After they left, Bill lingered while he drank the coffee. He had until midnight before he was off duty.

Molly politely kept him company, but she wished he'd leave. She wanted to go to her husband.

"Well, one thing for sure—Sam won't have to worry about his father-in-law anymore," Bill commented.

"Do you think he's seen the error of his ways?"

"I don't know about that, but when this comes out, Tisdale will be ruined in this community. Sam's name will be cleared."

Chapter Thirteen

Molly woke the next morning to a loud banging. She sat straight up in bed and looked around wildly.

"Someone's at the door," Sam said, pushing the covers back. "I hope they have a damn good reason for waking us up." He groaned when he rose from the bed.

She noted the bruise on his side had spread roughly into the size of a soccer ball. "You're lucky you didn't break something when you fell."

"Yeah, good thing I took most of the fall on my head."

She grimaced at his levity. He treated his injuries lightly because of her, she suspected.

The banging rattled through the house.

"Coming," Sam yelled.

"They'll wake up Lass," she grumbled, pulling on

her robe and slippers. She pulled a comb through her hair and washed her face, then helped Sam with a pair of jeans and a shirt, then shoes and socks.

He followed her to the kitchen.

They could see the shape of a man silhouetted against the dawn on the other side of the door. Sam went over and opened it.

"Good morning. You out for a snipe hunt?" he asked with dry humor when Bill Merritt stepped inside.

"Morning, Sam, Molly," the deputy said.

Molly, busy putting on a pot of coffee, returned his greeting. "What *are* you doing out at five o'clock?"

"We got your rustlers."

"Tom and Sandy? Where'd you catch them?" Sam asked.

"Down by your stable."

Molly whipped around and stared at the deputy. "Here? On our place? Had they come back for more cattle?"

"No. They were returning the truck they'd borrowed." Bill nodded toward the outdoors. "I've got a man on them."

"Now?" Molly couldn't believe the two cowboys would have the nerve to show up on the ranch.

"Yeah. Turns out they weren't rustling."

"How do you figure that?" Sam eased down in a chair at the table and motioned the deputy to a seat.

Molly brought coffee to the table and poured them each a mug before she started breakfast.

"According to their story, they borrowed the truck to transport their cattle to their place about a hundred miles from here. My man picked up on the truck li-

cense when they were on their way back and called
me. I told him to follow and keep me posted. When I
realized they were heading this way, I came on over
to see what was happening.'' His eyes gleamed with
amusement. ''They filled your tank with gas when
they came through town. Thoughtful crooks, huh?''

Sam snorted. ''How about bringing them in and
let's see if we can get to the bottom of this?''

Bill went outside. In a minute, he returned with the
two culprits behind him. The other cop took up a
guard position on the porch. The cowboys took their
hats off and stood in the middle of the room, shuffling
from foot to foot.

''You may as well sit down,'' Sam advised.

Molly cooked a pound of bacon, then started the
pancakes. She set mugs out for the two rustlers and
poured coffee for them.

''You boys want to tell me your story before I shoot
you?'' Sam asked cordially.

Molly gave him a startled glance.

The two men looked at each other, then Tom
started. ''We weren't stealing. Those cows belonged
to us, free and clear.''

''Yeah,'' Sandy asserted.

''How do you figure that?''

''We found 'em. They were range cattle.''

''No brands?'' Sam asked. He studied the two men
while he sipped the hot coffee.

''That's right,'' Tom said while Sandy nodded vigorously.

Sam peered at Bill. Bill shrugged. ''I have a man
checking it out.''

''If they were range cattle, why'd you hide them

and make off in the middle of the night?'' Sam demanded.

An uncomfortable silence ensued. Finally Tom burst out, ''We didn't want you to steal 'em from us.''

Sam's eyebrows rose at this statement. He shook his head slightly when Molly would have pounced on the ridiculous claim.

''Why would I do that?''

''Our last boss did.'' With that, the two men braced themselves as if expecting to have to fight their way out of the kitchen. They watched Sam warily.

''Hmm.'' Sam turned sideways, grimacing as he did and placing a hand against his sore ribs. He straightened his legs. ''I guess you're going to have to help me out. You'd collected a herd of range cattle, but your boss stole them from you?''

''He said they were his, that we found 'em on his property. That was a lie. We didn't. We rounded them up in our spare time on open range and moved them to a pen. That was the deal.''

Sandy broke in. ''We worked for less wages so we'd have time to start our own herd. We were supposed to have the use of a pasture to keep them in until we had enough to move them to our place. He threatened to have us arrested for rustling if we took one cow off his land.''

''Ah,'' Sam said.

Molly brought plates and silverware to the table. ''Sit still,'' she told Bill when he started to rise. ''You might as well eat, too. Unless you've had breakfast?''

''No, ma'am.'' He sniffed loudly. ''That sure smells good.''

"Tell your assistant to come in," she suggested. "He's probably hungry, too."

Bill called the man in. She put syrup and pancakes and bacon on the table, then replenished the coffee mugs and took her place by Sam.

She smiled happily. "This looks like a family meal."

"I'm gonna miss your cooking, Molly," Tom said with a great deal of sorrow in his voice.

"Why is that?" Sam asked. "Are you going to do your own cooking at the bunkhouse?"

Tom and Sandy looked at him, puzzlement appearing on their forlorn faces.

"It takes money to start a ranching operation," he continued thoughtfully. "You might want to keep up your jobs here...unless you have a big hunk of savings."

Bill poured a pond of syrup over his stack of pancakes. "I take it you're not going to press charges?"

"No." Sam poured an equal amount of syrup over his stack. "No law against moving your own cattle, is there?"

"No, but what about the truck?"

"Tom is the *segundo*. You give Sandy permission to borrow the truck?" he asked his new foreman.

Tom nodded slowly. He looked as if he were dreaming and was afraid he might wake up at any second.

"There," Sam said to Bill, "he had permission."

"Well, hell, it seems I got out of bed at four for nothing. And I have the midnight shift again tonight. I ought to charge you for my overtime," he told Sam before forking a big bite of pancake into his mouth.

Sam merely grinned.

The other deputy laughed. Molly did, too, then she leaned over and kissed Sam's cheek.

"Mmm," he murmured, "what was that for?"

"For being wonderful. Lass would never have forgiven you if you'd driven Tom away, and Porsche has a weakness for Sandy. He lets her sleep with her head in his boot at night."

"That probably works better than a flea collar," Sam mused.

That produced guffaws from everyone but Sandy, who turned a brilliant shade of red.

Molly ate her breakfast, her heart at ease about their two cowhands. She and Lass had come to love them. "But what about the other rancher?" she asked, recalling the wounded man. "Did you shoot him when he found you?"

"That weren't us." Tom shook his head vehemently. "Me and Sandy, we didn't do no shooting and we weren't on anybody's property but ours, yours and the open range."

"Then who did it?"

"Real rustlers," Bill told them. "We've been keeping more than one outfit under surveillance this week. They were using old homesteads around here to hold stolen stock until they could get them moved. The state police caught up with them last night. That's where I was when you called, Molly, helping out on a stakeout and arrest."

"Oh. So you knew Tom and Sandy weren't part of it."

"Well, I knew they weren't part of that gang, but I assumed they had a scam of their own going."

"All's well that ends well," she murmured with a

glad smile at Tom and Sandy. Her faith in them had been restored. She heard Lass cry out. "There's our girl. I'll get her."

She went to the bedroom. Lass was standing up in the crib, looking like a prisoner planning an escape. "Hello, darling," she said, bustling around the room.

After opening the blinds, she washed the baby's face, then dressed her in rompers and warm socks with grippers on the bottom. "Ma-ma," Lass said.

Molly paused, then finished fastening the snaps on the rompers. "Let's go see Daddy and Tom and Sandy."

"Da-da." Lass patted Molly's cheek as they entered the kitchen. "Ma-ma."

Molly quickly looked at Sam. His gaze flicked to hers, but she couldn't tell what he was thinking. Would he mind if Lass called her *Mother?*

She'd better ask before it became ingrained with the child. So far she'd referred to herself as Molly, but she wanted Lass to call her mother. It seemed natural and right to her.

After setting Lass in the high chair, she spooned cereal and fruit into the rosebud mouth, feeling very maternal with the eyes of the men on her.

Bill sighed and rose. "Time to go," he told his assistant. "We need to get some sleep. No telling what adventures we'll have in this crime-ridden county tonight." Chuckling he and the other officer left.

Tom and Sandy stood, too. "Do we really have a job here for the rest of the summer?" Tom asked.

"If you want it."

The men looked at each other, then at Sam. "We sure do." They picked up their hats and headed out.

"Well, that leaves us," he said when they were alone.

"Yes," she said, spooning the last bite into Lass's mouth. "I have a plan to help the Tisdales," she told him and waited to see if he would explode in anger.

"Now why doesn't that surprise me?" he murmured, watching her with a pensive look in his eyes.

She couldn't tell if he was angry or not. "Do you want to hear it?"

"Oh, yes. Please, continue."

"Well, I have a thousand shares of stock my grandmother gave me. I thought I'd sell part of it. I'll invest the money in the Tisdale land and combine it with ours. They could live there as long as they want. What do you think?"

He studied her for a long minute. "How much is that stock worth?"

"About a million."

"Dollars?"

"Yes." She wiped Lass's face with a damp cloth and put her in the playpen. Picking up her cup, she took a drink, then turned to face Sam. "You look sort of funny," she said. "Are you coming down with something?"

He pushed himself to his feet. "Why didn't you tell me?" he asked, his voice quiet and devoid of expression.

"Tell you what?"

"About the money. People thought you were a good catch before, now they'll be sure I married you because of it."

"So what?" she said, not seeing the problem he evidently did. "We'll know better."

"Do you?"

She smiled across the table at him. "Of course. You're way too smart to marry someone for money."

He walked across the room and out the door.

She went after him. "It isn't polite to walk out on someone in the midst of a quarrel," she informed him. Not that she was angry, but he seemed troubled. "If we have a difference, it's better to air the problem than let it fester."

"Later," he said. "We'll talk later." He headed for the barn while she stared at his back.

Sam leaned on the fence and watched the stallion. The big horse eyed him, its ears twitching back and forth. Slowly it crossed the paddock and came to him. It sniffed a time or two, then nuzzled his shirt, probably catching Molly's scent on him.

He moved back a step so the stallion wouldn't nudge his sore shoulder while it searched for Molly.

A million dollars. He hadn't guessed. Stupid. The signs had been there. The sophistication of her parents. Her brother who had argued cases in front of the Supreme Court. Her grandmother who was off on a world tour or something like that. Molly's education in a private girl's academy. Her degrees from an Ivy League university. He should have known.

A million dollars. He'd have to think about that. Would a woman like her really want to stay with a man like him? He couldn't give her a mansion or a fancy car. He didn't need to. She could buy all that for herself.

He pressed a hand over his eyes, thinking of her cooking for him and the hands. She'd washed his clothes and lectured him on hanging up his damp towels. How long would she be content playing the rancher's wife?

Six months. He'd give her six months. Then she'd be tired of him and want to be free.

For a moment, he considered trying to hold her with sex, with the child she thought she wanted. But he wouldn't do that.

The knowledge sat heavily on his shoulders as he went to check the calves in the barn. Tom and Sandy had finished the chores. Now they were restoring their possessions in the bunkhouse and discussing plans for the future.

It wasn't fair—to be handed a slice of paradise and have it jerked away before he'd gotten more than a taste. No matter. He'd have to do whatever was fair to Molly.

Right now she had the idea she wanted to buy a ranch. He'd have to talk her out of that. Her money was safer where it was.

He'd talk to his former in-laws and see what he could do for them. William might be arrested as an instigator of the rustling incidents that had happened recently. The ringleader had been the man he'd paid to start the rumors, according to the deputy.

He gripped the railing and stared at the sky, the rancher part of him noting the clouds blowing before the wind. They'd have a storm that night.

"Here, hold Lass," Molly told him, stopping by the fence.

He hadn't heard her approach. His heart squeezed into a tight ball of longing. He recognized the symptom.

Fool that he was, he'd fallen in love with his wife.

He couldn't say the words. If he told her now, she'd think it was because of the money, even though she said she didn't. He knew how people's minds worked. If a man's own mother hadn't believed him, why would anyone else?

Lass patted his cheek and tried to hold on to his nose. "Da-da," she said, giving him her biggest grin.

He rubbed his cheek on her soft curls while Molly went into the stable. She called the stallion by banging a pail against a post. The stallion headed for the open door.

Inside Sam could hear Molly talking to the horse, calling him pet names and laughing when he tried to nuzzle her. The stallion liked to snuffle along her neck. Sam thought the horse liked the scent of Molly's soap.

"Here I come, ready or not," she called.

Before he had time to think what this meant, Molly came out of the stable. She was riding the stallion.

Sam went utterly still. Fear beat its way to his throat and lodged there. "Molly, be careful," he said softly, trying not to show his worry.

"It's okay. I've been riding him for a week. I wanted to surprise you."

"You have," he told her, "in more ways than one."

"Can we keep him? Perhaps for a stud?"

"He's your horse. You can do whatever you want with him."

"Oh, Sam, really? He's mine?"

He nodded, then swallowed hard. She looked as if he'd given her the moon. Would she be as thrilled with his love?

She'd said she loved him, but sex could make a person think that. It was so good between them... The heat began to pump through him. He tried to turn the thoughts off.

"Watch," she called. She rode the mustang around the paddock in a circle, then she had him back up. "That's all I've taught him so far. I haven't taken him outside yet. I was afraid he'd head for the hills." She grinned.

"Ma-ma," Lass said and waved at Molly. "Ma-ma."

Molly glanced at him, then away. The mustang was acting up, prancing and shying at imaginary enemies. She had her hands full trying to rein him in.

"He needs a good run," Sam called to her. "Do you want to take him out in the pasture?"

She nodded.

He went around and opened the gate, then stood behind it while she coaxed the mustang outside. The stallion was suspicious of this sudden freedom.

Molly clicked at him and urged him forward. He broke into a canter, then swung into a loping run. Molly stretched out over his neck, her hair blowing wildly. Sam heard her laughter as they bounded away.

Going to the porch, he sat on the steps with Lass and watched the horse and rider. Molly was everything he wanted in a woman—an enthusiastic lover, a sympathetic companion, a loving mother, an accomplished rider, teacher, citizen. And friend.

How long before she tired of ranch life?

Molly brushed the tangle of hair back from her temples. The ride had been exhilarating. The mustang was calm, his excess energy spent. He looked around with a keen eye, interested in everything on the ranch. An intelligent animal.

She smiled with pride when she rode back into the paddock and waved at Sam. Lass was crawling on the porch, inspecting everything she came across. He hadn't said anything when the baby had called her Mama.

Wanting to be with them, she hurriedly dismounted and put the gear away, then brushed the stallion until he was dry. She left him with a bucket of feed in his stall.

After washing up at the utility sink in the stable, she and the cats joined the other two on the porch. Porsche jumped to the railing and settled into a ball of contentment. Persnickety rubbed against Lass and purred loudly when Lass grabbed a handful of fur.

Molly settled beside Sam with a happy sigh. "That was fun, but I might not be able to climb out of bed tomorrow. It's been years since I've ridden like that."

"You're good. You must have had a horse when you were a kid." There was a question in his voice.

She shook her head. "Summer camps."

"Oh, of course." His tone was sardonic.

"We need to talk, I think," she said. "Why does it bother you that I have money?"

"It doesn't."

She searched his eyes, wondering at the darkness of his mood. "I can't figure you out. You should be happy that the rustling has been solved and our men cleared, yet something is eating at you. If it's not the money, then what is it?"

"It's nothing." He gave her a half smile filled with irony. "Just a little quandary of my own."

He wasn't going to tell her. Disappointment bit into her. She'd thought they were growing close. She was obviously mistaken. Well, she'd been wrong before.

She studied her silent husband with quick glances at his face. He grimaced when he reached over to collect Lass, who was peering at a mesquite branch hanging over the railing.

"Poor darling," she murmured, remembering his injuries.

He was tired and out of sorts and probably aching all over. Neither of them had had a great deal of sleep last night.

She ran her fingers up and down his back. "Why don't you take a nap?" she suggested. "Lass will want one after she has her bottle, so the house should be quiet."

"That sounds good." He didn't look at her or take notice of her caresses.

Remembering how he'd embraced her during the shower, she tried to figure out his change in mood. Surely money couldn't make that much difference to him. It wasn't as if she'd lied. She'd listed all her assets in the prenuptial agreement.

"It wasn't my fault if you didn't realize the thousand shares were worth a lot," she said aloud.

He stiffened. "I realize that."

"So why should it make any difference now?"

"It doesn't."

"Good." Springing up, she lifted Lass and took her inside. She warmed a bottle and, going to the nursery, sat in the recliner rocker and fed Lass the formula.

The child gazed up at her, one plump hand patting the bottle while she drank.

"Your father is a hard man to figure out," she told her.

Lass stopped sucking and grinned up at her. Molly's heart contracted with love. She couldn't imagine being anywhere but here, in this house, with this family.

But what if Sam didn't want her?

Now that he was clear of all threats from his father-in-law, he no longer needed to worry about anyone taking Lass from him. Certainly he didn't need a spinsterish teacher who lectured on everything from table manners to bath towels in his life.

As Lass's eyes drooped, then closed in sleep, Molly wrestled with the problem of understanding her husband. Well, she'd take it one day at a time and see what developed. She grimaced at her own optimistic attitude. Molly, the great philosopher.

After laying Lass down, she went to the master bedroom. Sam was there. He'd undressed to his briefs and was lying under the sheet, one arm over his face.

She stripped to her underwear and joined him.

To her surprise, he rolled toward her and laid his arm over her waist. She turned to her side and snuggled into his body, spoon-fashion. His breath sighed against her hair, then deepened. She realized he was asleep.

For a few moments, she pondered the way he'd looked at her yesterday when he arrived home and found out she and the baby were all right. It had been fierce, yet tender. She'd thought it was because he was injured and vulnerable, but maybe...maybe she was wrong...

* * *

Molly and Lass stood at the window and waved one last time. Nana waved from the window of the plane. The plane moved away from the gate. Behind them, Sam waited silently to drive them back to the ranch.

"I hate to see her go, but truthfully, I'm exhausted," Molly admitted, heaving a sigh of part sadness, part weariness.

"Your grandmother is an energetic lady," he commented, taking Lass from her and guiding them toward the door.

"Fortunately she doesn't stay in one place longer than ten days, as a rule. She says that's the limit of her patience. I think that's all ordinary people can last with her."

During the past ten days, they'd made a thorough tour of the area, looking at landmarks, ghost towns, museums and meeting all the local citizens. The last thing Nana had whispered to her was, "He's a keeper, your young man. Makes me miss my Bertie."

Molly blinked away the mist from her eyes. "We'd better hurry. Chuck and Janice will be at the house before we get back. I'd like to have a leisurely dinner with them before the Tisdales arrive to discuss the legalities."

The two ranches were forming a joint project where their land met at the river. They were going to open a limited area to wilderness camping for families, plus a youth work camp for city kids to build trails, clear brush from campsites and learn to ride and herd cattle and get paid for it.

They arrived at the ranch five minutes before their dinner guests. The other couple pitched in. Soon the meal was on the table. Afterward, they went into the living room and discussed the project over coffee while waiting for the older couple.

"You sure you want to do this?" Chuck asked.

Sam glanced at Molly, smiled and nodded.

Chuck perused one, then the other. He started laughing.

"What's so funny?" his wife demanded. She smoothed her maternity smock over her rounded tummy.

"I gave Sam some advice once. He wasn't sure it was the best advice, but he took it."

"What was the advice?" Janice asked.

"How about another cup of coffee?" Sam interrupted, springing to his feet.

Molly looked from one man to the other. "I detect a devious plot here, Janice. Do you?"

"Absolutely. We'll tickle you to death if you don't tell us right now."

Chuck nodded to Sam. "It's his secret. Shall I tell?"

Sam refilled their cups and replaced the pot on the tray. He shrugged. "Why not? They'll bug us from now until eternity or until they find out, whichever comes first."

"I advised Sam to marry the nursery schoolteacher as a way to solve his problems with his former father-in-law."

Molly's smile retreated. She pushed it back on her face.

"Told him it was my best advice. And it was." Chuck beamed at them, quite pleased with his legal counseling.

"Yeah, it was," Sam agreed.

A beat of silence followed while he gazed at Molly. She felt the tenderness of his look and swallowed against the emotion that closed her throat.

Marriage was good, she mused as the conversation flowed around her. She and Sam had a solid relationship. Tomorrow, they would have made it six months. Six months of marriage to a man she loved more than anything. She sighed. Yes, it was good.

The Tisdales arrived, and the talk grew lively. There had been times during the past months when she and Elsie had had to intervene between the two strong-minded men.

Moving around the kitchen, cutting the pie and serving dessert, she wondered if anyone noticed she always included food during their meetings. The ritual stemmed from ancient times.

Sitting down to a feast symbolized peace and a measure of trust between two warring factions. Only the lowest form of humanity would betray this sacred treaty. She'd found it worked as well in modern times.

William had shed his anger slowly, like a snake shuffling off its old skin. It had been interesting to watch the transformation. Gradually the charming man he had once been had emerged from the twin shadows of resentment and frustration.

As for Elsie… Molly studied her friend while she placed the plates on the table. Elsie was positively blooming under the gentle warmth of Lass's love.

Yes, life was good. Tomorrow, on the day of their six-month anniversary, she had a favor to ask of Sam. A hint of the nervousness she felt deep inside penetrated her poise.

She would soon be thirty-three. It was time.

Chapter Fourteen

The day had been hot for October, but now the shadows were long under the mesquite branches, and the air had cooled. Molly smiled as Lass followed the cat around the porch.

The "yearling," as Sam had called her since her birthday, walked with that all-out gait toddlers used to get from one place to another, her eyes always on the prize she was after and never on her feet. She wore sneakers—her first pair of real shoes and a gift from Elsie.

Across the pasture, she could see Sam and the two cowhands pulling barbed wire tight and stapling it to posts. They were moving the cattle in close for the winter. During the summer the field had grown alfalfa, now stored in a huge barn as hay.

She'd planned a special supper for the men.

Chicken-fried steak and mashed potatoes, with gravy smothering everything. Also baking powder biscuits, which she'd learned to make just right by trial and error.

She grinned. Terrible tastes these Western men had, but once a month she indulged it. She had grown to like gravy and biscuits herself.

Nana, who was originally from the South, had laughed about that. ''You'll make a cowgirl out of her yet,'' she'd said to Sam.

''I hope so,'' he'd replied, giving Molly one of those mysterious glances that stopped her heart. If only Western men weren't so darn silent!

When the men headed in, she set the table and had their supper laid out by the time they came to the house.

''Next year, I'd like a garden,'' she said, taking her place beside Lass. She'd found it was easier to sit beside Sam with Lass in the high chair between them at the corner of the table.

Sam paused as if studying the idea from every angle. ''It's a lot of work,'' he finally said.

''I know, but I'd like to try it one time. Maybe Mrs. Stevens would come more often.''

''We could plow it for you,'' Tom volunteered. He paused. ''Uh, if we're here next year.''

''You'd better be,'' Sam ordered. ''You'll have most of the responsibility for the ranch while the resort is getting off the ground. If it does.''

Molly grinned at his skepticism. ''It'll be fun. We'll use camp hosts like the National Park Service does to keep an eye on the campers and report any problems.''

''We'll probably spend half our time rescuing lost

kids.'' Sam smiled when she started laughing. ''All right, I'll quit being such a pessimist.''

When dinner was over, he gave Lass a bath and got her ready for bed while Molly cleaned the kitchen. She listened with a deep inner contentment to Lass's shouts of glee as she splashed in the tub. Sam's deeper rumble scored a vibrant counterpoint to the child's treble tones.

She hummed while she finished up. After a while, feeling another presence, she looked up. Sam lounged against the doorframe, watching her work. She smiled at him.

''Lass is ready for her story,'' he said.

She rubbed lotion into her hands and went to the bedroom. Holding the child in her lap, she read a bedtime story about some bears going into the woods at night. Lass pointed to the pictures and growled in imitation of her father.

''That's right. The bears go *grrrr*,'' Molly agreed.

Once again Sam watched from the door with an unreadable expression in his eyes. A shiver sluiced down Molly's back. There'd been such a depth of emotion in his glances of late. She couldn't figure out if it forebode trouble or not.

After Lass was settled with her blanket and a thumb in her mouth, Molly slipped out of the room and closed the door.

Going to the master bedroom, she found Sam in the sitting room, which doubled as the ranch office, watching the news on television. He'd showered and put on a blue sweat suit.

Her heart skipped, then settled down. She flew into

the shower and out again in five minutes, eager to be with her husband. They still made love nearly every night, but Saturday night was their "date" night.

After blow-drying her hair, she added cologne at a few strategic locations and slipped into a new night-gown frothy with lace and the color of champagne. With the robe, she was modestly covered, but everything about the outfit whispered "seduction."

That's exactly what she meant to do.

She glided into the sitting room in her bare feet and sat beside Sam on the daybed, curling her body toward his and resting her legs across his.

"You smell good," he said, dropping an arm around her shoulders. He rubbed a smoothly shaven jaw against her head.

"You do, too." She took a breath. "Sam—"

"Molly—"

They stopped and looked at each other expectantly.

"Ladies first," he offered.

"No. You." She was about to chicken out.

He nodded. He reached behind him and pulled a box from under a pillow. "For our six-month anniversary."

"Oh, Sam," she whispered, touched that he'd noted the date. The box contained a necklace and earrings that matched her engagement ring. "Oh, how beautiful. I can't imagine a more perfect gift."

"I can," he murmured.

She looked up. Her gaze was trapped by his.

"I watched you and Lass tonight. She's your daughter in every way that counts. I thought…I wondered if you'd be willing to make it legal."

"Adopt her?" Her heart soared like a helium balloon. ''Of course I will. I've thought about it, but I wasn't sure...I didn't want you to think I was pushing... Oh, Sam, you know how much I love her.'' She set the box on the table and kissed him rapturously all over his smiling face.

He chuckled and caught her mouth in a shattering kiss. She sighed and laid her head on his chest when it ended. His heart was pounding hard. Against her thigh, she felt the arousal that always followed their kisses. That reminded her...

''I have a request,'' she murmured, no longer shy about asking for her favor.

''Ask away.'' He idly smoothed her hair.

''Could we start a baby now, tonight?''

She felt him stiffen and wondered if she'd read the situation wrong. She lifted her head and gazed at him.

Time stopped, just stopped, and lingered suspended in the dark blaze of his eyes for an eternity.

''Sam?'' she said and heard her voice tremble.

He didn't speak. She suspected he couldn't. She saw him swallow, then take a deep breath. His heart knocked against her breasts in a pagan beat that started an answering beat in her.

She didn't need the words. She saw it in his eyes—the love he couldn't, didn't try to hide, the fierce protective love that was utterly sweet and utterly tender.

This time it was for her.

''Sam, my love.'' She raised her face, needing his kiss.

He kissed her lips, her cheek, her ear. Then he said the words. ''Molly...I love you.''

So softly. A whisper of sound. Words. Tender. Loving.

Words. For her.

"You're the only woman I've ever loved, truly loved."

She couldn't believe it was possible for one body to hold so much happiness. "I believe you."

Laughing, Sam lifted her into his arms and carried her to their bed. He laid her down as if she was precious. To him, she was…this woman who believed in him, who'd taken his part and kept faith with him, who'd made each day a joy and showed him in a thousand ways that she was in for the long haul…this woman who loved him and Lass with a deep, abiding love that they'd come to trust and depend on.

Yeah, he loved her.

He gathered her close, needing to say the words in his heart. "Molly. Molly, darling."

"Love me," she said, restless for him. "Just love me."

"Forever," he promised.

And he did.

* * * * *

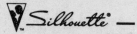